THE SOUTH SIDE TOUR GUIDE

SHELTER SOMERSET

Dreamspinner Press

Published by
Dreamspinner Press
5032 Capital Circle SW
Ste 2, PMB# 279
Tallahassee, FL 32305-7886
USA
http://www.dreamspinnerpress.com/

The South Side Tour Guide
Copyright © 2013 by Shelter Somerset

Cover Art by Brooke Albrecht
http://brookealbrechtstudio.blogspot.com

ISBN: 978-1-62380-696-5
Digital ISBN: 978-1-62380-697-2

Printed in the United States of America
First Edition
May 2013

To J.C.

CHAPTER
ONE

WITH glares from the streetlamps ricocheting off the windshield, Andy clutched the steering wheel of his van and floored the gas pedal to keep up with the beefed-up Honda Accord careening down Sixty-Third Street. After two months working nights, he'd become accustomed to the bright lights. Three, four gunshots rang out from the Honda's backseat. Andy smiled. This was the big time. His grand show. "Make sure those seatbelts are strapped tight," he said to the eight passengers in the backseats. "You're going to get what you paid for tonight."

A half block away, the shooter's target, a scrawny teenage boy, ran for his life down South Aberdeen Street, a narrow one-way riddled with abandoned homes, vacant lots, and weeds punching through pavement. *Idiot, you should've taken a one-way street with opposing traffic.* Tires screeching, the Accord turned after him. Andy maintained a reasonable distance but made sure to keep the Honda and the youth in view.

Andy reached for his cell phone and dialed 911 while keeping a tight grip on the steering wheel. He reported into his headset what he saw and the Englewood location. He clicked off the phone and set it aside before the operator had the chance to ask if he wanted to give his name. Of course, he never did. If word hit the streets he was a "snitch," it might spoil his budding business.

A golden Buick LeSabre maintained a steady speed alongside Andy's van. Andy's detailer had blacked out the passenger windows for added security, so the driver and the Buick's four or five passengers could not see them. But they could see Andy, and they recognized him from past confrontations. Andy had no fear. The teens knew by now that shooting at his bulletproofed van, already pockmarked from dozens of attempts, wasted their valuable lead slugs.

One youth lowered the back window and brandished a Glock nonetheless. Behind him, Andy's passengers gasped. "No worries, folks," Andy said. "We're the Fort Knox of security on wheels."

He slowed to let the Buick move ahead, where it faced off with the Honda. Andy turned down an alley that connected to a street dotted with elms and bungalows, upscale compared to Aberdeen Street. Pedestrians shot glances Andy's way. Some hurried to see where he was going, for they knew wherever Andy's van traveled excitement wasn't far behind. Others ran inside their homes or ducked behind gutted cars or spindly bushes.

Andy idled in another darkened alley and allowed his passengers to watch the shooting match on Aberdeen without interfering in the action. He barely noticed the boy running for the alley. The Accord and LeSabre pursued, heading straight for Andy's van.

"Hang on!" Andy shifted gears and jolted the van in a swift reverse move to evade a head-on. The drivers hurled expletives at Andy as they maneuvered past. Andy laughed aloud, whooped, and cheered with a few of his passengers.

He made a U-turn on Aberdeen and trailed the tire tread marks. At the tee, he braked to avoid the Honda shooter targeting the Buick. A stray bullet grazed the side of the van, and two of the passengers screamed.

One Danish woman kept praying, "*Ah, min gud!*" while her male companion laughed and patted her shoulder with one hand and held his smartphone to the window to capture the action with the other.

The runner leaped into a nearby backyard. From there, he'd most likely scale fence after fence, imitating a deer, and disappear into the night. Andy suspected he'd received at least one nonfatal shot. Police would later pick up the blood trail, and he'd be treated and questioned, leaving Andy in the clear on that matter.

The two drivers sped toward Racine, probably hoping to cut off the runner on Fifty-Ninth Street. Andy aimed to follow, but two Chicago Police cruisers formed a "V" and hindered his passage. Andy recognized the officers, slowed to a stop, and wound down his window. The muggy July air hit his face hard against the cold air conditioning inside the van.

"Hello, Officers," he said, grinning. "It's good to see you again, but you might be more interested in the shooters getting away."

"We got other officers pursuing them," Officer Gonzalez said out the lowered window. He stretched his thick lips under his shot-glass-sized nose and smirked at Andy. "Haven't we warned you about trailing shooters?"

"I just happened to be in the neighborhood."

"Sure, and I'm on my way to a dance recital." Officer Gonzalez rolled his eyes at his colleague. Officer Kenneth Millpairs had already stepped outside his cruiser and was approaching Andy.

Under his flaming-orange eyebrows, Officer Millpairs's irises shone like blue headlights. His broad shoulders seemed to shrink the surrounding sycamore trees, but Andy was not about to let him rattle him for information.

"You wouldn't happen to have gotten their license plates this time," Officer Millpairs said to Andy.

Andy gazed at him and shrugged. "Sorry, didn't notice."

"We can haul you in, Wingal," Officer Gonzalez hollered. "You bet we can."

"For what?"

Officer Millpairs answered for his colleague. "Obstruction of justice, disturbing the peace, interfering with a crime scene...."

"I don't do those things. I'm conducting a free enterprise, that's all."

"We have one of the license plate numbers, Officer," a female passenger from the backseat said in a small voice. "We captured it on our camera."

Andy shot the woman from Evanston a look in the rearview mirror, but he kept his lips in a tight grin. He hopped out of the van and slid open the passenger door for Officer Millpairs with a flourish.

"You're going to hurt someone one of these days," Officer Millpairs whispered to him as he stepped up to the door.

"I've got a business to worry about, just like you," Andy replied under his breath. "You and I aren't all that different. Without criminals, we're both out of business."

"Keep your smart mouth shut."

Andy watched Officer Kenneth take out his notepad and rest his foot on the step bar, a smooth action which stretched the seat of his trousers to reveal a well-formed butt. Even his bulletproof vest failed to conceal that under his blue uniform lay firm pectoral muscles and a flat stomach. One of the few Chicago cops who didn't need an extensive stay at a fat farm.

Officer Millpairs finished jotting down the license plate number from the couple's digital camera and flashed his bright blues at Andy. "One of these days, you're going to be sorry, mark my words. These people might be misguided, but they don't deserve to die, either in a shooting or a car wreck."

"Safety is my number one concern. Always has been."

"I want you to head home. Your passengers have seen enough tonight."

"Yes, sir, Officer Ken."

Officer Millpairs strutted to his cruiser, his round butt snapping at Andy. While he radioed the license plate number to dispatch, Andy climbed back behind the steering wheel of his van and tipped an imaginary cap to the officers. "Have a good night," he said. He edged forward, and Officer Gonzalez backed up his cruiser so that Andy could maneuver past.

Five minutes later, he was keeping up with late-night northbound traffic on the Dan Ryan Expressway. The more he neared the exit for Congress Parkway, the taller the Chicago skyline loomed against the sapphire-blue sky. A dazzling kaleidoscope of steel and glass.

He dropped off the first two passengers at the Hotel Burnham. Andy jumped out, slid open the door, and grinned as they stepped onto the sidewalk. "I'm glad you enjoyed your Friday night. Hope it was everything you had expected."

"We take film of action," the Danish passenger said. "Like in American TV show."

His wife piped in, "*Ah, min gud*! Fun times, *ja*."

Andy pocketed a ten-dollar tip and headed across the Chicago River for the last hotel, the Red Roof Inn on Ontario Street, where two men got off, laughing and shaking their heads.

"Wild and crazy," one said in his thick southern drawl.

"Exceeded my expectations," his friend added.

With the remaining four passengers and an additional fifteen-dollar tip, he exited onto Lake Shore Drive for home base. Lake Michigan stood to the east, a shimmering sheet of iron reflecting the sparkling lights of the skyscrapers and late-night boaters. The summer air was warm and thick, and many pedestrians strolled arm in arm along the lakefront beaches and bike path, spotlighted with orange orbs from the occasional streetlamps.

"More exciting than a roller coaster," the man from Evanston said once Andy pulled into the Clock Tower parking lot in Lakeview ten minutes later. His wife, nudging him out of the van, nodded in agreement.

"I still can't catch my breath," she said, her hand cupped to her breast.

"There's no doubting that," the Wisconsinite added, climbing out after them. "What a ride."

"Amazing," the man from Elk Grove Village uttered.

Andy pointed to the fresh bullet indent directly under the "y" in "Andy Wingal's South Side Tours." The logo and phone number underneath were painted on both sides of the sleek black Ford Econoline in bold white and yellow lettering, evoking the sense of moonlight. Next to that was a silhouette of a man pointing a gun sideways, like those found on old gangster movie posters. His glossy black van with the tinted windows possessed an edginess that even gave Andy goose pimples. "Take a look," he said. "That's from our excursion tonight."

The four passengers ran their fingers over the fresh bullet marking, oohing and ahing in disbelief.

"Glad you enjoyed the tour, folks. Don't hesitate to come back, and make sure you tell your friends about it."

Andy recounted his tips, a total of fifty-five dollars, in addition to the two hundred eighty he'd made from his thirty-five dollar per person fee. Happy for another eventful night, he watched the passengers head for their parked cars, their voices fading as they continued to chatter about their adventure.

"This is how you make a living," he whispered to the upscale condominiums rising above Lake Shore Drive. "This is how you grab life by the balls and yank hard."

CHAPTER
TWO

OFFICER Kenneth Millpairs gripped the fitted sheets of the futon mattress and pumped Andy until Andy worried Ken might push him through the wall into his neighbor's apartment. Andy clutched onto Ken's flexing butt muscles and copied his rhythm. Perspiring and breathing heavily, Ken tensed, grunted, and collapsed with a final spasm.

He lay motionless for several minutes, his shaved chest scratching Andy's nipples.

"You better get up," Andy said, struggling for breath. "You're about thirty pounds heavier than me."

Ken raised his head, sweat trickling from his temples. "You love it. You know it." He jumped up, stripped off the loaded condom with his fingertips, and strolled into the bathroom, where Andy heard the toilet flush, followed by the shower pipes screeching.

Exhausted from his long night, Andy pulled his knees to his chin and fiddled with the blond hairs on his toe knuckles. Another fervent session with Officer Ken. Almost two months they'd officially dated, and they were still no more emotionally connected than that first time they had fooled around. And fool around was the perfect term to describe their sexual interludes.

He had figured Ken for a starchy control freak when he'd first run into him on his second week of giving South Side tours. Like earlier that night, he had impeded Andy on a hot pursuit. He'd lectured him about his "recklessness" and endangering the passengers. But Officer Ken's cockiness had failed to discourage Andy. Nor had he dissuaded Andy from finding him hotter than a Maserati in sixth gear.

They'd crossed paths a second time, a week later at a Halsted Street bar. Standing well over six feet, Ken had swaggered his masculine physique to where Andy and his friend Skeet had been sipping cocktails against the wall, enjoying a midweek respite during "video night."

"Having a good time?" Ken had asked in his gravelly baritone, as if he hadn't been the slightest bit surprised to find the infamous Andrew Wingal at a gay bar—the man who had become one of the South Side's most notorious operators and the police department's biggest pest.

Andy had acted unsurprised to see Ken, but Ken had taken his teasing in stride. Gay men of his bulk were probably used to playful games. Skeet, taking the hint, had vanished into the smattering of posing men and fruit flies, and Andy and Ken had spent the next three hours getting to know each other, ending up at Andy's Uptown studio apartment, where they'd thrashed and tossed about on his futon until the sun rose over Lake Michigan.

Andy would have liked more from Ken than sexual gratification. But the sex was rather enjoyable, he had to admit. Their passion pulsed like a steady stream—on Ken's terms. Loving emotions escaped Ken. Andy had concluded police officers learned to repress their true feelings to cope with their volatile jobs.

Andy stood naked outside the shower stall and hollered above the rush of water. "You mind if I jump in with you?"

"You know I hate that. I'll be out in a minute."

Didn't hurt to give it another try. One of Ken's peeves—he loathed showering with anyone. Perhaps it had to do with his military and police background. He'd spent half his twenty-nine years showering with other males.

Andy didn't mind that Ken was seven years younger than him. Despite the age difference, Ken had become the more dominant partner. Andy had accepted it. He preferred stronger men. Ken sometimes stepped over the lines of aggression, and that had added to Andy's questioning what might come from a long-term relationship with him.

He pulled on his robe and started the coffee brewing in the galley kitchen, mere steps away. He liked his small studio but longed for something grander. Why should others have all the fun?

Such thinking had led him to start his tour guide business. He'd invested more than fifteen thousand bucks for the scheme—bulletproofing, tinting, and painting the used van he'd bought for four thousand dollars—and applied the effort required for his CDL and public utilities license. Once word had spread, a mêlée of media attention sprang up. Five interviews his first week of operations, including a scornful *Sun-Times* write-up.

"He seeks to profit off the unfortunate," the reporter had written. Hate mail and threats came next. But so did the flow of tourist dollars.

For the first time since his layoff from the public relations firm a year ago, Andy had a surplus in his bank account.

The diminutive studio was dark, for he kept the curtains drawn to block the bright sunlight and the city noise that seeped through his second-floor window. His days were his nights, and he usually slept from six until about two in the afternoon. He thought it fortunate that he and Ken worked the same hours. He'd been asleep when Ken had stepped inside his apartment at eleven o'clock in the morning, the keys Andy had given him a week after they'd begun dating clenched in hand. The redheaded Chicago native from a southwest Irish neighborhood resembled Thor in his irresistible police uniform. Andy couldn't wait to strip it off him.

The window air conditioner hummed and rattled, beating back the heat that accumulated in his small studio at night, while the police scanner on his laptop murmured with sporadic reports. Although few street criminals were awake during the day, Andy had acquired the habit of turning on the scanner at home. The crack of incoming dispatches—mostly minor disturbances—and the air conditioner mingled with the prattling old woman who lived in the studio above him. Her sneezing came so loudly through the ventilation system Andy swore she was standing by his ear.

He grabbed a mug, poured the coffee. The hot liquid flowing down his throat refreshed his tired limbs.

"Pour me a cup, will you?" Ken said, toweling off his football-sized calves.

Andy poured Ken some coffee and left the steaming mug for him on the counter. "You want to hang out a while?"

"I think I'll just get dressed, finish off this coffee—" He took a swig. "—and be on my way."

"I can cook us up a nice dinner before work later, or we could go out and—"

"Told you I can't. Got too much to do. I need some good sleep at home before my shift starts."

"How would you know you couldn't get good sleep here? You've never tried."

Ken pulled on his tight whites. "Don't start."

"I guess I need my sleep too," Andy said, shuffling to the dining table. "I have another full booking tonight."

"You're going to get yourself or someone else killed doing that crazy tour business of yours."

"Your job is way more dangerous than mine."

Ken buttoned his cop shirt and glared at Andy. "I'm expected to stand in harm's way. I'm a police officer. You're a civilian messing around where you don't belong. You better wise up."

"I made over fifty bucks in tips alone last night," Andy said. "I'm starting to bring in almost two thousand a week, more than in my entire life. I'm not about to give that up. Not for some inane moral code that means nothing to anyone anymore."

Andy had once read in a survival manual that the best way to avoid being crushed in a stampede was to run with the flow. That's what Andy was doing. Scurrying alongside the charge of scavenging humanity.

Fully dressed in his blue uniform again, Ken examined his Glock and reholstered it. "It's more than just moral codes and money, bozo," Ken said, slapping the top of Andy's head. Ken had meant to give him a playful pat, Andy suspected, but it had come hard enough to make him wince.

"If you really care so much about me," Andy said, rubbing his sore head, "why don't we move in together?"

"You know how I feel about that."

Numerous times, Ken had explained his dilemma: as the youngest of eight siblings, coming out to his family might cause unwarranted anguish for everyone, "Possibly even one of my parents having a heart attack." Andy had heard the justifications until his ears had gone numb.

Ken carried his coffee to the table opposite Andy. "Don't take me not wanting to move in with you personally. I like you a lot. I want you all to myself. You got a killer body for a thirty-six-year-old. And, man, gotta love your cleft chin. But you could use a haircut. I've told you before I like it off your neck and ears."

"You want me like a toy you keep on a shelf," Andy said. "You take me down when you want to play, and when I'm not convenient, you store me away again."

"Is that some kind of bullshit pop psychiatry you heard on TV?"

Andy gulped his coffee, which had already turned tepid and bitter. "Never mind. It's no big deal. I gotta get back to bed, Officer Ken."

Ken leaned over the table and seized Andy's arm. "That's another thing. I told you never to call me that, especially in front of my colleagues. I almost bopped you tonight, the way you were mocking me in front of Ramiro."

Pulling back from Ken's tight grip, Andy said, "I wasn't mocking you. I thought I was being cute."

Ken sat back. "I don't want you acting cute in front of my colleagues. You need to wise up."

Andy deposited his empty mug in the kitchen sink and lay atop the mussed futon mattress, which he almost never folded away, and cinched his robe tighter across his waist. Ken shadowed him and gazed down at him like an ominous redwood.

"Things are good between us, Andy. You're just too ignorant to realize."

"I'm not complaining," Andy said to the white stucco ceiling.

"I'll hold back from telling you what I really think of you for now."

"I've already gotten enough of a browbeating from people," Andy mumbled. "I've been called racist, uncaring, opportunistic. Join in. Tell me what you think of me. I'm a horrible citizen, right?"

Ken gazed into the mirror, straightening his uniform. "You said it, not me."

"I always show civic responsibility. I report all the crimes I witness to 911. More than what many others might do."

"You could do a lot more, and you know it," Ken said, standing beside him.

Andy propped himself up on his elbows. "How?"

"You know how."

"I told you over and over. There's no way I can do that."

"You've avoided it for too long."

"The South Side is bombarded with shootings," Andy grumbled, "and they make it sound like I'm the single man who can end it all. I'm not about to squeal and louse things up just to make some prosecutor feel less guilty for taking bribes."

"I'm on your side, Andy. Don't forget that. But I won't be able to hold them back. I'm tired of making excuses on your behalf. They're getting suspicious."

"Give me one good legal reason why I should talk."

"You'd help us do our jobs."

Andy dropped his head back on the pillow. "That's not a legal reason. Besides, why don't you help me do my job?"

"The city will put an end to your nonsense soon enough, anyway. You might as well go easy. That's how things work around here." Ken took one final gulp from his coffee and set the mug on Andy's tiny desk. "Get ready to chat with prosecutors when the time comes. That's all I'm saying."

Ken moved to leave. Andy sat upright. "You sure you have to go?"

"Got lots to do." He gave Andy a wet coffee kiss. "Do me, yourself, and everyone else a favor. Stay home tonight." Seconds later, the door thumped shut behind him.

Andy dropped back onto the mattress and switched on the television with the remote, hoping to soothe the dull ache of loneliness that had pierced him without warning. An old syndicated sitcom agitated him more. As kids, he and his sister, Lillian, used to watch that very show. Even those days had disintegrated into dust.

The police scanner crackled alive. Two youths in Humboldt Park were behaving suspiciously. Nothing interesting. Andy got up, turned down the volume, and lay back in bed. The old lady above sneezed and dropped what sounded like a bowling ball. In the murkiness of his Uptown studio, Andy forced himself to chuckle along with the canned laughs coming from the television set.

CHAPTER
THREE

"DAD, where're my sneakers?"

Coffee in hand, Harden turned toward his son, Mason, staring at him through the screen on the storm door. "In the closet," he said in a voice that struck him as overly detached.

"Not those, my baseball cleats."

Harden marveled at how his boy resembled him. Light-blue eyes, sandy-colored hair, cheeks that puffed out like an autumn foraging squirrel's. "Can't you ask Kamila?"

"She doesn't know."

His rare morning of peace on the front porch interrupted, Harden trudged inside the house, the storm door slapping shut behind him. The buzz from the kitchen television drowned out his thoughts. Olivia was giggling at the cartoons while she ate her cereal. If only he had more time to clear his head. Always so many distractions. Never enough time to breathe. To think.

He rummaged through the pile of shoes and jackets knotted on the foyer bench. "Didn't I tell you to clean this stuff up?"

"Kamila said she'd do it. Besides, I already looked through all that. They're not there."

"Kamila can't be expected to do everything." Harden lifted a plastic bag containing a pair of faded, grungy cleats. "You mean these aren't here?"

Mason blushed in a way only an eleven-year-old could get away with. "Guess I didn't see them. Must've put them there and forgot." He snatched the bag and fled upstairs.

Tiny awards, like a smile from his only son after finding a pair of soiled cleats, were all that Harden might expect to lift his spirits nowadays.

He could see into the kitchen. Kamila was urging Olivia to finish her cereal so that she could load the dishwasher. He almost dreaded facing them. His seven-year-old's messes irked his inner fussbudget. "A big slob," Mason, who exemplified his father's penchant for order, would call her.

I love you, I love you, he repeated to his children inside his head while stepping into the kitchen. *I know I don't always show it, but I love you.*

"Look, Daddy." Olivia reached for a picture she'd drawn but nearly upset her glass of plum juice.

"Watch it, Olivia," Harden said. "Try to be more careful, won't you?"

She continued to wave her drawing. "Do you like it?"

"It's nice, sweetheart," he said, barely glancing at it. "You're a good artist."

"I'm going to write a play to go with it. I'm going to call it 'The Kranes'."

"That's good." He turned to Kamila. "I might be home a little later today. Can you stay until about seven? If not, I can ask my mom to take off work early and stop in for an hour or two."

"Yes, I can stay."

Kamila—a godsend. His Bosnian housekeeper kept the family from fraying into tatters. She wasn't the neatest housekeeper, but she was better than nothing. Besides, it was nice to have a female around the house for the kids. He'd hired her last summer after his promotion so he'd be less of a burden on family and friends. She worked full time five days a week in summer, part-time afternoons and every other Saturday once school commenced.

Despite her embarrassingly meager salary, he had to cut back on a few things to afford her. (At-home haircuts became more frequent.) He'd considered asking her to move into the basement bedroom and become a live-in housekeeper, but he feared the negative ramifications of her constant presence might surpass the plusses.

Kamila, in her own way—like all of them—brought another level of anxiety to him. The forty-something-year-old Eastern European transplant wanted more from him than the typical employee-employer relationship, Harden was certain. He'd done his best to pretend he never noticed.

Harden arranged the contents of his briefcase while the TV cartoon clonked, clunked, and guffawed. Kamila rinsed Olivia's bowl and juice glass and cranked on the dishwasher. The added commotion stretched Harden's patience. "Didn't Mason turn on that dishwasher last night before bed like I asked him? We couldn't possibly have used up that many dishes this morning."

"Mason never does what he's told," Olivia said, adding finishing touches to her drawing.

"Don't be supercilious, Olivia."

Olivia repeated the word "supercilious" over and over under her breath and giggled. "Daddy, can we go to the swimming pool?"

"Let me have two seconds to think, please. I haven't even had a chance to finish my first cup of coffee yet. Where's that.... Olivia, is that my pen?"

Olivia, eyeing the pen in her small dough-like fist, frowned.

"I told you never to take anything out of Daddy's briefcase." Harden snatched the pen and placed it in its proper slot. "I need my things for work. You don't want me to lose my job, do you?"

Kamila moved to help Harden with his briefcase, but he gestured for her to back off. Instead, she tried to entertain Olivia using her typical low-key voice with an accent that had become more commonplace to the Krane household than the hum of cornfield crickets.

"When will you get home, Daddy?"

"I just told you, about seven."

"Can we get a dog?" Mason strolled into the kitchen, clenching his baseball mitt.

"We've been over that, Mason."

"Why do we live on a farm if we have no animals? All my friends have at least a dog."

"You can visit theirs. We've got too much going on here without needing to worry about a bunch of grungy animals. And you forgot to turn on the dishwasher last night like I asked you. I told you, if you have a bowl of ice cream before bed, you're the last to stack the dishwasher and turn it on. How hard is that?"

"Daddy, I want you to help me write my play," Olivia said, kicking her feet under the table, which caused Harden to almost drop the briefcase lid on his arm.

"Be careful, Olivia. Now get upstairs like Daddy's sweet little girl and brush your teeth. Try not to make a mess."

"My *Raving Rhino* app is stuck again."

Exasperated, Harden pushed aside his present needs and tried to fix Mason's favorite app game for the umpteenth time since the boy had downloaded it on his iPod last month. "Christ, Mason, why don't you play another game, one that works?"

"I like this one."

"I will try," Kamila said.

Mason swiped the iPod from Harden before Kamila could grab it and began tinkering with the dials. Glad to have his hands back, Harden snapped the briefcase shut and swallowed the last of his lukewarm coffee. "Who's driving you to your game this afternoon?"

"Mr. Hart again."

"Make sure you—"

"Thank him for taking me to the game and for driving me home," Mason said almost verbatim, since Harden had told him many times.

Harden chuckled and rubbed Mason's hair. "Just do as you're told, smart aleck." He thanked Kamila in advance for staying later, instructed Mason to keep his sister out of trouble, and hopped in his Jeep Patriot.

Green cornstalks, taller than Mason, flanked the driveway as he turned onto the country road for the short drive to work. He longed to dirty his hands on his two-hundred-twenty-acre farm with the white L-shaped old Craftsman-style house and semiwraparound porch that he'd inherited from his grandparents. But the world had different prospects for Harden Krane.

Once he'd earned his master's in biotechnology from the University of Minnesota, a hometown enterprise offered Harden a magnificent job that Lillian had insisted he accept. The next thing Harden knew, he was living on the farm like he might a suburban cul-de-sac and commuting to work. Now, with two children to raise solo, farming dreams seemed forever tucked inside sticky, stubborn drawers.

It was a wispy fantasy he'd clung to since he was a boy growing up in nearby Duncan, a town with fewer people than most big city high schools. When visiting his grandparents, he'd spent hours exploring each nook and cranny of the farm, certain the wind blowing through the towering burr oak, the farm's namesake, whispered his name.

His inability to farm full time was a blessing, he figured, keeping his speed steady. Farming entailed countless hours of hard work. His grandfather had spent so much time in the field he'd often fallen asleep on his tractor. In addition, there were the endless hours bent over accounting ledgers and logs. With two active children and no wife, that would be impossible for Harden.

For now, he had to make do with Dick Carelli's quarterly rent payments. After Grandpa's death, Grandma had rented Dick the land, since she could no longer farm alone. Harden, embarking on his suit-and-tie career, had extended the lease. At least he enjoyed watching the family farm put to good use.

He slowed enough to wave to Burt Anders, who was unloading wood planks from the back of his pickup. He wanted to build a bridge at the bottom of his driveway to stave off flood damage. Good neighbors, Burt and his wife, Alicia. They had always been there for Harden during the tough times. He made a mental note to help Burt with the modest construction project, but then remembered he had to work late.

Yellow prairie asters along the edge of the road whizzed past in a blur as he turned onto the wider thoroughfare and picked up speed for work. The lush Iowa farmland stretched in a sea of green cornfields. Billboards dotting the road hawked ethanol gasoline distilled from those yields. Harden wondered how many corn-for-fuel lobbyists were in Washington at that moment buying lap dances for politicians.

The Jeep's air conditioner sucked in odors of the beleaguered, blistering summer. *I used to worship this time of year. What happened?* Life elbowed him in the jaw and left him with two demanding children and a house to maintain; that's what happened. Since finding himself a single father, Harden looked forward to the end of summer and the start of school more and more. *Let someone else fuss over Mason and Olivia.*

Three years ago, the school district had required that Mason, still coping with the upheaval of his home life, attend summer school. Harden had lectured him before the start of each subsequent spring term, "Don't start slipping again. You'll have to go to summer school. You don't want that, do you?" Yet the dastardly voice taunting Harden inside his head had always whispered, "You'd like it, wouldn't you, if Mason could go to summer school like last time so he'd be out of your hair."

Harden didn't want to be the kind of father who would wish for his son's scholastic failure so he'd get a little more peace. "Thank God for Loretta Ficklemeyer suggesting Kamila," he whispered toward the windshield.

He made the final turn for work, and Marshall Farming Enterprises' one-story office building emerged ahead. He parked his Jeep by the usual maple sapling and headed inside. The stench of solvents assaulted his nose. He never grew used to the stink that clung to the walls, floors, ceilings. Nothing matched it, other than the stench people leave behind in bars after the Super Bowl.

Arty Ficklemeyer greeted him with a light pat and a reek of cigarette smoke almost more irritating than the office stench. "Good weekend, Harden?"

"Hectic but nice. And yours?"

"Good. Lunch later?"

"Okay, sure, Arty. Come get me."

Lucinda Jamison smiled at him from the copying machine. "Hi, Harden. Hope you had a good weekend."

Harden's cheeks burned. "Thanks, Lucinda, you too." He waved to Charlie Marshall, the company's owner, who was speaking with one of the new Bosnian machine-parts workers, and picked up his pace for his office. Behind the closed door, he sat at his desk and situated his mind. Thank God for work.

His position as senior agronomist required he hustle ethanol, which he judged limited in value. But on the brighter side, his job was basic nine-to-five, and he could set his own hours if needed, with occasional overtime and even a rarer scouting or business trip. As an added consolation, his coworkers and customers knew him well. They trusted each other. The camaraderie was important to him for a job that he disliked.

As much as he wished he were riding a tractor, without his work he'd be a lost man. He loved his kids (*I do, I do. I really love them*), but a daily reprieve from the chaos they stirred proved essential to his mental health.

Life's a kick in the crotch, he thought while hunkering down to another Monday.

CHAPTER
FOUR

HARDEN was rushing to ready himself for his late afternoon teleconference with an ethanol buyer from California when he received a call from Mason's baseball coach, Tyler Phelps. Mason and another boy had scrapped over a few poorly chosen words. He had tossed both from the game. Mr. Hart, at the game with his son, couldn't leave, so Harden would have to pick him up.

Christ!

Harden considered calling Kamila, but he didn't want her to haul Olivia cross county. Embarrassed and angry that he had to postpone his teleconference, he marched out of the office with the ripe taste of rage on his tongue.

Strangled with fury, Harden found Mason standing next to Mr. Phelps's assistant, Gabe Jackerman. He kept a civil tone in front of Gabe, but once he pulled out of the parking lot with Mason strapped in the passenger seat, Harden's anger coalesced into a fist inside his gut. He barely noticed the purple bruise germinating over Mason's left cheek.

"Not one word, you hear me. I'm too angry with you right now to handle this properly. So you just sit there quiet and don't even move a hair on your head."

Back at home, he set his briefcase and laptop on the foyer console and, before he'd even loosened his tie, pointed up the stairs. "You better spend your time saying your prayers."

Kamila was putting dinner into the oven. She flashed him one of her soulful expressions.

"Another fight," Harden said before she'd even asked.

"Is he good?"

"He'll be okay, maybe some ice."

Kamila retrieved the cold compress from the freezer and began wrapping it in a hand towel. Harden appreciated the house's rare silence before he had to face Mason. Kamila wasn't one for much speaking, most likely because English was a second language to her.

He glanced out the window at Olivia swinging in the backyard next to the burr oak. He'd bought the kids the swing set three years ago to lighten their emotional upheaval. Yet he'd also purchased it for himself. *It'll give them a reason to get out of the house.*

The sight of his daughter lifted his spirits. He loosened his tie and tapped the windowpane. She looked up and waved back.

After letting his temper cool, he took the icepack from Kamila and made the arduous trek to Mason's bedroom to pronounce a punishment, one he hoped would be the last.

Mason, still in his soiled baseball uniform, sat on the edge of his twin bed, his gaze cast to the blue shag carpet. Harden studied his son's bruised cheek from the doorway. The swelling had spread to his upturned nose. Deep down, Harden hoped Mason had given the other boy an equally big wallop but refrained from asking. "Here, put this on your face."

Mason took the icepack from Harden's outstretched hand, but he let it dangle between his knees.

Harden peered around the bedroom. Red, white, blue, and neat and orderly. Too orderly for an eleven-year-old boy.

"I thought you were done with this," Harden said to him. "Mr. Phelps tells me the county might bar you from playing if this happens again. Would you like that? What will you do for the rest of summer?" *What will* I *do?*

Mason shrugged. "He deserved it. Mike called me a—"

"I don't care what he called you. Every time you react to what some bully says to you, I ultimately pay the price. Do you want that for me? Christ, Mason, I had to cancel an important meeting because of this. I could lose my job," he said. "Then what do we have, huh?"

More silence.

"You better shape up, Mason. I'll put you in one of those military schools. You just wait and see."

Mason lifted his blue and black cheek to his father. "You can't do that."

"Then smarten up. You're stronger than this, Mason."

Harden had lost count of how many lectures he'd given Mason over the past few years to discourage his angry outbursts when the other kids teased him. His pool of punishments was running dry. Poor kid. The past few years had been torture enough.

Rather than confine him to his room without dinner (Harden's old standard), he told him he couldn't play any of his electronic games for a week. As a bonus for Harden, he wouldn't have to hear Mason complain if they failed to work.

"Now get that uniform off and clean up," Harden added. "And stay up here until I call you for dinner."

Downstairs, Kamila poured Harden coffee. Silently, she set it before him at the table, where he tried to clear his head. Harden disliked the overt service from Kamila. He'd hired her mostly for the kids and to straighten the house—he needed that for mental peace. But she doted on him more and more.

Olivia interrupted his short moment of calm and leaped onto his lap, nearly spilling his coffee.

"Watch out, Olivia."

"Come help me write my play."

"How much have you gotten done?"

"Most of it, but I need you to correct grammar."

"Okay, okay. Wait a bit now. I just got home." He repositioned her so that he could feel his legs. "What did you do today?"

Same old question. No one ever asked Harden how his workdays went, not even Kamila. Good enough, he figured. He had little to share with them about his days at Marshall Farming Enterprises.

He was more interested in Olivia. Especially since Mason's old troubles had crept to the foreground again. The bright boy had fallen far. Last school term he'd shown signs of improvement, but Harden worried he might be slipping again with the latest clash. He needed to ensure Olivia didn't follow after her brother.

"I played in the backyard, and I tracked a rabbit to the creek," she said while twiddling with his loosened necktie. "Did you know the creek is almost empty?"

Harden removed her hand. "We need rain."

"Where do the fish go?"

"They hide in deep gullies protected by stones. They'll be okay."

"What about the rabbits? Where do they drink when there's no water?"

"They know where to look. Don't worry about them."

"Where do they look?"

Harden set Olivia onto her feet with an exaggerated movement. "The refrigerator, where else?"

Olivia giggled. "You're silly, Daddy. Rabbits don't have refrigerators."

"That's why they use ours."

Even the staid Kamila smiled at Olivia's joyful reaction. Kamila made one of her unusual gestures (hand raised, palm down, and a clawlike movement with her fingers), and Olivia shuffled to her. She said something to her, and Olivia raced off. Kamila used Bosnian commands around the children that only they understood. Harden supposed Kamila had instructed her to wash her hands before dinner. Olivia returned minutes later, the front of her T-shirt wet, waving her play before Harden's eyes.

She hopped on his lap again, and together they read through the play, neatly typed and printed from the family computer. He suggested minor revisions until his lap went numb.

"Go make the changes while Daddy gets out of his work clothes before dinner."

Upstairs, he slipped into his sweatpants and T-shirt and pondered how much easier life had been with a wife. He found few women as intriguing as he once had Lillian. He gazed at their portrait on the bureau. How much time had passed since then? Twelve years?

"A mother's the best thing for the kids," Harden's own mother had told him many times. "Lillian's gone. Isn't it time to move forward?"

"But he needs to find the right girl, Mom," his older brother, Lance, would often insert on his behalf. "Give him space."

"I'm just thinking about Olivia and Mason."

"So is Harden. That's why he doesn't want to rush into another marriage."

Crushed between their shoulders, Harden had listened to their discussions of his personal life too often. In many ways, his life had unraveled without his noticing, too late to fix it.

He'd even stopped worrying over his nonexistent sex life. He'd been with only two women since Lillian. Two short, quick interludes. The first, a woman from Dubuque, he'd met through an old college friend. They'd enjoyed a simple dinner, and afterward she'd agreed to follow him in her car to Burr Oak Farm. She'd waited patiently while he'd thanked his sister-in-law Holly for babysitting and then undertook the cumbersome job of tucking the children into bed. Perhaps he'd rushed things. She'd appeared stiffer once he'd come back downstairs and sat beside her.

They had talked until the moon left wedge marks on the carpet. By one, they'd ended up in the basement bedroom to avoid waking the kids. The first woman to have lain beside him since Lilly. He'd made sure to lower the noise level. She'd bailed before sunrise. At breakfast, he'd never noticed if Mason or Olivia had suspected anything. A few days later, his two text messages to the Dubuque woman went unanswered.

The other woman he'd met while on a rare business trip to Rockford, Illinois. Separated from the children, the seduction of the saleswoman from St. Louis had come easier. Their encounter had fulfilled him more, but in a way that had made it worse. She too had ignored his voice messages.

The smell of roasting spiced meat told him dinner was close to ready. Another one of Kamila's Bosnian recipes. She made so many meat dishes Harden worried he might metamorphose into a side of beef. Sausages, ribs, kabobs, anything but pork. She even put ground beef in her homemade pastries. Although Harden confessed he adored her delicate pita breads.

On the way downstairs, he poked his head inside Mason's bedroom. The icepack lay unused on his night table where a small puddle accumulated. Changed into shorts and a T-shirt, Mason twiddled his thumbs at his desk. His tanned hands looked forlorn without a handheld electronic device in them.

Mason refused eye contact with Harden even when he uttered his name and draped an arm over his shoulder to walk him to dinner.

Things could be a lot worse between father and son, he imagined.

A lot worse.

Kamila had dinner waiting for them buffet style, as was her custom, and Harden waited for the storm door to slam shut behind her before they served themselves. He asked Mason to lead grace, for Harden never felt comfortable speaking prayers aloud himself. Hypocrite, he considered himself. Although raised Catholic, as were eighty percent of those in northeastern Iowa, he never put much faith in religion. Nevertheless, he made sure that Mason and Olivia attended Mass each Sunday, even if it meant asking his mother to take them on his behalf.

Church—something Harden had at one time believed he could live without. That was, until he found himself alone with two kids.

CHAPTER
FIVE

ANDY had carried a total of thirty-seven passengers for the week, translating to nearly thirteen hundred dollars. That Friday was his largest load to date. Fifteen squeezed inside his van. Five from the suburbs, three from Indiana, two from Connecticut, two from Germany, two from Japan, and a solo traveler from South Carolina. They had all read about his business in the newspapers and on the Internet.

Streetlamps reflecting off the damp pavement from an earlier rain shower gave the night that added verve Andy loved for his passengers. He anticipated another fast-paced tour. The air was hot and steamy, and local inhabitants streamed onto the sticky streets. His cell phone, tuned onto the local police scanner, crackled and hissed. Most weekends, violence was common enough he'd come across a crime before the police or dispatchers ever got word. Muggy South Side weekends always provided action.

Litter stuck to the wet streets, and the stench from the overflowing garbage bins wafted inside the van. He stayed clear of the occasional police cruisers before they spotted him. By now, the area had become familiar with Andy's sleek black van with "Andy Wingal's South Side Tours" etched on the sides. Pedestrians and drivers waved and honked or flashed him and his passengers the digital salute.

He took the typical streets that crime logs showed had the most homicides. From his experience, dawn on Saturdays and Sundays proved the deadliest. That was when burned-out partiers stumbled about, desperate for transportation, money, and more drugs. But few passengers wanted to remain out beyond three, so he kept to the "high profile" sections of the South Side, searching for some midnight action.

The first came from a group of youths throwing empty pop cans at a small convenience store. The passengers ducked, and laughed, and snapped photographs. The owner had long slammed shut and locked the metal shop gates, but the youths apparently had some ongoing grudge against him. Andy had witnessed his shop targeted before.

Vacant lots. Cracked and battered driveways that led to nowhere. Boarded-up homes and apartment buildings. The passengers snapped photos or filmed through the bulletproofed tinted windows while craning their heads to view one of Chicago's most infamous ghettos.

Andy's ears had become acclimated to the sound of gunshots versus a car backfiring or a firecracker set off. One such sound came from the east. He turned in that direction, careful to maintain a safe speed, and alerted his passengers to a possible shooting.

Hushed intensity filled the van, along with fear, excitement, perhaps even self-loathing.

"Like exploring the homes of Hollywood stars," Andy had once replied to his friend Skeet, who'd asked why on earth Andy wanted to embark on a business cruising the dangerous South Side hoods. "Some people show mansions of the rich and famous. Some show where the Amish live. For me, it's the ghetto. We're all marketers to the curious, one way or the other."

He passed through a block with clusters of evergreens and maple trees abutting well-kept bungalows and Victorians. Andy had noted the intermittent manicured side to the South Side. Like small towns plucked straight out of the pastoral Midwest and dropped in the midst of a slum.

One house in particular struck Andy as anomalous to those on adjacent blocks. Tall trees, planter boxes overflowing with pink and lavender flowers, lattice trim, gingerbread overhang, contrasting white shutters against the blue wood panels, and a white picket fence neatly framed the proud owner's home. The eternal push and shove for normalcy and beauty in a sea of decay.

Another distant gunshot rang out. This time many of the passengers had heard it and expressed their enthusiasm.

"I think it came from that way," one of the men from Indiana said, pressing his finger to the window.

Andy made a U-turn and turned onto a darkened street where weed-choked vacant lots outnumbered habitable homes. Few of the homes kept their lights on in rooms facing the street. Many South Siders used their living rooms as storage while the families gathered in other rooms, away from the possible stray bullet that might shatter their front windows and take out an innocent life.

Shadows stalked them as Andy continued at a prowler's pace. At any moment, frantic prey running for his life might appear, hunted by one or more gunmen. Three or four blocks in, the headlights hit a dark mass lying in the middle of the street. He idled closer, pulled to the curb, and shifted to park.

The passengers gasped. Two women sniffled back tears. He heard the mutter of German and Japanese and the snap of a few cameras.

They'd missed the shooting but beheld the aftermath. An eerie corpse left unnoticed, facedown in a puddle of blood.

He turned off the van, instructed his passengers to stay put, and hopped out. *Woopa woopa* echoed through the dark street as he locked the doors with his automatic key and jogged to the scene. He peered around, fell to a squat. A fresh kill. He could not see a visible wound, but the bullets must have penetrated his head and torso. Blood puddled by his right side and head and had begun to stream down a gutter gushing with rainwater.

The victim appeared no older than seventeen. He did not look like the typical street punk or gang member. He wore tight jeans, from what Andy could see, rather than the loose clothing popular with gang members. No gang colors or emblems were visible. Perhaps that's what had made him a target. Shot dead for no reason other than abiding by the good side of the law. A bunny rabbit surrounded by ravenous foxes.

Poor kid. Probably never stood a chance.

Screaming sirens from Ashland sent Andy scurrying for the van. He revved the engine and headed north on Aberdeen toward Sherman Park, away from the shrill of the police. He called 911 to ensure they knew where to look for the victim. Once again, he clicked off before the operator had a chance to ask for his name.

The passengers remained speechless during most of the drive north on the Dan Ryan Expressway. But once the multicolored stalagmite-looking skyscrapers loomed in full view, the tension released, and they began chatting and chuckling about what they'd experienced.

Admittedly, the homicide unnerved Andy more than he'd have expected (he'd seen plenty of dead bodies that summer), but he maintained light banter with the passengers while he dropped off those staying at downtown hotels. The Japanese man, stepping off the van, said with a chuckle, "We have no urban decay like that. We better than you."

"I'm sure you are," Andy said while he took the man's five dollar tip and slid the door shut after his wife.

He collected sixty dollars total from the out-of-town tourists and headed north along Lake Shore Drive for the Clock Tower parking lot to drop off the remaining six passengers. Andy again expressed his delight that they had gotten their money's worth. "Like I warned, you might get what you pay for."

"I'll never forget it," the man from Skokie said with a low-key tone. "I'm still shaking. I got lots of pictures. My relatives in North Dakota won't believe it."

With his passengers driving off or wandering toward Broadway through the Lake Shore Drive pedestrian underpass, Andy gazed into the Chicago night, a canopy of expanding light. Under the half moon, the city beat with a harried pace. He could feel the city's hot and steady breath on him. Each exhale loaded his pockets with more riches.

The night had proved exciting. Even better for Andy since Ken and the cops had stayed clear of him. He glanced at his wristwatch. Two o'clock. An early night for a Friday. But the passengers had expressed satisfaction with the one dead body, a ghastly image for anyone.

Pocketing the one hundred dollars in tips, he turned for his van. Before he reached the driver's door, two police cruisers jolted to a halt behind him. Like a cornered deer, he jerked around, startled by the flashing lights and quick-pulse sirens.

CHAPTER
SIX

THE bright fluorescent lights of the Nineteenth District police station flickered in Andy's eyes. Seated in a steel "reception" chair, he stared at the officers who surrounded him. Under the glare of the lights, they appeared pale and sickly.

"Why am I here?" he asked for what seemed the twentieth time. "You know I haven't done anything illegal."

"What have you done?" the silver-haired, square-jawed sergeant with blank blue eyes asked. The nameplate above his right pocket read: Robert I. Peterson.

Andy furrowed his brow at the middle-aged sergeant. *Not bad looking for a guy his age.* He tried to inflect reverence in his voice, although his patience with the typical police nonsense began to wane. "I don't understand any of this."

"We have a warrant out on you."

"But what for? That's all I ask."

"We've got you for obstruction of justice."

"That's ridiculous. You're just trying to shut down my business, and you can't do that legally."

"We can revoke your public utilities license. But if you cooperate, you might get your van back."

The pack of police officers meandered back and forth between the maze of desks, answering buzzing telephones, chatting with officers in cubicles, and listening in on Andy's interrogation, as if the sluggishness of the law weighed on their slumping shoulders. Typical police-style chitchat questioning. Never really demonstrating a single concern for what they were asking but unleashing pinpricking demands nonetheless.

An overweight officer with the nameplate Maximilian Wozniski yawned and scratched his thigh. "You think we should jail him?"

His fitter colleague, Officer Brian Larsen, one of the two officers who'd cornered Andy at the Clock Tower parking lot, shrugged. "I don't know."

Since Andy's tour took him to the South Side (the single digit districts) he was unfamiliar with the officers stationed in Lakeview, except for one or two he recognized from the Halsted Street beat, who sometimes moonlighted by patrolling gay establishments.

"Did you happen to witness a homicide near Fifty-Ninth Street tonight?" Officer Wozniski asked.

"I did not."

"We've got your passenger list from your van," Sgt. Peterson said. "We can call and detain whoever you drove around tonight for questioning."

"You'd be harassing law-abiding citizens. Why don't you go after the criminals? You can start with city hall."

The officers laughed and nodded. "They write our checks," Officer Larsen said, dragging a hand across his well-groomed hair. "Can't do that. We're not the FBI."

"What did you see?" another pudgy officer asked Andy, his eyes wide and emanating more enthusiasm than his associates.

Andy hesitated and peered at Officer Calvin Walker. "None of us saw anything," he said with a grimace. "The boy was already dead."

"Good enough." The overhead lights reflected off Sgt. Peterson's star as he turned and wandered to a desk. Andy gripped the armrests while the sergeant fiddled with papers, answered a call, chatted with a fellow officer out of earshot. The other officers wandered off also, save for Officer Walker, who continued to stare at Andy wordlessly.

Andy turned away and let his gaze trace the cracks in the tiled floor. He couldn't believe he was in a police station, held against his will like a common criminal, facing accusations and harassment from big-city cops. How had it come to such a moment? Refusing to go on welfare and, to a larger extent, seeking to rebel against society by giving people what they wanted, he'd walked straight into a world far removed from his former way of life.

He almost laughed at being interrogated by a swarm of overworked and tired police officers. Officer Larsen shuffled over to his colleague, who still eyed Andy with a strange, cunning indifference that Andy had learned to associate with law enforcement.

"Maybe we can let him go," he said. "You think he might want to help us with that triple homicide from June thirtieth?" He looked to Andy. "Didn't you admit to being at the scene of that one too?"

Andy shook his head and suppressed a disbelieving grin. "I figured that's what this was about. Listen, I always call in crime scenes to 911, unless the police are already there. What more can I do?"

"Did you see anything?" Officer Walker asked again, using the same monotone.

"I've already admitted I was there," Andy said. "But the police arrived about the same time I showed up. I didn't even need to call for dispatch."

"You see anything before the police got there?"

Yes, Andy had seen something. Two youths in a Buick holding Glocks, followed by three successive flashes from a small opening in the window. But street life had taught Andy a hard-learned lesson—reveal little to the police.

Soon after that June incident, Andy had consulted a friend of a friend about his legal responsibility. The attorney, who had appeared appalled with Andy, had given him a quick response, and Andy was unsure if he could trust him. But Andy understood enough of the law that he accepted the man's callous advice. Imagine, Andy had thought after he'd taken his leave, an attorney who made his living by garnering city contracts for the mob, censuring Andy's career.

"Legally, I'm clear," Andy said. "I already know that."

Officer Walker focused his drowsy eyes on Andy. "We think whoever is responsible for those three homicides might be responsible for some others," he said. "We'd like to get whoever it is off the street. You help us, we help you. Quid pro quo."

Andy wavered, but only for as long as it took Wozniski to return with a cup of stale-smelling drip coffee.

"I told you what I saw," Andy said. "It's on record. I heard three pops, and three guys went down. Three shots. Perfect hits." *Now I'm starting to sound like a thug.* "I didn't see any of the shooters' actual faces."

"Shooters?" Officer Wozniski chuckled. "You didn't see, but you know there was more than one?"

Andy hated Officer Wozniski's overdone Chicago accent, almost as if he tailored it for him. "We got there seconds before it happened," Andy said, keeping his voice even. "Not a pedestrian in sight. Just the three victims. What more can I tell you?"

A youngish blond officer with the nameplate Jayson K. Adams sat opposite Andy and propped his legs on a chair. He straightened his trousers and eyed Andy as if Andy were a cat at a dog show. "What's this guy in for?"

"Obstruction of justice. He won't tell us what he knows about that triple seven-twenty down in the Seventh District."

"What's he doing up here?"

"We picked him up for questioning."

The newcomer snickered at Andy. "You afraid of something?"

Andy noticed his tight trousers. "Not at all."

"He's worried about his business," Walker said through thick lips.

"What business is that?"

"He's the South Side Tour Guide."

"The what?"

"The guy who takes people around on tours to see South Side crime. Don't you know anything, Adams?"

"You're kidding? Someone does that?"

"Where the hell you been?"

The officers began their usual insulting banter. The blond rookie took the brunt. One always wore the target, usually with an odd smile, as if he understood the position and perhaps even relished it. The younger officer named Adams peered at Andy with sharp green eyes.

"You really do that? You really give tours to see crimes like murders? People pay for that?"

Andy grew impatient. "Could I have my van and go, please?"

With tepid authority, Officer Walker shrugged and grunted. "Probably not."

The officers left Andy alone to stew. He began to regret having defended the police to his friends, who often grumbled that police officers liked to harass homosexuals. Yet Andy had never known any of them to have experienced overt mistreatment by the police. A rainbow of men and one woman in uniform surrounded him, maybe one or two who might be gay. He was in a neighborhood with the largest homosexual population in the Midwest, and the Nineteenth District recruited to fit the demographic.

He watched the police go about their night shift protocol. A crazy lot, Andy thought. They'd hold him through the next shift if he didn't provide what they wanted. He sat planted as their middle guy, between the criminals and the law.

I've stepped into the position as their go-to snitch.

The night impinged on Andy. Green pallor bloomed over the officers' mugs from the sickening lights. They guzzled coffee that lacked steam, wiped their mouths with steady hands.

He couldn't reveal to them that his boyfriend, Officer Ken Millpairs, worked the same night shift in a South Side district. Little that might help. Besides, Ken, sealed in the closet tighter than a hermetic jar of peach preserves, would kill him if he outed him to his colleagues.

Twenty minutes more of waiting, and Andy's head whirled in a dizzy spectacle of despondency. He cleared his throat, conjured enough courage to speak to the closest cop, the female officer who had tried to act extra tough. "Excuse me, ma'am, what can I do to get out of here?"

She flashed him wide black eyes and a sardonic smirk. Inadequate makeup failed to conceal her rosacea-covered face under the harsh lights. "Hey, Walker," she hollered with a thick Chicago accent. "Your guy is getting restless."

"Tell him to sit tight."

"If I promise to speak with prosecutors, can I have my van back?" *Promise to speak didn't mean testify.*

The female officer giggled and gestured for Walker. With his signature remote countenance, Officer Walker shuffled to Andy.

"Here's the deal," he said, tightening his features for the first time. "The prosecution won't prosecute without an eyewitness. You're the best we got. We need you on board for the case to go forward. See how much this rests on your shoulders? You want a killer to wander free?"

"I told you all that I know." Walker made to leave, but Andy stopped him. "What do I have to do?"

"We'll force you to talk, or you can talk willingly. We'd rather not have a hostile witness. Doesn't look good to judges. We already had to let the suspects go from lack of evidence. They've let their guard down because they think they're home free. You give us word, and we'll nab them this time with solid charges."

Their interchange piqued the interest of the good-looking sergeant. He wandered over and peered at them as if he were watching a tennis match. Walker continued to pressure Andy. Comply or face a term in jail for obstruction of justice. Either way, the cops screwed him.

Sighing, he said, "All right, I'll talk to the prosecutor. But I don't have much to tell. I didn't see anyone's face. And I won't give up my passenger list. I've got to hang onto some semblance of a business, right?"

Satisfied with Andy's response, Sgt. Peterson nodded toward Walker with a downturn of his mouth and strolled off.

A quick three days later, Andy sat shivering and rubbing his hands between his legs in the prosecutor's downtown office. Her stare came at him from across her pretentious mahogany desk, equally frigid. Despite his coming aboard, she eyed him with a calloused, distrustful look. He shared what he knew. She took notes. By two o'clock, he returned to his Uptown studio apartment without any sense of civic pride. Somehow, he imagined Miss Steinen got something extra on the side too.

Based on Andy's statement, police apprehended two suspects the next day. A subsequent arraignment set their bond at three hundred thousand dollars, a pittance to a duo that could unearth millions in a few days. Their bosses, drug kingpins with the clout of ombudsmen, had a cash flow more abundant than many movie stars.

By Wednesday, Andy, itching to forget about the impending trial the judge had set for January, was back in his van giving a tour to four passengers. Already he feared a dent in his business from the negative publicity his testimony might have given him. Nonetheless, they had a thrilling night for a midweek tour—two stabbings and a police chase. "Just like on TV," the passenger from downstate said.

He returned home exhausted and eager for a few cold beers, yet relieved the worst of the triple homicide ordeal wouldn't rear itself for another six months. Drowsy, he parked his van in the private garage two blocks away and was about to step inside his building when hot pain traveled along his upper back to his nape. Before he could turn and see what had caused the burning sensation, at least two people jumped on him, followed by a thrashing that knocked him flat to the concrete.

He pulled into a tight ball to ward off the kicks and punches and waited for the beating to stop. Moaning and writhing, he heard one of the men say in a deep baritone, "And that's what you get for squealing, punk." Through the fog of his pain, he watched two blurry images swaggering off.

CHAPTER
SEVEN

"*VOLIM te*, Daddy."

"What's that, sweetheart?"

"*Volim te*. Means 'I love you' in Bosnian. Kamila taught me."

Kamila glimpsed over her shoulder from the sink where she was hand washing the breakfast dishes. Harden had asked her to wait before cranking on the noisy dishwasher, but he hadn't meant for her to scrub them by hand. Preoccupied, he'd disregarded her. He wondered why his housekeeper had bothered to teach Olivia such a phrase. Did she feel that way toward him?

"*Volim te* back at you," Harden said under his breath. "Now let Daddy focus on this little bit of work."

"Are you being supercilious, Daddy?" Olivia asked.

Harden, surprised she'd articulated one of his favorite words, gave in to his chuckles despite his mounting aggravation. "I might be, but I need to concentrate. Why don't you watch *Thumb and Thumbelina?*"

"Okay." Olivia wandered toward the living room where she kept Harden's old laptop that he'd given her after Marshall Enterprises had bought his newer Toshiba.

He turned back to concentrate on the bevy of farming equipment reports scattered across the kitchen table, where he needed the extra space.

Local farmers had expressed interest in the manufacturer and they wanted Marshall to investigate them. The newer designs required less fuel, a major cost consideration in farming, especially lately. Dick Carelli had bellyached how fuel comprised almost a third of his operating costs.

Kamila replenished his coffee. She moved back to the counter and finished drying the dishes. Harden gazed at her backside. Her shoulders and butt shook while she swiped the damp rag over the bowls and plates. She wasn't so bad looking for a woman her age. About five feet five, feminine and solid. Sure, she was older, but Lillian had also been older by a few years. *Man, I must be desperate.*

She unplugged the sink, dried her hands on a towel, went to retrieve her purse from the laundry room cupboard where she stowed it, and stood before him. "I go to store now."

"Do you have the list?" Harden asked.

"Yes, and the money you put with."

He relaxed more once the purr of Kamila's Toyota faded down the driveway. She usually took her time shopping, but she knew to return before ten. He'd already told her he planned to head to work by that time. He'd wanted to examine the research material and type a rough draft for an acquisition proposal at home first.

The house was as still as it could be for a Friday morning. Mason had left for baseball practice in Mr. Hart's old pickup. Since his last altercation, Mason had managed to stick to his promise and evade trouble. Harden's threat to send him to military school seemed to have accomplished his objective. Harden did not like to use such weapons, but in desperate moments with little else at his disposal, he flung at him what he could.

But wouldn't he like to ship him off to military school and out of his hair?

No, not that badly. I couldn't be that overwrought. Besides, how would I even afford it?

"Look, Daddy." Olivia ran into the kitchen holding a piece of paper that flapped like a flag in a strong wind.

"Aren't you watching your show?"

"I drew a picture instead. See?" She held up the drawing to show him but upset a pot on the counter that Kamila had said contained herbs.

"Olivia!" Harden leaped from his chair and stood over the shattered pot. Soil and green shoots were splattered across the linoleum. In his anger, he ripped off a lengthy flow of paper towels and squatted to gather the mess into a manageable pile.

"See what happens when you're careless? You want me to look at your artwork, but this is what I have to do instead. I have to clean up after you." He went for the broom and swept the debris into the dustpan.

"This is the time I must spend with you now," he repeated, stooped over and sweeping. "You see? Cleaning up after you. If you weren't so sloppy and always in a hurry, I could be looking at your drawing right now. I have to clean up your mess instead."

He watched Olivia's red-stocking feet turn away. Nudging guilt aside, he replaced the broom with a wet paper towel to scrub what seemed like an endless mess. After he cleaned the floor and tossed the remains of the herb pot, he plopped down before his work. He sat staring at the opposing wall. Olivia hadn't really disrupted him. Worries had plagued his mind when she'd rushed in with her drawing.

A minute later, he pushed himself up from the table and strolled into the living room. "Let's see your picture, sweetheart," he said to Olivia, outstretched on her belly with her face inches from the laptop screen.

She jumped up and grabbed the drawing from the console. "Here."

Harden brought her closer to his side, his arm wrapped around her waist, and gazed at the colorful crayon drawing. "Is that the swing set and burr oak?"

"Yes," she said, nodding like a bobblehead. "Do you think it's good?"

"Sure do. It's the nicest rendition I've seen. We'll have to add it to the refrigerator."

Harden set the drawing aside and sat with his daughter to watch *Thumb and Thumbelina*. He ignored the clutter around him. Toys, clothes, shoes. Most belonging to Olivia. *Why was she such a slob?* For fifteen minutes he feigned interest in the digitally animated cartoon before he insisted he needed to get back to his work. By that time, Olivia was so entranced by her show (a movie she'd seen dozens of times) Harden eased himself away without objection.

He sat back at the table and compiled a rough draft from the reports. He was readying his briefcase to leave for work when Mr. Hart's truck pulled into the driveway. Mason was home from his Friday game.

He was surprised when Mr. Hart escorted Mason to the front door rather than leaving him in a plume of dust. Harden went to meet them. Mr. Hart's son remained seated in the truck bed, gaping above the rim.

"Hi, Mr. Hart." In the midst of shaking his hand, Harden realized why he'd walked Mason to the door. Black and blue swelling practically sealed Mason's left eye. Instinct told him that Mason had not gotten clobbered by a fast pitch.

Harden kept his cool in front of the man he'd known since high school. Mr. Hart had been Harden's eleventh grade woodshop teacher. He and his classmates had thought of him as a grown-up man. Later, they'd realized he was only eight years older than them. Out of habit, Harden still referred to him as "Mr. Hart."

"We were just about to collect the equipment and head home after the scrimmage," Mr. Hart said, "when Mason and another boy got into a fight. Same boy as last time. Mike Tuelong. He's a hot mouth. Coach suspended both for a week."

Mason stood clutching the plastic bag that contained his dirty cleats. He wiggled his toes, which protruded from his sandals. Harden gazed at his smarting eye. Another humdinger. *Not this all over again.*

"Get on up to your room," he said, sighing. Once Mason's clunky steps receded upstairs, Harden shook his head at Mr. Hart. "He's been acting up again, I'm afraid."

Mr. Hart laid a reassuring hand on Harden's shoulder, the way he had when Harden would come to him with questions about his lopsided birdhouses. "He's a good kid. He just needs to figure out how to handle these boys. Have you considered therapy?"

"He seemed to have snapped out of it the last time he went through this," Harden said. Did he really need therapy?

"Don't worry over it much. Maybe it'll pass for good this time. Meanwhile, we adults will try to keep an eye on those bullies. They'll most likely grow bored, like last time. And then hopefully they'll be matured by then."

"I appreciate your help, Mr. Hart. Thanks for driving Mason back."

Kamila pulled up to the house just as Mr. Hart was walking to his pickup. Harden spotted her expression. She sensed something unpleasant, not even accounting for her poor herb plant that waited to greet her from atop the kitchen's overstuffed garbage pail.

Mr. Hart drove down the driveway, and Harden helped Kamila unload the groceries. He grabbed the cold compress out of the freezer and lumbered upstairs. A standard routine lately.

"I'll have this on my mind all day at work," he said to Mason from the doorway, peering at the back of his head where he sat at his desk. "You really are trying to make things tough for us. Here, put this on your eye." Mason reached for the compress from Harden's outstretched hand without turning. "You've gone and gotten yourself suspended from the team. Next time it'll be expulsion. You're stronger than this, Mason. You're stronger. Stay in your room the rest of the day and think about it. No playing outside, no bike riding, no television. I'll make sure Kamila sticks by my word."

At work, Harden did spend most of his time pondering Mason. He submitted his equipment proposal to his boss, Marshall's owner, Charlie Marshall, and smiled and chatted with coworkers, ensuring he tucked away his pained thoughts. They already knew too much about his personal life.

Thank God the weekend neared. He wanted to salvage the week somehow. Perhaps he'd take the kids to the aquatic center in Dyersville to lift their droopy moods. They all could use quality time together before the summer's end.

Had Harden been neglecting Mason and Olivia?

Maybe I am supercilious.

That evening, Harden entered the house, leery of what to expect. He recognized the smell of Kamila's dinner—more spiced kabobs. Olivia lay on the living room floor playing *Let's Go Shopping*. She giggled and slapped the carpet after each failed attempt to maneuver through the checkout line. She always took failure lighter than Mason. *If only she wasn't so messy.*

On her way out the door, Kamila reminded him that she planned to take Monday off. Harden made a mental note to ask his mother when he saw her on Sunday to use a personal day from her job and stay with the kids. Kamila informed him that Mason had remained in his room as ordered.

Satisfied, Harden pulled himself up the stair railing and found Mason lying faceup in bed, playing with his iPod. Harden probably should've forbid him from using electronic gadgets like last time. Not that it had done any good.

His eye appeared less swollen, but the blue-green discoloration remained. The last torment he needed was a visit to the doctor's office. "You can come downstairs for dinner now," he said to Mason. "Let me know if that eye gives you any trouble."

In his room, Harden changed into his typical evening attire—sweatpants and T-shirt. Tired and unhappy, he ate dinner alongside the kids, trying his best to appear content. Olivia was the only one animated among them. They ate, and Mason cleared the table and switched on the dishwasher as instructed. Harden rested on the living room sofa, breathing easier.

Mason spread across the easy chair, reading a puzzle book that pinpointed state capitals Harden had given him for his eleventh birthday in February. Unusual to see something in his hands other than an electronic gadget. He seemed satisfied, considering.

Harden gazed at Olivia, innocent and quiet, doodling in her notepad. Rare warmth and satisfaction expanded around him. Times like these gave him the most pleasure. When the children played peacefully without stress, parenting wasn't so bad. Everything appeared calm and harmonious. Any hard feelings harbored by either of them must have evaporated, forgotten like a wispy dream.

He fixed his eyes on them, absorbing the moment. The now. He tried to inhale the scene, to freeze the instant like a snapshot and hold onto it so he might never forget. Perhaps Grandpa had observed his family at the same spot with similar emotions, smiling over Harden's father when he was a boy. This was what he liked about parenting. He cracked a grin. Maybe he wasn't such a bad father, after all.

CHAPTER
EIGHT

ORANGE light from the streetlamps cut through the gap in the drawn curtains. The police scanner and television were turned off, and his apartment remained mostly silent save for the light rattling of the air conditioner. Even with the microwave's interior light on, he could see on the door the reflection of his bruised left eye and scrapes on his forehead. He touched the swelling on the back of his head and winced.

The microwave dinged, and he reached in for the mug of steaming water. He steeped a tea bag and carried the mug to his bed. Grunting, he sat back against the wall and blew into the hot liquid.

Andy had already provided a reluctant description of his two attackers to the police. He was able to capture a view of them before they left him for dead on the sidewalk. They had trailed Andy from the Clock Tower parking lot, the police had pieced together, and ambushed him while he had turned the doorknob to his apartment building. But Andy blamed the Chicago Police Department more than his assailants. If not for them, he'd still be able to run his business—and move his head without the swirling nausea.

They'd forced him to provide evidence for a case that would knock less than a decimal point off Chicago's homicide rate. And the suspects probably would plea bargain and face a lesser charge of second degree murder, spending fewer than six years in prison. Then back to the crime circuit.

Idiots!

The waste sickened Andy worse than the lumps on his back.

None of it made sense.

Andy had spent the past twenty-four hours trying to figure out why he'd allowed the police to use him like a sacrificial lamb to fight a disease that would never go away. A disease that, for some, bore too great a profit to end.

Andy had become one of those profiteers. He didn't care. He'd already paid a stiffer price than the killers or the city. And he had the achy body to prove it.

Tea, for now, plugged the hole in his soul. He sipped and tried to allow the orange pekoe to mollify his anger and pain. He had turned off his cell phone for some added peace. No use answering it. Six callers had inquired about weekend tours since his attack. Andy had to tell them "maybe" with the awful possibility of canceling additional bookings.

The door swung open. Andy strained to turn his head and see who'd entered. Ken stood by the galley kitchen and stared at him with an arrogant sheen in his blue eyes. Dressed in his street clothes (black tank and khaki cargo shorts), Ken appeared almost unrecognizable. Ken usually kept himself scarce on his nights off.

Ken switched on the kitchen light. "You look horrible," he said, dropping the keys into his shorts pocket and strutting to the bed. A genuine glint of concern washed over his complexion. His bulging biceps flexed when he scratched at the orange stubble on his chin. "You should still be in the hospital."

"They didn't find anything wrong." Andy squinted from the light and set aside his tea. "Just scrapes and bruises. I'll mend. They gave me a prescription for pain, but I haven't bothered to fill it."

"It's that damn tour business of yours."

Andy slumped onto the futon and rolled his back to Ken. "My business had less to do with this than yours. If it wasn't for the cops, I wouldn't be lying here with a black eye and a knot on the back of my head the size of Soldier Field."

"You bitch about the police, yet they were the first ones you called after your attack."

Andy slurped up a small pool of saliva on his pillow. "Sure, sure," he said. "Just don't talk too loud."

"You've been asking for it since you started this garbage, and you know it." The refrigerator door opened and closed, coinciding with the snap and hiss of a beer can opening. His voice louder, Ken added, "You're lucky those punks didn't kill you."

Andy regarded Ken through blurry eyes. "Don't lecture me, please." He reached up with a shaky hand for Ken's beer. Ken held the can steady to Andy's trembling lips. The refreshing, cold liquid invigorated him, and he sat upright again, wiped his mouth with the back of his hand, and watched Ken kick back on the small love seat. Large brown calf muscles tensed from his crossing one leg over the other. Ken was one of the few natural redheads Andy had known who tanned easily.

"You really did this to yourself," Ken said.

The back of Andy's head found the pillow. "I don't even want to testify. The prosecution put my business in jeopardy."

"Is that all you care about?"

"It's how I earn a living. Plus I'm helping the overall economy. I've brought tourists to Chicago."

"They would've come whether you had your asinine business or not. Do you even ever stop and let your passengers patronize South Side establishments? No one profits from your tour business down there but you."

Andy hated Ken's rare stumbling onto righteous high ground. "There's only one economy the city of Chicago recognizes," he said in defiance, "and that's what takes place under the table."

"So you'd rather be low and dirty?"

"There're different classes of lowlife." Andy felt his face twitch with one of his latest self-effacing smirks. "I'm a lowlife of the highest sort."

"You're a bozo."

"You could've been a little help." Andy turned to reface the wall. "Why didn't you do something so I wouldn't have had to talk to that prosecutor in the first place?"

"What was I to do? Step in and say, 'Hey, guys, that's my boyfriend you're badgering. Please let him go.'?"

"Are we really boyfriends, Ken? You and I, huh?"

"What's that mean?"

"Nothing," Andy murmured into his pillow. "Forget it."

The old lady who lived upstairs coughed, sneezed, and prattled about. *What does she keep up there, the Chicago Bulls?* He sipped his tea, set the mug aside, and fixed his bare feet on the carpet. Even his toes ached. "What are you doing here, Ken? I didn't ask you to come."

"I wanted to check on you. And to let you know we have a fix on your assailants. Twentieth District doesn't think it's the triple homicide guys you fingered, but two who work for them, anyway, or who work for their ringleader. It's a whole chain of command out there. We'll nail them for battery and witness tampering. We don't know where they are, but we're looking for them. Your defendants refuse to talk."

"But I talked, didn't I? Look what it got me."

"You made yourself a target for a lot of people before that."

"The cops made me a target, you mean."

"Stop blaming the police department. We might be the only ones who can save your butt at this point. The drug dealers are the least of your concerns."

"What am I supposed to do?" Andy rubbed his temples. "Give up my business until the trial is over in January? I won't have a business by then."

Andy watched Ken's Adam's apple wobble up and down while he sipped his beer and swallowed. His underarm hair seemed extra red. "That's another thing I wanted to talk to you about," he said. "You have to leave."

"Huh?"

"You have to ditch town for a while."

"But it's the middle of summer. I've got tourists lined up from Japan, Germany, Sweden, all over North America. More people have called for this weekend. I have a career to consider."

"Career? More like a scam."

"The whole world is a scam, Ken. What's the point?" Andy grimaced from his own raised voice. Quieter, he said, "Why do I have to sit out life while everyone else is having a grand time doing whatever they want without concern for the consequences?"

"You have no choice this time." Ken moved to the kitchen and popped open another beer. "You've got the entire South Side buzzing," he said, returning to the sofa, his bare knees, coated with tiny red hairs, pointing toward the ceiling. "Take a trip somewhere. A week or two should simmer things down. We'll nab those punks."

"A week or two? That'll be the end of my business, for sure."

"So much the better."

"That's what you guys really want."

"You're in deep shit, Andy. You should take that beating you got as a warning."

"Maybe the city sent those thugs after me."

Ken smirked and shrugged. "Could be. Either way, you need to hightail it."

"Those punks were just blowing off steam. No one's going to bother me again. Not as long as I refrain from letting you guys force me to testify in court."

Ken reached over and seized Andy's arm. "The prosecutor is counting on you. You don't have a choice."

Andy freed his arm, winced, and said, "I've counted on a lot of people in my life too, and they didn't always come through either. Life's like that."

Ken settled back against the sofa. "You're leaving town for a while, case closed. You won't have anything left if you stay, business or otherwise. Where is it you're from?"

"Streamwood," Andy mumbled toward his toes.

Snickering, Ken scratched his nose. "Suburban boy. Figures. That's too close, anyway. Best if you desert the whole area, to be safe. Get out of state."

"Where out of state? South America?"

"You'll think of somewhere. Rest up here a few days, then hit the road. I'll keep an eye on your place, collect your mail and all that. Don't tell anyone where you're going except for me."

Andy placed a hand on his stomach and eased back against the mattress. "This is ridiculous."

"It's either take a trip or face more harassment, jail time, or possibly another beating, from virtually anyone. It's not a suggestion, Andy, it's an exact order. Listen, this town doesn't like bad publicity."

Sleepy sickness pressed on Andy's head. He pulled himself into a ball. Badgered to flee. And to where? The dark side of the moon?

CHAPTER
NINE

HARDEN watched from the porch as a thin sheet of sunlight sliced through the heavy cloud cover and draped a yellow haze across the far end of the cornfield like a curtain. The gray and white stratus clouds turned the remainder of the field dark green. Rain would fall by late morning. The farmers would be overjoyed. They needed the rain for their crops. The corn had stopped growing the past week.

Mason and Olivia were watching television. They'd remain indoors if it rained. Mason was suspended from Saturday's baseball game, but even if he wasn't, the game would certainly be postponed. Harden hoped the kids stayed quiet and out of his way while he fine-tuned his machinery acquisitions proposal.

He settled at the kitchen table to focus on the work spread before him. He worked fast, accomplishing more than expected by noon. Pleased, he cleaned up his work space and called the kids for lunch. They prepared peanut butter and jelly sandwiches while the predicted downpour smacked the windows.

Olivia gazed out the rain-shellacked windowpane. "The creek will overflow and the fish'll get lost."

"A few days ago you were worried they lacked water," Harden said.

"But now they might drown."

"You always say that, dumbhead," Mason said. "Fish can't drown."

"They'll wiggle their way back to the creek once the rain stops, sweetheart," Harden assured her.

"Unless the crows eat them first," Mason said with a snicker.

"Daddy, make Mason stop saying nasty things."

"Mason, stop needling your sister. He was only joking, sweetheart. Now come and finish making your sandwich."

Olivia stuck out her tongue at Mason and finished spreading the jelly atop the peanut butter. They plopped their sandwiches onto plates and carried them to the table. He warned Olivia to sit up and not to drop crumbs, and Mason not to drum the tabletop with his fingers. The bruise on Mason's left eye had faded to an ochre color, and the swelling was visible only when Harden looked hard enough. He appeared in good spirits, otherwise.

"What has eighteen legs and catches flies?" he said.

Olivia stretched her neck, and the dab of peanut butter stuck on her cheek crumbled and fell to her plate. "A big ugly caterpillar."

"Wrong, dumbhead. And besides, caterpillars don't catch flies. They eat leaves."

"What is it?"

"Wait for Dad to answer."

"I don't know," Harden said, chewing with contrived interest.

"A baseball team!"

Mason and Olivia laughed and laughed, slopping their sandwiches against the roofs of their mouths. Harden wondered if they were as fidgety as him and tried to inject their home with silly jokes to fill the void carved by their mother's absence. The ongoing rain matched the artificial cheerfulness.

Determined to conjure some genuine levity, Harden rubbed his hands together and worked up the gregariousness more familiar to his friends and coworkers. "Hurry and eat so we can play."

"A game?" Olivia's blue eyes expanded.

"Only if you eat your sandwich and don't make a mess."

"Hurray!" Olivia cheered.

They finished eating, cleaned the table, and stacked their lunch dishes in the dishwasher. Next they spread out on the living room carpet to play Monopoly Junior, with the gurgle of rainwater rushing down the gutters.

Four turns in, Olivia said, "Will Uncle Andy want to play games with us too?"

"I'm sure he will, sweetheart."

"He played games with us last time he was here," Mason joined in. "We played that dumb game where you have to draw."

"Pictionary," Olivia sang out and raised her arms in a strange show of victory. "I want to play it again with him. I love to draw."

"You remember that?" Harden was surprised his daughter could recollect something from when she was four years old. The thought first tickled him, but he wondered what else she might remember from a time period that held traumatic memories for a little girl. For every one of them.

"I want him to take us to the pool while he's here," Mason said.

"I'm sure your Uncle Andy will take you once he gets here."

Mason and Olivia raved their approval, and they played the game until Mason collected the last of the properties. While the kids scampered around upstairs, Harden was left to clean up, but he valued the moment alone to focus on something other than work and his personal life.

The remainder of the afternoon passed much the same. Tedious and smooth, save for the minor scuffle between Mason and Olivia. The rain still trapped them indoors, so Harden suggested they bake brownies from the mix Kamila had bought from the grocery store. Mason especially liked to experiment in the kitchen, and the distraction kept them busy for an additional hour. The only mishap: Olivia dropped an egg while carrying it from the refrigerator.

Harden allowed the kids to slip into their swimsuits and frolic outside under the sticky rain. Clutching a mug of coffee, he watched from the porch while they splashed in puddles in grassy areas and hopped and yelped. Olivia raced to the back and returned with good news. The creek fish appeared alive. He recalled playing similar summertime games with his brothers. A mixture of delight, regret, and dreariness settled over his soul.

After a light dinner of Kamila's leftover kabobs, they watched television until the kids' eyes drooped. Harden ushered them upstairs to bed and read to Olivia from one of her favorite books. Once they were tucked in, he loped to the kitchen and cracked open a beer. In midsip, he caught a glimpse of his reflection on the door leading to the backyard. Dressed in his sweatpants and T-shirt, he looked the image of the frumpy dad. *No wonder I feel so secondhand.*

His gloominess tracked him into Sunday morning and through church, where he sat with the kids, his mother, and Lance's family. He decided he needed to make a show at Mass alongside his children that morning to satisfy his mother, who'd been pestering him more. The sermon failed to lift his slumping spirits. But he was glad to see old friends and spend time with his big brother.

Afterward, they met at the family home on Third Street in Duncan. Corralled indoors by a nagging drizzle, they brunched on tomato slices, corn pancakes, scrambled eggs, and fried slices of leftover ham roast. Later, Lance's only child, Damon, entertained the kids in the basement while the adults played several hands of Hearts.

When Harden mentioned in passing that Andrew Wingal planned a short visit to Burr Oak Farm, the card table fell silent, but their forced smiles amused Harden more than irked him. His mother squared her hand.

"I haven't seen him in quite some time," she said, fanning out the cards in front of her nose. "It'll be good to see him again."

"He was always nice to me," Lance's wife, Holly, said in her typical relaxed manner.

His brother brought out a more boisterous response. "Andy's a good guy," Lance said. "Hope I get a chance to see him while he's here."

"Did he say what's bringing him?" his mom asked, gaze unmoved from her hand.

Harden shrugged. "Just that he was coming out for a visit. Probably wants to see the kids. It's been a while."

"How long did he say he was staying for?"

"Not long, Mom."

They passed their cards, and Harden waited for more comments about Andrew. But Harden suspected they bit their tongues. Several more hands played out, and eventually his mother voiced her concern for Mason's swollen eye. Harden refrained from mentioning his prior bruised cheek, but Lance, who had probably heard it through the Duncan grapevine, uttered it on his behalf. *Thanks, Bro!*

His mother expressed her typical reserved concern. "I hope you're able to spend enough time with him."

"He's with his kids more than anyone, Mom," Lance said, slapping down a discard. "He does the best he can."

"I was merely expressing an interest," she said toward her cards. "I know Kamila does her best, but a housekeeper cannot replace a mother or a father."

Harden endured the Mom-Lance sandwich for a few more hands before leaving them to play three-man Hearts. The rest of the afternoon he lounged with Dad, who'd been sitting and smoking his Don Diegos in the garage with the door raised, since Mom couldn't stand the stench.

His father, certifiably obese, appeared happy in his nascent retirement from Healey Dairy, but Harden worried more and more about the sixty-six-year-old's health. The last ordeal any of them needed was the untimely death of Dad.

Together, they watched the drizzle and sucked down a few beers while chatting about farming, the weather, Harden's youngest brother, Jordan, who lived in Kansas City, and Harden's job at Marshall. They rarely discussed anything personal, although Harden understood behind his father's defiant blue eyes, sealed near shut now with rivulets of flesh, resided a man who'd endured the pain and happiness of a full life. His father always danced the thin line between sense and sentimentality. It was with his big brother, Lance, a fireman in adjacent Buchanan County, that

Harden could reveal his inner thoughts—those needing a good shaking out.

Despite living twenty miles apart, the duties of parenthood had separated Harden from his brother. Emotionally, their lives as modern fathers united them closer than ever. Somehow they managed to check on each other enough to reassure them neither lacked for moral support.

Before leaving for the night and while waiting for everyone to gather, they snatched a short, private hallway chat by the front door. Lance gave Harden one of his, "so how're things" looks. Harden peered at his loafers and shrugged.

"Mom's right. I wish I was around more. I'd catch one of those punks teasing Mason. Probably wallop him before Mason had a chance."

"Sorry for squealing about Mason's other fight. You know how things are around here. She'd find out anyway."

Harden shook his head. "I just don't want this to get out of hand like last time."

"What about Olivia? Does she get any of the teasing or bullying that Mason gets?"

"If she does, she keeps it to herself and handles it much better than Mason. It's been three years. Why won't they leave them be?"

"Most of the kids are okay, aren't they? Only a few bully them. Don't fret over it too much."

"Christ, I try. But I worry about Mason getting older. He'll be a teenager in a few years. Imagine things then."

"Brother, you're doing the best you can with what you got. You have enough on your plate without worrying about what-ifs."

Harden trusted that his levelheaded fireman brother had made a good point.

That evening back at Burr Oak Farm, the children settled, somber and quiet. Typical after a full day of Sunday socializing. They remained in their rooms most of the night and made not a peep. But rather than relish the stillness, Harden moped about downstairs in his sweatpants and slippers, agitated and uncertain.

What-ifs. He'd spent a lifetime tripping over unforeseen fears. He'd failed at warding off the ones that had proved too real. Why bother worrying about ones that had yet to materialize?

He stood on the porch leaning against the railing, listening to the crickets and watching the lightning bugs. Harden never sat while alone on the porch. Seemed silly to swing without someone beside him, like Olivia, who liked to kick her legs and make the swing wobble.

The rain had stopped, and the corn appeared to have grown two or three inches in the past twenty-four hours. Probably an illusion from the purple blooming over the cornfield from the setting sun. Sometimes as a boy Harden had sworn he could hear the corn grow after a good rain shower. Out in the field, Dick Carelli's tractor rumbled. He must be tending to the soggy crop.

Gazing off into the fields, with the smell of moist soil thick and tantalizing, he contemplated the odd text message he'd received late Friday night from his former brother-in-law. At first, he hadn't recognized the number with the 312 area code. After a second's thought, a name had scrolled across his mind. Spit had sapped from his mouth when he'd linked to the message, and, sure enough, the message had come from him.

Andy Wingal here, he'd written. *How r u? Would like 2 come 4 visit next week. Ok?* Harden had replied after ten minutes of pondering, not wanting to appear too eager: *Hey, you! Kids would luv it.* Andrew had added he'd be there Thursday afternoon, *for no more than a week.*

Excitement had grabbed hold of the kids after Harden had relayed the news. Lillian's side of the family had faded, and they yearned to reconnect, he was sure. Surprised Andrew still carried around his number, Harden had saved the message on his phone and had reread it several times, like he did now.

The more Harden considered Andrew's coming, the more expectant he became too, like the kids. A relative stranger was going to visit Burr Oak Farm, and Harden looked forward to something to break up their monotony. Andrew might bring a much-needed added distraction for Olivia and Mason. Yet he also harbored reservations.

Harden wondered what was up with Andrew. He hadn't seen or heard from him in three years. His text, even without voice inflections or facial expressions, had an oddity to it. Desperate and sudden.

Harden hoped that Andrew wasn't in any trouble. He'd had enough of the Wingals' issues.

A comfortable breeze broke the muggy night and rustled the corn tassels and leaves, like the wind chime on his parents' porch. Crickets competed with the distant call of thrushes and warblers. The sun disappeared completely, and the sky transformed from a purple to a cobalt stain across the horizon. He pocketed his cell phone and wondered how things might be with Andrew visiting their little farm.

How strange it would be to see him again—along with the painful memories he might bring with him.

CHAPTER
TEN

THE drive from Uptown to the Mississippi River crossing in Dubuque took four hours, longer than Andy had recalled from his last trip to Iowa three years ago. He still didn't want to go. He'd felt like a fool texting Harden when he'd failed to think of an alternative. He had to search for his old Motorola to find Harden's number, unsure if he still had it. Such a long span of time had lapsed since he'd last spoken with his former brother-in-law. But his current trip came under far more pleasant circumstances, considering.

He'd come to Dover County three times throughout Lillian and Harden's marriage. The first visit was for their September wedding, the second for Easter the following year, and seven years later when Harden had telephoned about Lillian.

At that time, his mind had fastened on the horrible events that had forced him to take a week off his public relations job and head for his sister's farmstead. The undulating terrain, like a windswept sea, had hurled him headlong into grief.

Still achy after his beating, but no worse than after a long night out with friends cruising the Halsted Street bars, the half-day drive hadn't exacerbated his injuries like he'd feared. Resentment toward Ken and the police for forcing him to leave dogged him more. He couldn't help but agonize over the mounds of money he was losing by leaving Chicago. Dozens of tourists and thousands of dollars—flushed down the toilet.

Each mile along Iowa's choppy Route 20, and his misgivings grew greater. He wondered how Harden and the children had fared without Lillian. Guilt forced him to clutch the steering wheel, and he tried to stifle the nagging voice inside his head.

You should've made yourself more available to them. You shouldn't have allowed three years to pass without a single visit or even a phone call.

The rolling hills of northeastern Iowa carried him along. Silos, far from the highway, reminded him of "magic mushrooms" from his high school days. He chuckled to himself, seeing the foreign landscape. Yet some of it looked familiar. Estate homes, like those in Chicago's upper-class suburbs, sat closer to the highway atop what was probably former farmland. Where did the residents work? How had they come into their money out in the middle of nowhere?

Soon, the green signage welcoming drivers to Dover County appeared ahead. He had his Magellan switched on, but once Andy exited for the small town of Duncan, he realized he'd have no difficulty locating the Krane farm, and he clicked off the annoying voice.

Cornfield after cornfield flanked the country roads. For a while, Andy allowed the pastoral landscape to soothe his nerves. But as soon as he spotted the Kranes' mailbox, his heart began krumping inside his chest.

Hesitantly he turned toward the driveway. The crunch of gravel under the van's heavy tires sounded like an army march. He slowed and took in the small white farmhouse with the green roof, semiwraparound porch, and nearby silo and barn. Everything exactly as he had last seen it. As if on cue, Harden Krane, still dressed in his office attire, stepped outside.

Worries that he might be unwelcome vanished upon recognizing Harden's signature grin, one that seemed to extend wider than the cornfields. Andy matched Harden's smile even before he had a chance to set the brake and exit the van.

They approached each other, hands extended. "How you been, Andrew?" Harden said, clasping two warm hands over Andy's. He had the same cheery blue eyes (perhaps with less sparkle), and those irresistibly pinchable cheeks that had always made Andy succumb to chuckles. As they did now.

"Good to see you, Harden. Been too long," Andy said, unable to stop laughing from the mixture of good feelings and released tension.

Harden shared in Andy's drunk-like laughter, but then he stifled himself and moved his face within inches of Andy's. "Looks like you've had a little scuffle. What happened? You didn't get mugged in the big city, did you?"

Andy had hoped his bruised eye would have completely healed before the trip. The black and blue that had faded into a green ring was, in some ways, more noticeable. "It's a long story that would bore the pants off you."

Harden released Andy's hand and gazed over his shoulder. "Some mode of transportation you got there. Big enough to haul ten head of cattle."

Andy relished Harden's country vernacular and glanced at his iconic van, his laughter fading into light coughs. "It's the only vehicle I got," he said.

"I've read about your unusual business." Harden snickered. "South Side Tours, huh?"

"We haven't spoken in so long I forgot you might've learned."

"We get the Internet in Iowa too, you know. The modern computer originated here, in fact. Iowa State University. Ever heard of the Atanasoff-Berry computer?"

The storm door slapped shut, and a little girl with long blonde ponytails fluttering behind her rushed outside. Olivia immediately threw her arms around Andy's legs. Taken aback by her greeting, Andy hesitated before lifting his niece and returning her hug. "I can't believe how big you've gotten," he said, noticing how she smelled of peanut butter. "How old are you now?"

"Seven."

"Wow, that's old."

The storm door shut again, but softer. Mason ogled them from the top of the stoop. Andy let Olivia slide from his embrace, and Mason shuffled closer and gave him a timid hug.

"You're almost as tall your dad, Mason."

"He's growing faster than the corn," Harden said.

"I see you've got something on your face too," Andy said, glancing at Mason with a squinty smile. "Looks like we're twins."

Blushing, Mason stepped back from Andy. "Just a little fight with some guy from my baseball team."

"A baseball brawl, huh? What does the other boy look like?"

"A lot worse than me."

Andy poked Mason's ribcage. "That's the business."

"Why don't we get your stuff inside?" Harden said, scratching his nose. "Mason, fetch your uncle's bags from the van."

"Don't worry, I got it." Andy retrieved his duffel bag and laptop and walked with the family toward the house, which seemed to grow by meters with each encroaching step.

"Did you find us okay?" Harden asked.

"I remembered every road. Didn't even need the GPS."

"How was the drive?"

"Other than traffic through I-90, not too bad. I always forget how mountainous northwestern Illinois is. Gorgeous. Even around Dubuque."

"Careful driving it in the snow."

Andy knew firsthand the treacherous conditions of windy Route 20 in wintertime. Early November, almost three years ago, he'd last traveled to Burr Oak Farm. But why bring up awkward memories so soon after his arrival?

Inside, Harden introduced Andy to a woman working in the kitchen as his housekeeper. They nodded to each other. Andy at once took note of her cold dark eyes, and icy fingers kneaded along his spine. Kamila spoke something under her breath to the children. Sounded like a foreign language. Whatever she told them, they paid her no mind and focused more on Andy.

Harden escorted Andy to the basement with Olivia bouncing at their heels. "You'll be bunking here," he said. "I think you stayed down here the last time you came."

Andy suppressed the unpleasant pang and gazed about with a tight smile. "Candy on the pillow, Harden? You're not watching too much Martha Stewart, are you?"

Harden's face turned pink. "That must be one of Mom's ideas. She watched the kids for me on Monday, and I asked her to ready the room. Mom tries so hard to make people feel at home, she makes them feel like paying guests."

Andy unwrapped the chocolate mint and popped it in his mouth. "I like it."

Back in the kitchen, Kamila the housekeeper had already taken dinner out of the oven. It sat steaming on the counter. Using an even voice, she told them dinner was ready and disappeared into what looked like the laundry room. A minute later, she returned with her purse snug on her shoulder.

"Smells great," Andy said with a high tone to lighten up Kamila. "What do you call it?"

"Ćevapi."

Andy tried to pronounce it but gave up. "Looks and smells good, anyway."

Kamila left without a formal good-bye, and she pulled out of the driveway in her Toyota Corolla. She left behind a chill plainer than the swollen eye on his and Mason's faces. Lucky that the children created a wave of energy that kept the mood uplifted. Olivia grabbed Andy's hand and pulled him toward the living room.

"It's dinnertime, Olivia. Let your uncle have a moment."

"I don't mind, really," Andy said over his shoulder, allowing Olivia to drag him before a laptop on the carpet.

They played a quick game of *Let's Go Shopping* before Harden insisted they stop. Already out of breath, Andy sat with the family at the formal dining table. He watched them as Olivia, her small hands pressed together like the wings of an origami bird, muttered grace. His face heated when she thanked God for his visit. Harden gave him a soulful glance through one open eye, and Andy smiled and choked back his chuckles.

Dinner conversation revolved around the kids wanting to know more about Andy's "funny-looking van," which he explained—in partial truth—that he'd bought secondhand, with no other elucidation. Mason and Olivia announced what they expected to do with their uncle during his stay.

"He's only going to be here a week. I don't think he'll have much time for all those things," Harden said.

"I'm up for it all. I'm on vacation, and I plan on having some fun."

And indeed Andy, despite the knowledge that he was losing money each day, hoped to make the best of his short visit. Across the table, Harden's sidelong glance told Andy that he might already have guessed the real reason for Andy's coming to Iowa.

After dinner, the kids again insisted Andy play with them. He spread out on the living room floor while the kids fought over which games. Mason complained about playing Pictionary but relented to his little sister's wishes.

"Don't you play, Harden?" Andy asked.

"I'll sit up here on the sofa and let you have all the fun tonight, Andrew. My job will be to make sure no one cheats."

They played about five rounds, until Mason insisted on a game of Monopoly Junior, and for another two hours Mason amassed a small fortune until Harden—*thank God*—herded them to bed. Andy tucked Olivia under the bedcovers and read to her from one of her picture books. She was sure to demand he flip back when he tried to skip a few pages to speed things along. Mason had warmed up to Andy enough they shared scar stories, pointing out their cuts and bruises. Andy embellished a scenario in which he'd trounced two burglars.

Andy found Harden downstairs. He plopped down beside him on the sofa and breathed. "Can't believe how much the kids have grown," he said. "Mason's turning into a spitting image of you. And Olivia looks exactly like…." Awkwardness reached through the cushions and seized Andy. He couldn't broach that topic, not yet, if ever. "Like… like the Wingal side of the family."

"I've noticed that too. She's even got the budding of your dimpled chin." There was a moment more silence. Harden smiled at him. "You sure did run them ragged tonight."

"You kidding? They wore me out. I'm exhausted."

"Kamila's a good mother hen, but she doesn't enjoy games with the kids much. Wish I could be around more, but work has me busy lately. I'm senior agronomist now."

"Awesome. Congrats. You still working at that industrial shop? Marshall…?"

"Marshall Farming Enterprises. Keeps the family fed and under a roof."

"What about your dream of farming? You give up on that?"

Harden shook his head, grinned, and lowered his gaze to his lap. "Unfortunately, that's still a distant fantasy. Not possible with just me and two young kids. Requires much too much work."

Andy nodded toward the french doors. "That man still renting your land? Dick something-Italian?"

"Dick Carelli. Still comes all the way from Fayette County."

"Guess it's a good way to bring in some extra cash."

"Things could be a lot worse. That's what I tell myself. So what about you, Andrew?" Harden tapped his leg. "Expound on this tour business of yours."

"It's no big deal. Just a job. Something to keep me—" He snorted. "—out of trouble. I had to find a way to bring in an income. I was laid off about a year ago and couldn't find any other work."

Harden flexed his eyebrows. "I guess we haven't kept in touch, have we?"

Andy peered at the cold, dark television set. "It's been a while. But I promise I won't stay too long. I don't want to be a nuisance."

"No bother. Stay as long as you like. In case you haven't noticed, the kids are crazy about you being here."

"Your housekeeper isn't too happy I'm here, though."

"Kamila? What do you expect?" Harden snorted. "You show up in a van riddled with bullet holes and with a bruised eye. Besides, she does that silent nagging to everyone she meets. She's become rather territorial over the house and the kids. She's taken a shine to them. I must say, I appreciate it. Lightens my load. But don't let her bother you. That's her way. I think she lost a husband and child during the war in Bosnia. She never talks about it, and I'm not about to ask."

"I think she likes you."

Harden gaped at Andy. "Who? Kamila? What makes you say that?"

"She's taken a shine to more than the kids and the house, I can see. That's why she's territorial."

His face reddening, Harden ogled his shoes and scratched at his temple. Feet pattered about upstairs, followed by a toilet flushing. Andy glanced at the ceiling, suppressed a chuckle.

"It's embarrassing," Harden said. "I try to act as if I don't notice. She's at least ten years older than me, much older than…. That's not a big deal. But still, she's not quite my type. Don't try to marry me off. Mom does that and it drives me nuts."

"I'm the last one to play matchmaker."

"So how's your love life? A guy like you has to have them lined up, right? How does that work living in a big city like Chicago? A date each night?"

Andrew tossed his head back and rolled his eyes. "Not that easy. Hard to explain to straight people. Things are different. You wouldn't understand."

"Doubt it's all that much different. I haven't had a serious date in... I can't remember when. Nobody wants to date a guy with two small kids. Women come around with good intentions, but ultimately they realize it's not for them."

"Maybe things aren't that much different out here," Andy said, speculating. "Guys in Chicago avoid settling down. I'm sort of dating a guy, going on about two months, but he's not exactly ready for the suburbs or anything like that."

"Speaking of the suburbs, how's your mom doing? She still sends the kids gifts for their birthdays and Christmases, but I haven't talked to her in a few years."

"I guess there's still some awkwardness there, what with... with...." Someone had to mention her name. Andy figured it might as well be him. It would sound better falling from his lips first. "With Lillian," he spit out.

Her name plodded through the air, heavier than the Magnetism perfume she used to squirt herself with. Harden flinched but remained poised. He clenched his hands in his lap.

"I suppose that has changed things for all of us," he said toward the coffee table.

Andy studied Harden's profile. From the side, his features bunched toward the middle, leaving those paunchy and vulnerable cheeks exposed. Still looked youthful. He resisted laying a hand on his shoulder. "I'm sorry about staying away for so long," he said. "I should've visited before now, or at least called."

"What could you do? You were in another state two hundred miles away with your own life. Besides, it hasn't really been... that long." Harden tried to bite back a yawn. "Sorry, buddy," he said, "guess I'm not used to staying up past ten these days."

"Back in Chicago, my day would be just starting."

"I should get to bed. Gotta get up early for work. Feel free to stay up. Make yourself at home. If you get hungry, the kitchen's yours." Harden stood and stretched. "We'll talk more tomorrow. Good night, Andrew."

"Hey, Harden. Call me Andy. I always hated it when you called me by my full name."

"All right." Harden chuckled. "Good night, Andy."

"Good night, Harden."

CHAPTER
ELEVEN

ANDY lay in bed, listening to the unfamiliar, muted banter and the background noise seeping through the kitchen floor. Different from the morning rush of cars honking on the street below or the sneezing and grunting of the faceless old woman who lived above him. That feeling of being someplace new descended over him as he stared toward the ceiling. Similar to waking in a strange bed on vacation, although this was no holiday. Andy had come to Iowa against his will.

Light patters scurried away from the basement door, accompanied by a little girl's mischievous tittering.

"He's still sleeping" came Mason's voice. "Don't go down there."

"Be good now, sweetheart," Harden said.

Maybe they wouldn't mind if he slept longer. Unused to early bedtime hours, Andy had spent most of the night texting with Ken after Harden had gone upstairs. He still resented Ken for forcing him to leave Chicago. It was nice to see the kids—and Harden. But what would a misfit like him do in Iowa for an entire week? He'd pleaded with Ken to allow him to return to his tour business. Ken had ended their text thread with the implicit warning: "Keep your head."

What time was it, anyway? No alarm clock. He checked his cell phone. Nine thirty! He tossed the covers aside and scooted to the edge of the bed. He winced from an unexpected soreness in his muscles. He gazed around, rubbing his thighs, unsure what to do first.

Sudden bursts of flickering sunlight pierced the high hopper windows, and he turned in irritation. He smelled something like toasted frozen blueberry waffles and coffee.

Coffee. Now *that* was familiar.

Olivia's gentle giggling roused him to his feet. Adjusting his crotch, he slumped to the bathroom. The house was weird to him. Too snug and overly warm. And the basement smelled of mildew. At least he had a private bathroom.

He brushed his teeth, washed his face. Louder echoing voices traveled through the shower vent.

"He just got here, Kamila," Harden was saying. "Are you sure you just don't like him horning in?"

"Horny in?"

"Horning…. It's an expression. You don't like him being in your space."

"I cannot watch him and the house all the same time."

"You don't have to watch him," Harden said.

"Uncle Andy played games with us, Kamila," Olivia explained to her, which seemed to have shut the housekeeper's mouth long enough for Andy to drag a comb through his hair and change into clothes.

Dressed in his cargo shorts and T-shirt, he stood at the door to the basement, staring at a group of strangers. "Good morning, all."

Four sets of eyes turned to him. Silent a moment, no one seemed to know which move to make, as if they'd forgotten he slept in the basement. Kamila wore the smirk on her round face that Andy had envisioned from downstairs. Olivia leaped from the kitchen table and tugged his hand, insisting that he sit beside her. "We're finishing up breakfast. You can eat fast and help me draw."

"Good morning," Harden said, chuckling. "You sleep okay?"

"Great, thanks. Sorry about sleeping in so late."

"Don't worry about it," Harden said in a light voice. "We're running a bit late this morning too. Fridays are like that around here. Wish I could spend more time with you today, but I have to head into work. Mason and Olivia will keep you entertained, I'm sure."

"Looking forward to a day with the kids."

"Dad, fix my iPod."

"Mason, I'm on my way out the door."

"It's stuck again."

"Christ, Mason, I'm sick and tired of hearing about that godforsaken thing."

"Let me look at it." Andy toyed with Mason's iPod, and within seconds the blue light flashed. "You have to toggle it sometimes. It's all in the thumb action. See? Mine does the same thing."

Smiling, Mason held the iPod in his palm. He thanked Andy, and next Harden ordered him and Olivia upstairs to clean up. Kamila followed after them. "Help yourself to whatever you want," he said once the kids and Kamila cleared the room. "Kamila or one of the kids will let you know where things are. I'll be home around six. Kamila will be here until I get back."

Broad shouldered and masculine, Harden stood under the doorframe to the kitchen, looking handsome in his casual Friday attire. Red polo shirt, khaki slacks, brown loafers, like a country gentleman. His apple cheeks lifted higher when he grinned.

"By the way," he said. "I kind of volunteered you to take the kids to the aquatic center in Dubuque County. It's not far from here. Hope you don't mind."

"No problems," Andy said. "But I didn't think to bring a swimsuit."

"You can wear my trunks." Harden sized up Andy. "We're about the same height and weight. You'll find a pair in my top drawer upstairs. Here're a few bucks." He took two twenties from his wallet and handed them to Andy, but Andy refused with a raised hand.

"It's on me," he said.

Stuffing the bills back in his wallet, Harden shrugged. "I never grapple over a bill. Have a good time. See you this evening. And make sure the kids get covered in suntan lotion before you head out. Olivia especially. She's got your side of the family's skin."

With the master of the house out of the way, Andy sat at the kitchen table and inhaled. Surrounded by the house's silence, he realized how odd the circumstances for his visit were, and that perhaps he really did not belong there. He turned to a sudden rustling. Kamila had returned downstairs and was straightening the foyer. She worked with one eye tacked on him. Circumventing her leer, he reached for coffee.

He should probably make nice with her, despite Andy tiring of people flaunting moral airs that they failed to live by. So what if she'd survived a war and might have lost her family. Life everywhere roared as a battlefield. He'd seen it firsthand in Chicago's South Side. People had blamed him for that. Was Andy responsible for religious and political upheavals ten thousand miles away too?

He noticed crumbs scattered around the warm toaster. Should he ask for something to eat? He grabbed for a banana instead.

Kamila eyed him. With his best patronizing face, he took a bite of the banana and said, "What's keeping the kids?"

"They clean like father tell them," she said with a furrowed brow. "They are obedient children."

"When I was a kid, I'd go a week in the summer without washing. I'd be outside from dawn to dusk, like a rabid wolf, kicking up dirt everywhere." Andy realized he was causing Kamila more distress and loved it. He took three big bites of the banana and tossed the peel.

Coffee in hand, he stood at the bottom of the stairs. Kamila had moved to the kitchen but hovered within earshot. "Olivia! Mason!"

"What's up?" Mason asked from the top step.

"A scarecrow told me about some swimming pool not far from here."

"The aquatic center," Olivia shouted beside her brother. "Daddy said you'll take us."

"Yup, I heard it from him too. Get your suits on. And don't forget sunblock."

The kids squandered no time rushing back to their rooms, stomping about like two bison calves. Andy climbed the stairs and peered around the master suite, the room his sister had once shared with Harden. Neat and tidy. No further signs of Lilly or her featured scent, or anything he might construe as feminine. Other than maybe a portrait of Harden and Lillian in a silver frame etched with fleur-de-lis that sat on the bureau.

He set down his coffee mug and lifted the photograph, gazing at the happy and smiling couple. The picture had been taken in Cancun at what appeared to be an outdoor nightclub, where Harden and Lillian had first met while vacationing with friends. Tanned, grinning faces and sparkling eyes stared back at Andy. They were much younger then, in their midtwenties, healthy and alive. Six months after meeting, they'd married.

The photo, Andy knew, was twelve years old. It might have been taken last week. Harden looked much the same, maybe ten pounds heavier today with a rounder face. But those same puffy cheeks! He mentally kicked himself for not being more available to him and the kids. Time stood still, but it also raced headlong. A lifetime had passed.

Heartaches and disappointments had shaped Andy into a different person from those times—a man he'd like to keep hidden away during the daylight hours and bring out only at night. He'd learned to profit from his self-loathing and discontent with the world. Harden? He faced special challenges. How had he changed?

Life's bumps must have altered him in profound ways too, although Andy found him much the same as he remembered him. The good-natured, laidback country boy with a heart of gold had greeted Andy yesterday afternoon, busting a grin and ready with a firm handshake.

Andy had read somewhere that if you stretch before exercising you should always stretch; if you never practice stretching then you should avoid it altogether. In other words, either for eternity or never. And here he stood in his sister's former bedroom, inserting himself in the Krane household after a three-year absence. Stretching and stretching.... He could hear and feel the crack of his joints.

He replaced the photograph and found Harden's swimming "trunks" in the top drawer. Dark-blue, basic board shorts. Typical Harden Krane style. They still held onto a musky odor. *Why do straight men believe they never have to wash swimsuits because they get wet?*

Andy carried the trunks into the master bathroom, which looked exactly how Andy had imagined for a bachelor like Harden. Organized, yet everything within easy reach. Deodorant, toothpaste, lotions—even a near-empty jar of Vaseline, which gave Andy's heart an unanticipated palpitation—all arranged on top of the counter. The smell of Harden's spicy aftershave still lingered.

He stripped off his clothes and coated himself with the suntan lotion he found on the counter. Checking his reflection (leg rested on toilet seat, rounded butt profiled nicely), he decided he looked pretty good. "A killer body for a thirty-six-year-old," Ken had mentioned from time to time. But he could use some sun. With his new career working nights, he'd slept much of the days away and hadn't gotten as tan as previous summers. At least the bruises from his beating had faded to a faint jaundice.

Funny how he'd become aroused once he slipped on Harden's funky trunks. Perhaps it was the snug fit. The trunks highlighted one of his better assets. He adjusted himself, squatting three or four times to loosen the seat. But who would care how he looked in Bumfuck, Iowa?

Just don't go shaking your ass all over the place, Andrew.

Olivia and Mason were waiting for him in the entrance foyer when Andy, dressed again in his T-shirt and cargo shorts over his swimsuit, galloped downstairs. The kids clutched their tote bags, bounced on toes comfy-looking inside colorful flip-flops.

Outside, while ushering the kids into the van, Andy noticed Kamila glaring at him from the kitchen window. He hooked his Oakleys over his ears and waved to her with a touch of sarcasm. She grimaced and turned away.

They arrived just after the park opened, and the place was empty save for a small group of children playing in the shallow end of the main pool. Andy and the kids placed their belongings on three corner lounge chairs and undressed down to their swimsuits.

Olivia spotted an eagle perched in a tree outside the pool grounds and shouted for them to look. Andy's cell phone dinged at the precise moment the eagle flew off. Ken with a text message. *Feeling better this morning?*

Andy replied: *Not bad, at pool, saw eagle.*

Fun, Ken responded. He added that they had no new leads in Andy's assault and battery case. As if Andy expected them to nab anyone.

With kids, talk later, Andy wrote and clicked off.

"Hey, Krane," one of the towheaded boys in the pool shouted. "Where's your mom, huh? Is that guy your new mommy?"

Mason squinted from the sun sparkling off the surface of the water. "You just keep talking, Randy Lederman. I'll sock you like I did Mike Tuelong."

"You barely pinched him."

Andy dropped to his haunches, eye level with Olivia. "Who's that?"

"That's one of the boys who always teases us."

Andy straightened and squared his shoulders. "Hey, little boy," he hollered to him. "I see your mom. Over there, in the trees, swinging from the branches."

The children looked where Andy pointed. "What're you talking about? My mother's not even here," Randy Lederman said, his face souring.

"She's swinging in the trees, like a monkey."

The other children began laughing along with Olivia and Mason. Red-faced, Randy slapped the water and swam away. On the far side of the pool, Andy could see him climb out and tattle to a lifeguard. She glared in Andy's direction and went back to surveying the swimming pool without budging from her tall chair.

"Well," Andy said, wiping his hands dramatically, "I guess that takes care of little Randy what's his name."

Mason grinned at him. "Thanks, Uncle Andy."

"No problem, Mason. Now, who wants to play dive for the nickel?"

Mason and Olivia jumped into the pool without a care for testing it first. *Kids must have the skin of hippopotamuses.* Andy dug through his cargo shorts and stood poolside. The other children joined them, five altogether.

"The first one to surface with the nickel wins." He tossed the coin, and the children disappeared under sparkling splashes and gurgling bubbles. Olivia struggled to the bottom. She kicked and slapped the surface. Another boy came up for air, showcasing the nickel pinched between pudgy fingers.

Andy set aside his sunglasses and eased himself into the tepid water, keeping his arms above the surface until he acclimated to the temperature. He took the nickel from the boy and said, "Keep a close eye on it, now." He tossed it again, this time farther out toward the shallower end.

With the water barely above chin level, poor Olivia looked to be tiring fast while she struggled to dog paddle. She gave a gallant effort and never once showed signs of disappointment each of the times she came up empty. Mason berated himself the times he failed at retrieving the coin. But he cheered louder than the others the two times he clenched it first. Andy arbitrated a minor scuffle between Mason and another boy when the coin slipped from one of their fingers. To keep the peace, Andy said, "Do over." They played the nickel game until his arm tired.

"You guys play amongst yourselves now," he said, giving one final toss of the coin.

He used the side ladder to climb out of the pool while the kids scrambled for the nickel, and stretched over Mason's Spider-Man beach towel. Replacing his sunglasses, he rested the back of his head on the lounge chair and sighed. Relaxation.

The children's giggles and the familiar scent of chlorine and wet cement brought back bittersweet memories for Andy. He could almost see him and Lillian playing at Streamwood's public pool. They used to spend hours swimming, until their skin wrinkled like a shar-pei's. Afterward, they'd climb the mulberry trees abutting the facility and nibble the succulent, dark fruit. Other children would join them, and from a distance they must have looked like a swarm of monkeys. They cared little that their fingers were coated in black and the sticky berry juice ran down their chins and necks.

Pool water drying on his skin gave him a tingle. Thank goodness the awakening yellow jackets kept to the bushes. More arriving children added to the giggles that merged with the singing of the birds in the trees bordering the center. Occasional whiffs of honeysuckle from the trellis outside the bathrooms masked the ever-present smell of livestock dung that lingered even in town.

Mason and Olivia raced up to him. Puddles of water accumulated at their feet. "Can we play under the mushroom waterfall?" Mason asked.

Andy glanced toward the wading pool with the protruding mushroom sculpture that oozed water from its sides. "Sure." He shrugged. "Have fun and be careful."

He stretched back over the lounge chair and the sound of the kids' bare feet slapping against the pavement faded. But before he closed his eyes, a strange awareness forced his head toward the cluster of elms outside the pool. He sat upright, peered harder over his lowered sunglasses. He couldn't distinguish a figure, but a pair of cold eyes gazed at him. He knew the difference between a casual glance and a penetrating, harsh glare, even from a stealthy distance.

He looked over at little Randy, wrapped in a towel and shivering on the side of the pool next to the lifeguard chair. Mason and Olivia and a few other children darted in and out under the mushroom. By the time Andy turned back to the elm trees, the eyes had vanished.

Don't get paranoid, Andy boy. Chicago is two hundred miles away. No one out here wants to get you.

CHAPTER
TWELVE

THE solvent stench at work bothered Harden less that day. Andrew's—Andy's—company at the house after such a long absence blossomed like a fragrant orchid and provided longed-for peace of mind. Last night, realizing Andy slept beneath the family gave Harden an added sense of serenity. Another adult to help him with his load. Even if for a short week.

It was approaching two o'clock, but knowing the kids' love of water, Harden guessed they must still be swimming. He was going to send a text to Mason or Andy but decided to leave them alone. The happy knowledge the kids were playing with someone who'd watch out for them proved enough to pacify Harden.

He liked that he had Andy to talk to last night. Kamila was never enough. As much as she involved herself in Mason and Olivia's lives, she was distant. An outsider. Andy was family.

Andy couldn't have come at a more perfect time. Their house hadn't exactly been the den of laughter lately. A stuffy oppression had loitered at Burr Oak Farm for many years. With summer at its apex—which demanded the children play, breathe, race outdoors—Andy had wrenched open their stuck lives.

He chuckled to himself, recalling how Andy had remembered where he worked and that his dream was to farm. He sighed at his desk, feeling a genuine smile curl his lips for the first time in quite a while.

Initially, he'd worried that Andy's return might force the kids to pine for their mother, but there had been no sign of that. Certainly Kamila noticed the upswing of emotions. She had walked into the house that morning with a sour face.

Was it jealousy? Perhaps he needed to speak to her. Wouldn't that be a bit too aristocratic for Harden? Lecturing the help? No snootier than Kamila's behavior toward Andy, he convinced himself.

Andy was a male version of Lillian in some ways. Same dark-blue eyes. Same dirty blond hair (except years ago Lilly had begun to use peroxide). He worried Andy had become hardened by life. Was it a family curse?

Hadn't life walloped everyone?

He never worried over Andrew's homosexuality. Lillian had mentioned it in passing before he'd first met the family a few months before their wedding. He supposed it was natural to him. He'd be a different person if he weren't gay. Harden had concluded if Andy were heterosexual he'd be less prone to open up to him. The only other man he could reveal his emotions to was Lance. But their one-on-ones came less frequently, what with life's everyday urgencies.

A slight yawn pulled Harden from his desk. He stretched and headed for the kitchenette. Leftover cupcakes from the surprise party they'd thrown Marshall's office manager, Stacey Glisten, sat waiting on a tray. The ones with pink and blue frosting had already been eaten, but a few of the yellows and greens remained. They'd celebrated Stacey's twentieth anniversary at Marshall (almost as old as the company itself) with a robust chorus of "For She's a Jolly Good Fellow." Harden had mouthed the lyrics, hating the sound of his singing voice.

"Hi there, Harden." Arty Ficklemeyer shuffled into the kitchenette, distinctive large grin on his thin ruddy face. He had been outside smoking a cigarette. Harden could smell the signature stench on his clothes.

"Nice out?" Harden asked him.

"Hot and muggy. Good, there're some cupcakes left. Need that sugar fix." He grabbed a green cupcake with his nicotine-stained fingers and took a bite. "Imagine," he said with a full mouth, "twenty years with the same company."

Arty had worked for Marshall almost as long, fourteen years. In another three, Harden would match his record. Difficult to comprehend a decade had raced ahead, while his dreams faded.

From the small kitchenette window, he viewed the cornfield across the road. Bright sunshine and a stunning blue sky seemed to mock him. "You'll never get to farm, Harden Krane," the outdoors was saying. Harden turned his back on the window and began to make a single-serve coffee. The aroma of Vanilla Roast wafted from under the spout.

"Be grateful we have jobs," Harden uttered.

"That's for sure. With the way things are? Whew!"

Harden listened to the coffee percolate, waiting patiently for it to finish. Arty shuffled behind him, his jaw cracking from eating a second cupcake. Thinner than a fencepost, Arty could mow down cupcake after cupcake and never gain a gram.

"Word is you have a relative of Lillian's visiting," he said.

"That's right. Her brother." Though his back was to Arty, Harden sensed Arty shifting his eyes in his typical style.

"Good to hear," Arty said in a high voice. "Kids glad to see him?"

Harden removed the mug before the drip was complete and lifted the steaming coffee to his lips. "They're at the aquatic center in Dyersville right now, having a great time, I bet."

Arty's rectangular face stretched with a full grin. "Now that sounds like summer. What I wouldn't do for a few more years of those days back. You and the kids looking forward to tomorrow's corn roast?"

"You kidding? I'm the head grill master this year. Got a freezer full of chicken. You're joining our group like last year, right?"

"If you're doing the grilling. I wash my hands from that responsibility. Everyone is always trying to tell you what you're doing wrong. I promise I won't hassle you." He gazed downward. "Will your brother-in-law still be in town for it?"

Harden nodded over the rim of his mug. "Yep."

Arty lifted his head and chuckled. "That's good. That's good. Have him come along."

The dull click of approaching heels on the hallway's Berber carpet stiffened Harden. Too late for an escape. Lucinda Jamison, the twentysomething woman whose flirtations caused him anguish and delighted Harden's officemates, strutted into the kitchenette. She carried in her characteristic smell of jasmine perfume, so sweet and strong it gave Harden an instant headache.

Upon seeing Harden, she grinned between lofty, rosy cheeks. "Hi, Harden. How are you?"

"Good, thanks. Having a good day?"

"Sure am. Hi, there, Arty."

"Hi, Lucinda."

Bleached blonde hair, slim physique, stylish attire, she was the best looking girl at Marshall. Perhaps that's why Harden wanted to avoid her. She was too flashy for him. She even dressed slick on casual Fridays. Early in their romance, Lillian had been more down to earth. When he'd first spotted her in Cancun, sitting with a group of girlfriends, in an instant her robust personality and far-reaching voice had attracted him.

Age differences never mattered to him (Lilly was two years older), but considering he wanted to evade Lucinda's passes, age was a good enough excuse.

Lucinda slipped her mug under the coffeemaker spout and leaned against the counter, slender arms folded beneath her blouse sleeves, while the machine hissed and sighed. "Can't wait until five o'clock," she said, eyes locked on Harden.

"Been a long week," Harden agreed.

Arty made wide eyes at him. Married thirty years, Arty probably yearned for the romance more than Harden. Arty had nudged Lucinda toward Harden her first day at Marshall, a little more than a year ago. Harden hated the jollies her attraction brought Arty and his coworkers.

"You going to the corn roast tomorrow, Lucinda?" Arty asked.

"I haven't thought of it."

"Harden's going to be this year's grill master for our group. Why don't you join us?"

Harden mentally rolled his eyes. *I'll get you one of these days, Arty Ficklemeyer.*

"Really?" she said. "That sounds like fun."

A puff of steam shot up from under the coffee spout, indicating her coffee had finished brewing. She added sugar and cream and stirred it. "I think I might go."

"We'd love to see you there," Arty said.

"I better get back to work," Harden said, sensing the fatigue settling over him again, despite the hot coffee. "I'll talk to you guys later."

"See you maybe at the corn roast, Harden."

"Sure, Lucinda, see you."

Back at his desk, Harden's head cleared from Lucinda's perfume. Other matters needed attention. The short stack of paperwork on ethanol sat under his elbows. He sighed and flipped through the research. Not typically a clock-watcher, Harden glanced at his wristwatch. He snickered under his breath, gripped his red pen, and aimed the fine point toward his paperwork.

CHAPTER
THIRTEEN

KAMILA fed the kids a snack of apple slices and peanut butter at the kitchen counter while Andy explored the farmstead outside. He'd eaten plenty of the aquatic center's junk food and had enough of the housekeeper's disapproving glares.

In the barn, he gazed at Dick Carelli's odd-looking equipment and tools. Rusty rake-like contraptions, plows, rigs, welding equipment, hitches, and machine parts glinted from the wedges of sunlight that cut through the barn clefts. The stable holds that Mason wanted to load with farm animals were stuffed with seed sacks.

Everything looked and smelled the same as last time, yet so alien.

He envisaged sharing Harden's strange dream of farming. He'd found farm life fascinating like he might ants at a picnic. No way could he imagine living on a farm full time. He shared Lillian's dislike for rural living.

At least Harden had a dream. What was Andy's?

To live in self-pity and profit from the world's bloodletting.

He waved away gnats swarming in tight balls around his face and inspected a pitchfork. Next he kicked a sack of dirt. He ran his fingers over the solid body of the tractor, still warm to the touch, and formed a soft ball with the sticky dirt stuck on his fingertips. Cobwebs high on the rafters, resembling silk latticework, brought his attention to the barn loft. He fixated on it, unable to comprehend....

Had life at Burr Oak Farm been that horrible for Lillian?

A crow flying from under the door eave startled him. He watched it launch for the blue sky, beyond the swaying corn. Chest-high corn. As far as the eye could see.

Almost as if he were peering inside a stranger's house, he stepped closer to the cornfield and squinted down a row, wondering.... What resided in there? Gnomes? He pulled back one of the leaves, examined the texture without committing himself to holding it. He noted the yellow corn.... *What did they call them? Corncobs? Cornhusks?* Only about the size of a small child's forearm, he supposed the corn needed a good few weeks to reach harvesting stage if Dick was going to use it for people food.

He dared to twist off one, and clenched it in his fist, firm and girthy.

He pictured Lillian again, occupying her days at the white farmhouse with the barn and silo so close. Why hadn't he spent more time with her, driven out for visits to lessen her loneliness? Those days could never be dug up and relived.

He tossed the corn to the ground, wandered to the side of the house, and stood in the silo's shadow. He peered along the gray-white structure to the rounded cap and realized that no fancy towers with rooftop swimming pools and tennis courts existed in Iowa. Silos were the predominant high-rises in that country.

In the backyard, he studied the mighty burr oak. No change, of course. Still thick trunked and wide reaching. He'd remembered the lofty, expansive tree from his other trips. The swing set was new, he believed. Maybe he failed to remember it from his last visit. So much drama had transpired then. Probably hadn't even noticed.

Olivia raced to him from the kitchen, her golden ponytails fluttering behind her. "Uncle Andy!"

Happy suddenly for the distraction, he opened his arms to her, and she fell against his body at full speed. Grunting, he lifted her and gave her cheek a peck. "Yum! You taste like peanut butter."

"I ate some for a snack," she said, squirming out of his embrace. "Let's swing."

He pushed her on the swing, obeying her commands to go higher and higher. The tips of her tiny sneakers touched a solitary fluffy cloud that eased across the sky as if she were nudging it with her toes. In an instant, he saw himself and Lillian kicking their legs back and forth on their old swing set back in Streamwood, each trying to outdo the other. Where had those innocent, tender moments fled? Vanished more inconspicuously than the cloud.

The nasty yellow jackets darting around his exposed legs irritated him, and Andy jolted the giggling Olivia to a stop.

"We better get inside," Andy insisted. "I've got a surprise for you and Mason."

"What kind of a surprise?"

"You'll have to wait and see."

Andy carried the cheerful Olivia inside. Kamila shot him one of her askance looks from the laundry room where he noted she was on the last load. Meanwhile, he played electronic games with Olivia and Mason. After Kamila finished the wash, he insisted she go home, guaranteeing he'd look after the kids and have dinner ready for Harden. Wearing a sour frown, she left the house at four o'clock, purse rigidly high on her shoulders and brow low.

"What's the big surprise Olivia talked about?" Mason said.

"Come on." Andy led them into the kitchen. "We're going to make a special dinner, and you're going to help."

With the kids' enthusiastic assistance, Andy jumbled together dinner. Now and then he glanced out the kitchen window, certain eyes peered in at them. He shrugged it off and kept his spirits high. Forty-five minutes later, four fresh Frisbee-sized pizzas, piled high with sauce, cheese, and a whole lot of other stuff, waited on the counter. Harden pulled his Jeep Patriot into the driveway right on time.

He stood, framed by the kitchen's doorway, staring at Andy with an amused countenance. "I see you're finding your way around the kitchen."

"Hello, Harden. Dinner will be ready in about twenty minutes. I'm waiting for the oven to heat to five hundred so I can stick the pizzas in."

"Looks great," Harden said.

"I hope you don't mind I sent Kamila home."

"You guys get in a fight?"

"Nothing like that. Just thought with me here she could use the afternoon off."

"Hey, you got some sun today. Covered over most of your bruised eye."

"We had a great time at the pool. Kamila washed your trunks, and they're hanging up in the laundry room. How was your day at work?"

Harden gazed at the floor. A slow-moving smile lifted his strong cheek muscles. "Not bad. Got what I needed to do done."

Mason hurried into the kitchen. "Dad, we made homemade pizzas, and we each get our own."

"So I see."

"Uncle Andy said we could put on them whatever we wanted. I put black olives, tomato slices, and some of Kamila's leftover ćevapi."

"And I put mayonnaise and American cheese on mine," Olivia said beside her brother.

Andy grimaced. "She insisted. Don't worry. We made one special for you too. Four different types of cheese."

"Guess what Uncle Andy did at the pool today."

"What's that, Mason?" Harden set aside his laptop case and draped an arm around his son.

"He called Randy Lederman's mom a monkey."

Harden snickered, looked at Andy, and said, "No wonder you have a black eye. You go around calling people's moms monkeys in Chicago?"

"It wasn't quite like that," Andy said. "I intervened on Mason's behalf to stop his friend from bullying him. Maybe I should've held my tongue, but I couldn't help myself. This kid was a real punk."

Andy noticed a sober stain replace Harden's unabashed grin. Harden forced a wobbly smile and said, "I'll wash up and change for dinner. Don't eat without me."

A half hour later, the four were eating their hot pizzas with gusto. A wedge of gooey American cheese slid from Olivia's slice when she lifted it to her mouth and fell to her lap. Harden rolled his eyes but joined in everyone's laughter. Olivia, giggling, peeled the cheese from her pants and popped it in her mouth.

"Can we have some Pop-Ice, Dad?" Mason asked after they'd cleared their plates.

"I want some too," Olivia chimed in.

"Okay, but take them outside so you don't make a mess."

The kids sprinted for the freezer, rummaged through a box, and carried the frozen treats to the porch. Harden and Andy, grabbing drinks, decided to join them.

Harden and Olivia sat on the porch swing together, while Mason sat on the top step and Andy leaned against the railing nursing a pop, the setting sun warm on his back. He observed how sweet Olivia and Harden looked side by side, Harden's arm snug over her square little shoulders, the glow of the pink and orange sun reflecting off their faces. Harden held a beer in his free hand and took small sips between contended smiles. Olivia sucked on her red Pop-Ice, kicking her feet to make the swing wobble. The unnatural color of the ice shimmered gemlike in the sun. Sticky, sugary juice ran down her chin and fingers. Harden nudged her, grimacing.

"Stop wobbling, Olivia. You're making a mess. Why don't you go sit with Mason on the stoop?"

Wordlessly, Olivia complied. She dropped beside Mason, who was sucking a green Pop-Ice, Andy's all-time favorite. Mason helped Olivia push up her ice, much like when Andy and Lillian were kids, only the roles reversed. It was Lillian, the big sister, who'd helped her little brother master the fine art of sliding Pop-Ice from the plastic wrap, ensuring none of the precious ice liquefied until the very end, when they'd make a slurry and slurp it up. Lilly had taught him how to suck the juice without needing to tilt his head, preventing all that exquisite syrup from spilling along his neck and clothes.

Seemed only yesterday he and Lillian were sharing summertime treats on their front porch, their dirtied and bruised knees from playing outdoors pointing toward the pink and blue sky. Summers used to drift along, slow, like a dandelion seed floating on a windless day. A lifetime would pass before school commenced again. Now, summers hastened past with an ugly urgency.

And these days, Andy's bruises came from other sources.

"Hey, Uncle Andy, what did the old chimney say to the young chimney?"

"I don't know, Mason. What?"

"You're too young to smoke."

Andy tossed his head back and laughed. "Good one."

"I know a riddle," Olivia said. "How can you tell if there's an elephant under your bed?"

Mason tittered. "I know that one, dumbhead."

"Wait for Uncle Andy to answer."

Andy made a face of concentration. "I give up."

"Your nose hits the ceiling." And Olivia laughed and laughed.

"That was a good one too, Olivia. Okay, here's one. What does a house wear?"

The kids peered around, their lips sealed to their Pop-Ices. Shrugging, they looked to Andy for an answer.

"A dress. Get it? Address."

Hoots and giggles parted the kids' red and green stained lips. "That's silly," Olivia said.

"I think my kids have your side of the family's sense of humor," Harden said.

The kids finished slurping the precious Pop-Ice slurry, and Harden ordered them to wash their hands and faces with the barn hose, "before you get that sticky stuff everywhere."

Andy took Olivia's former spot beside Harden. The moment he sat on the swing, he noticed Harden's hand flinch where it had rested by Olivia's shoulder. He kept it there for a moment longer, moving it slowly to his lap while mentioning the muggy evening.

Andy grinned toward the cornfield, replete with shadows from the setting sun. "Feels nice," he said, pretending not to notice Harden's tensing. "I always liked hot and humid summers. Brings back a flood of memories. Remember being a kid and things like sticky hands were no big deal?"

"Now I curse myself for getting red marker on my fingers," Harden said.

"I used to hate that at work," Andy agreed.

"My brothers and I used to live outdoors during summertime," Harden said. "I remember spending weekends here at the farm and maybe going inside only to sleep, sometimes not even then. A few times, we camped in sleeping bags under the burr oak."

"Same with me and Lilly back in Streamwood. Maybe we'll do that with the kids while I'm here. Camp out back."

Harden let out a light snort. "You know, I've never once thought about doing that with my own kids. Imagine." He shook his head. "Guess my mind's been on other things."

"The kids seem well adjusted," Andy said, sipping his pop with steady, condensed movements.

"They're coping better. As well as can be expected. Olivia is a wonder, a sloppy wonder. She takes things in stride. Sometimes I'm afraid she might be too laid-back. And Mason, well…."

"He's been getting into a lot of fights?"

"I thought things were settling down," Harden said, "but two fights in as many weeks have me worried."

"Hope I didn't make matters worse by insulting that kid today."

Harden shook his head. "Randy Lederman had it coming. I'm glad you told him off. Something I couldn't get away with as a father."

"What if he tells his mom?"

"She'll probably laugh. Besides, what he and some of those other kids say to Mason is a lot worse. No good reason to tease like that, just because… well, Christ, there's just no reason."

"Don't worry about Mason. He'll do okay."

"That's what everyone keeps telling me."

The porch swing was swaying. Andy hadn't noticed until that moment. He and Harden were toeing the floor planks, falling in rhythm with the breeze rustling the corn and the birds calling to each other from the oaks and elms that edged the house. Andy sipped his pop. Sticky caramel remained on his lips longer than he'd wanted, and he swiped the syrup with his tongue.

Harden brought his beer into his lap. "So how did you get your black eye, for real?"

"Saw something I shouldn't have, and they roughed me up a little."

"Is that the reason for your visit? Kind of a sabbatical?"

"Sort of. I did miss the kids. I'm glad I've gotten the chance to hang out with them again. I forgot how much fun they are."

"It's tough on them, living so far from most of their friends who live in town or on farther away farms. I have to take them into Duncan and stay with my parents for trick-or-treating and things like that. Kamila drives them around sometimes, like to the pool, but she hates it. They ride their bikes, but alone, without adult supervision, sometimes that worries me."

Mason reprimanded Olivia out of sight by the water spigot. Lillian had a way of taking charge that had made Andy feel safe. Where was she now to protect him from bullies, like Andy had with Mason today? He swallowed a mouthful of pop, set the can in his lap, and snickered.

"Do you remember when you and Lilly came to Streamwood that Thanksgiving? It was only the third time you'd been out there, I think, and you worried someone had broken into Mom's house. You pulled a kitchen knife on that poor short, bow-legged man who was fixing the garage door opener. Remember?"

"I had no idea anyone was supposed to be there." Harden flushed pink and scratched at his head. "No one told me."

"You came to the Chicago area expecting to be mugged at every corner. There's no crime in Streamwood."

"That wasn't as bad as that time you came out here for Easter and you drove through our neighbor's cornfield."

"Looked like a driveway."

"We call them corn rows," Harden said. "We usually don't drive cars down them."

"Blame it on Mom. She's the one who told me to take the turn."

Their laughter faded, and Andy gazed at his sneakers. He remembered another embarrassing incident, one he was unsure he should raise. He'd never quite understood it. Happened during one of Harden's earlier visits to Streamwood.

Lillian was pregnant with Mason, and he and Harden were drinking beers and joking while Lillian laughed along. Andy had gone to the kitchen to wash a few of their dishes at the sink. Shortly after, Harden had come in for another beer. Out of the blue, Andy had felt two hands clutch his shoulders. Next he'd realized, Harden had turned him around and planted a kiss right on his lips.

Harden had walked off as if nothing had happened, and neither of them had ever mentioned it since. Andy suspected he'd been drunk. Just one of those things. Straight men often showed few inhibitions around gay men, especially after drinking. Andy took nothing more from it than that.

He chose to remain mute about the sink incident from so many years ago. Why make Harden uncomfortable? Most likely he wouldn't even remember. Instead, he said, "It's a different lifestyle out here. That's for sure."

"Not much different, not anymore." Harden swigged from his beer and released a harsh breath. "Satellite dishes and cable and the Internet and social media expose big city people and country folks to the same things. Yet, funny thing, we've never been more divided."

Appreciating his former brother-in-law's intelligence, Andy added, "That's because most of the images we get of each other are probably no more realistic than *Grimm's Fairy Tales*."

Harden's snicker rode in the wake of a crow scampering from the cornfield. "Hey, Andy, I forgot to mention our annual corn roast at the county fairgrounds tomorrow. It's far more down to earth than our technology-driven world. You interested in going? Kids won't have it any other way, I'm afraid."

"Sounds corny."

"Now I know for sure where Mason and Olivia get their humor. Anyway, it's a big summer affair. People bring their own food and grills, kind of like a tailgate party."

"Sure, might be fun," Andy said with a shrug.

"I have to admit it's been a load off knowing you're spending time with the kids. It's almost nice Mason was suspended from his baseball team. Gives you a chance to spend extra time with him."

"The kids have been great."

Harden let out a long sigh that mingled with the barnyard-scented breeze and the aroma of canned beer. "I'd be lying if I said I don't sometimes dream of a life without kids, like yours."

Andy shook his head. "People think that, because you aren't married with children, you have all this free time, no responsibilities. The truth is, you have just as much to do as anyone else, if not more. You can't divide up the workload. You have to do everything on your own. Cook, clean, do the shopping. It can be exhausting."

"Never thought of it like that."

"Count your blessings, Harden. Despite everything, you're a lucky guy."

Olivia and Mason dashed back to the porch. Mason looked dry, but the front of Olivia's clothing was soaked.

"Mason, why didn't you watch her?"

"She's a slob, Dad. I tried."

"Okay, you guys, you might as well head inside and get baths before bed. Mason, you can use my bathroom."

The kids gave a mild protest but caved to their father's orders. The storm door slapped behind them, followed by four feet stomping up the steps. Several seconds passed, and Harden planted his feet to stop the swing. "I better get upstairs before Olivia floods the bathroom."

Andy grabbed his pop. "I'll finish cleaning up the kitchen." He edged behind Harden inside the house, letting the storm door close on his backside to reduce the slamming. A comforting pat, like a man slapping his teammate's rear end after hitting a home run.

CHAPTER
FOURTEEN

HARDEN tossed a lit match onto the coals and almost leaped into the arms of his coworker from Marshall Farming Enterprises to escape the hot flames.

"I told you, too much lighter fluid," Arty Ficklemeyer said.

"I know what I'm doing," Harden grunted, straightening his shoulders before the flaming grill.

"Watch out, Harden," Harden's neighbor from a quarter mile down the road, Burt Anders, said with a chuckle. "You don't want to lose those nice eyebrows of yours."

"Get those gas grills," his brother, Lance, said. "Those work real nice."

"No hassling me," Harden barked.

"We're not hassling," Arty said. "Merely giving you some handy information."

"You should get those new charcoals that already come with fuel on them," Burt said.

Harden turned to the men, brandishing his stainless steel grill fork as the smell of smoking lighter fluid hovered thick over their heads. "Back off, you guys. A real barbeque chef uses none of those newfangled things.

We authentic barbeque chefs have been known to behead anyone who suggests such a thing."

"Let the king reign over his grill," Lance said, patting his younger brother's back. "He'll banish us if we don't."

Standing apart from the men, Andy lifted his sunglasses for a clearer view. The "grill sergeant" (as Andy had teased Harden earlier, to the delight of the others, when Harden had stepped up to the grill, wearing his apron and clutching his utensils) absorbed Andy's attention.

Although Andy hadn't really looked forward to the corn roast when Harden had mentioned it while they had sat on the porch swing yesterday evening, he liked watching Harden at play. Pride welled inside Andy as Harden stood his ground before his grill with a hint of self-effacing humor. He'd always admired Harden. He embodied a disposition Andy wished most men possessed, especially Ken. Decisive, laidback. All-American. Andy's kind of guy.

He dropped his Oakleys over his nose and tried to disregard the spontaneous notion that pinched him like one of the black flies buzzing around his bare legs. He hadn't meant to fantasize Harden in such a desirable way. Of course, Andy had thought Lilly had made a nice find when she'd first brought him to Streamwood and introduced him to the family. But that didn't mean anything then. Harden had belonged to his sister.

He's not off limits anymore, Andy Wingal.

Harden threw his head back and laughed. His eyes squeezed toward the blue sky, where smoke from the grill and the fire pit loaded with sweating cornhusks disappeared among the tree branches. Andy concentrated on his wobbling and protruding Adam's apple. The veins on his neck coiled like slim roots.

Andy carried his weird thoughts to the beer vat. He raked for one of the low calorie beers and snapped open the can, but his eyes remained pinned on Harden. What did it mean, if anything, that Harden acted differently around him than his friends and brother? Andy noticed many heterosexual men sometimes demonstrated a gentler consideration with him. Maybe some kind of subconscious awareness, a pheromone, motivated them.

Harden had always doted on him with an interested attention, like a protective big brother, despite being only a year older. Perhaps he cared enough to step in as Andy's male role model once he'd learned Andy's father had run off to live in New Mexico with a woman from Thailand when Andy was about Mason's age.

And there was that time Harden had kissed him full on the mouth at the kitchen sink back in Streamwood....

He watched Harden poke the charcoal, then wave the fork around his head, laughing with his buddies. Star of his own show, grounded on his stage of soft soil, surrounded by corn that, if steadily nourished and left unharvested, might grow until it choked the world.

Where did Andy stand among the Iowa farmland? Already, he separated himself from the men at the grill and their wives who sat in foldout chairs in a snug circle under an elm tree. They had been kind to him, but in a dismissive way. Harden's brother, Lance, had shaken his hand with a firm grip, but behind his robust greeting lurked suspicion and possibly fear.

Lance, the fireman. Taller than Harden. But the same posture and disposition. He came across more condescending than genuine. Whenever Andy spoke to Lance or made a comment that Lance had wanted to respond to, he never answered Andy directly. He'd raise his voice and seemed to speak to the crowns of the trees to ensure the entire gathering could hear.

He wondered how much they might understand about Lillian and Harden, and how they might blame him and the entire Wingal family for Harden's suffering. Such a small community knew everyone's business. Certainly, they held sympathy for poor Harden. But not for Andy. Maybe some in their cluster had been the ones who'd tried to fix up Harden with their unwed daughters and female friends.

One of those meddling females sitting with the small sphere of friends raised her dark eyes and called to Andy.

"Sit with us, you," Arty Ficklemeyer's wife said.

Boisterous with the flare for Midwestern gab and familiarity, Loretta waved Andy over, her flabby triceps wobbling like globs of jelly. She had farm matriarch blazoned on her puffy face, adorned with nothing fancier than a pair of pearl-framed round eyeglasses. "You look just like Olivia," she said as Andy edged closer. "We were just talking about it, don't you know."

Andy stood by a chair vacated by a woman he'd overheard earlier announcing her plans to shop the fairground for handmade clocks and artisan cheese. Only when he noticed the crumpling of the aluminum can in his tightening grip did he relax his fingers. "You think so?"

"You betcha! We used to think she was a spitting image of her mother." The shadow that passed behind Loretta's eyeglasses vanished faster than the condescending smile that appeared in its place, and she lifted her eyes like squeezed lemons. "You two weren't twins, huh?" Loretta said.

Andy sipped his beer, savoring the icy burn. "I'm one of a kind, you'll be glad to know."

"The kids are lucky to have you back," another woman with fierce red hair and freckles said. He'd forgotten her name and hoped one of the women might mention it. But Andy had noted they seldom addressed each other by name. It seemed they knew by intuition when someone addressed them. A gentle roll of the tongue or a voice inflection replaced the need for names.

"I betcha you're having loads of fun with them," Burt Anders's wife, Alicia, said with a tight, lippy grin. (Andy remembered the Anders as the people whose cornfield he and his mother had driven through that embarrassing Easter.)

They were trying to be kind. A kindness that Andy was unused to. Were they sincere? So difficult to judge. Best he went along with them, one way or the other.

"I haven't had this much fun in…. I don't know when," he said, shrugging. "Those kids are something."

"Just yesterday they went to the aquatic center in Dubuque County," Lance's wife, Holly, said. Like her husband, Holly used the most animated voice, always the kindest words, while speaking to Andy—but never would she hold his eyes. She spoke to the wind, as if Andy were a moth fluttering from view. *Yoo-hoo! I'm over here, yoo-hoo!* he'd wanted to shout many times in either of their company. She smoothed over her jeans legs and peered at the tips of her white sneakers. "We know just about everything that happens around here. Little birds tell us things."

Loretta tapped the thigh of a chunky dark-haired woman named Betty. Betty's knees protruded from under her skirt like two ripe melons. "Way things are around here, huh?"

The women laughed, and Andy's legs tired. He sat and sipped his beer, keeping a furtive eye on Harden. *It's because he's the only adult I really know here. Psychologically, it's called imprinting.*

"My mother used to say she couldn't burn coffee without someone from town asking her if she'd cleaned the pot okay," Betty said.

The redhead whose name Andy couldn't remember said, "Things are much better today. I'll say that, for sure. You're too young to understand."

"People are nosy today too," Holly responded. "Maybe not as bad, but they're nosy."

Loretta seesawed her broad shoulders. "I don't mind a little interest in my life from a kind neighbor."

"Never quite thought of it that way," the redhead said. "You got a good point, doesn't she?"

Alicia Anders nodded in agreement. "She does. I'd hate to think about taking ill or growing old with no one to care for me."

"Get one of those Life Alerts," the redhead said.

Loretta extended her arms and wiggled her fingers. "I've fallen and I can't get up!"

The women howled with laughter. Andy couldn't help but join in. He pictured the television commercial that sold medical alerts to the elderly and shut-ins and shook his head. He wondered if the old woman who lived above him in Chicago carried one, and how long she might lay dead before her stink alarmed neighbors.

Then he saw himself after his beating, mere steps from the front door to his apartment building. Not one of his neighbors had bothered to come to his aid or check on him during his recuperation.

"Back in my grandmamma's days," the red-haired woman said, "nosy sometimes meant living a way others told you to. A girl only had so much liberty back then. Remember the story of what happened to my grandmamma?"

"Sure do," Betty answered.

"What happened?" Andy asked, leaning forward in his chair.

The redhead brought her hands to her round, freckly face. "Grandmamma lived with her husband and his mother and his only surviving brother. Newlyweds when her husband died of tuberculosis. Two months later, her mother-in-law passed on. Grandmamma found herself living in a house with just her and her brother-in-law. Scandalous back then that a widowed woman would live alone with a man not her husband, even an in-law."

"What did she do?" Andy asked.

"She had no choice but to move out. The brother-in-law inherited the farm, so she lived alone in a motel outside Waterloo, living off beans, working whatever odd jobs she could get, or so she said. Her family had all died from polio, except for one younger brother who lived in an iron lung till he died at thirty. Hardly had much of a pension or whatever she got from her husband's GI Bill."

"That's horrible," Andy said.

"Nowadays we mind our own businesses more," she said, "but you can picture back in those days, things like that were... well... scandalous."

Andy massaged the condensation forming over his beer can. "What eventually happened to your grandmother?"

"She wound up marrying her brother-in-law," the woman said, nodding with her chin flush against her freckled neck. "That's my grandpapa! After that, Grandmamma could move back into the farmhouse, about the only home she'd ever known, and they raised a family, which eventually included my mother. Oh, she told us she grew to love

Grandpapa, in her own way. He was five years younger than her but provided well. Never said a mean thing to me in my life, never even recall a sour face. He'd done her a great favor by marrying her."

Andy widened his eyes and drew in his lips. "Wouldn't that be even more scandalous? I mean, marrying your brother-in-law?"

Loretta adjusted her eyeglasses "Honey, in those days, widows used to marry their deceased husbands' brothers all the time. People considered it proper, even encouraged it. Come a long way from the days a woman had to run off because she couldn't live unwed in a house with a bachelor. Nowadays, two bachelors can up and marry each other."

The ring of women laughed, and Andy's cheeks burned. He understood Loretta had referenced Iowa's same-sex marriage law. But how much did they care? Loretta and the others hadn't expressed condemnation. Arty Ficklemeyer's wife had merely stated a fact, along with a rather shrewd philosophical observation. He figured most of the women seated among the casual circle were Catholic, as were virtually everyone in that part of Iowa, yet Loretta's brazen comment had set them giggling like schoolgirls, rather than fuming with religious zealotry.

Somehow, the discussion of same-sex marriage evolved into chatter about a new stitch the redhead had learned during her crochet circle.

Disinterested in needlecrafts, Andy took the opportunity and excused himself to join Harden and his man friends around the grill. Harden greeted Andy with a light pat on his shoulder, and the other men's smiles widened. Too wide, Andy thought. Anxious, twitchy grins.

"Guess I'll go see what's got those women all giggly over there," Burt said, backing off.

Arty and Lance straggled behind him. "They're having too much fun," Arty said.

"You have enough room on there for all that food?" Andy asked Harden, wanting to keep the mood uplifted, although he feared he had pissed on Harden's fun.

Focused on the smoldering charcoals, Harden said with a snicker, "I'll be here most of the afternoon. Patty after patty, chicken breast after chicken breast."

"I'll keep the ice cold beers coming for you."

Harden swigged his can empty and shook it upside down. "Keep the grill sergeant well nourished."

"I'll go get you another one."

Andy grinned, thinking that Harden had adopted his nickname. But a young woman approached the group, and a sudden—and unsettling—bright burst of energy smacked the smile off his face. The friends raised their heads and voices while the younger woman chatted with them. Their laughter lifted high above the local cornfields and merged with the neighboring partiers.

The new arrival, wearing tight jeans and a yellow half-sleeve shirt that showcased her tanned shoulders, set a pie on the table and strutted over to Harden. Only when he noticed his burning hand submerged in the vat's slushy ice did he accept that he'd been glowering at her. Andy found Harden's favorite brand, shook the blood back into his frigid hand, and beelined for the grill. "Here you go, Harden."

"Thanks." Harden snapped open the can with a spit of foam. "Lucinda, have you met Andrew? Andy, this is Lucinda Jamison. She's a coworker from Marshall."

"Nice to meet you, Lucinda." They shook hands. He noted her blond hair pulled into a bun to accentuate her long neck and the hoop earrings that captured the sun. "Sorry, my hand's a bit cold."

"That's okay, mine's a bit warm." She laid her fingertips (her nails were painted hot pink with flecks of gold) to the back of Harden's neck, and he flinched and chuckled. "I was baking all morning. My pie's still warm."

"Sounds great," Harden said. "What kind?"

"Strawberry rhubarb."

"My mouth's watering just thinking about it," Harden said.

"First time I tried baking one of those."

Harden stated that some farmers refer to rhubarb as "pieplant" because of its popularity with bakers. Lucinda mentioned her girlfriend's grandparents grew rhubarb in Minnesota, and "they earn gross profit returns of up to seventeen dollars per crown each year." Andy worried his phony smile might melt onto the grill.

Someone shouted his name, and he turned to see Mason and Olivia rushing toward him. His grin felt more genuine, and he asked what the fuss was about. Breathless, Mason told Andy about the corn maze, insisting he come along. Andy had never heard of a corn maze, and when he asked, Harden poked the charcoals and said, "You don't want to know."

"It's a maze they cut through the cornfield so it looks like a crossword puzzle from an airplane," Mason explained. "You have to find your way through, that's all."

"That's simple," Andy said. "The entire city of Chicago is a maze. A maze of super-tall buildings, and I can find my way through that pretty good."

Olivia grabbed Andy's hand. "Then let's go."

Andy held back, hesitant to leave Harden and Lucinda alone. But he shook himself, realizing the foolishness of his sentiments. He guzzled what remained of his beer, tossed the empty can into a receptacle, and relinquished himself to Olivia's hold until they stood before what looked like the maze's front entrance.

Flanked by cornstalks, the entrance deepened into darkness.

"Let's go," Mason said.

Andy placed his sunglasses atop his head and stepped inside the maze behind Mason and Olivia and a few other kids. Dry duff and green clover crunched under their sneakers as they made their way down the first row. The sun barely penetrated the tall stalks, two heads taller than Andy. The maze consumed the kids' voices, and a vacuous, strange hush slowed his movements. His nose tickled from the smell of sweet earth and fertilizer.

The first turn, they hit a dead end. Giggling, the kids retraced their steps and proceeded down another row.

"This way." Mason and a companion raced off.

"Slow up, guys."

"Don't worry, Uncle Andy. We'll stay with you." Olivia took hold of his hand, and they, alongside another little girl whose features resembled Kamila's, shuffled down the row.

The rows filled an arm span of about two yards, enough room for one adult and two small children to walk side by side. Andy gripped both girls' hands. They winced and let go. More children raced ahead. Indistinguishable shouts came at him from unseen mouths.

Somewhere, he was certain Mason cried out, "Try to find us!"

"Mason? Where are you?"

Olivia and her friend nudged him down another row. He turned his head a moment, and the girls had vanished.

"No playing games, girls."

Olivia and her friend appeared around a corner. "Wrong turn. Let's try this way."

"Hold up, you guys."

Olivia raced back to him. "Isn't this fun, Uncle Andy?"

"Sure. Where are Mason and the others?"

"Mason's probably already out. He's done it so many times, he knows his way even in the dark."

Other children rushed past them, twisting and chuckling as they plotted their escape.

"I don't think this is the right way," Andy said.

"It's over here," Olivia's friend said. "I remember now."

Though the tall stalks blocked much of the sun, humidity built high, and Andy mopped his forehead. One impasse after another and Andy wondered if they'd ever see the outside world again. "The fairgrounds need to provide maps for this place," he mumbled.

Olivia's little friend grasped her hand and hurried her off. Andy followed, calling after them to slow down and not to get lost. Yet it was he who he worried the maze might consume without a trace.

He tired, and the girls rushed ahead. As he straggled behind, his thoughts turned to what Loretta and the other ladies had said about marrying in-laws. He laughed to himself. His crush on Harden hadn't become that severe. It wasn't like he really wanted Harden the same way he wanted Ken. Yet when he pictured Lucinda and Harden alone at the grill, blood burned his eyes.

Each turn brought his ruminations down more unfamiliar terrain. He began to compare Ken and Harden. Head to head, he had to give favorites to Harden. Ken was…. What was Ken? A bully, in some ways. Ken had been rough with Andy from the beginning, even while they had "fooled around" that first time. Years ago, Andy wouldn't have given a man like Ken two minutes of his time. Had his sinister nature taken on such a deep root—like the corn around him—that he believed he deserved a man like Kenneth Millpairs?

He visualized Harden again, tossing his head back with the force of laughter, patting his buddies on their backs, beer gripped in hand, grill fork raised with poise. Good-old-boy fun. Andy had enjoyed observing him.

Suddenly, there stood Lucinda. Not only pretty and well-groomed, but bright. She spoke the language of farming, Harden's cherished first love.

You belong in Chicago, bozo. Not in Iowa.

Gazing around, Andy realized the voice he heard came from inside his own head. The children's giggles had evaporated amidst the breezes teasing the stalks. The only noise—the beating of his heart.

"Hello? Where did everyone go? Olivia?"

He traipsed down row after row, each time facing a wall of formidable green stalks. His breath came in scarce spasms. He'd forgotten to exhale. When he swallowed the thick, hot air, his tongue sealed to the roof of his mouth. All his spit had evaporated.

Far off giggles jerked his head. Vaporous laughter, like the breeze. His heart pounded inside his chest and he began to grow disoriented and dizzy.

"Where the hell am I?" he muttered loud enough for a flock of crows to flutter out from the cornstalks. He flinched back, cursing the birds. Although he wished he could fly away with similar ease.

The more he shouted for the kids, the more his voice sounded empty, the sole human utterance on earth. The walls of corn swallowed his voice. Almost as if he were drowning in a vast sea. A speck no larger than nothing.

He could navigate his way through the gritty, litter-strewn streets of Chicago's crime-ridden ghettos, but he couldn't find his way out of a corn maze in the middle of Iowa.

Pathetic!

He worked the saliva around inside his mouth. Laboring to orient himself, he peered from side to side, up along the massive stalks and down the endless rows. What sadistic freak had conjured up such a labyrinth?

Slices of sunlight against the clover-covered ground summoned his hope and courage. Somewhere out there, the world wagged. The sun, the sky, the trees, the people, the food piled high on picnic tables.

Stalks snatched at his T-shirt and hair as he traipsed along. *No wonder they call them stalks!* The elbows of corn seemed to thump his nose, scorning him. He swatted away the spindly appendages and annoying gnats.

He stopped and breathed. Beyond the stalks, the vinegar-like aroma of roasting corn tickled his nose. The gala was going on without him. He checked his wristwatch. He'd trudged inside the damn maze alone and lost for more than fifteen minutes. How long did a person need to reach the other side?

"Anyone hear me?"

A pile of bones lay to the side of one row. Nice sign, Andy brooded. At a closer look, he realized the bones were from someone's chicken picnic. Discarded in a dash for the exit. Ants scurried over the bones in a crazed pursuit to devour leftover flesh. Trapped in their own maze.

A sudden impulse to bushwhack through the stalks took hold of him. Had to be quicker than racing around like a rat.

Each row led nowhere. More dead ends. More mocking corn. He imagined the stalks coming alive, chasing and grabbing him like devilish phantoms.

Silly to experience anxiety in a corn maze. They had built it for fun, not torture. *Where are those damn kids?*

"Olivia! Mason!"

The distant cawing of a crow dug a hole the size of a swimming pool in Andy's soul. He wiped the sweat from his forehead and inhaled. His shirt and sweaty legs were coated with corn straw and dead bugs. Defeated, he fell to his haunches and dragged his fingers through the clover.

A few yards off, a candy bar wrapper lay on the ground, trampled by many feet. Another reminder that humans existed, yet had abandoned him in some strange parallel world.

"Andrew...."

He stood tall and jerked his head toward the sound of a man's voice. Familiar, but too remote to judge.

"I'm here!"

"Andy?"

"Over here!"

"Stay where you are," he said. "Keep talking and I'll find you."

Andy stood motionless and repeated, "I'm over here, I'm over here," until the crunch of duff amplified and he beheld the sight of his former brother-in-law, Harden Krane, walking toward him and wearing a wrinkly forehead.

He stopped several paces away. "You get lost?"

Andy began chuckling in relief. "I was about to resort to eating crow, but I think I have in a way. I'm an idiot."

"Everyone gets lost in here their first try," Harden said. "The kids shouldn't have left you alone."

"They made it out?"

"Sure, they're already eating. I asked where you were, and they thought you had gotten out."

"What made you think to come after me?"

Harden flushed. "You were gone so long I worried. No one had seen you since Mason and Olivia dragged you off." Sunlight bathed Harden's blond hair when he turned to make room for Andy to walk alongside him. "Come on. I bet you're hungry."

They shared a light chuckle, and together they hiked down the corridor of cornstalks toward the exit, where the outside world awaited, among good food and much needed ice-cold beer.

CHAPTER
FIFTEEN

EXHAUSTED after a long day under the hot sun and trying to find his way out of that godforsaken corn maze, Andy relaxed beside Harden on the living room sofa. They had tucked the children in bed, and now they sat shoulder to shoulder, knee to knee, smelling of sweat and corn and grill smoke, striving to remove the kernels from between their teeth with toothpicks.

Harden—toothpick pinched between index finger and thumb, pointy end wedged between two front teeth—elbowed Andy. "What did you think of our corn roast, huh?"

Their elbows working in unison, Andy smiled. "I had a good time, really, I did."

"Even after getting lost in the corn maze?"

The blood taste annoyed Andy. He tossed his toothpick on a napkin atop the coffee table and wiped his hands. "Quite an experience. I'll concede that," he said, and he roved his tongue over his gums. "Thanks again for rescuing me."

"Not quite like a weekend in Chicago, though, I bet."

"Everything's fun in its own way. The food was awesome. That's for sure."

"I'm stuffed." Harden patted his belly. Andy noted the small bulge overlapping his jeans—his papa pack, Andy called it. "I shouldn't have eaten so much. I had one too many slices of Lucinda's strawberry rhubarb pie. It was horrible, but I didn't want to appear rude."

"She likes you," Andy stated with a downturn of his mouth.

Andy liked the red that streaked across Harden's sun-bronzed face. "Lucinda's a flirt," Harden said.

"Not interested in her?"

"Way too young for me."

Harden's admission gave Andy a strange sense of gladness and relief, yet he needled him. "Kamila is too old, Lucinda is too young. Picky guy."

"Guess I'm fickle," Harden said, his voice earnest. "I don't even know what I want these days."

Andy exhaled and brought his hand closer to his side. "Don't worry over it too much. All that matters is you're a good guy."

Harden continued to pick at his teeth. "You think?"

Nodding unhurriedly, Andy said, "I think."

Harden chortled and again poked Andy's side with his elbow. "Jane was sure giving you some looks. You can't tell me you didn't notice her."

Andy *had* noticed Burt Anders's eldest daughter, Jane. She had joined their party while Andy was fighting his way through the corn maze. The moment he'd scooted his legs under the picnic table she'd begun staring at him. Offset by the others, Jane had acted outright flirty. He'd tried to ignore her, but she had made it impossible.

"Don't people around here know I'm gay?" Andy said.

Harden brought his picking hand to his lap and chuckled. "I took out an aerial advertisement after Lillian told me. Seriously, it's nobody's business. I have no idea if they know or not. Clearly, Jane Anders doesn't. Why do you ask?"

"I got an impression Loretta might know. People are more indirect here, I guess. I don't mind anyone knowing. Did it ever bother you?"

Harden shrugged and began picking his teeth again. "Why would it? None of my business either."

"I'm guessing the kids know by now."

"Kids know everything."

Andy prodded Harden further. "Be honest, what did you think after you found out?"

"I figured it's a part of nature, like corn."

"Being gay is like corn?" Andy threw his head against the backrest and howled to the ceiling. He cupped his mouth with his hand when he feared he might wake the kids. Softer, he said, "That's a new one. But I can see a reasonable simile there."

They chuckled under their breaths and for a moment Andy fancied Harden might tickle his ribs when someone knocked on the living room's french doors.

"Who's that?"

"Must be Dick," Harden said, setting his toothpick next to Andy's and getting to his feet.

Harden and Dick spoke a few minutes at the door, but Andy failed to decipher what they were saying. Over Harden's shoulder, Dick eyed Andy. Flushing, Andy turned his gaze to Olivia's laptop on the carpet.

"Why's he knocking at this hour?" Andy asked once Harden sat back beside him.

"He likes to let me know when he's working the field at night," Harden said.

"Working so late?"

"He's using the full moon to get extra work in. It's cooler to work nights. Haven't you ever heard of a Corn Moon? Native folklore suggests the soil turns richer under full moons too. I took a course on farming folklore in college. Very interesting."

"I should've known," Andy said, nodding. "A full moon. That's why we're so punchy. I make my best money on nights like this. Shootings always increase during full moons. Did you know that? Farmers and gangsters share similarities. Both come out at night to accomplish their best work."

Harden shook his head. "You and that tour business of yours. I can't believe people pay for that kind of service."

"People see shootings and crime all the time on TV. Why not see it in person? Is what I'm doing any different than providing tours through Auschwitz or Lizzie Borden's house?"

"I know you better than this, Andy. You're doing this for more than the money. This is your own way of...."

"Of what?"

Harden faced Andy. "Admit it, you hate what you're doing."

Andy crossed his arms across his chest and peered at his stocking feet. "I'm tired of taking the straight and narrow road. What do I get out of it? Poverty? Rejection? Layoffs from people who practice the identical political correctness as corrupt politicians? Even prisoners have pen pals and celebrity endorsements. What do I have? I have a right to a life too, don't I?"

"Hey, take it easy, buddy. I wasn't judging you. In case you haven't figured it out, I have a high regard for you. I always have. That's why I question what you're doing."

Andy turned his warming face to Harden. He loosened his arms and in slow motion brought them to his sides. "A high regard for me?"

"Sure. I've always liked your unique way of seeing things. I'd hate to see you toss aside your convictions just because you're angry at the world."

Andy stared back at his feet. "I'm not angry at the world."

"You just proved you are with your outburst. I know you well enough that it's against your nature to be doing this nonsense in Chicago. It's good you came here to get away from it."

"I'm just trying to make a living."

"We all are. I work at an office I dislike. Sure, I like the people. That's what makes it tolerable. Right now I'd do anything to swap places with Dick Carelli. But I'm not going to throw my life into the gutter because I can't have everything I want." Harden eyed Andy like he might Mason after one of his fights. "You once told me that's what's wrong with this world, that we're all too spoiled and selfish. More is never enough. Didn't you say we act like kids in a candy store who are told they can't have a tenth piece of caramel, and then we throw temper tantrums, destroying everything in sight?"

Andy recalled many past philosophical discussions with Harden. One aspect of Harden's personality Andy had always appreciated. He wasn't one to draw blank stares whenever Andy mentioned topics heavier than what movie star wore whose gown at which award show.

Even more impressive, Harden remembered some of those conversations. Andy, equally self-conscious and tickled, grinned at him, but he grew worried when Harden's face muscles lost their tautness.

He shook his head toward his lap. "I shouldn't preach. I'm just as bad. It's my job to peddle ethanol, although I know it's a waste of tax dollars."

"What's wrong with ethanol?" Andy asked sympathetically.

"Requires more energy to distill corn into ethanol than what you get out of it. My company has me exaggerate the research to prove it's cost effective and more environmentally sound, despite the industry knowing otherwise. The great collective lie, we call it. I guess everyone sells out at some point." He craned a smile Andy accepted was for his benefit. "I better get some sleep. Kids will be up bright and early. We have to go to church. I kind of promised Mom I'd go again. You want to tag along?"

"To church? I'd rather not, if that's okay."

Harden pushed himself up by his thighs with a deep sigh. "Do what you please. It's your vacation. See you in the morning. Sleep well, Andy."

"I'm not too far behind you, Harden. See you in the morning."

Downstairs in his room, Andy lay in bed after a fantastically long, hot shower and stared at the ceiling. Pitch black silence. As if he'd fallen through a gaping fracture. Had he disappointed Harden? Maybe he should have accepted his invitation to attend church. Especially after the somber turn to their conversation.

The pull of Chicago suddenly became stronger. The excitement, the bright lights, the hot pursuit of criminals for his passengers. There was zero nightlife in Dover County. Days passed fine. Replete with sunshine and oddities to explore. But the nights?

Harden had said his business went against his nature. He had "high regard" for him all these years. What did a country boy know? A country boy who had earned a full scholarship to a major university. Still, Harden lacked the know-how to move mountains or to change Andy's destiny.

The proprietor of South Side Tours had become a part of Andy's identity. His van, parked out front for anyone to see, a monument to his self-defeat. Andy Wingal, the peddler of dirt. Would it be so easy to shake off that image, no matter how much his business dwindled to nothing?

He pictured Harden lying in his bed two floors above him. Certainly Harden deserved happiness and fulfillment. Maybe Lucinda what's her name wasn't a bad choice. She at least understood farming.

He switched on the table lamp and texted Ken. *How r u?* he wrote.

Ken's text arrived a few minutes later. *How's Iowa?*

Quiet.

Let me get back to you.

A minute later, Andy's phone rang. Surprised, he answered. "Hello, Officer Ken. What makes you call tonight? You never use that end of your phone."

"I'm on the handless, taking a break at Benny's Chicken and Fish Hut. My hands are messy."

"Sounds yummy. How's the South Side?"

"Hot weather keeping things busy. So you're liking your first weekend in Iowa? It's a bit conservative for you, isn't it? Don't they drive those pickup trucks?"

"They're more conventional than conservative. There's a difference. And they drive pickups because they have stuff to haul around. People out here still do much of their own manual labor."

"They don't even wear tank tops or shorts from what I remember that summer I drove through there on my way to Colorado."

Andy glanced at the scratches on his arms and legs from his stint battling through the corn maze. "That's because they work hard here. Farmers especially, even into the night. You try toiling the soil in one of your muscle shirts, cargo shorts, and sandals. And they have gay marriage too, Kenneth. The courts here legalized it before New York and Sweden did. Not that that means anything to you."

"Don't start on me about that, not when I'm in public. Maybe I ought to come out for a visit and knock you around. I have Wednesday and Thursday off this week."

"I'll be back in Chicago by then."

"No you won't."

"What do you mean?"

"You stay put."

"But I've already been here for—" *Has it only been three days?* "—for long enough."

"You need to keep out of Chicago until things settle down with your assailants."

Assailants. The word sounded strange while lying snug in a basement bedroom, with Iowa's farmland outside. "I don't care about those punks," Andy said. "They won't bother me anymore. I should be out right now escorting my passengers. I'm ready to come home."

"If you do, the city will probably find a way to confiscate your license."

"They can't do that."

"They sure can. Stay in Iowa where it's safe. Relax. I'll keep checking your mailbox. So far you've only gotten about four pieces of junk."

Andy sighed. "I can't stay here too much longer. Who visits people for two weeks? It's not like I'm in some Jane Austen novel."

"Then go somewhere else for a week or two. Visit an old college friend."

"They all live in the Chicago area. Can you tell me how I'm to pay for this extended holiday? I've already lost tons of money because of you forcing me to come here. It'll take me weeks to make up the income."

"Stop bellyaching. If you don't want to waste more money, stay put. So how long a drive is it to where you're at?"

Andy hesitated. "About five hours. You have to take back roads once you get past Rockford. It's very windy and hilly. If you're not used to it, the driving can be treacherous."

"Sweet. I'll let you know if I can make it. Gotta run. Meanwhile, keep your head."

Andy set the phone aside and envisioned Ken with his tight "beater" shirt and bronzed muscles and shaved chest in Iowa. He'd really rather not merge his Chicago world with life at Burr Oak Farm. Despite what Harden had said about technology colliding their two cultures, Ken in Iowa would be like marrying a mouse with an elephant.

The rural landscape moved slowly, unforced, easy, and natural. Ken was a jittery, quick-tempered blaze of muscle. Nothing like the way Harden must appear snoozing above him. His chest rising and falling slower and slower, infused with the dreams of a trouble-free youth and renewal for better things to come.

The corn roast ladies had hinted at an Iowa like that. With its dichotomy of gay marriage and crocheting circles, Iowa ebbed and flowed between the past and the future. A land where, as Harden had mentioned, the modern computer was invented, yet the phases of the moon still ruled many people's movements.

Officer Ken Millpairs, city boy from Chicago's southwest side, could never fit into that setting.

Andy switched off the table lamp and squirmed under the bedcovers. How long, he wondered, before Iowa's countryside caught him between its undulations, leaving him abandoned and shattered. The same as what had happened to him earlier that day. Lost and knocked to his haunches inside a corn maze.

He stretched his mouth into a tight grin. He visualized Harden coming to his rescue. Of course, sooner or later, he would have found his way out of the tangled grid. But that Harden had sought to locate him made his unanticipated and extended stay in Iowa less annoying.

Stay in Iowa where it's safe, Ken had said.

Andy supposed worse scenarios had beleaguered him before.

CHAPTER
SIXTEEN

NEXT morning at the kitchen table, Harden asked Andy for a second time if he'd like to attend Mass with him and the kids. "I'm not a churchgoer," he replied.

"I'm not much of one either, but, well, with the kids...."

"Don't explain," Andy said, raising his hand. "I understand."

They had already finished chocolate chip pancakes and salty Baltic beef sausages, and now they sat sipping coffee while the kids dressed for church. Harden looked handsome in his brown slacks and light-blue Oxford, the sleeves rolled to the elbows to expose yesterday's sun on his forearms. Rich brown forearms, dusted with the perfect amount of blondish hair.

"Funny how you want to protect your kids from all the things you used to think were cool," Harden said with a modest snicker.

Andy chuckled. "That's all part of getting older. I'll hold down the fort while you guys are out. Don't worry about me."

"We usually spend time at my parents' after Mass. Mom cooks up something to eat, and we play a few hands of cards. If you want, you can drive over there and meet us. I can give you the address."

"Honestly, I don't think I'd be comfortable. But, Harden, before you go, I wanted to ask you something."

Harden had stood, ready to leave the kitchen. At present, he stared down at Andy, his hand clasped on the back of Andy's ladder-back chair. "What is it, Andy?"

"If it won't be any trouble… I was thinking. I'd like to stay on here a few more extra days than what I had planned, maybe even until the end of next week."

Harden shrugged. "Sure. That would be great. Any more trouble back in Chicago?"

"Nothing like that. I was just thinking I'd hang out a while longer, spend more time with the kids. Make up for lost time. Although I'm sure Kamila the Hun won't approve."

Harden threw back his head and laughed. "I told you not to worry over her." He squeezed Andy's shoulder. "I'm glad you're staying on board a while longer. The kids will love the news."

Andy resisted placing a hand on top of his. "Thanks, Harden."

The house grew dead still with everyone gone. Bored and antsy, Andy finished his coffee and stretched on the sofa to watch television. Nothing much on Sunday morning other than political talking heads who shouted at each other from across shiny round tables. If only they'd shut up long enough to listen to each other, they'd realize they echoed the same positions.

Maybe he should have tagged along to Mass. Would Harden think less of him for refusing? Even Harden had confessed he lacked an ardent belief. The kids had looked adorable in their church clothes. Mason, dressed in khakis and a brown polo shirt, had been a pint-sized carbon copy of his father. And Olivia in her green little-girl summer dress had resembled a princess. But the more he imagined facing Harden's family, with their cold country cordiality, he realized he'd made the correct decision to stay behind.

His eyes began to itch. Next thing he knew, he'd rolled to his side and nearly fallen off the sofa. He sat upright and tried to shake off the post-nap fog. The clock above the computer desk read nine-thirty-five. He'd slept a meager twenty minutes. He would still be sound asleep in Chicago if he had his tour business to run through the night, deep into the dark morning hours. He switched off the yakking political PEZ-heads and wandered downstairs.

More restless after his nap than before, he changed into nylon basketball shorts and a sleeveless T-shirt with "Illini" embroidered across the chest. A few minutes later, Burr Oak Farm grew smaller and smaller in his rearview mirror as he headed down the road. His goal: to find a gym in the town of Duncan.

Thick-stalked yellow wildflowers edged the narrow country roads. Cawing and hemming crows perched on wooden fences faced the sturdy breeze. Heavy farming equipment dipped and rolled with the land through the braids of corn. Distant puffs of smoke from the exhaust pipes pumped with the power of man-made machinery meeting earth. A typical Sunday for Iowa, Andy figured.

Different from his prowls along the streets of Chicago, that's for sure. Deep down, Andy knew Harden was right when he'd said his job as the South Side Tour Guide wasn't suited to him. But hadn't that been the idea? To go against his nature, fling convictions and decency aside? To lose himself in the moral rot and feed off the carcass like everyone else until nothing remained but splintered bones?

He recalled standing alongside the body of the boy shot near Aberdeen Street, watching his blood stream toward the gutter. Andy had learned later, the boy, seventeen, had been a gifted student who'd attended one of those inner city magnet schools with a curriculum focused on engineering. Had that been the reason his peers had targeted him? Because he had a future? A lamb surrounded by resentful, covetous wolves. Destruction for destruction's sake.

And Andy cashed in on that ravenous, wanton annihilation.

At least I'm no hypocrite. At least I don't cheat and steal and lie. My biggest sin is I give people what they demand.

He drove past a good-sized office building with the signpost: "Marshall Farming Enterprises." Harden's worksite. Made Andy feel good looking at the modern facility. A place where Harden rolled his sleeves to his elbows, clenched a pencil between fingers pumped with blood, and sweat beads exposed his churning mind. Good, sincere work. But what had Harden said about selling out to ethanol investors? Maybe only honest work came from self-subsistence, isolated from society's games.

Duncan's sole Catholic church emerged. Andy had always thought it odd a town Duncan's size should have a cathedral with a steeple taller than most of the surrounding silos. In nearby Dyersville, the church Harden and Lillian had wed in had a massive steeple also—two of them—visible from a mile down the road.

Many cars lined the street outside the church and filled the small parking lot. He spotted Harden's forest green Jeep Patriot. Another twinge of regret for refusing to attend church with the family needled him. *Maybe I'll go next Sunday, if I'm still here. It won't be so bad to face his family's condescension.*

He cruised the short shopping district and scanned for a gym. Nothing but food joints and retail stores, most of them closed.

He drove on and noticed a barbershop with an "open" sign. Remembering he needed a haircut, he parked and headed inside. The employees and patrons chatted in both English and what he gathered was Bosnian. They seemed to know Andy, and they waved and hollered greetings. He overheard one of the barbers mentioning a man who'd gotten lost in the maze during yesterday's corn roast, but Andy was unsure if the barber meant to tease him. No one indicated they recognized him as the infamous fool.

After a short five minute wait, a female barber waved him to her chair. She draped the smock over him and asked in a thick accent what kind of a haircut he'd like. "Off the neck and ears," he said, considering how Ken preferred it. And no, she and the others didn't know of any gyms other than the one in Concord, fifteen miles away.

Twenty minutes later (and ten dollars and fifty cents lighter), he left the barbershop and checked his Magellan for a gym. The display concurred with the barbershop folks. Unwilling to drive fifteen miles for what might prove to be a closet-sized facility with nothing but cardio equipment, he turned back for Burr Oak Farm. He'd only been home ten minutes when the kids rushed inside the house.

"Uncle Andy!" Olivia hurried to him. "Is it true? You're going to stay with us for longer?"

Andy patted the top of her head. "You got me to tug around a few extra days."

Grinning like a truant schoolboy, Harden stepped behind Olivia and explained they'd agreed to skip his parents' brunch and head for home, not wanting to leave Andy home alone. "We just saw Lance yesterday, anyway," he added.

"You look different, Uncle Andy," Mason said, squinting at him.

"Hey, you got a haircut," Harden said. "When did you get that done?"

"I went out for a drive and found a barber in town."

"Looks real nice. That reminds me, Mason, you're due for a cut. Now that it's on my mind, we better get it over with so we can have a free day ahead of us. Head upstairs and change. Meet me out back."

"I'll do it," Andy said.

"You?"

"Sure, I've cut hair before. He's got straight hair like yours, can't be too difficult. Just hand over the clippers."

For the next half hour, Andy trimmed Mason's hair in the backyard, using a twenty-dollar clipper Harden had said paid off tenfold on haircuts its first year. Andy recommended Mason fly down the slide and swing to shake loose the hairs. Olivia rushed to join him.

The remainder of the afternoon, they explored by the creek and played board games. Later, they ate the dinner Andy had made: Chicken a la Andy, with some of the yummy leftover sides the women handed them before they'd left the corn roast. Afterward, Harden permitted the kids to put on their swimsuits and run through the sprinkler. Harden and Andy watched from the porch steps, sipping pops under the hot sun that had turned the western sky lavender.

"You know how long it's been since I ran through a sprinkler?" Harden said.

Andy eyed him. "A while, I'd guess."

They sat quiet, sipping their drinks.

"You thinking what I'm thinking?" Harden said.

Andy's grin hurt his sunbaked face. "Let's do it."

They both set aside their pops and jumped to their feet. Harden kicked off his slippers and socks, stripped off his shirt and jeans, and ran through the sprinkler in his light-blue boxers. Andy flung off his shirt and sandals and scurried after him. He was still wearing his nylon gym shorts and cared little if they got wet. Overjoyed with the antics of the adults, the kids laughed and leaped higher over the tiny pulsating jets. They jumped on Harden's back, begging that he act like a show horse, and he leaped with them through the sprinkler.

Not bad for a single dad, Andy mused, catching glimpses of Harden's naked torso and legs—and wet boxers that adhered to his solid-looking butt. *Even with his papa pack and farmer's tan, not bad.*

Their fun continued into Monday. Harden had decided to take the day off work, and last night Andy had overheard him telephone Kamila, asking her to remain home. Once they'd finished storing the last of the cleaned breakfast pans, Harden suggested the aquatic center. The kids raced to see who could get ready faster. They arrived an hour later. Harden and Andy played "catch the kid" in the near-empty pool. Last night, Andy had fallen asleep picturing Harden running through the sprinkler, and here he was again, in full view, the sun radiating off his wet skin and the light brown hairs on his chest.

Wearing Harden's same dark-blue trunks from last time, Andy also felt sexier. Who needed a gym when he could tread water for a lactic burn? Harden and Andy tossed the kids airborne, and the water splashed and sparkled. Their laughter faded in and out each time Olivia or Mason dragged Andy under the water. Harden blew water from his mouth, impersonating a spitting fountain.

Mason and Olivia climbed on Andy's and Harden's shoulders to play chicken until the lifeguard blew his whistle and demanded they stop. The aquatic center filled with more people. Some of the same children from Andy's last visit played with them, but Randy Lederman stayed out of sight. Andy was delighted to see Olivia and Mason get along better with the other children. Olivia insisted they play find the nickel. Harden raised his hand and, breathing heavily, begged off. "I need a rest," he said, his wet hair dripping down his heaving chest.

"I'm with Dad," Andy said. "I'll toss you a nickel and you guys can play with it yourselves."

He trailed Harden out of the pool and rummaged through his shorts pockets. While the children swam for the coin, Andy lay by Harden on a lounge chair. Oakleys secured on nose, he found himself examining more of Harden's body.

He wore a pair of light-blue cargo trunks with a double white stripe along the outside legs that accentuated his thighs. He lacked Ken's bulging, taut muscles, but he had a natural man's look. A body that worked when needed and was well fed. Solid meat on his bones. Biceps round and full. Not marble hard, but enough to…. *Sink my teeth into?*

He looked straight ahead when Harden turned to him.

"Nice to see the kids all smiles and laughs," he said. "Come to think of it, I haven't seen the kids with their noses buried in a hand-held game since you got here." Harden lowered his sunglasses with the orange mirrored lenses and eyeballed Andy. "I guess you make a better plaything."

Andy spread his arms. "And I don't need toggling."

"Sure about that?" Harden jabbed Andy's ribs, and Andy shrunk back, chuckling.

They settled into their chairs and absorbed the sun while the aromas of honeysuckle and chlorine and suntan lotion drifted over their heads. In the background, a chorus of shouting and giggling kids ebbed with the sound of splashing. Andy quivered from a combination of the sun drying his skin and good feelings. They remained like that, side by side, their toes pointing toward the blue sky, relaxing and chatting and chuckling, until shadows vanished under their lounge chairs.

Harden stretched to a stand. "Guess we better get going before the kids turn into prunes. We can grab lunch on the way home. Sound good?"

Andy agreed, and he collected their gear while Harden waved in the kids. The four left the pool, laughing and ribbing each other and talking about their fun morning and how they looked ahead to an even more enjoyable afternoon.

No prying eyes had bothered Andy at the aquatic center that day.

"I promised the kids a movie and dinner," Harden told Andy later that evening, once Andy had climbed from the basement, fresh and clean from a hot shower. "There's a seven-thirty showing in Concord."

Andy shrugged. "I have no other plans."

They piled in Harden's Jeep and headed for Concord, where they ate at a local diner and watched a G-rated animated feature at the town's twin theater (four dollars for adults, three for children). Afterward, they crossed the street for ice creams and sat outside at one of the parlor's boutique tables. Andy scanned for the gym and saw that it was as small as he'd expected.

Olivia, dripping cheesecake-flavored ice cream down her forearm, said she liked the movie better than other cartoons she'd seen but insisted she could have drawn the characters by hand with more detail than "some stupid computer."

A conventional girl, Andy reflected. Much like her father, a man who he couldn't help watching as he swirled his thick tongue around his ice cream cone with unbridled enthusiasm.

CHAPTER
SEVENTEEN

TUESDAY after work, Harden returned home to a lifeless house. His anticipatory smile after a long day faded. Loosening his tie, he called for Andy, the kids, and finally Kamila. No response. He peered at the backyard's swing set. Empty and still. Then he realized Andy's black van was missing from the driveway. They must have gone out, extending their fun from Monday.

He smelled cleaning solvent. Kamila probably had taken advantage of the empty house and spent a good part of the day scrubbing with Pine-Sol. He called for her again, certain she would not have tagged along with the others. He glanced out the window and noticed her car, too, was gone. In the kitchen, he found a note left on the counter. "I told Kamila she could go home since the kids begged me to take them to McDonald's for dinner. We'll bring you back something. Andy."

An old-fashioned, handwritten note. Text messages and voice mails took the spontaneity out of life for a crazy guy like Andrew, Harden supposed. Harden's smile returned.

The storm door slammed shut. He looked over his shoulder, expecting to see Andy and the kids.

"Kamila?" He gaped at her. "Andy wrote that you'd gone home."

"I run errands," she said, setting down her purse and a bag of groceries. "I do not accept his telling me to go home when things need doing. How do I trust? He messes around with the kids too much."

"What do you expect him to do while he's here?"

Kamila said nothing, and she moved to put away the groceries.

"Daddy!" The storm door slammed again, and Olivia fell into Harden's arms before he had a chance to counter Kamila's hostile silence.

"How's Daddy's sweet little girl?" He twirled Olivia and kissed her sun-warmed cheek.

"We went to McDonald's Playland."

"I read your nice note. Did you have fun?"

Olivia nodded, her ponytails bobbing up and down. "We played in the ballroom and Mason got lost under the balls."

"I hope you found him."

"Don't worry. He came back up."

"That's good."

Andy and Mason trailed behind Olivia. Mason looked ready for more action, but Andy's expression lacked the good nature of the kids. He set a greasy McDonald's bag on the table and asked Olivia and Mason to run upstairs to "wash off those yucky germs." Harden stood silent, questioning him with his eyes. Andy went straight to the counter where Kamila was putting away the groceries and intercepted her arm to prevent her from sliding a box of cereal into a cabinet. Rooted to the floor, Harden stared.

"Were you following me and the kids today?"

Kamila rotated her shoulder so that her arm freed itself from Andy's grip. She did not appear angry or insulted by Andy's inquisition. Her eyes drooped, and her mouth pulled into a subtle frown. She kept her back to him. Andy repeated himself and added, "You followed us to McDonald's, didn't you? And watched from your car through the window."

Still no answer. Harden stepped in. "Andy, what's going on?"

"I'm used to being trailed, Harden. But not by someone like her." He faced Kamila's back. "It's the truth, isn't it? It hasn't been my imagination. You've been following me and the kids around in your Toyota since I got here."

Kamila glanced at him, but her mouth remained closed, and she resumed putting away the groceries.

"Andy—"

"No, Harden. If I'm going to stay here longer, then we need to have this out." He edged closer to Kamila, on the brink of pinning her to the cabinet. "Why have you been spying on me and the kids? I want to hear you speak the truth."

Kamila snapped her head toward Andy. "I worry over them. We do not know you. Who are you? We still do not know. No one in town knows you."

"And I don't know who you are either," Andy said. "What does that have to do with anything? I haven't been following you around like an escaped mental patient."

"I am here with them." Kamila went back to the groceries but stopped before putting any more away. "You are stranger. What do you bring here?"

"I bring myself, which I think isn't such a bad contribution."

Kamila gazed out the window toward the driveway, her hand clutched on a can of peas. "I only worry for the children."

"And I worry for them too."

"Christ, Kamila, of course he does." Harden stepped in closer behind Andy. The kids rambled upstairs, out of earshot. "Why do you think he stood up to Randy Lederman? His instincts are to protect the kids too, as much as mine or yours. I must insist you stop this unwarranted behavior of yours."

Kamila remained quiet. Like a slow moving lazy Susan, she faced them. A semblance of a simper twitched her lips. "I am wrong. Forgive me. I go now." She set down the can and made to leave.

Harden reached to her but could not will himself to move his feet. "You don't have to leave, Kamila. I don't mean to come across as bossy. It's just that...."

"I go. Please, put groceries away."

She grabbed her purse and headed for the door. Protocol demanded Harden stop her, yet other emotions prevented him from calling or chasing after her. Kamila had worked like a loyal employee for him for almost a year, but Andy Wingal was family and had brought something special to their home.

Kamila's sudden departure left behind a shadow of silence. Harden finally budged to put away the remaining groceries. No words came to mind. Even if they had, Andy had stomped downstairs before he might have had the nerve to speak them.

Harden finished storing the groceries and resisted going downstairs to Andy. He waited the fifteen minutes he knew it would take Kamila to arrive home before telephoning her. After speaking with her for a few minutes, he hung up and reluctantly warmed the Big Mac and fries Andy had brought him. Andy returned upstairs in the middle of his eating. A light chuckle fluttered from between his tight lips.

"Sorry about the dramatics," he said.

Harden swallowed a bite. "Don't worry about it. I've already spoken with Kamila on the phone. She's fine with everything and apologized again for following you like she did. She's going to take tomorrow off but will be back on Thursday. She's promised to stop following you."

Fortunately, Mason and Olivia remained oblivious to the minor family fracture. They were watching television. Light canned laughter from a sitcom drifted in from the living room.

"Lately I've been testy about people judging me," Andy said. "I had no right to yell at her."

"She had no business doing what she did."

Andy apologized again and went to see Mason and Olivia. Harden finished his meal and tossed the wrappers. Upstairs, he changed into a nice pair of cargo shorts and a T-shirt and headed back down to watch television alongside Andy and the kids.

Once the sun settled beyond the cornfield and the blue glow from the television covered the living room, he ordered the kids to bed. He and Andy tucked them in, and afterward they sat on the porch swing, swaying so subtly that Harden hadn't noticed they were moving until Andy stopped it with his foot. He stood with his hands thrust inside his shorts pockets and walked to the railing, where he gazed over the cornfield blanketed by a cobalt sky.

Harden studied him from behind. His glassy-smooth calves revealed the beginnings of a tan. He noted his plaid shorts draped his physique in a fashion he wished his own might. *You're a frumpy dad racing toward middle age, and that's all, Harden Krane.*

He hoped a sip of beer might cool his heating cheeks. He settled the can between his legs and turned his gaze alongside Andy's. Indeed, the cornfield resembled something magical during dusk. Often he would stand on the porch and watch the sky change from pink to purple and ultimately to black. Alone, with the children asleep, he'd admire the stars as they freckled the sky and stare at the moon, fascinated by the dancing shadows among the cornstalks. During those quiet moments, he'd dream of bygone days, when life harbored an innocent expectation that made day to day living more tolerable.

Andy turned to Harden with a toothy grin and leaned against the railing with his hands behind his back. "Have to admit," he said, "it's really amazing. Almost nicer with the evening sky. The corn looks lavender."

"Not as exciting as a night in Chicago, huh?"

"Right at this moment, I can't think of anywhere else I'd like to be, believe it or not."

"Even with all that lost income?"

A blush darkened Andy's already reddened cheeks. He gazed at his sneakers while bugs snapped against the porch lamps. "If I don't think about that, I'm cool."

Harden judged from the glint in Andy's irises that he spoke the truth. He never knew Andy to bend to spurious words or deeds. One of his better traits. "And Kamila?" he dared to ask. "She hasn't forced you to change your mind about staying longer, has she?"

Andy shook his head. "I just feel bad about confronting her like I did."

"I told you not to worry. You had a right." Harden shifted his gaze to the nighttime sky, where a black crow flew noiselessly against the purple spread above the pink corn. Crickets chirping fluctuated with the warm breeze and more lightning bugs dotted the night. "I can't get over her following you around like she did. I guess I should be grateful for her dedication to the kids, but there's really no excuse for that kind of behavior."

"I was really steamed when I realized it was her," Andy said, smiling again. "I probably should've counted to ten and taken a deep breath, same with before I mouthed off to that Randy what's his name. I find more trouble that way."

"It's all good. Don't worry. I sense a calm coming over the horizon." And though his last words had flowed from his wetted lips barely audible, lighter than the breeze tickling the corn silk, Harden had uttered a truth.

Something of a truce had been reached between Andy Wingal and Kamila Becic. Earlier, when he'd spoken with Kamila, her voice had suggested a yielding to Andy's presence. Perhaps she'd learned to realize that his standing up to her also meant he possessed the same fortitude to face others on behalf of the kids, the way he had proved with the bully, Randy Lederman.

Mild cohesion had somehow formed. The family ventured toward the realm of honesty and openness, what any social unit required for survival. Harden sighed with relief, picturing a more peaceful household. He chuckled.

"What's so funny?" Andy said, gazing at Harden. His fresh haircut accentuated the strong shape to his oval face and his wild dimpled chin.

"You should've seen the kids Sunday when I told them you were prolonging your stay. They even hugged each other."

Andy sat back next to Harden. Harden caught himself flinching but willed himself to relax. He sipped his beer, licked his lips.

"They're the greatest kids in the world," Andy said, his stare fixed over the top of the porch railing. "You should commend yourself for holding things together as well as you have."

Uncomfortable with compliments, Harden gripped his beer tighter and nodded. "You wear them out for me. I'm used to them attacking me when I get home. It's wonderful having you around."

"I'm glad I can help. I should have contributed more a long time ago."

"Stop apologizing, will you."

Andy snickered. "Okay, I promise. No more regrets."

Together they sat, staring at the indigo cornfield.

Gentler than the sweet breeze, the swing began to move back and forth again, keeping in rhythm with the bowing corn and Harden's curiously whimsical thoughts.

CHAPTER
EIGHTEEN

Uncle Andy: Hello. I am here.

Daddy: We are glad you are here.

Olivia: It is fun you are here.

Mason: It is good.

Uncle Andy: We go outside and play now.

Olivia: OK.

Daddy: OK.

Kamila: I will stay and cook in the kitchen.

Daddy: OK.

Uncle Andy: OK.

Olivia: OK.

Mason: OK. Let's go now. I want to go outside and play with Uncle Andy.

Olivia: I want that too. We better go now.

Daddy: Come follow Uncle Andy and me outside so that we can play together.

Olivia: I like that.

Mason: I like that too.

Olivia: We are playing on the swings now.

Uncle Andy: It is fun.

Daddy: Be careful you do not swing too high, Daddy's sweet little girl.

Olivia: I will be careful, Daddy.

Mason: I can swing higher.

Daddy: Uncle Andy and I will watch you together.

Uncle Andy: We are watching you together.
Olivia: Watch us!
Uncle Andy: You are swinging nicely.
Daddy: Yes, you are swinging better than anyone in the world.
Olivia: Thank you Daddy and Uncle Andy.

"She's captured your personality to a tee," Andy said with a sarcastic lilt, while he read over Harden's shoulder. "I like the way she highlighted the dynamic of her and Mason's relationship too. And her Kamila couldn't have been more spot on."

"It's the cutest thing I've ever read," Harden uttered.

Andy swallowed a chuckle. "She's another Hellman in the making. I helped her with the grammar. She insisted on giving me a part."

"You should be flattered."

Andy allowed Harden to finish reading Olivia's play. For another five pages, her characters bantered back and forth on the swing set, at the dinner table, during a game of Pictionary, and ending with:

Daddy: It is time for bed.
Mason: I hate to go to bed, but I will go.
Olivia: We are in bed now. Good night, Daddy. Good night, Uncle Andy. Sleep tight and don't have any bad dreams.
Uncle Andy: Good night. We are going to bed now.
Daddy: We are in bed now.
Uncle Andy: Yes, we are in bed.
Olivia: That is good. Good night.

Harden laughed and laid the play on the computer console. "It's funny the way she made us out at the end, like we're sharing a bedroom. I think she forgot you sleep downstairs."

Andy had failed to notice Olivia's ambiguous ending until that moment. His face heating, he said, "Kids can be silly, I guess."

"She certainly enjoys writing," Harden said. "I like to encourage her."

"Maybe, once she learns stage directions, she'll grow up and become rich and famous."

Harden made a strange grunt from deep inside his throat. "I can't picture Olivia and Mason grown up." His attention remained fixed on Olivia's play, as if he'd entered his young daughter's innocent, two-dimensional world and, like Andy trapped in the corn maze, found himself unable to escape. Or perhaps he didn't wish to. "I suffer the guilt of wanting them to grow up and get out of the house so I no longer have to worry over them, and wanting to hold back time and keep them children forever. It's so confusing."

Andy failed to fully comprehend Harden's angst, but he sensed Harden was seeking consolation. "I'm sure other parents feel the same," he said.

"Moments like this I cherish, though."

Andy felt a hand press on his shoulder. He looked into Harden's blue irises and turned away before Harden might catch the flush that burned his neck and threatened to travel to his cheeks. "Why's that?" he asked, stifling a shudder.

"It's nice to have another adult to share sweet times," Harden said matter-of-factly. "So often, I just compliment the kids on something they've done and that's that. I feel so empty afterward, like I'm some sort of horrible hypocrite."

"You're anything but that, Harden," Andy said toward the desk, where his fingertips stroked Olivia's play. He caught himself fidgeting and brought his hand to his side. "What about Kamila? Doesn't she help out enough?"

"It's different with her," Harden replied. "We're not quite... equals. We come from different worlds."

"Don't you and I? I'm from Chicago and you're from Iowa farm country."

Harden moved to the sofa. A cold, empty sensation remained where his hand had rested against Andy's shoulder.

"I meant she and I don't relate to each other," Harden said, sitting and cupping his hands over his knees. "It's hard to explain. Maybe it's just her personality, or maybe it's mine."

Andy followed Harden to the sofa and mirrored his posture. They sat together like any couple might after a long day, discussing the children, the future. Knee to knee, knuckles mere inches from each other's. But Andy realized that Kamila and he—childless, far from home, strangers in Iowa—shared more in common than he and Harden. The notion made him wish his life had fallen onto a different path.

Upstairs, Mason and Olivia trampled about, cleaning their rooms before dinner like Andy had asked. Harden sighed and said with a tremulous shake of his head, "I realize it's tough for the kids to be out here, so far from their friends and relatives. But I just can't bring myself to dump this place, not yet."

Andy stepped up to the challenge. "It would be different if you had another person… someone in place of Lilly?"

"Of course."

Olivia, dressed in her pajamas, ambled downstairs and fell onto the sofa on top of them. "I want to watch TV."

Harden stroked her hair, long and flowing freely from the typical ponytails. "Did you clean your room like Uncle Andy asked?" She nodded, and Harden said, "Why don't you watch *Thumb and Thumbelina* on your laptop and let me and your uncle have some quiet time before dinner?"

Olivia placed her tiny index finger to her plump pink lips and gazed upward, as if musing over her father's suggestion. Finally, she sat erect. "Okay." She jumped from the sofa and sprawled prostrate on the floor before her laptop, the soles of her stocking feet parallel with the ceiling.

"She's adorable," Andy muttered.

"If she wasn't, I doubt she'd survive."

"I'm getting passionate about them both. I'm starting to understand Kamila's motives for following us."

"They're kind of like a basketful of puppies," Harden said, gazing at his daughter with wistful eyes. "A burden, but too cute to get rid of."

Andy chuckled at Harden's humor. "She helped me make the french fries for dinner to go with our hamburgers," he said. "You'd be happy to know she only dropped about three or four of the potatoes."

"How many fingers does she have left?" Harden said with a snort.

"Don't worry about that. I did the chopping. She rolled the wedges in salt and garlic powder. Mason made the patties. He put special spices in them. Wouldn't let me know what."

"The kids are full of surprises."

"You're talking about us," Olivia said, using her maternal voice. She kept her eyes on her video cartoon. "You're being supercilious."

Andy blew out a chortle. "She's right, you know."

"Kids are right about everything," Harden said.

And that night, Andy dozed, thinking of Olivia and Mason. In his dreams, he chased after them in a cornfield brimming with purple stalks, while they laughed and squinted from the white sun bursting through a burnt orange sky. Andy's job was to steer the children away from the broad fissures in the earth. But all at once, he was driving them in his glossy black van through a dirty, seamy street. Bright streetlamps pelting the windows and gunshots blasting against the van's sides replaced the sunshine and chatter of birds. Ken Millpairs appeared before the windshield, Glock raised at shoulder level. Andy slammed on the brakes, and he awoke panting and confused.

Slashes of sunlight cut across the bed. He sat up against the headboard and steadied his breathing. His cell phone read close to seven thirty. But he did not emerge from the basement until quarter past nine, when he knew Harden had gone to work.

Detached and frustrated, he climbed the stairs. The murmuring of unfamiliar adult male voices commingled with Kamila's forced him to pause before opening the door. He waited a good minute, then, inhaling, found Dick Carelli seated at the kitchen table alongside another man, sipping coffee. Kamila, without acknowledging Andy, carried a steaming mug and sat across from them.

He was unsure what to say to her after their altercation from Tuesday. He expected her to initiate the first sign of an armistice. Yet she remained fixed, her eyes far away like the times before, unwilling to express the most basic salutation or even bother to introduce the men to him.

"Good morning," Andy said in his over-the-top singsong voice, knowing he might irk them.

Too tired and still reeling from his dream to care about any of their mumbled responses, Andy poured himself coffee and headed for the front porch, void of any further words. What difference did civility make in an uncivil world?

Andy leaned against the porch railing and watched the corn. Little else to do. The landscape offered limited visuals: cornfields or sky, or the barn and silo if he turned his head sharply to the right. He visualized Lilly standing on the front porch, coffee in hand, like he was now, dulled by the same scene day after day after day.

When his coffee went lukewarm, he tramped back inside, set down his mug with a thud, and marched to his basement bedroom. With the taste of toothpaste fresh in his mouth, he lay in bed and listened to the murmurings of Kamila and the two men flow through the ceiling.

"I best get home," Dick Carelli said. "The wife will be wondering what happened to me. I been working too many nights." A chair skidded. "Thanks for the breakfast, Kamila."

"Thanks, Kamila" came the other man's voice, followed by two more chairs pushed out from the table.

Three sets of feet slapped the floor above and faded toward the front door. Next, the door slammed shut and a single set of steps grew louder. He jumped from bed and beelined up the stairs. Kamila sat firm at the kitchen table with her coffee. This time, he was less suave. "Where're the kids?"

"Upstairs to play."

He sensed her cold brown European eyes burning holes into his back as he went to the bottom of the steps and shouted for Mason and Olivia. He cared little for her disapproval, but he needed to get away from the farm, from Kamila.

"What is it, Uncle Andy?" Olivia said.

"We're taking a day trip."

Olivia's blue eyes shone. "Where to?"

"Get your brother and let's go."

"You take the kids?" Kamila said from the kitchen.

"Nothing to concern yourself over." He wanted to face her again and say, "You plan on following us?" but rather than unleash his anger in the manner he wanted, he checked his tongue. In a way, his taking the kids on a joyride was more to test Kamila than to get out of the stuffy house.

He waited, noting Kamila's unchanged stony countenance. The kids trampled downstairs, dressed and ready. For a good three hours, Andy chauffeured them around northeastern Iowa. His Magellan piloted the way past Holbert Park, where the kids had said they sledded in winter if they could find rides, next through a small Amish settlement, and to a Trappist monastery southwest of Dubuque, where a lone monk dressed in a black-and-white tunic came out to provide them a quick tour of the lush grounds. Andy balked from allowing him to show them inside.

Much like his life back in Chicago, Andy played the tour guide. The kids seemed to enjoy themselves, but he turned for home after Olivia and Mason stretched and yawned. To his odd sense of disappointment, there was no sign of Kamila tailing them that day. She was still silently stewing when they returned home.

The remainder of the week passed much the same. Andy threw himself into domestic life, doing his best to avoid Kamila. Harden went to work each morning, and Andy stayed behind to entertain the kids, and they him. Wednesday, they rode their bikes through the Iowa countryside, and the kids took a turn at playing tour guide. He and Harden were the same size, and Harden's three-speed needed minimal adjustments. Pungent odors of sticky sweet earth and livestock followed them along the rolling farmland.

He and Kamila continued their silent face-off. Her presence bothered him less and less. She had become like one of the bruises from his beating. A dull ache, fading to a barely noticeable tawny color.

Ken had no additional news from Chicago. Andy suspected whoever had clobbered him would evade justice. Without informing Ken, he'd concluded he'd return to Chicago by next Wednesday. That would give him a solid two weeks visiting the Kranes, in compliance with Ken's original command.

On Friday, he drove Mason to his first baseball practice since his suspension and encouraged him to avoid any altercations with the nasty boys who teased him. "This time, let them throw the first punch," he said before the game. Luckily, no one did. Before reaching home, they stopped at the grocery store. They returned home with three bulging plastic bags, and Andy insisted Kamila again leave early. With the housekeeper out of the way, he took over the kitchen. Olivia and Mason assisted.

"What are you making?" Harden, bordered by the kitchen's doorway, said a few hours later when he returned home from work. He looked handsome in his usual dress-down Friday attire.

"Mexican vegetarian fare," Andy said. "Soup's on the stove and bean burritos are baking in the oven."

"Nice to have something other than Balkan food," Harden said. "Kamila makes so many meals with beef I worry I might turn into a sausage link. I take it you sent her home early again? Wish she would lighten up."

"We get along okay."

"How was Mason's scrimmage? Any trouble?"

"As smooth as asphalt. His side lost, though. How was your day?"

Harden stepped to the stove and inhaled the steam rising from the pot of pumpkin soup. "One of these days, buddy, I'm going to quit," he said, sitting at the kitchen table with a sigh. He stretched out his legs and rested his left arm over the top. "I finally had that teleconference with the big ethanol buyer from California. I felt like I was selling him snake oil."

"You gotta do what you gotta do," Andy said into the pot, which smelled of cinnamon and cumin. "Think of Mason and Olivia."

"Sure, sure. They're the only things I do think about. You plan on sticking around past next week?"

Andy faced him. "You kidding? I've been here too long already. I got my business back in Chicago waiting for me."

"That's some life you got."

Andy returned to stirring the pot without responding. Behind him, Harden sighed and said with a patronizing tone, "They say there's more money in nation destroying than nation building."

Andy's cell phone *ding dinged* just in time. Despite the determination to hang onto his career, his face flushed when he dug deep inside his cargo pocket to see who was calling. He deduced who it might be even before seeing the unrecognizable number: a caller for his tour business. He clicked "refuse call" (what difference did it make while in Iowa?) and went back to stirring the soup.

"You know what I've discovered?" he said, steam tickling his nose. "What success requires is a certain lack of emotion. A detachment in what you do."

"You're probably right, buddy. You're probably right."

Mason raced inside, carrying with him the smells of body heat and the outdoors. "Is dinner ready? I'm starving?"

"Almost, Mason."

He turned to his dad. "I helped make it."

"Go wash up," Harden said. "You smell."

Olivia entered, dirtier than her brother. Harden insisted she wash up for dinner too, and he scooted her upstairs. By the time Andy plated the vegetarian meal, the awkwardness brought up by Harden's disapproval for Andy's career had left. Everyone gathered around the kitchen table, their hands scrubbed and shiny—and the front of Olivia's blouse soaked— eager to eat. Harden asked Mason to lead the prayer. Like the other times, Andy respected their beliefs and bowed his head, although he refused to fold his hands or close his eyes.

Halfway through the meal, Mason said, "You should move in with us, Uncle Andy. You can make yummy dinners like this all the time. It's better than Kamila's."

Andy required extra effort to swallow a bite of his bean burrito. "I'm glad you like my cooking, Mason, and I appreciate your offer, but I don't think so."

"Do we bother you?" Olivia said. "We're not being too supercilious, are we?"

Andy chuckled. "No, you're not. But I worry I might be."

"It's fun with you here," Olivia said. "I like playing Pictionary."

"I do too."

"Keep quiet, dumbhead," Mason barked. "Every time you open your mouth you spit food at me."

"Knock it off, you two," Harden said. "Olivia, you're dripping soup down your chin."

Andy was about to bring humor back to the table with a riddle when the sound of crunching gravel forced him to look out of the window. A compact hatchback hobbled to a stop in the driveway. Harden mirrored his gaze.

"Who's that?"

"Beats me," Andy said. "Looks like someone in a beat-up car. It's got Michigan tags. Maybe they're lost, like that time Mom and I drove through Burt Anders's cornfield."

Andy tipped his head for a better look, but he could hardly distinguish anyone sitting inside through the smudgy windshield. Difficult to tell if the car was beige or coated in dirt. Not until Olivia pushed out her chair—upsetting her plum juice in the process—and ran shouting for the front porch, did Andy realize who had come calling.

"Mommy! Mommy! Mommy's home! It's Mommy!"

CHAPTER
NINETEEN

ANDY sat, unable to move from the kitchen table while Olivia's blood-red plum juice trickled onto the linoleum floor beside him. Through the kitchen window, he watched his sister, Lillian, stumble from the car and squat to scoop Olivia into her arms. A court order mandated that she keep away from the children without Harden's consent. He was certain Harden had not given it. He would have told Andy if he had. And Harden's subsequent actions confirmed he wanted Lillian nowhere near Burr Oak Farm.

Harden leaped from his chair and made a mad dash after Olivia. Andy followed. He peered through the screen on the storm door that still vibrated from Harden having swung it open. Harden tripped on his feet to reach Olivia, his arms stretched before him, like a man under a spell. His ashen face twisted in pain and agony that caused Andy to step backward, bumping Mason, who'd edged beside him, trembling.

Pure desperation exuded from Harden's eyes. He fumbled for Olivia, trying to tear her from her mother as if his arms were made of wet noodles. "You're not supposed to be here, Lillian. Lillian, put her down."

"I want Mommy!" Olivia clung to Lillian with one arm and pushed Harden back with the other.

"Hello, my little darling." Lillian lifted Olivia toward the blue sky and swung her around, ignoring Harden's pleading and nearly falling over.

Even from the door, Andy noticed Lilly's inebriation. She struggled to keep her eyes open, and one of those odd half-wit grins contorted her unrecognizable face, which had aged beyond her thirty-nine years. Though dressed in clean, stylish blue jeans and a beige camisole, Lillian's clothes hung off her underweight frame and creased with her movements. Her teeth had been narrow and jagged when he'd last seen her three years ago. She must have had them capped since. Now they gleamed perfectly white and absurd, mocked by the sunlight.

Premature age lines still cut into her pink, narrow face, and gaunt cheeks revealed the bones underneath. Haphazardly applied makeup failed to cover the blemishes along her jawline, which had taken a sharp masculine contortion. Her hair remained the typical platinum from the last time he'd seen her. Ken had once told him that female crystal methamphetamine users often resorted to prostitution to support their habits, and they bleached their hair platinum to stand out.

"Put her down, Lillian." Resignation scorched Harden's whimpering voice. "We've been over this. You're not allowed to come here. Put her down. Put her down, Lillian."

In his attempts to lift his daughter from Lillian's tightening arms, Harden vacillated between clawing for Olivia and throwing his head into his hands. From his vantage point, Andy noted Harden's delirium. He was clearly weakened from the anguish of his ex-wife's imposition. He was like a man sleepwalking.

"Put her down, Lillian. Put her down. Christ, look what you're doing. You're doing it to them all over again, Lilly. Put her down. Please, stop this. Stop this before you cause them more harm. Please stop, Lilly."

Blood pounded in Andy's ears. His feet remained stationary, as if fierce claws held him fixed to the floor. For the first time, he wished for Kamila's presence. Her iciness alone might push Lillian back into her derelict car, where a shabby-looking man sat reading a magazine behind the steering wheel, disinterested in the family drama taking place beyond the smudgy windows.

"She's my baby girl," Lillian muttered, acknowledging Harden for the first time. "Let me kiss her. Let me kiss my baby."

"Mommy, come inside. Come inside."

"Mommy can't come inside," Harden said, his voice faltering. "You know she can't. Mommy can't come inside."

"I want Mommy."

"Let me hold my baby," Lillian squealed.

"You can't, Lilly. You know you can't." He pried loose Olivia's grip and pushed her sideways, but she ran back for her mother's arms. Harden's expression demonstrated a desperation Andy had never witnessed before, not even among the urban youth in Chicago's South Side. Stricken with disbelief and helplessness, Andy watched, unable to move a muscle.

Mason nudged Andy out of the way and ran outside. He stopped on the stoop, began sniveling, and rushed across the driveway. "Mom! Mom!"

With his arms spread-eagle, Harden attempted to block his son from reaching his mother. But with the nimbleness of a cat, Mason dodged Harden's grasps and collapsed into Lillian's wobbly arms.

"Mason, my love. Hug and kiss your mother."

The three of them coalesced into a singular embrace. Harden circled them, like a policeman trying to break up a brawl. Joyful and horrified sobbing poured into Andy's ears.

Harden dislodged Mason from the group and dragged him kicking and squealing up the porch and into the house. Andy tried to restrain him with a light clamp on his shoulders, but he jerked free and ran back outside, straight into Lillian's arms. Again, Harden extricated him and forced him to the porch. But Mason slapped at his father's arms and rushed to his mother's side. Andy willed his feet to move, and he marched straight to Lillian.

Affecting nonchalance, he grinned, wanting her to think he was happy to see his big sister after three years, which on some level he was. Immediately, he winced from the unidentified stench he recalled from the last time he'd seen her that she tried to mask with Magnetism.

"Lilly, how have you been?" He patted her shoulder and, in doing so, tried to grab Olivia from her tight grip and pass her over to Harden, whose flimsy arms still came at them with intermittent lunges. "Don't you recognize me, Lilly? It's Andy."

She stopped struggling and looked into Andy's face. Her smile disappeared, and a shadow of a frown emerged. "Andrew?"

"Yes, it's me." His smile muscles convulsed. "It's your baby brother."

Her tiny specks for pupils met Andy's frozen gaze. She shook her head, as if trying to identify him. Andy forced a firmer smile.

"Let's go for a stroll around the farm, Lilly," he said in a light voice. "I haven't seen you in so long. Leave the kids behind and come with me." Andy tried to pull her hand, but she shook loose and clung fiercely to Olivia.

"You're trying to take my children from me." Her voice came at him, strained and cavernous. "Stay away. Stay away."

Harden stomped his foot, looked to the blue sky. "Christ, Lilly, look what you're doing to the kids. You're doing it all over again. Why, Lilly? Why?" Helpless in his pleas, he slumped onto the bottom step and concealed his face with his hands. His shoulders shook. He lifted his tear moistened red face and hollered, "Lilly, Lilly, you're destroying everything."

Andy pushed in closer to wedge apart Lillian and the kids. "You're in no condition to see the kids, Lillian," he said with defiance now. "Come with me, and you can see them another time. Don't you want to spend time with me, your baby brother?"

He wrenched Olivia from Lilly's arms and threw his own around her. Why had she allowed herself to become a wasted person? Andy at his worst could never have stooped to such a low-down level, especially if it meant risking losing his own flesh and blood. Where was his Lilly?

Lillian pushed Andy off her. He stumbled backward and fell on his butt to the gravel. Olivia jumped back into her mother's arms. The children hugged her tighter, clinging to her shoulders and legs.

Harden leaped to his feet and, with newfound conviction, swatted Lilly's hands from Mason and Olivia. "Leave them alone, Lilly. Leave them alone. I'm telling you. Listen to me, now. Leave them be."

Silent tears fell hot down Andy's cheeks. Even the green, lofty cornstalks seemed to shake with mushrooming dread. Lillian tripped and began to weep. All of them were in tears, but each for different reasons. Torn between saving Harden and wanting to see more of his sister, Andy chose to defend Harden, the man whom he trusted at that moment more than anyone on earth.

He stood, brushed himself clean, and forced his way inside the circle of mother and children. The kids kicked and screamed, ear-shattering screeches that sent the crows cawing from the cornfield.

Harden pushed Lillian toward the hatchback. "Get out of here, Lillian," he cried. "Get in your car and leave us. Get out of here. Don't come back unless I say."

Off balance, Lillian tumbled backward. She flashed Harden the finger. "Fuck you, Harden Krane. Mr. Perfect. Mr. Man Who Knows Everything. You're a perfect asshole, that's what you are, you fucking bastard."

Lillian charged him with her head down. Harden dodged her sloppy attack and, catching her around the waist, again pinned her against the car.

"Leave Mommy alone! Leave her alone!"

Olivia kicked at her father's shins. Harden swept away her fury and continued to subdue Lilly. Mason rushed in and jumped on his father's back.

Immobilized against the car, Lillian turned her rage to Andy.

"You faggot," she said, slurring her words. "You... you faggot! You're nothing but a faggot."

Harden ordered the kids to cover their ears and hide inside the house. They defied him. Olivia bit his arm, causing him to recoil. Mason began to kick his legs and elbow him.

"Leave here, Lillian," Harden said, disregarding his children's assault. "Leave us in peace. I'm going to call the police if your latest boyfriend doesn't drive you out of here now."

Harden pulled his cell phone from his pocket. Mason swatted it from his hand. Teary eyed, Harden crawled on all fours over the gravel after it. Mason jumped on his back, trying to stop him. Andy recalled the kids climbing on Harden's back while they'd jumped through the sprinkler and later when they'd played at the swimming pool. Fresh tears rolled down Andy's face seeing how they attacked him now.

Andy could bear witness no further. He pulled Mason from Harden's back, setting him on his feet and demanding he stay put, and dragged Lillian to the car. He looked to the man seated behind the steering wheel. "Get her out of here, will you!"

Only then did the driver bother to notice the commotion. "Hey, all cool here? What's up?"

"Get her in your car and leave now before the cops show up. And don't bring her back. Go back where you came from!"

Lillian's voice, raspy and deep from years of smoking drugs and the throat infections that resulted, bit at the driveway dust agitated by everyone's flailing arms and legs. "You bastard. You can't stop me from seeing my children… my children. You… you can't stop me. You fucking bastard."

Her companion succeeded in planting her in the passenger seat. Olivia ran for her. Andy held her back, clutching her arm to the point he could feel the blood pulse through her veins. From an open window, Lilly continued to curse and rave at Harden and Andy.

"You faggots. You can't take my kids. I'll come back for them. I'll come back."

She appeared ready to pass out once the man backed up and drove down the driveway. Exhaust and dust from the Toyota's wake seemed to mute the crying and commotion. They stood unable to move, speechless. Sporadic sobs choked Olivia.

Suddenly, "I hate you, Daddy. I hate you!" Olivia sprinted inside with a harsh slap of the storm door. Mason ran after her, followed by another strident slamming.

Harden, still on his knees, curled into a ball and wept. Andy, almost afraid to approach him, stood stiff. Finally, the breeze seemed to push him closer, and he dropped to his haunches beside Harden and placed a hand on his quivering back.

"It's okay, Harden. It's going to be okay."

"Why did she have to come back?" Harden said to the ground. "Christ. Everything was going okay for once. Why did she have to come back, right when things start to go good?"

"It's okay, Harden. It'll be okay."

CHAPTER
TWENTY

MASON and Olivia remained sealed behind their bedroom doors. They ignored Harden's knocking until he insisted they answer. Curt, murmured responses indicated they continued to breathe. Harden allowed them to sulk without finishing their dinners.

Downstairs, Andy lowered himself to his knees and wiped the spilt plum juice from the linoleum. He figured bleach would take out the stubborn stain. He walked for the laundry room past Harden, who was rinsing the dishes and stacking them in the dishwasher. He seemed shaken beyond anything Andy had ever seen of him—seen of anyone. A man marred from old battle scars that had emerged to assail him again.

They remained detached and quiet throughout the evening. Any words Andy longed to express wedged somewhere between his mind and throat. What might he say? Harden's flimsy attempts to smile and act as if nothing had happened exacerbated Andy's torment. Shadows replaced the setting sunlight that had filtered through the windowpanes and fixed the furnishings into rock hard uncertainty.

Over and over, Andy rehashed in his mind the ugly scene that had played out on the driveway. Harden's fighting Lillian to keep her from the kids had both shocked and excited him. But he could not speak his thoughts. The silence stood impenetrable, like a steel wall. With the swish of shuffling feet and the occasional opening and closing of the refrigerator,

Andy also feigned he'd witnessed nothing more than a movie. A terrible and ghastly tragedy.

By nine, Harden, weakened and battered, pulled himself upstairs by the railing and uttered a pathetic, "Good night, Andy." Andy remained downstairs alone, sitting at the cold and austere kitchen table, sipping beer without tasting it.

As a brother, Andy had experienced the disappointment and sadness of losing a sister. But Lillian's drug addiction had ripped the soul from her children and ex-husband. Her sickness weighed on Harden more than any of them, for no more reason than he was cognizant of its awfulness and had stood helpless against it. He had resided cheek to cheek with the demons.

The last time Harden and Lillian had visited Streamwood, four years ago, Andy had realized something was wrong. Unable to hold a person's stare, Lillian had seemed agitated, distracted. She had lost discernible weight and looked wild-eyed, and had smoked her mentholated Virginia Slims to excess. The children seemed to sidetrack her more than concern her. At that time, he'd chosen to reject the warning signs.

Harden had telephoned Andy a year later and confessed he too had understood the symptoms but refused acting. He'd gone to work each day while Lillian had gotten high in her "happy place" in the barn loft. She'd begun an open-door policy with paying tricks she'd met on the Internet (some traveling from as far as southern Minnesota), often while the children were at home. That's when Harden had butted heads with reality and intervened.

Neither Harden nor Andy had been successful in convincing her. She'd refused treatment and had run away. Two weeks later, she'd turned up in Streamwood, disheveled and pitiable. Mom had called Andy, fresh back from Iowa, and had begged for his aid. Before he'd arrived, Lillian had fled again. Today had been the first time he'd seen her since.

Andy had checked off Lillian from his list of reliable people years ago, realizing that she had gone from his life and might never return. He'd relegated her tragedy as a dusty artifact from the past and had wiped his hands clean from it, relieved, almost, that she'd vanished. After all, he had his own melodrama to perform.

Now she hovered in his life anew. An unrecognizable apparition of her former self.

Andy figured the kids hadn't understood Lillian's outbursts. Her harsh words must have buzzed over their heads. Or perhaps they had heard her rantings often at the height of her drug abuse and paid them scant attention. Or they had wanted to see her so badly she could have pointed guns to their temples and they'd still have clung to her, demanding she remain at their sides.

With a sigh, Andy finished his beer, tossed the empty can into the trash, and slumped into the basement. That night, he relished the cool and vacuous darkness that enveloped him. He turned off his cell phone, uninterested in returning the calls for his tour business or reading Ken's inane text messages that had "dinged" throughout the evening, ricocheting through the silence. Dreams came in sharp whispers, like ghosts seeking reparations for former harm.

The next morning, the children scuffled downstairs an hour later than normal, after Andy had shaved and showered and helped Harden prepare breakfast. Harden had refrained from calling for them. Olivia ate her cold cereal so slowly that she made hardly a mess. She refused the toasted waffles and sausage Harden placed before her. Mason kept his eyes on his toast and orange juice, never looking up long enough to notice that Harden and Andy had begun to clear the table. Afterward, Olivia and Mason wandered into the backyard and sat on the swing set, which had become their refuge. They barely moved on the swings. From the back window, Andy noticed they spoke little to each other, even while alone.

He was glad for Saturday so he would not have to face the kids' present funk alone with Kamila. Despite Harden's condition, Andy was relieved to have him around to shoulder the burden of the anguish that masqueraded as a family. Harden was still in a somnambulistic state. Eyes vacant, mouth tense, save for an occasional synthetic smile to appease Andy. He went about caring for the children, working at the family computer, stacking the dishwasher, as if set on automatic.

He assumed nonchalance. Yet Harden looked as casual as a man who just had his ears cut off. Andy supposed the best support would come in the form of silent understanding. He refreshed his coffee, washed a load of clothes, scrubbed again the annoying plum juice stain from the kitchen floor that refused to completely come out, and provided Harden the space he seemed to crave while he moped about the house.

As the morning sloughed ahead, the kids remained outside on the swing with their feet barely moving off the ground. When that bored them, they wandered to the creek. Mason had once told Andy he liked to take off his shoes and socks and kick the water to spur the spotted fish to bite and tickle his toes. Andy imagined he hadn't done that that morning. Later, they returned upstairs and stewed behind their bedroom doors. Harden's lighthearted attempts to engage them failed miserably.

Finally, after preparing a lunch the children had declined, Harden sat at the kitchen table alongside Andy and inhaled. "I talked to my brother," he said, staring at the cheese and bologna sandwiches untouched on plates. "He and Holly are going to keep the kids tonight and take them to church in the morning. It'll be good for them to get off the farm. I should have sent them to summer camp. They'd be there now, and Lilly would have missed them, and she would never have given them false hope."

"That's a good idea they get away a while," Andy said, matching Harden's soft and reserved tone. "For you too. I'm guessing you told Lance the details?"

Early afternoon sun oozing through the windows eked sweat from Harden's troubled brow. He mopped his forehead with a napkin and let his hand drop with a thud onto the table. "He knows. Lance understands. It's like this each time she's come back."

"How often has that been?"

"Twice before, same scenario. The last time was last year, just before Christmas."

Harden stood and walked out of the room. Andy stared after him and knew it was best to leave him alone. Perhaps, in his desperation, Harden searched for a miraculous remedy that might ease his pain.

Andy hoped relief might rise above the horizon close to four o'clock, when Mason turned to him before hopping into Lance's Ford Escape and spoke without needing prompting for the first time since Lillian's unplanned visit. "At Uncle Lance's house, the pigeons singing under the roof and the traffic on Main Street makes me feel good," he said apathetically. "I don't really know why, just does."

In the children's absence, the tension lessened, but the quiet remained. When Harden's mother telephoned, he stood talking into the landline like a scarecrow. He barely spoke, although he held the receiver to his impassive face and fiddled with the cord a good fifteen minutes. "No, don't come over.... I'm okay.... I'm sure.... Maybe, Mom.... All right.... Talk to you later."

At five o'clock, Andy grabbed his wallet and van keys. "I'm going to do some food shopping," he said to Harden, who brooded at the computer console with a televised baseball game playing in the background that Andy was certain Harden paid little attention to. "Anything you need?"

Harden raised his head to look at Andy, and his eyes, vacant and sad, tried to sparkle with gratitude. "There's the beginning of a list on the fridge. I'll give you some money."

"Don't bother. I'll be back shortly."

Andy relished the reprieve away from the Krane house. Under the supermarket's bright fluorescent lights, his mind cleared from the gloom. The multicolored towers of foodstuffs, the hum of humanity charging with purpose and life, provided him the resolve to end the death knell darkening Burr Oak Farm. He spent extra money on specialty foods (filet mignon, local-grown asparagus, russet potatoes the size of fists), along with taper candles and two bottles of cabernet from a local vineyard.

Back at the farm, he went about preparing the special meal for Harden. The working oven filled the kitchen with the warmth of labor and decisiveness. Harden shuffled in from the living room, his gray sweatpants stretched in the knees and seat. "What are you cooking?" he asked, his voice grainy and low.

Andy kept his pitch upbeat. "I'm making us dinner."

Harden edged closer to the stove. A shadow of a smile lifted his fallen face. "Smells good. What is it?"

"Stay back now," Andy teased with a raise of his elbow to keep Harden from getting too close. "It's a surprise. Go back to the TV. I'll call you when everything's ready." He took two steps to the refrigerator, tossed Harden a can of beer. "Here. That'll tide you over for another hour."

By the time Andy set the table (complete with dimmed lighting, glittering silverware, and woven placemats), Harden had showered, shaved his day-old beard, and dressed. Dark-blue jeans and a red polo shirt replaced his grungy sweatpants and T-shirt. Andy, still in cargo shorts, snuck downstairs and changed into slacks and the one Oxford he'd packed. Not until they sat down to the candlelit spread did Andy's mouth go dry and his head spin.

What do you think you're doing, you idiot? Dating him?

Harden appeared unfazed by Andy's fussing over dinner. He licked his lips at the juicy filet mignons wrapped in butcher bacon, twice-baked potatoes oozing with cheddar cheese and sour cream, and green bushels of asparagus bound with slices of lemon rinds that sat steaming on porcelain plates. Flickering candlelight glistened in his wide blue eyes. "Looks amazing," he said, unfolding the cloth napkin across his lap. "I haven't had a dinner like this since… since…."

Andy guessed how far into the past Harden might have to travel for the last time he'd enjoyed a fancy meal. He saved Harden embarrassment by saying, "Don't be afraid to eat up. There's more warming in the oven."

Andy poured them each cabernet in long-stemmed glasses. The gurgle of the plum-red wine resonated in his ears like the gentle sound of wind chimes. Outside, the last pink blush of sun submitted to a cobalt sky. The orbs of candlelight illuminated their shrinking world.

"Cheers," Andy said, raising his glass.

Harden reciprocated his toast and sipped. "Good stuff. What is it?"

"From a local vineyard," Andy said, setting aside his wine and feeling his face flush like a schoolboy's.

"I've never tried any of the wines from here." He cut into the filet and smiled across the table. "Steak is just the way I like it."

"I remembered," Andy said. "Whenever we would all go out to eat, you'd order your steaks medium rare."

"Nice to have meat I can sink my teeth into. Kamila's spicy ground beef gets old after a while. This is delicious."

Delicious. Harden's choice word tickled Andy. The vocabulary of a mature adult male. Not a boy. But someone responsible and unafraid of his image, devoid of pretense. A word that embodied a universe Andy wished more lived in. *Delicious.*

"More wine?"

Harden swallowed. "Just a little."

The cabernet shimmered under the dancing candlelight, and the weekend's anguish lifted above the massaging lighted spheres. The children were miles away, at Uncle Lance's. Tonight would be one of gentleness, warmth. The darkening night outside brought them a secluded asylum. No intrusive arms could reach inside and subdue them.

Yet Andy noted that Harden's eyes, reflecting the candlelight, narrowed, and his lips had tightened over his fork. With the passing of the awfulness, his mind loosened, sought solace. Andy foresaw he wanted to unburden himself even before he opened his mouth to speak.

"They'll need days to get back to normal," he said without lifting his gaze off his plate. Andy understood he'd meant Mason and Olivia. "Like the last two times she showed up unannounced. Always the same. I work so hard keeping the family together. Each of Lillian's arrivals threatens to unravel all my efforts. I feel I have to start at square one."

Andy continued to eat and watch Harden from under his brow, encouraging Harden to continue with his eyes widened. He knew from Harden's past confessions that he intended to separate Mason and Olivia from their mother until—or *if*—she recovered from her addiction to crystal methamphetamine.

"She got the drugs from dealers in Chicago. Did I ever tell you that?" Harden flashed Andy blue eyes. "They sometimes travel to the boonies and peddle it, mostly to teens. They convince them they are bored living out here and that the drugs will bring sparkle to their humdrum lives. They are like the old snake oil salesmen, but with much more dire consequences. Most people rally together and chase them out, but some manage to leave a mark. Like with Lilly. I tried to keep the family together for the kids' sakes, but I realized they'd be worse off with her around."

Andy had never learned the exact details of Lillian's fall. They'd stopped sharing years before her addiction took hold of her. Lilly never said much to Andy about hating life at Burr Oak Farm. He'd read through her demeanor and understood she had disconnected with most everything in life. But he had chosen to pretend none of it mattered.

Her announcement that she planned to marry Harden and move to Dover County had shocked the entire family. Andy had bit his tongue from making sarcastic comments. Wild, fun-craving Lilly, a farmer's wife?

But in a way he'd envied her decision to cut ties and start fresh. But she hadn't really. The first suspicions came from her unpredictable phone calls. Neither he nor his mother had taken them seriously. The next time he'd seen her, she had looked like she'd lost twenty pounds and had her spirit sucked out of her.

Lilly had yearned for adventure her entire life. Bright lights, music, laughter. Anything to drown out the reality of the present. She was never happy unless her life emulated glamour. She'd once told Andy, shortly after Mason's birth, "My life is nothing like those people on MTV's *Cribs*." He pictured her nursing Mason, her eyes riveted on the television, her only source of companionship while Harden toiled at work, day in and day out.

Andy admitted he'd started to appreciate the rural flavor of Iowa and the farmhouses and estate homes that dotted the prairie of hardworking, genuine people. The vineyards on rolling green landscapes that erupted lush, spilling with abundance, like a horn of plenty, and the small towns with towering steeples and state-of-the-art public libraries. It had a clean, rustic feel to it.

The smell of cow poop and biting grasshoppers had begun to energize him. Even the people's honesty and down-to-earth daily routines stirred him into accepting their world. He'd thought such lifestyles and attitudes had disappeared from American life. He'd only missed it living in the city.

He'd become narrow-minded and disillusioned. But what about Lilly? Iowa had failed to solve her problems. Didn't Harden just say that drug dealers from Chicago often traveled to rural communities to get them hooked?

"Olivia and Mason must know how bad off she is by now," Andy said, keeping with Harden's hushed manner. "Surely they understand why they shouldn't see her, despite how badly they want to."

"I had no choice but to kick her out," Harden said again, raising his voice slightly, wanting the entire world to understand, as if he believed Andy still needed convincing. "Lilly drained our accounts of over ten thousand dollars before I could accept what was really going on."

Andy peered at him. Harden had told him that once. At the time, he had said nothing. "I'm so sorry, Harden. I know how bad things have been for you. I wish I had done more." Was that a bold-faced lie? Had Andy only wanted to suppress and bury all that he understood about his drug-addicted older sister and renounce any association with her?

I had my own life to lead, didn't I?

"What really worries me, in a selfish way," Harden said, "is that when they grow up they'll prefer her over me, after everything. They already hate me for keeping her away. Even with all the teasing Mason gets from his friends because of his drug-addicted mom, he still longs for her."

A sharp remorse pinched Andy's insides. "He wishes she was different and probably pretends on some level she is. Any kid would. A kid's imagination is sometimes all that can save him. But they won't be kids forever, Harden. They'll grow up and realize you did what was best for them. Harden, many fathers in your position would have handed their kids to foster care. There's no way Mason and Olivia won't love you for that. They must know you're better for them than she is."

"Kids grow up and cling to resentment," Harden stated toward the glossy tabletop that captured the candlelight. "I find even myself having a hard time getting past things my parents did. Little things like not allowing me to go out on a Saturday night with my friends. And here I am all grown up with my own kids, and sometimes, out of nowhere, I find myself fuming over it like they'd just punished me yesterday. Isn't that ridiculous?"

"I do that too sometimes, but my parents never really made the effort to nurture me and Lilly. You're different, Harden. Olivia and Mason will see that someday, if they don't already."

"Am I really that different? I'm so busy with work. I brush them aside more and more. Haven't I sent them away just today?"

"Who said being a single parent was easy? You also spend most of your free time with them."

Harden took several bites of his meal, washing down each one with a swig of wine. From the enthusiasm of his chewing and drinking, he still relished the taste in spite of their conversation's gravity. "I blame myself for what's happened. I brought Lillian to this farmhouse. It was my dream, not hers. She got lost here. At least she didn't start the meth until after Olivia was born. I guess life out here was too slow and boring for her. I never considered that."

"A place can't drive a person to drugs," Andy said, wanting to believe his own words.

"But boredom can, can't it?"

Andy recalled their youth, how his capricious sister had bounced from one toy or game to the other, and once she'd reached her teen years, she seemed unable to spend time at home for more than an hour at one stretch without going nuts.

"Lilly was easily distracted even as a little girl," he said, biting into his steak with determination. "Wherever she was, she wanted to be somewhere else. Where she wasn't, she wanted to be there. You could have moved to Hawaii and she'd have found an excuse to hate everything. Sure, she liked to party, but parties come to an end. She'd be displeased anywhere."

In an instant, Andy realized his alliance stood rooted with Harden rather than Lillian. She was possessed by something that took her from him and everyone else. Andy needed to protect Harden, steeped in the reality of those struggling to survive. Lillian marched with the dead.

Harden gazed into Andy's eyes, as if he understood for the first time too. Andy returned his fixed stare, smiling upon him warmly. He swallowed, dabbed the sides of his mouth with his napkin. Harden's somber countenance prompted Andy to say more. Anything to alleviate his misery.

"You keep telling me to stop feeling guilty for not doing enough for you and the kids," Andy said. "Take your own advice, why don't you? Life elbows you in the face, you have to take it. Just like how locusts and droughts once decimated farmland like this. Or even the floods that happen today. It's just part of life, right? You can't blame yourself for any of those things."

Harden's pupils shrunk behind the flames of candlelight. Shadows outlined his features, and his expression turned faraway once again. "When I first met her on vacation in Cancun," he murmured, "she seemed so exotic. A city girl. I was a country boy looking for adventure away from the grind of college. She was a spitfire who looked great in a bikini." He chuckled and shook his head. "We partied a bit. Drank too much, even smoked some local pot. I could take it or leave it. I know that dating someone you meet on vacation, especially a tropical resort where people party, is not always a good idea. But we hit it off, we really did. There were warning bells, of course. But aren't there always between two people getting to know each other? I really thought she was the one. I thought I found her. How is anyone to know things like that?"

"You have to take a leap of faith with people. Either you trust someone or you don't."

"Funny thing, the worst part of it all was that day last spring telling Mason and Olivia we were divorcing. Maybe it's the Catholic in me, but I never conceived telling my children that."

Determined to ease the mood, Andy said in a singsong voice, "As John Steinbeck once wrote, 'A man's got to do what a man's got to do.'

Now eat up and have some more cabernet." He topped off their wine glasses, unconcerned if he spilt any.

"I'm getting a little light-headed," Harden said, grinning at his overflowing wineglass.

"Just as good. Go ahead. Enjoy. You deserve it."

Harden sipped, wiped his mouth, chuckled. "Remember that time Lilly and I came to Streamwood, just before Mason was born, and you and I got to drinking beer? We got really wasted, if I recall. I think that was the last time I really got drunk."

"In those days, two beers would've set me off. I was about ten pounds lighter."

"That was a fun time." Harden's gaze fell to the candles. "So many responsibilities ahead of us. You in college, me fresh out of grad school with the baby coming, yet we still acted like immature kids in some ways."

The wine, in addition to the dimmed lighting and the night pushing in on them, tempted Andy's courage. "That was the same trip you...." He poked his fork at his asparagus. "Oh, never mind."

"You can't start something like that and then stop. Tell me."

Andy shook his head. "It's nothing, really."

"Spit it out, Andy. What did I do that has you turning redder than a cabbage?"

Andy set his fork down with a clink against his plate and breathed. Bolstered by the cabernet and Harden's prodding, he said, "That was when you kissed me by the kitchen sink."

Harden's eyes turned into gaping blue holes. "I did what?"

"Don't you remember? I was washing dishes, and you came in for another beer. You grabbed my shoulders, swung me around, and kissed me on the lips."

Harden peered toward the ceiling. A flush germinated over his protruding jowls. "Christ, I think I do remember that." He chuckled and lowered his eyes to his plate, avoiding Andy's gaze. "What was I thinking? I must've been drunker than I realized."

"That's what I thought," Andy said, and he looked away from Harden and began eating again. "We'd been acting goofy all afternoon. Poor Lilly, being pregnant, could only laugh with us."

"Who knows," Harden said, shrugging and sniggering, "maybe that's why I did it. Lilly's pregnancy made her less affectionate." Harden's laughter seemed to raise the ceiling, the same unrestrained laughter that Andy had relished while ogling him at the corn roast.

"You were attracted to my dashing charm. Admit it," Andy said, chuckling alongside him.

Harden rested his fork on his plate and checked his laughter until he coughed. "Maybe I always wanted to know what it was like to kiss a man with a cleft chin."

Andy snickered. "I've always liked your jaw muscles."

"My jaw muscles?"

"The way they protrude."

An abrupt silence pierced the table faster than the flicker of the candle flames. Andy wanted to replace the resulting discomfort with some levity. "Hey, I bought a dessert," he said. "Don't let me forget. Should be enough leftovers for the kids unless you pig yourself full."

"What did you get?"

"What else? Your favorite."

"Baked Alaska? How did you remember?"

"Same way I remembered you like your steaks medium rare. I'd have baked it myself, but I wouldn't have had time."

Red blotchiness popped over Harden's neck and forehead. "You go to so much trouble around here, Andy. You've been a godsend."

"I like to help," Andy said. "I have a lot of time to make up to you and the kids."

"Do we have to go through that again?" Harden said emphatically. "I never once expected you to do anything extraordinary once Lilly and I split up. I'm just glad you're here now."

"I'm glad I'm here too."

They finished their meal without mentioning Andy's guilt or Harden's kissing him again. After emptying the bottle of cabernet and downing two thick slices of the store-bought pie, they left the smoke from the snuffed out candles curling toward the ceiling and retired to the porch with the second bottle of cabernet.

Andy allowed Harden the porch swing, and he sat on the steps, looking into the descending darkness. Stars glowed like tiny orbs of taper candles from distant light years. Someone else in the universe, perhaps another lonely being, was concocting a silly dinner for two.

He joined Harden in polishing off his glass. They both licked their lips, breathed deeply. The night comforted Andy, yet made him antsy. Gray shadows cast from the porch lamps crept up on Andy and seemed to prod him. Chilly knuckles kneaded his nape, despite the mugginess.

Sweet corn scent rode high on the wind, and the entire countryside seemed to thrust upward and meet where Harden and Andy sat. Nighttime encapsulated their corner of the world. Andy imagined putting it in a tiny vial and wearing it on a silver chain around his neck. Perhaps the wine helped shrink everything into charm-sized nuggets.

Andy would be prepping for his South Side Saturday tour about now. Thrills came in many forms. Tonight, hot mounds of cash and the buzz of carting suburbanites and foreign tourists into the sticky crime-ridden streets of Chicago would be replaced by corn growing, crickets chirping, and the dumb bugs smacking against the inside of the lamp globes.

Andy tried to feign nonchalance when Harden got up from the swing, sat next to him, and topped off their glasses. He rested the crook of his arm on Andy's shoulder. "I guess a man can't predict what will happen to his future," Harden said. "Not with my kids or anything else. I guess we all have intuition, but at some point, you have to trust someone, like you said, right?"

"That's true," Andy said, sipping his wine. "I'm glad you're coming around and not beating yourself up over everything that's happened."

Harden stood with a reverberating crack of his joints. "Easier to give advice than to take it."

He walked inside the house, the slap of the storm door swallowed by the night.

After rinsing out his wine glass in the kitchen sink, Andy found Harden sitting on the edge of his bed upstairs, his gaze on the carpet, still looking as if he were brooding over Lillian's visit. Andy stood at the threshold, watching him. "Harden, are you sure you're okay?"

Harden looked up and tweaked a smile. "I'm okay. A lot on my mind, that's all. Don't worry. Thanks again for an amazing dinner."

Andy stepped inside the bedroom. The photograph of Lilly and Harden in Cancun leered at him from the bureau. Overhead light reflected off the glazing and blurred Lillian's face. Harden must have noticed him staring at it.

"I keep it mostly for the kids' sake," he said, gazing at the photograph with Andy, his voice distant. "That way they can see her in a good way, with her bright eyes and happy smile, a time before they even knew her. Poor Olivia, most of her life has been during Lillian's drug abuse."

Edging closer to Harden, Andy said, "She's handling things well. She'll get over this latest setback, you'll see. Both of them will. You've done a wonderful job raising the kids."

Harden stared back to his hands in his lap, and he began twiddling his thumbs. "I just want everything to work out okay. That's all. I just want to know in the end everything that I've done was right. What I would do for a little relief from the constant worrying about tomorrow."

Andy stood planted before Harden. He peered down at his head, with his blond hair combed to the side, conventional and sleek. A hint of his spicy cologne wafted from him. Harden had preened himself for their night together. Like he might any date. Had he done it out of habit, out of desperation? Did Harden wish Andy was Lillian or one of his women friends, like his coworker Lucinda Jamison?

His heart beating inside his ears, Andy sat beside Harden, like Harden had with him moments earlier on the porch. But Andy refrained from placing his arm on his shoulder, despite his muscles crying out that he do so. Instead, he leaned against him to keep himself from falling forward. "Harden…."

Andy felt Harden flinch, but his head remained downturned. "What is it?"

Tremors raced along Andy's body. He did not speak. Impulsively, he clasped Harden's bare forearm. Each pounding throb, each course of blue vessels streaming with heated blood sent shockwaves through Andy. He looked toward Harden's profile, with his wonderful, plump jowls. "Please, just let me, Harden."

Harden stiffened. "Let… let you what?"

"Let me give you a little relief."

"What do you mean?"

"Remember in the kitchen in Streamwood? Remember, Harden?"

"But Andy…."

Andy slumped before Harden, abandoning any iota of coordination or reserve. His head, sloping and seemingly without a neck to hold it upright, fell onto Harden's lap.

"Andrew…. Why?"

Andy moved his arms closer to Harden's sides and held onto him. "Let me. Please, Harden. Let me. We both knew it was coming to this. Let me please you. It's what you need. What you want."

Andy glanced up, but only for an instant, so that he might discern Harden's liquid blue eyes and the truth stirring behind them. Firm and inert, Harden stared off where wall and carpet met, far from the portrait of he and Lillian. His lips, moist and drooping, quivered. His ultimate response—a relinquishing of breath.

Using the gentlest of movements, a butterfly's wings folding, Andy nudged his hands closer toward Harden's lap. "Let me give you relief tonight, Harden. Let me please you the way you deserve."

He half expected Harden to brush his hand aside and rush horrified from the room. But he did not. Andy, his heart pounding and his fingers trembling, undid the first of what seemed an endless row of buttons on Harden's fly. One by one, he unfastened them, until the glow of Harden's light-blue boxers appeared, and Andy, catching the first scent of Harden, swooned in a near stupor of his heart's pounding and quickening blood.

CHAPTER
TWENTY-ONE

THE scent of Harden's pheromones and cologne came heavier once Andy unfastened the last of the buttons. Andy wanted to believe maybe Harden had sprayed himself down there, not out of habit before an elaborate evening, but knowing—or hoping—Andy might ask to relieve him that night. Perhaps Harden had sent the kids away for more than one purpose too?

Driven by daring and passion, Andy reached inside Harden's boxers and gripped him. Harden let go a groan, and his head drooped forward. The heat of his thick sex, pulsating with blood, sent Andy's heart into a tailspin. He squeezed harder, gauging Harden's expression as he stiffened. Save for a slight shudder that worked through his limbs, Harden no longer budged. He kept his eyes shut and his hands curled around the edge of the bed.

Andy peeled back the elastic waistband and slowly freed Harden's semierection, exposing him to the full light. Exactly how Andy had fantasized. Without thinking, he licked the head. He glanced up after his tongue's initial swipe. Harden's lower lip had fallen open, and his eyelids quivered. Determined, Andy massaged Harden, forcing more blood flow. Then he positioned his lips over the tip and swallowed him.

Harden's right leg kicked out. Moans came more erratically. Hot breath from his nostrils shot over Andy's neck. Harden clutched the bedcovers, mumbled something, whimpered. Andy's mind spun with disbelief as Harden grew more turgid.

Smells of spicy cologne and pheromones prodded him to work his tongue and lips firmer. He relished the feel of Harden's golden tufts of pubic hair tickling his chin and nose. He focused on Harden as if nothing else mattered, until Harden suddenly stood and flopped from his mouth.

Andy feared he'd had enough. But Harden remained standing, his stiff sex pointing inches from Andy's face. Rolling his shirt higher, Harden gripped himself and aimed his pulsating head closer to Andy's mouth.

Without hesitation, Andy devoured him again. He rolled his eyeballs upward, delighting in Harden's reaction. Harden squeezed his eyes shut, and his nostrils flared. Subtle lines pulled the sides of his tightening lips. His robust jowl muscles tensed. He had the look of sheer helplessness. Lost, confused. Yet his feet remained stationary and his arms taut by his sides.

And then the moment Andy had savored whenever he'd given oral to a straight man. Harden stripped off his shirt entirely and placed a hand behind Andy's head, holding him steady.

"You shouldn't be doing this," Harden whispered from deep within his throat. "But don't stop. Don't stop, buddy. Take it all."

Andy held his hips and swallowed him until his lips pressed against his pelvis, moist with fragrant perspiration. Long, shimmering strings of saliva fell onto the carpet before Andy's knees, and Harden grew thicker and lengthier.

He kept at it, forgetting the choking tears that poured from his eyes. He serviced Harden the way he believed he was due. Harden shuddered. A quivering moan floated from his lips. Bolder now, Harden kept a solid grip on the back of Andy's head and thrust in and out of Andy's mouth until Andy gagged and gasped for breath.

Wanting more of him, Andy inched his lips and tongue along Harden's length and tasted his balls, which had pulled up against his body. Harden's hands remained firm on the back of Andy's head while Andy took in his balls one by one and rubbed his wet lips the length of his stiffness. He swallowed him fully again. Harden tossed his head back and grunted.

He fell backward onto the bed, and Andy descended with him, keeping his mouth locked on him. He reached for Harden's pectoral muscles and cupped the furry mounds in his hands. Harden leaned on one elbow and fixed his hand behind Andy's head, holding him firm on him and sighing and moaning in rhythm to Andy's movements.

"Christ," he groaned. "Feels so good. Why didn't I ever know? Why didn't I ever know...?" His words trailed off, and Andy continued to gulp him.

Unable to hold back, Andy unzipped his fly and stroked himself, using Harden's precome, which came in long, salty strings, as lubricant. He pulled Harden's jeans and boxers down to his knees, with Harden giving only the slightest inkling of resistance. Andy finally needed air, and he took a respite by roving his face over Harden's sex, covering himself with Harden's stickiness and his own warm spit.

Harden sat upright, his legs spread, with Andy's face poised between them, and gazed deep into Andy's eyes. Andy froze, waiting. Had Harden come to the endpoint? But Harden surprised Andy by reaching under his arms and pulling his face closer to him. And like that afternoon in Streamwood while Andy had washed dishes at the kitchen sink, Harden kissed him.

Their tongues touching shocked Andy, and he worried he might melt into oblivion. Bubbles seemed to pop around his ears, emitting powerful messages to submit. The slightest sound vanished into a vacuum. Andy's heart beat more wildly.

They pulled apart long enough to regard each other. Andy trembled violently, but Harden, his hot hands firm under Andy's arms, held him steady. Harden leaned in and kissed him again, this time more gently. Harden's lips were electrifying, tasting of wine and his own saltiness. Andy gave in to him then, and allowed his strength to hold him upright so that he would not slip into unconsciousness.

But Harden stopped a second time, pulled back his hands, and looked away. Andy locked his elbows to keep from falling over.

"What's wrong?" he asked, stunned by the sensation of Harden's sudden yanking away from him.

Harden glanced out the darkened windowpane where the night beat with a hot pulse. "You kiss and do all that very well. It's just that...."

"What, Harden? Don't you trust me?"

"More than anyone I know."

"Then what is it? You don't think it's wrong that I want to make you feel good?"

Andy shifted his eyes to their exposed erections, throbbing and painful, within inches of each other. He admired his former brother-in-law, looked up to him, wanted him more at that moment than any man before. Wished he could be more like him in many ways. Harden's firm masculinity pumped with indecision, fear, and despair. Andy needed to hold him this time, to erase all his loneliness and dread.

In slow motion, Andy wrapped his arms around him tighter, feeling the warmth of his naked torso. Harden remained mute. Andy felt Harden's facial muscles tense on his shoulder, and the durability and power of his magnificent jowls. Andy eased his embrace and beheld him, nose to nose. The firmness of his jawline lengthened into a sharp contrast with his lopping lips. Slowly, Harden met Andy's eyes. With both hands, he guided Andy's mouth back to his throbbing sex, and Andy, wanting nothing more, slipped his lips around his impressive girth.

Having forever erased the impenetrable line, Harden moaned and groaned and seemed lost in passion. His grunts came louder, more dauntless. In response, Andy worked his lips over him faster and faster. More tears streamed down his cheeks, and snot ran along his chin, merging with the saliva that coated Harden. He did not care. It was for Harden.

Dizzy from lack of oxygen, Andy lifted his head and breathed. Instantly, Harden pulled him to meet his lips, and he swathed him with more kisses. They fell backward and rolled about the bed, their arms locked around each other, finding their lips with probing tongues.

They kicked off their shoes and socks, yanked off the pants and underwear that had shackled them at the ankles. Harden unbuttoned Andy's Oxford, tossed it with a devil-may-care flourish into the air.

Naked and pressed against each other, they kissed deeper and harder. Andy rubbed his hands through Harden's hair, mussing it so he looked even more frenzied and youthful. He moved his tongue along Harden's chest and stopped to nibble on his quarter-sized nipples. Harden squirmed and yelped and directed his mouth farther down his torso, where Andy left a shimmering kiss trail over his little papa pouch and across the tan line. Harden squeezed his purple hardness so that it stood firmer. Almost trancelike, Andy bobbed up and down on him faster with firmer pursed lips.

"Feels so good," Harden uttered. "You're really getting me going. Maybe we shouldn't be doing this." But Harden's strong handhold on the back of Andy's head stated otherwise. Like a vise, he held Andy on him, rising up and thrusting to meet Andy's lips.

"I want all of you," Andy panted between sucking and licking and roving his head over Harden's sex. "I'll do whatever you want."

"You want me inside you?" Harden whispered, keeping a hold on Andy's head. "Do you?"

Andy said nothing. His body went limp, and he languished between Harden's legs, dizzy with disbelief and longing. His passion surpassed any remaining inhibition he might have had at that point. Somehow, Andy managed to move his head with one or two nods.

"How do I do it?" Harden said simply.

Wanting to laugh at Harden's naivety, Andy stood and jogged for the bathroom. He remembered seeing the jar of Vaseline on the counter when he'd dressed in Harden's swim trunks, but now it was gone. "Do you have any lube?" he asked.

Harden stood beside him, his penis still erect, matting the small hairy pouch below his belly with dapples of precome and Andy's spit. He opened a few cabinets. "I'm all out. Will suntan lotion do?"

Andy swiped the lotion from the counter, seized Harden by his erection, and guided him to bed. "We should probably use a condom," he said, desperate to get Harden inside him before Harden changed his mind. "It's no big deal, but people use them. Not that I don't trust you."

"I think I have one or two left." Harden rolled to his side and reached inside the night table drawer. He pulled out a familiar-looking shiny package and glanced at the back. "Expires next month. I haven't had much occasion to use any."

"Perfect timing." Andy wasted not another minute to grab the package from Harden, rip open the contents, and spread lotion over both of them. Enjoying the pleasure of Harden's squirming, Andy unrolled the condom onto him. It barely made it past the thickness, but the prophylactic would suffice.

Andy lubed it up and immediately straddled him, allowing his penis head to enter millimeter by millimeter. Harden's eyes grew wider, his hands loose on Andy's hips. Andy sat down further, taking his time to allow Harden to enter him fully without the gut-wrenching pain. Harden released a guttural sigh when he broke through. A shock of pleasure and pain ripped along Andy's spine and shattered his mind. The inevitable release of energy fluttered from his mouth, and he moaned.

"Tell me if I hurt you," Harden said.

"You can't hurt me now," Andy muttered. "Go as hard and deep as you want. Show me what a stud you are."

Harden gripped Andy's waist tighter and moved up and down with him. Andy, grunting and groaning, maintained the cadence of Harden's thrusting. Throwing his head back and closing his eyes, he grabbed hold of Harden's shoulders so that they might stay locked forever.

"Christ!" Harden screamed. "I can't believe how good this feels. Christ, you're tight."

Harden lost himself inside Andy, pumping and pushing more fiercely. Each thrust was more powerful than the one prior. Andy had never before seen Harden's current expression: pure ecstasy etched across his sweat-shellacked face. He pulled Andy down on him to get more fully inside, to push more of his man power deeper into him.

"Andrew...," Harden grunted. "Is this what you need?"

Andy, close to reaching climax, shouted that it was. Harden sat up so that their chests pressed against each other. Their tongues dug into each other's mouths, while Harden's drives came quicker and sharper. Harden nibbled on Andy's cleft chin and seemed fixated on it. Overwhelmed with pleasure, Andy clutched Harden's deltoids and presented his neck for Harden's mouth.

With a rapid succession of thrusts, Andy felt Harden's sex pulse and fill the condom. But before Harden's final spurt, Andy lowered his face so that he might see, eye to eye, the wonderful glow eclipse Harden's countenance. It was at that moment that Andy realized Harden had given as much of himself to Andy as Andy had given him.

Stroking himself, Andy shot onto Harden's hairy chest and fell forward. They lay still, stiff like mannequins, except for the rise and fall of their heaving chests. Andy stirred, and their stickiness made a strange sucking noise when he sat upright. Disbelief seared into Harden's face, he stared blankly at Andy. But the corners of his lips quivered into something resembling a smile. Andy copied his expression.

"Are you okay?" he asked.

Harden nodded, his breathing easing. "Felt amazing. But I better take a shower."

"You have to now?"

"I'd feel better if I did."

Before rising, Harden kissed him on his dimpled chin, and a few seconds later Andy heard the rush of water from the shower.

Alone in bed and unsure what to do next, Andy withdrew from the room and showered in his own basement bathroom. Lathering his body, he felt no regret for what he and Harden had done. He had given him what he'd needed, what he'd deserved. And Andy had received something glorious too. The need for a man—a man like Harden—was so intense that having that desire satisfied filled him not with sorrow but with a tremor that continued even as he toweled off.

Andy was drying his legs when Harden walked into the bathroom. He did not speak. Wearing only the same light-blue boxers, he embraced Andy from behind and held him firm to his damp body. His thickness began to grow again. Yes, a long time had passed since Harden had had sex. Realizing this, Andy dropped the towel, turned to him, and, equally and painfully hard again, held him tight, kissing him.

Harden rotated him back to face the sink. In the mirror, Andy could see Harden drop his boxers and grip his thick mass. He smacked it over Andy and then flourished a condom package that he'd held clenched in his fist.

Andy shivered, watching him roll on the condom and use spit to lubricate himself. Andy reached back and exposed himself more to Harden. Despite the initial pain, Andy had enough residual suntan lotion inside him he permitted Harden to push into him. Harden grabbed Andy's hands and forced his stomach against the sink. Andy's fingers curled around the edge of the counter, and Harden thrust faster.

Andy twisted his neck in search of Harden's mouth with his probing tongue. They shared several kisses, and Harden stood straighter, focusing on taking Andy as much as he could.

Grunting and heaving and shouting how much he loved Andy's tightness, he pulled out—which caused Andy to wince—and he shredded the condom before spewing hot globs on Andy's back. Andy even felt some strike his nape.

Spent over Andy's curved form, Harden wrapped his arms around his ribcage, his breath sour and his hair cold and damp. "I can't believe we're doing this," he whispered into Andy's ear. "But it feels so damn good. So amazingly good." He inhaled hard breaths a moment more, then whispered, "I'm glad you're here, Andy. I'm really glad you're here."

Andy gazed at Harden's image. Harden showed no sign that he wanted to ease off him. The first pang of remorse sapped Andy from the ability to respond.

CHAPTER
TWENTY-TWO

ANDY awoke to dead quiet. Not a stir upstairs. No patter of feet or muted singsong voices or the murmur of cartoons. A pinkish flush filled the hopper windows, but the room swirled with shadows. He looked to his left, and there lay Harden, tangled in the top sheet and breathing lightly. It took a good few seconds for the reality of everything that had transpired the previous night to penetrate his consciousness.

They had made love—twice!

Andy's desire to give Harden oral pleasure had been eclipsed by something more. Harden had responded with kisses, and they had rolled atop Harden's bed, which had led to intercourse, beyond anything Andy had ever expected. Eventually, their lovemaking had carried them into Andy's bed, where they had collapsed, holding each other until their bodies had faded with exhaustion.

Sex with Harden was no "fooling around." It had proved to be serious business. Maybe too intense. Languid eyes, watering mouths, grasping hands. Harden Krane, a country poet in lovemaking.

Way better than I ever fantasized.

They had dissolved the boundaries of friendship and family. Where would they go now?

Harden's eyes popped open. Andy expected him to glare at him, turn away sickened with shame once the recollection of what they had done surfaced, and dash upstairs. Instead, he smiled through the dawn's light that brightened the room in a smokelike haze.

"Good morning," he said with a grainy voice.

"Good morning," Andy muttered.

Harden rubbed his eyes, and they stared at each other. Andy realized he'd never seen Harden in bed for the first glimpse of his bright blue eyes fluttering open. The same confusion and fear that had bothered him after their second bout of lovemaking in the bathroom returned. The rising sun failed to lessen the anxiety, but exacerbated it.

"You're not upset with everything, are you?" Harden asked.

Funny, Andy had imagined asking Harden that question. "Maybe more stunned," he said. "Are you?"

Harden glanced away. "Kind of crazy. We drank a lot of wine. Maybe that was it."

Harden made to untangled himself from the sheet and stand. Andy grabbed his arm. "Don't go." He loosened his grip and smiled. Regardless of his misgivings, Andy did not wish for Harden to leave him cold and alone in bed. Not yet. "The kids aren't here."

"They aren't, are they?" Harden snickered and hunkered back under the sheet. "I was thinking I had to make them breakfast." He leaned on his right elbow and gazed at Andy. Without warning, he placed his free hand behind Andy's head and brought their lips together. He broke off and looked at him. "Okay that I kissed you?"

Andy nodded.

He inhaled more of Harden's sour morning breath, and Harden began to explore Andy's dimpled chin with his lips and tongue, causing Andy to chuckle and fidget. The jerky light movements brought Andy on top of him.

They had slept naked, and they were aroused and ready. Harden traced his hands along the entire length of Andy's back, stopping to squeeze Andy's tensing butt muscles. Andy reciprocated by reaching between them and clutching Harden. For a moment, he'd forgotten his doubts—and Harden's girth. Anointed with Harden's precome, they embraced and kissed for what seemed endless minutes.

Harden kicked the sheets to the floor and, grasping Andy's hands, pinned him onto his back with their woven fingers near Andy's ears. The sun rose higher, and slivers of light through the elms marked their bodies in a lattice pattern.

Harden peered down at Andy with his blue eyes. "Those times watching you run through the sprinkler and then later at the pool, I couldn't help but notice your ass. I didn't want to admit it then."

Andy snickered nervously. "You were checking me out, huh?"

"More like a barely conscious observation. Like after you got your hair cut. Really brings out the dimple in your chin. I wanted to touch it." And he kissed it with soft lips.

Andy's body tingled with desire. His thickening and lengthening arousal stifled shrewdness. He spread his legs apart, an act that goaded Harden to grind against him.

"Do you have any lubricant and condoms down here?" Harden asked.

Andy hoped that Harden wouldn't think of him as promiscuous once he told him he always kept a supply in his travel bag. "I might have some lube in my toiletry case for when I jerk off," he said as Harden leaped to his feet and dashed for the bathroom. "I might have some condoms too, but I don't know how old they are."

Seconds later, Harden returned, holding Andy's near-empty, gnarly tube of ID Glide and a package of condoms. "Are you sure you're okay with this?" he asked, gazing at Andy from the foot of the bed.

"Are you?"

Harden slipped on the condom, which looked painfully tight on him, lubricated himself, tossed the tube aside, and gave his stiffness a few quick squeezes. Next, he mounted Andy and looked down into his eyes. "I'm okay, and ready."

"I'm all yours, then."

"Can we do it this way?"

"You mean missionary? Just watch."

Andy positioned a pillow under his lower back. His torso rose, and Harden watched as if he were witnessing a modern marvel. Using his strong thighs, he spread Andy's legs farther apart. Gently, he began to insert his glistening sex into Andy, and Andy helped aim it in.

There was a spasm of pain as Harden crossed the sphincter, but soon the fleeting cramp gave way to complete and total rapture. Once inside, Harden no longer needed instructions from Andy.

Propped by his locked arms, Harden threw his head back and pushed into Andy hard, grinding and wiggling his hips from side to side. Typical straight move, Andy surmised, thinking back to his dalliances with other heterosexual or bisexual men and the way they'd simulate movements they used when making love to a woman. But a man did not need such outer stimulation. Nonetheless, Andy, enraptured by Harden's masculinity, tightened his legs around Harden so that he could feel more of him.

"Let me know if I'm hurting you," Harden said.

"You're doing great," Andy said as pleasurable ripples shot through him. "Don't stop. Give me all you got."

Those coaxing words drove Harden. He slammed Andy hard and rotated his hips faster and fuller. His subtle facial lines and muscles contorted into something surreal to Andy.

"Feels so good to be inside you," Harden groaned. "Feels so good."

Andy enveloped Harden with his arms and reached for his butt. The firmness of his glutes as he flexed sent Andy squirming. He wriggled and writhed under Harden's manly weight. Power and truth were revealed behind those thrusts, and Andy was not sure how long he could go without screaming loud enough for the angels in Heaven to cover their ears with their wings.

He spread his legs as wide as he could, his toes curled. Harden responded by lifting him off the pillow and thrusting deeper and unyieldingly. Gasping in the throes of passion, Harden simply stated, "I want to give it to you."

Harden began pounding into Andy as the man Andy always knew Harden to be. He was not heavy like Ken, who often crushed Andy, causing him to fear he might suffocate. Harden covered him like a comforting shroud, soft yet firm and purposeful.

He maneuvered Andy onto his left side, sandwiching Andy's leg with his own, and then onto his stomach. Andy clutched the fitted sheet and allowed his grunts and groans to match the ferocity of Harden's pumping.

Harden rolled him faceup again, and seemed to prefer the missionary position more than any other. Andy grabbed hold of Harden, cherishing the feel of his contracting muscles as the commanding thrusts continued unabated.

"I'm going to give you what you want," Harden said, gnawing on his cleft chin. "I'm going to give it to you good."

Andy's throbbing heart seemed ready to explode. He received Harden's mouth as if to ensure Harden exhaled life into him. Their lips fused and, with the brightening sun soaking the room and wringing extra sweat from their bodies, they orgasmed together.

"Christ!"

Harden's body shook and, languishing like a leaf before falling from a branch, he buckled and collapsed on top of Andy. Something like weeping broke from him. But when he lifted his face from Andy's perspiring chest, Andy realized he had been snickering.

"I get why the French call sex *le petit mort*," Harden said.

Andy smiled. He too understood the utter fatigue from lovemaking, as if he had suffered a tiny death each time.

Harden laid his forehead on Andy's shoulder. Other than breathing heavily, they lay still. Andy continued to clench down to prevent Harden from slipping out. Their sweat and Andy's semen helped to adhere them.

Finally, Harden slipped out of Andy, and he budged to sit upright. "I need another shower," he said. "Do you mind if I hop in yours? Kamila's keeping you stocked with clean towels under the sink?"

"Go ahead," Andy said, not bothering to question Harden's practice of showering immediately after sex, like Ken. "Let me know when you've finished. I could use another one myself."

Harden stood planted by the side of the bed. He stripped off the spent condom, which had hung from his thick, flaccid penis like a leaf heavy with dew, and clenched it in his fist. His casual movement for some reason charmed Andy.

"Why don't you join me?" Harden said. "We can save some water."

"You sure?"

"You don't like showering with anyone?"

Andy gazed into his blue eyes. "I do, a lot. But no one has ever asked me."

"Let's go, then."

Beneath the hot rush of water, they lathered each other's hair and traced dollops of liquid soap along their slick bodies. Standing face to face under the bathroom's fluorescent lights, Harden seemed to grow bashful. He smiled, flushed, fixed his gaze toward the suds gushing between their toes.

Andy fought the nagging misgivings. Whatever they were doing, he didn't want it to stop. At least not at that moment. Why worry about it now? He tweaked Harden's chin to meet his eyes and kissed him with tender lips.

Andy knelt before Harden and took him into his mouth. Thrusting unrelentingly, Harden clasped Andy's head with both hands. His grunts rose above the rushing water from the showerhead. Andy wanted to swallow him, devour his entire body and soul.

Harden pulled Andy to his feet. They kissed, a communion of tongues. Andy turned his back to Harden and pressed against him, tilting his neck so that their cheeks touched. Harden folded his arms around him, massaged his pectoral muscles, and nibbled the sides of his neck, landing on his chin.

Andy arched his back, roving against Harden. Harden slapped his sex against Andy's best feature and rubbed it between his legs. Then he slowly began to insert it.

"Is this okay?" he asked, breathless.

Moaning, Andy said, "I'm all yours."

Slippery with soap, Harden slid inside him. The feeling of his rawness sent a new sensation of electricity through Andy. It had been ages since anyone had penetrated him without a condom, and he'd forgotten the intensified pleasure of flesh intersecting flesh.

Andy pushed back to underline his consent, submitting to him for the fourth time in fewer than twelve hours. Harden responded by flexing his pelvis, moaning and sighing above the din of cascading water. He clutched Andy's shoulders and intensified his thrusting, forcing Andy's face against the shower wall tiles.

The pummeling water traveled down Andy's back and streamed over his face. He trembled, pressed his palms flatter against the tiles. Steam and the aroma of the woodsy soap and the rawness of Harden weakened him. His arms fell flaccid, and his hands slipped. Bent completely over, Andy relented to Harden's increased force.

He used his fingertips on the shower floor to keep his balance, and Harden pumped and pumped, his grip stronger on Andy's waist.

"Do you want it inside or outside?" Harden said, never letting up his heaving thrusts.

"Inside," Andy cried. "Inside!"

As if Andy had pressed a magic button, the first hot blasts ejected into Andy, and Harden screamed out. A fierce burning Andy hadn't experienced in many years pushed him beyond boundaries, and he stroked himself to another orgasm. He watched as his semen swirled down the drain.

Harden slackened, quivered, and melded with Andy's bowed form. Harden chuckled, cried a country boy "whoop," and stood straight. "So much for saving water," he murmured between heavy breaths, helping Andy upright. "Christ, that felt intense without a rubber."

Sapped of strength, Andy turned and leaned into Harden's chest. Their foreheads slumped against each other's, and Harden stroked Andy's dripping hair. Soon their echoing chuckles faded, and all that Andy heard was the continuing rush of water and the small puddle gurgling down the drain by their overlapping feet.

CHAPTER
TWENTY-THREE

ANDY carried two steaming mugs of coffee to the kitchen table and placed one under Harden's nose. The other he brought with him to a chair opposite him. Andy was dressed in cargo shorts and Oxford, which still smelled of their night together; Harden wore light-blue jeans and a T-shirt. Ready for any Sunday in late summer. But it wasn't any Sunday. Andy understood that.

He was unsure how Harden might behave now that they were dressed and settled upstairs, the full light of day pouring through the windows. He waited, not wishing to be the first to mention what they'd done.

Finally, Harden muttered, "I guess we got a little carried away."

Lost in his coffee's glossiness, Andy shook his head. "There's nothing to be ashamed of. You'd be surprised how common this is. Don't worry about it."

"It's strange, that's all," Harden said, his stare locked on the table.

A marquee of pain circled Andy's head, and his lips throbbed. He slurped his coffee. "Try not to think about it too much," he said. "That's not always a good idea for anything, whether you enjoyed it or not."

His voice came even, perhaps too much. As if he were counseling a stranger rather than chatting with his former brother-in-law, a man with whom he'd just shared a weekend of incredible sex.

Andy swallowed a gulp of coffee and said, "Was that your first time with a guy?"

Harden nodded. "I came close once. In college, some guy in my dorm asked me if I wanted to… well, you know…. But I said no. I was too surprised." He peered through the south-facing window toward the Anders's farm. "I actually wondered about him over the years, wondering if I'd missed out on something." He flushed. "I guess maybe I had."

"Did you ever think of me that way? I mean," Andy snickered, "before you couldn't take your eyes off me wearing your swim trunks."

Harden's ears turned scarlet. "Once or twice in the past, I might've pictured what it would be like. You're gay and good looking with a great body. What's a guy to think?"

Andy chuckled. "I was kinda checking you out in your bathing suit too. Guess I always found you hot. But that never really meant anything while you were married. Just so you know, I don't go around seducing every guy I find attractive."

Harden sighed. "If I thought you were a person like that, Andy, I would never have let things go as far as they did."

Another silence. Andy looked in Harden's direction, but more over the top of his damp hair and out the window, where he could see part of an airplane's vapor trail streaking across the blue sky. He wanted to give the impression of looking at Harden without letting on to his wavering doubts. What should they do until the kids arrived? And then, how would they go about their lives as if nothing had ever happened between them?

Andy could see Harden lift his eyes to him. Inhaling, he dared to meet his stare.

"I've got a bad case of blue balls," Harden said.

"Try some ice."

"Ice down there?"

Harden's eyes narrowed, and his grin faded to a fine line. His fingers, positioned over the tabletop, flexed as if he were searching for something to grab. Perhaps he was reliving the pleasure Andy had given him, when Andy had taken him with his mouth the first time and Harden had clasped the bedcovers to control his squirming.

Andy's heart beat faster. He savored the elation, the amorous delight that kicked his brain into a dizzy spell, but he also craved a semblance of normalcy. He managed to guzzle what remained of his coffee without dropping the cup and stand. "All right," he said, breathing in all the air his lungs could hold. "Meanwhile, we better make some breakfast. I'm starving."

"I'm with you, buddy."

Andy noticed Harden adjust himself after he'd stood. Andy too had to fix the front of his shorts. He set two pans on the burners and was about to ask Harden how he wanted his eggs, when the sound of a car in the driveway made them jerk their heads toward the window.

The last time Andy had heard a car pulling up, Lillian had showed.

Harden set the carton of eggs aside and peered out the kitchen window. Olivia and Mason were climbing from Lance's SUV, clutching their small overnight bags. Holly jumped out from the passenger side and escorted the kids to the house. Harden went to meet them at the front door.

Holly, dressed in nice slacks and a long-sleeve blouse, appropriate for church, followed Harden and the kids into the kitchen. Andy noticed she immediately spotted the two empty bottles of Iowa cabernet sitting on the kitchen counter. Next, she shifted her gaze to the formal dining room, where the partially melted taper candles still sat. All a testament to Harden and Andy's romantic weekend. A snapshot of time.

But what would Holly assume from any of it? Her grin remained, but her eyes widened. Too wide. More of her whites were visible than the black pupils or the blue of her irises. She gave Andy a boisterous greeting and brought her arms to her sides.

"Can't stay," she said, after refusing Harden's offer for coffee and breakfast. "Lance and Damon are waiting for me in the truck. We got to get Damon to Dyersville for some Scout meeting. Had to skip brunch at your mom and dad's. Don't worry. We got Mason and Olivia to church okay."

"Let me say hello to Brother," Harden said, accompanying Holly outside.

With Holly out of the way, Andy ruffled Mason's hair and lifted Olivia with a twirl, seeking their old routine. The breeze caught her hair, which was out of her typical ponytails and teeming with golden curls. Andy commented on how she resembled a movie star.

She kept her arms by her sides and spoke with a cavalier air. "Aunt Holly did my hair for me before church. She curled it with her wand."

"Certainly looks magical," Andy said.

He held onto Olivia, staring through the window to Lance's truck. Harden was leaning his head into the passenger side. Andy suspected they were discussing the kids. The brake light released, and Harden stepped back from the truck and waved.

Lance gave a final toot with the horn, and the SUV disappeared down the driveway. Harden returned to the kitchen and asked the kids if they had enjoyed their stay with Uncle Lance and Aunt Holly. They answered through pursed lips that they had. Difficult to judge if the lingering uneasiness came more from Lillian's visit or from Harden and Andy, who now, together, harbored an unmentionable secret.

"Did you get any breakfast?" Harden asked them.

Mason nodded like a polite—but indifferent—gentleman. "We ate breakfast before church."

"Your Dad and I haven't, and we're starving." Andy set Olivia down. "I was just in the middle of preparing something. You can help me."

Andy heated the pans, and Olivia and he scrambled a western omelet big enough for two and fried potatoes. Olivia managed to drop not a single vegetable or egg. Her movements came slower, more methodical, showcasing a haughty lack of interest which Andy figured for a sign of her slow recovery.

The kids watched their favorite television shows while Harden and Andy ate at the kitchen counter. Their stout appetites kept their mouths busy, although Andy wondered what they might say with the kids in the next room. Surely Harden's head must have been clogged with the same images of the two of them together as Andy's.

After breakfast, Harden offered the kids Pop-Ice. They accepted resignedly, despite the initial enthusiasm that bubbled behind their blue eyes. Harden and Andy sat on the porch swing drinking coffee and watched the kids on the steps slurp their treats. Once washed up and back in front of the television set, Mason and Olivia suggested in low voices after each colorful "back to school" commercial what they wanted or needed before their first day. It would be Olivia's first time in school without Mason. Mason was attending middle school, almost a teenager.

The day moved ahead like any other. Harden focused on work at the family computer. Andy washed three loads of laundry. Sheets needed a good cleaning. Olivia and Mason played outdoors, swinging or chasing squirrels up trees. With dinner out of the way, Harden and Andy stood shoulder to shoulder at the kitchen sink, scrubbing the pots and pans.

"Where does this serving tray go?" Andy asked.

Harden, his hands submerged in the sudsy water, pointed with his head. "Above the refrigerator."

Andy stored the tray and said, "I'll go up and read a story to Olivia before bed."

The moment Andy closed Olivia's book about growing pumpkins, Harden stepped into the bedroom. They kissed her good night and made sure Mason was asleep. The television was still buzzing when they returned downstairs. Harden switched the channel to the Chicago Cubs versus the Colorado Rockies. Together, they sat on the sofa, a blue blush from the television spreading around them. Andy wanted to hunker down closer to Harden, but he refrained.

By the seventh inning, Andy stretched his arms and suppressed a yawn. "I guess I better get to bed. My sleep patterns are starting to match yours."

For the first time since his coming, Andy left Harden sitting up alone, and not the other way around.

Wrestling with his conflicting thoughts, Andy settled into bed with the lights on and read the text Ken had sent him an hour before, one he didn't want to read in front of Harden: *Getting ready for the return?*

I can come back? Andy wrote.

Took long enough to reply.

Sorry, was busy.

Ken's response came several minutes later. Perhaps he wanted to teach Andy a lesson. The text was replete with typos, but Andy deciphered it. *Still haven't caught suspects. All is quiet with your business shut down.*

Andy gulped. Was his enterprise through for good? Did he even care anymore?

Maybe I stay longer in case? he wrote with a shaky index finger, surprising himself.

Andy barely breathed, waiting for Ken's reply. He took another few minutes. Finally, *Get back. No need to stay.*

He considered Lillian's awful visit and the family's struggles to maintain a happy home. *Still loose ends here.*

You gone three weeks. Pack and leave.

Andy waited, holding the phone in the hollow of his hand, as if expecting it to explode. *I'll let you know*, he texted.

See you in a few days, was Ken's closing response, leaving Andy scant room for dissent.

Andy had always been faithful to Ken. True to all his boyfriends. But he and Ken never officially stated a commitment. Not the kind Andy desired. Officer Ken Millpairs wanted a possession. Andy had allowed him to capture him and keep him as his plaything. Like a yo-yo.

Andy had believed he deserved nothing more.

Now, someone novel and wonderful stood between them. Harden Krane. Their lovemaking had been hot, breathtaking, and Andy delighted in the images. But should they do it again?

He knew he couldn't stay forever at Burr Oak Farm. It would be impractical. Maybe Ken was right in forcing him to return to Chicago and whatever scraps of a life remained for him there.

He was about to switch off the light and roll over to sleep when the door creaked open. Framed by the door, Harden stood in his sweatpants and bare chest like a little boy wanting one last glass of water before bed.

"Feels weird to sleep alone all of the sudden," he said.

Andy, his heart rasping in his ears, sat upright. "I was thinking the same. But what if the kids need something in the middle of the night and they can't find you? Especially Olivia?"

"They ought to be okay."

Against his better judgment, Andy said, "Go back to your room. I'll follow you up in a minute."

He combed his hair and, for a second time, brushed his teeth, then slinked to Harden's room and carefully locked the door behind him. The minute he turned around, Harden flung off the bedcovers and revealed his nakedness. Andy slipped off his nylon shorts and, without vacillating, took Harden into his mouth.

Harden grunted and murmured words of passion. Andy stopped and gazed up at him.

"Careful not to make too much noise," he said.

"We have thick country walls," Harden said, guiding Andy's lips back onto him.

Andy resisted. "What if they see the light under the door and think you're awake?"

"We'll turn it off."

Andy held him from reaching for the table lamp. "I hate sex in the dark." He scurried into the bathroom, grabbed a towel from the holder, and stuffed it under the door like a draft snake. "There, that should work," he whispered, skulking back to bed.

Harden pulled Andy tight against him. Affection, comingled with lust and need, drew Andy deeper into Harden's arms. But also anger lured him. In a sense, he sought vengeance against Lillian. Andy saw in Harden a prize of sorts (he always credited his sister for making quite a catch while vacationing in Cancun), and Lillian had forsaken that trophy. Her and Harden's portrait sat on the bureau behind them. Andy wanted to rescue Harden from her stupid selfishness.

They used what remained of the suntan lotion, and soon moonlight slitting through the curtains' small opening reminded them they needed sleep. The upcoming day was Monday, and Harden wanted to get to work extra early to make up for the Monday he had missed last week.

They slept after showering and arose before the sun peeked above the cornfields. While Harden dressed, Andy tiptoed downstairs and started on breakfast. Ahead of the kids stampeding to the kitchen, Harden ate and rushed off for work. Andy left the dishes for Kamila and absconded to his basement bedroom, where he lay on the bed and stared toward the ceiling, his mind occupied with what he and Harden were embarking upon.

Kamila entered the house above, and the kids' voices seeped through the ceiling, mingling with the sound of the kitchen's small television set, which Olivia switched on automatically each morning. Much of life at Burr Oak Farm continued unchanged. He dressed and made the long ascent up the stairs to meet Kamila's harsh glare.

But when Kamila looked at him, her wide brown eyes suggested something else. Fear and sadness oozed from her pupils. The fine lines around her mouth appeared deeper and filled with shadows. The kids were out of sight, and she looked to be about to carry a basket of fruit to the porch. Andy knew the instant he saw her that she sensed drastic events had happened to the family during the weekend.

He feared she might read his mind and see what he'd been picturing almost without ceasing: him and Harden naked and thrashing about the house, powerless to overcome their need for each other. He understood news traveled fast in small towns, like the women during the corn roast had implied. But how on earth would anyone know about him and Harden? And so soon?

Kamila set the fruit basket on the side porch where the sun shone and returned to the kitchen at the same time Olivia raced downstairs, her hair, back in the familiar ponytails, bouncing above her shoulders.

"Where's Daddy? Kamila said he'd already gone before she got here."

"That's right. He left early for work," Andy said. "With me here he felt comfortable letting you get some sleep."

"Do you want to push me on the swing?"

"In a little while, sweetheart." Andy kept an eye on Kamila, who'd begun to finish clearing the kitchen table. "Why don't you go ahead? I'll be out in a bit. See if you can reach the tips of your sneakers to the line of the roof."

Kamila began wiping the cleared table with a damp rag, but she seemed to lack focus. Andy switched off the television, which had been on low, showcasing a parade of singing and dancing cartoon animals.

"Tell me, Andy," she said, addressing him by name for the first time, "what has happened here? I know something. I was afraid to ask the children."

Andy clenched his fists by his sides, worked the spit in his mouth. Kamila needed to be told something. Housekeepers deserved at least a partial truth. She almost fell backward, her dark eyes wide and her mouth puckered, when he recounted Lillian's appearance. In an instant, Kamila dropped into the nearest chair and raised the hand holding the rag to her chin.

"That *vještica*!" she said in a fierce whisper. "Why she do that to the children again? Why?"

Andy said, "I don't know, Kamila. The need to see them. But she only harms them, knowing she can't stay here in her condition."

Kamila let go of the rag and lowered her hand to her lap. Certain now that Kamila had detected only the ugliness of Lillian's visit, Andy sat across from her.

"Was she on the drugs?" she asked.

Andy nodded. "I've seen enough of it to know."

"And Mr. Krane? I did not see him this morning. Is he in bad way like last time?"

Andy shuffled his feet under the table. The somber gesture set off a sheath of quiet over the kitchen. No words were needed for him to describe the ugly details of that Friday evening.

"He's coping better," he said, staring at the tabletop. "He was bad off at first, but now... he's fine."

"That is good."

The sound of Olivia swinging screeched in a steady and sober rhythm. Andy lifted his gaze to Kamila's glum expression. She eyed him back.

"You are her brother," she stated through thin lips.

Unsure what she'd meant, Andy said, "Yes, I am her brother."

Kamila kept her vacant brown eyes on him. Andy supposed Kamila's dislike for Lillian and the troubles she'd caused the household might have incited her suspicions. That was why she had shadowed Andy and the kids around the countryside. She had worried that brother and sister shared similarities beyond physical appearance. Andy had wondered about that himself at times.

He wanted to turn from her steady gaze, but he chose to keep his head poised so that he might absorb the full brunt of her scrutiny.

Her eyes wide and glistening, she said, "Then as her brother, you suffer the loss like Mr. Krane and the children."

Andy's heart sank. He had not expected her to utter such a statement, for her to comprehend so completely. He'd assumed she associated him with Lillian and blamed him and the entire Wingal family for the bad things that had befallen the Kranes. Now he understood. If the stories of Kamila losing her family during the war were true, then she'd recognize his agony too.

From across the table, he expressed himself with a soft smile and nod. They got up and went about their day, no longer flashing each other grimaces.

CHAPTER
TWENTY-FOUR

HARDEN sat at his desk, compiling more excruciating reports for ethanol investors. Although the effort came smooth enough, considering, his mind kept returning to one matter: Andy. The more he pondered what had happened between them, the more an odd peace of mind lifted his spirits.

Shouldn't I be freaking out?

If Andy had asked him, point blank, his opinion about their weekend together, Harden might have told him: "Made me feel grounded to connect with someone I know and trust. Sometimes I'm so busy earning a wage and parenting, I forget I'm a man with needs."

And Harden certainly hadn't felt like the frumpy, supercilious dad while Andy had knelt before him and….

Andy had advised him not to think too hard on what they had done. Perhaps he was right. Their sexual venture had happened, and Harden had taken pleasure in it. (Was their weekend together any worse than when he'd brought home that woman from Dubuque and had had sex with her on the same bed he had with Andy?) Just let it be. Let it exist. Don't stew over it. *Whether you enjoyed it or not.*

He almost didn't care about altering the ethanol reports to look more favorable above what the research revealed. The office was a place to earn a buck, and hardworking men and women did what they were told while they dreamed of home.

The back of Harden's mind clamped on nothing more than Burr Oak Farm and his loved ones who waited for him there—including Andy.

Nothing in life proved better.

"Hi there." Arty popped his head into Harden's office. "Hadn't seen you come in. How are you this morning?"

Harden smiled, tried to act casual. "Got in kinda early," he said, wincing from the fresh cigarette stench wafting off Arty.

"You seem in good spirits."

"Really? I guess I am."

"I'm rather surprised. I mean, well… I heard that…." Arty gazed at the carpet. "I heard about Lilly's coming back."

Harden snorted. "That didn't take long to get around. I'm used to her games. It's over. She's gone again."

"Mason and Olivia are doing well?"

"Better. They stayed with Lance over the weekend, if you haven't already learned."

"Her brother is still with you at the farm? He didn't leave with Lilly?"

"Of course not. They have nothing to do with each other. Without Andrew, the situation might have been worse, for me and the kids."

"He's been there a while."

"I don't know how I've gotten along without him. He's a godsend."

Arty forced a smile. "Well, I'm glad everyone's fine. Just wanted to say hello and see that you're doing okay. Lots of work today. You know Mondays."

"Unfortunately, Mondays and I are far too familiar with each other. See you later, Arty. And thanks for the concern."

Arty's head vanished, and Harden snickered under his breath. He had every reason to praise Andy to Arty Ficklemeyer. He'd spoken the truth. Lillian's impromptu visit had brought him to his knees. Without Andy, Harden would most likely still be a broken man.

He settled, trying to concentrate on work. He didn't believe the nonsense about ethanol, yet work was work, and he squared the proposal on his desk, inhaled, and hunkered down.

The long morning progressed. By eleven o'clock, coffee lured him to the kitchenette. He made himself a single serve Vanilla Roast, savoring a moment away from his desk. When he lifted the steaming mug to his lips, Lucinda Jamison walked in, carrying her signature jasmine scent.

She wore a beige blouse, opened to her cleavage, and slick black slacks that fitted tight through her hips and thighs and fanned out over the pumps that clicked against the thin Berber carpet. Yes, he found her sexy. He'd even imagined them in bed a few times. But something felt lacking. What was it?

She's too easy. I prefer a challenge.

That was what had attracted him to a wild woman like Lillian. And ultimately, to her brother, who exhibited a profound understanding of life—and love. Had he really seen their weekend coming like Andy had said?

Don't think about it, Andy's voice chimed in his mind, or the enjoyment might fade.

"How was your weekend?" Lucinda asked cheerfully.

"Very nice, thanks," he said, suppressing the heat building under his collar. "And yours?"

"Not bad. I sat home, mostly. It's that time of year. Summer's winding down and I'm no longer sure what to do. Looking forward to cooler weather."

Lucinda seemed to have come to the kitchenette for no good purpose. She didn't make coffee or rummage through one of Marshall's two refrigerators searching for something to eat. Instead, she stood by the doorway, posing with a strange solicitous expression.

Arty or someone had probably tipped her off about Lilly's coming back, for no reason but to provoke her to swoon over him in his "time of need." Harden swallowed his resentment and tweaked a smile.

"I guess we're all getting antsy for the autumn and school to start up," he said.

"That's probably it."

"It's been a long, hot summer."

"Certainly has."

He was acting too haughty. Normally, he stood on a stage with his colleagues, gregarious and prone to laugh, at times even with Lucinda. They might assume he was fibbing about his ex-wife's visit not bothering him. He wasn't, of course. If they had seen him Friday night or Saturday during the day, they would have been correct. At that time, he'd been certain he'd suffered a catastrophic setback, like the last times Lillian had showed up unannounced. But after Saturday night.... Everything seemed different now.

He turned from Lucinda and allowed his gaze to wander out the small window. The cornfield across the road, bright and green, merged into a blurry radiance, a watercolor painted by an invisible yet grand hand, and solely for Harden's enjoyment.

Lucinda shifted behind him. He swung back, smiled at her.

"Sorry, Lucinda. Guess I'm daydreaming." He sipped his coffee, held the mug with both hands before his chest. "Mondays are like that."

"I can understand, Harden," Lucinda said, her voice soft.

Harden nodded, his lips tight. "I better get back to my desk. Big pile of work waiting for me."

"Sure, Harden."

He eased passed her, and he could sense her eyes following him until he turned the corner for his office.

A few paces from his door, he hesitated. Save for a crack, the door was closed. When he'd gone to the kitchenette, he remembered having left it wide open. He took a full sip of coffee and stepped inside.

Christ!

Charlie Marshall, his boss, sat in the armchair across from his desk. Harden recognized the meaning of his hunched shoulders. Though eleven years in age separated them, they were friends more than employee and employer. Still, once or twice, Charlie had come down hard on Harden, as any boss might. He'd even terminated a few long-term employees, which Harden suspected Charlie wouldn't have done unless they had it coming.

Charlie dropped the report he was reading on Harden's desk and looked up at him. "Good morning, Harden."

"Hi there, Charlie." Harden motioned for him to stay seated and situated himself behind his desk. "What can I do for you this morning?"

Dumb question. He knew why Charlie was paying a visit. The ethanol issue was coming to a boil. Harden had expected it for some time. With a naïve government and the slew of zealous investment and special interest groups, Charlie had pushed him harder and harder to garner funding for corn distillation.

"Harden, I've been looking over these reports of yours." Charlie rotated the paperwork so that Harden could read it. "I worry that, with the way you're presenting this data, you couldn't give away a free bottled water to a man suffering dehydration. You're not trying hard enough."

Harden swallowed a lump. "These are only the rough drafts, Charlie. I hope to flesh it out."

Charlie stretched his neck to stress his stature. Standing six five, with the girth to match, Charlie knew how to use his mass for his own purpose, even when seated. In college, he'd been the linebacker for the Iowa State Cyclones. An all-American. That was in 1985. Now he was a middle-aged man with a business, and, as one of the Maquoketa River Valley's largest private employers, he lived with a set of his own bills and headaches.

"It's for the good of our community here in northeastern Iowa that we get these grants," he said. "Haven't we emphasized the importance?"

Harden nodded. "We have, Charlie. I respect your—"

Charlie waved him silent. "I know how you feel about ethanol, Harden. You have a right to your views. But I have a business to run. We live in the corn belt. More corn is produced in Iowa than anywhere on earth. Corn is king here. We can't change the eating habits of Americans and force them to eat more meat, but what corn farmers don't sell as feed they can distill into ethanol. It's our future. You're our chief agronomist. I expect more from you than this."

"I'll work extra hard on it, Charlie," Harden said, acquiescing to his boss's demands. "Trust me on that. I will give you what you want. I just need a few more days to tie everything together."

"It's vital enough that Vivian and I came around to your house Sunday morning on the way home from church so that I might speak with you. Vivian wanted to give you a pie she baked, anyway. It was before we heard about Lillian." He lowered his eyes. "I'm sorry about that."

Harden willed the blood from pumping into his neck and face. If only his office had a larger window, one that overlooked an expansive cornfield rather than the modest bungalows that abutted the outskirts of Duncan. Scenery to take his mind off his present discomfort.

"I knocked and no one answered," Charlie went on when Harden sat mute. "I saw your Jeep and figured you were still home and hadn't left for church. We saw that strange van of your brother-in-law's too. Anyway, I just wanted you to know how imperative this is and that I've been worried out of my mind about your dawdling."

Breath expired from Harden, and his heart quickened. "I understand, Charlie. And I'm sorry I didn't hear your knocking. I was most likely showering." *With my former brother-in-law!* "The kids were with Lance over the weekend."

"I assumed something like that." Charlie checked his wristwatch and stood. "I have a teleconference in ten minutes with some engineers in Georgia. Harden, I'd like to see a thorough report by midweek, one that showcases your training and education. Don't disappoint me." He stopped before stepping into the hallway and snapped his fingers. "One more thing. Vivian and I want to remind you to come for our annual Labor Day barbeque Monday."

Harden said he wouldn't miss it, and Charlie added that he could bring his brother-in-law if he was still around. Harden promised he would. Charlie walked away wearing a hearty smile. He always departed on good terms. That was Charlie's style. And his invitation was sincere too. Harden never knew him to offer for show. A man of his word. That also unnerved Harden.

He thought again about farming. If only he had someone special to share his life with, he could dump his work and live his dreams.

Meanwhile, he owed more to himself, his company, and Mason and Olivia than fanciful ambitions. He was the top dog in Marshall's science and technology department. Charlie had awarded him the promotion last year, in addition to hefty responsibilities.

Yet, despite his boss's reprimanding, his mood again perked up. The irritation of writing glowing reports on ethanol (for potential buyers from such diverse places as California and Brazil) suddenly appeared trivial.

He worked through lunch, and by six he had a partially written research proposal he was sure would meet Charlie's requirements. He tucked the report inside his desk drawer and hurried for his Jeep. But there was one stop he wanted to make along the way.

He gripped the steering wheel and shook his head. *Why aren't I feeling weirder about this?*

Good smells and pleasant chatter greeted Harden when he stepped inside the house thirty minutes later. But then it hit him again, almost the moment he'd crossed the threshold. He glanced at the plastic bag that contained his purchases and almost laughed aloud.

After eating, he and Andy played several rounds of Pictionary with the kids. Then they tucked them into bed and returned downstairs to hand wash the larger pots and pans from Kamila's buffet-style dinner.

"You got home a little later today," Andy said, drying once Harden washed.

"I had a big report that needed finishing, and then I stopped off at the store."

"I thought maybe you were avoiding coming home."

Harden dunked a pot in and out of the water until the soap rinsed clear and set it in the drying rack for Andy. "Complete opposite."

He was glad Andy didn't respond and continued to dry. He wasn't in the mood to analyze their weekend together while the kids were at home. Wasn't Andy the one who'd suggested they not discuss it? Instead, Harden asked him, "Things go okay between you and Kamila today?"

"She's not so bad once you break down her iron curtain."

"I figure most Europeans are like that," Harden said. "She can be a good friend once she gets to know and understand you."

Harden washed the last pot and unplugged the sink. The gurgle of water filled Harden's ears until Andy said, "What do you think we should do about tonight?"

Drying his hands, Harden replied, "You mean about the sleeping arrangements? I'm unsure. At work, everything seemed simple. I couldn't wait to get home. I still feel that way, but I'm unsure."

"You worry about the kids?"

Harden shrugged. "I don't know. Maybe we should move, change our address."

"That's a bit extreme."

"I'm thinking more about Lilly and her threat to come back." Yet Harden understood, in Iowa, her gaining custody of the kids was unlikely. Courts wouldn't side with a drug addict over…. He didn't dare think it. A same-sex couple? Or were they nothing more than two old friends who shared a few intimate moments?

"Lilly's gone and won't be back for some time," Andy said. "You said she last turned up at Christmas. That was more than eight months ago. Maybe she won't bother you and the kids for another year. Try not to think about her."

Harden sighed. Puzzled, he looked into the backyard. The shadowy swing set stood empty under the sapphire sky, the two seats barely moving in the mild breeze.

Fatigue overwhelmed his muscles and bones. "I think I'll turn in early tonight," he said, dropping the towel and moving for the stairs, knowing full well Andy's eyes burned into his back.

He stopped with his hand curled over the newel post and eyed Andy, still standing at the sink. Andy returned his smile. He laid aside the damp dish towel, stored the last pot, and together they climbed the stairs to Harden's bedroom.

Locked behind the door, Harden revealed his main purchase. Like a mischievous child, he drew it out from the plastic bag and dangled it before Andy's eyes.

Andy took the tube of KY from him and snickered. "Weren't you embarrassed?"

"That's why I bought a handful of other things I didn't need for camouflage." He pulled them out, one by one. "A tube of toothpaste, deodorant, contact lens cleaner, although I don't wear them, and a bag of gorp. If you get hungry, help yourself."

Andy smacked the tube of KY on his palm. "Guess we'll be working up another appetite tonight."

Harden did what he'd been yearning for the entire day. He wrapped his arms around Andy and held him tight to his chest. They slowly undressed each other while glazing their lips with lazy, wet kisses. They tumbled to the bed, and Harden explored more of Andy's body, fixating on his firm butt muscles. He was fascinated by the smooth mounds. He massaged each side, his fingers meandering around the marble-like curves and crevices.

Needing more of him, he pulled Andy from the bed, stood him up, palms flat against the wall that faced the cornfield, away from the hallway so Mason and Olivia would not hear, and knelt behind him. With soft lips, Harden kissed his butt cheeks and rubbed his face against the tight skin. He had never dreamed, never fantasized, about doing what he longed to do now—even to a woman. But he needed to. Desired nothing else.

As if venturing into a forbidden garden, Harden spread Andy. He stared, transfixed that the first word to come to his mind might be "beautiful." Still more redolent and cleaner than he'd guessed for a man. Powerless over what came next, he teased Andy with his tongue. Andy flinched forward. Harden pulled him back and licked him again. Andy began to thrust back farther, enticing Harden to take more. Harden dared to drive his tongue deeper.

He ravaged the smooth, perfect orifice that burned his prodding tongue. Andy clawed at the wall, released low moans. Harden nibbled more fiercely. Andy's fidgets intensified, and he tapped his forehead against the wall. So virile, yet so vulnerable. And there was something magnificent about it. Such utter intimacy.

Harden got to his feet, leaving a wet trace along Andy's back, and pressed hard against him. He teased him with the head of his sex, delighting in the wetness he'd left behind inside Andy and how Andy squirmed and begged for more. Harden lubricated himself with a healthy glob of the newly purchased KY and penetrated him.

Each thrust, each subdued groan convinced Harden he harbored no regrets about having sex with his former brother-in-law. He wanted Andy to submit to him. To yield control to him. He pushed and drove, their bodies quivering. Harden grabbed Andy's shoulders, clutched his waist, and forced his entire body as close to him as he could. Drove into the very mouthwatering mound that he had worshipped with his tongue.

Andy reached around for Harden's glutes, and the sensation of hot hands on him sent thrills through his body. He nearly laughed into Andy's ears, never letting up on his pounding.

He stopped, breathed, moved Andy to the bed—the exact spot where Andy had first come to him Saturday night—and positioned him faceup with his legs spread. Holding Andy steady by his solid calves, he entered him. Toes digging into the carpet, he relished the entire warm tightness of him. He tossed his head back, thrusting back and forth, and fell closer onto him and nibbled at Andy's chin. In minutes, Andy again came without stroking himself, an amazing sight that stirred Harden with a sense of his own masculinity, perhaps beyond what he'd ever felt with a woman, and drove him to swell Andy with powerful thrusts. Drunk with ecstasy, his knees buckled and he lay down upon him.

They breathed heavily. Soon they rose and showered. Back in bed, Harden's mind roiled. He had never experienced such draining, yet invigorating, lovemaking. He eyed the towel stuffed under the door. It had already become a habit for Andy to place it there. How wrong was it to go about the charade, covering what they were doing?

Olivia's juvenile five-act play had proved true. She'd written innocently that her father and uncle shared a bed. And here they were, side by side under the bedcovers. Writers possessed an uncanny ability to foresee the future, Harden mused. Or maybe children could see what adults were too preoccupied to notice.

Odd tapping on the roof startled Andy.

"What's that?" he whispered, glancing toward the ceiling.

"Acorns falling off the oak trees onto the roof. The squirrels will clean it up. That time of year again, thank goodness. School starts next week."

"They're excited about it," Andy said, relaxing under the covers. "I sure didn't look forward to the end of summer when I was a kid."

"I hate to admit," Harden said, "since being a single parent, I can't wait for the start of the school year. So much is lifted off my shoulders."

"They're kids for only a few years. Enjoy them while you can."

"Can't believe how fast they grow," Harden said. "Time flies the older you get, that's for sure."

"Just think, in the same amount of time Mason and Olivia reached their current ages, Olivia will be eighteen, about to start college, and Mason will be twenty-two and already graduated."

Harden clutched the bedcovers and pulled them down to his gut. "Christ, did you have to put it like that? I feel old as it is, and I'm only thirty-seven."

"You'll still be young by then. Forty-eight isn't old. They say the forties are the new twenties."

"Not exactly a tribute to our generation."

"Maybe it's about our appearance and not emotional development."

Harden traced his thumb over Andy's dimpled chin. "I'm sure you'll look pretty good in ten years."

Andy held Harden's hand steady and brought it to his chest. "I didn't come to Iowa for this, you know," he uttered. "I never intended to seduce you and cause you and the kids more heartache than you've already suffered."

He absorbed Andy's dark-blue eyes. "You haven't caused us any suffering," he said. "It's been wonderful with you here. I'm glad how things have turned out."

In an odd way, the moment he'd first read Andy's text message asking to visit, Harden had wondered if something might happen between him and his gay ex-brother-in-law. He couldn't really pinpoint what. Love? Affection? Sex? Domestic tranquility? But he'd sensed it.

Yes, Andy had spoken the truth when he'd said they both had foreseen their weekend. Maybe from the start he'd sent Andy signals. The same ones that Olivia had detected. Maybe he, and not Andy, had ignited their fervor Saturday night. Had Harden, in some way, gone to his bedroom that night, wanting Andy to follow?

He shushed Andy from saying more, fingers brushing his lips. "You've done nothing wrong. You have no reason to blame yourself for anything. Now stop worrying."

Andy lowered himself further under the covers and stared at the ceiling, mute and still. Harden switched off the light, and at some point during the night they fell asleep. Before dawn, Harden awoke and, through the half-open curtain, watched the rich twilight spread blue across the western sky.

He peered at Andy, barely noticing the portrait of Lilly and Harden that sat in shadows on the bureau. The subdued light cast a serene and stunning glow over Andy. Innocent looking, yet his breathing lifted the bedcovers with potency.

Inch by inch, he unrolled the bedcovers, exposing Andy's partial arousal. Andy opened his eyes, smiled through the emerging dawn. Harden sensed Andy surrender to his will when he laid a gentle hand on his smooth chest, warm to the touch.

He wanted to bury their fears, to wield a power not only over Andy, but the both of them. "You belong to me," he whispered. "We've crossed a threshold. I'll take you whenever I want."

Andy grew fully engorged, and Harden detected a slight ripple of muscles under his taut flesh. Lubed with KY, Harden slowly climbed on top of Andy and wedged his legs apart. He marked his words by again entering him, ensuring Andy did not experience pain by gauging his expression, yet showing no hesitation.

They made their first quiet, gentle love. Slow, decisive. Sandwiched together. He filled Andy, and afterward they catnapped, sticky and breathing lightly, until the pink dawn brushed the tops of the corn.

"I better hop in the shower before the kids wake up," he whispered to Andy.

He removed Andy's arm from his chest and got to his feet. Just then, he heard Olivia's footsteps in the hallway. Seconds later, the toilet flushed. Next came the creak of the middle step. She was heading downstairs.

Andy sat against the headboard, pulled his knees to his chin, and wrapped his arms around his legs. Harden slipped on his underwear and sweatpants, watching Andy yank the light hairs on his toe knuckles.

The first habit that annoyed him.

He wanted to chuckle but pursed his lips and said under his breath, "I'll go see about Olivia first. Wait a couple of minutes before coming down. You can say you had woken up early and had gone upstairs to look for something. They're kids. They won't require details unless it's about something you don't know anything about. See you in a few."

He toed aside the draft-snake towel, eased open the door, and, once safely reaching the stairwell, skulked downstairs, hoping Mason wouldn't stir from sleep until Andy made his way down.

CHAPTER
TWENTY-FIVE

THE week passed much the same. Each night after tucking in the kids, there was the longing, the loving, followed by the sneaking downstairs. The dizzying reality of Harden and Andy's newfangled bond augmented Andy's confusion. In painful ways, Harden and Andy came from different worlds. Other than the children, they had little in common. They didn't even share the same hopes for the future. Andy wanted to cash in on the rot—like vultures on a carcass—while Harden, seeking a higher existence, kicked and screamed against it.

School started the following Monday. Like he had all week, Harden hurried off for work. Andy walked the kids, with their colorful backpacks and Olivia clutching her brand new Bubble Guppies lunchbox, to the bottom of the driveway to await the school busses. Mason's arrived first, and he wished him good luck. A few minutes later, Olivia's pulled up. Andy scooted her up the steps and, swallowing a sudden lump in his throat, waved to her as she peered out the window. He stood, watching the iconic yellow bus grow smaller.

For most of the morning, Andy slumped around the house. It was his first full day alone at Burr Oak Farm. Now that the school term had started, Kamila worked from three until whenever Harden returned from work, and every other Saturday. Andy wished she was there that day, hating moping around an empty house. Dick Carelli's working the field came as a welcome distraction. Seated high atop his tractor in the distance,

Dick was the solitary human he saw or heard, except for what flashed across the television screen.

He finished his tepid coffee and checked his e-mail at the family computer. (The past few weeks, he'd failed to get an Internet connection for his laptop and had finally stowed it away in frustration.) Thirty people interested in his South Side tours had sent queries since his coming to Iowa, in addition to the one or two phone calls he still received each day. He hated thinking about losing money. He had more in his savings account than ever before in his entire life, but it wouldn't last forever.

Ken was pestering him more and more also.

One of his rare e-mails read in part: "What the hell are you doing out there? You should've gotten back days ago." Without responding, Andy signed off the computer.

He avoided answering Ken's texts and uncharacteristic calls. What might he tell him? Even his friend Skeet had telephoned Andy Saturday afternoon, baffled about what was going on.

"Ken keeps texting me," Skeet had said, with Chicago's energetic street traffic buzzing in the background. "He asks about you and where you are. He wanted to know if I knew when you were coming back. The first and second times I told him I didn't. The third time I ignored his text. So what's up? Have you two broken up? Are you staying in Idaho?"

"Iowa, and I'm unsure." Andy had told him he'd call Ken to straighten everything out, but he had yet to bother.

He puttered about the house, thinking, debating.

Much of Kamila's housework was completed by the time she showed at three. Bored out of his wits, Andy had washed two loads of sheets and towels, made the beds, and prepped dinner. He even had Olivia's school lunch ready for the next day.

Only after the kids returned from school, near four o'clock, did the house grow animated. They tripped over each other's talk about their first day. Mason loved middle school, where he had different classes for different subjects. And Olivia believed her second-grade class might be the best in the school's entire history. Andy tossed them as many questions as they could juggle. Later, he helped them with their first homework assignments while Kamila sorted fresh fruits and vegetables and set them on the porch to ripen in the afternoon sun.

Andy checked himself from throwing his arms around Harden when he returned home a tad past six. He stepped aside and allowed Olivia room instead.

They continued to share a bed. Their lovemaking had become a comfortable passion. Andy grew woozy realizing he touched or ogled the private orifices and body parts of a man who'd once been married to his sister. The same man who had fathered his nephew and niece. And, with the exception of those first two times, they made love stone cold sober.

Tuesday, Andy again walked the kids to where the driveway met the road. With the odd lonesomeness clogging his throat, he waved good-bye to the last bus and lumbered back up the long driveway. He found himself waiting for Kamila. The clocks ticked.

Was that how Lillian had felt before the Chicago drug dealers had enticed her?

On Wednesday, he met Harden for lunch, a wonderful midweek reprieve. After a short forty-five minutes, Harden saw Andy to his van. Melancholy shadowed him.

That night while Harden slept soundly, Andy crept downstairs to his old basement bedroom before the moon rose. Though he loathed his time alone during the day, he suddenly craved the solitude of night, to think.

Alone in the dark basement, with the hopper windows showcasing a swatch of white stars, the bedroom's walls opened to him. He lay awake most of the night, wondering....

Thursday morning, Harden refused eye contact with Andy and seemed more impatient with the kids. "Olivia, watch you don't put your sleeve in your cereal. You have no time to change into a new shirt. And what did I tell you about snatching Daddy's pen from his briefcase? Mason, keep your schoolbooks off the stairs. Someone might get hurt."

After walking the kids to the bus stop, Andy returned to the kitchen and watched Harden rinse the dishes and stack the dishwasher. He looked handsome in his black slacks and loosened baby-blue tie, the sleeves of his white Oxford rolled to expose hunky forearms.

Andy understood the silence between them. They had ascended to a new level of communication, as though the currents carried signals without the need for words. Andy stepped behind Harden and placed his hands on his shoulders.

Harden paused. He turned and looked into Andy's eyes, the first time that morning. The corners of his mouth struggled into a smile, and he shook his head, flushing.

"I'm sorry," he said. "I'm acting like one of the kids. When I saw you hadn't slept in the bed this morning, well... I...."

Andy fell into Harden and wrapped his arms around his waist. Harden squeezed back. As if they were slow dancing, Harden rotated them so that Andy's lower back pushed against the sink. Nothing existed but the breath exchanged between them and the pulsating of blood through their veins.

Their foreheads pressed against each other, and Andy savored the drive of bone against bone, the melding heat of something stronger than the both of them.

They kissed more, long and full.

Reflections from many years ago wafted through Andy's mind. Harden had first kissed him by the sink in Streamwood. It seemed impossible, surreal, that life had conveyed them to their present juncture.

Andy opened his eyes and looked over Harden's shoulder. A sudden and horrible dread smothered him. Standing on the porch, clutching a basket of fruits and vegetables, Kamila peered at them through the kitchen window with her dark eyes.

Andy shoved Harden back.

"What is it?" Harden asked, gripping his arms.

"Kamila, out on the porch. She just saw us kissing."

Harden spun around. Only dust from the wake of Kamila's Toyota remained.

"Are you sure it was her?"

Andy nodded, moisture sapped from his mouth. "Positive. The look on her face. She must be freaking out. I'm freaking out."

To Andy's surprise, Harden pulled him into his chest for another embrace. His lips brushed Andy's cheek. "Don't worry. It'll be okay."

Andy nudged Harden off enough that they could see into each other's eyes. "Aren't you worried?"

"Why should I be?"

"She'll tell the entire county. You know how things are around here."

"Not with Kamila." Harden softened his voice. "The Bosnians are as closemouthed as a people can get. She probably won't even tell her sister and brother-in-law. Besides, she's been a loyal employee."

Harden went off to work, reassuring Andy that their secret was safe between them. Andy remained housebound, expecting Kamila to barge in and assault him in a jealous woman's rage.

Suddenly, life in Iowa seemed more menacing than what he'd left behind in Chicago.

Thank goodness, the day passed without incident. When the kids raced inside the house, one behind the other, they asked about Kamila. Andy told them she'd been taken ill. Probably not far from the truth. Olivia said she wanted to draw her a "get well" card, and Andy couldn't help but chuckle.

Later that night in the bedroom, after they'd made sure the kids were asleep, Andy found Harden's sexual advances unsettling. He seemed little concerned about Kamila on the prowl, holding as a potential weapon the knowledge of his and Harden's relationship.

"I told you not to worry," he said, fumbling with Andy's shoes and socks, next yanking off his jeans. Andy relented, though his mind traveled far from Burr Oak Farm, over the miles of cornfields, worried how he might have brought shame to Harden and the kids, like his sister had.

But maybe Kamila realized that she had seen nothing unusual. European men were thought to be more affectionate, and she might be used to seeing men kiss, like Harden and Andy had by the sink.

Andy recalled her expression. The wide eyes, the tensed jaw muscles, the white knuckles from her clutching the basket handle to her chest. And her rushing off in her car, leaving a plume of dust.

Kamila had understood perfectly what he and Harden were doing.

And there was Harden's sister-in-law, Holly. She'd gathered the implications of the two empty cabernet bottles and the half-burned taper candles too, Andy was certain.

Harden succeeded in stripping Andy naked. Andy, chuckling, pushed him off. But soon he surrendered to Harden's tongue. He roamed along Andy's body, from his neck to his toes. Harden stopped midway working upward again, and for the first time took Andy into his mouth. Harden coughed, looked up at him, and smiled.

"Sorry. I've never done that before. Guess I'm no good."

"Feels awesome," Andy whispered, prodding Harden's mouth back onto him.

And soon, Andy forgot about Kamila Becic and Holly Krane, and their pestering eyes.

The next afternoon, Kamila again failed to show. Andy sent Harden an atypical text message, asking if he'd heard from her. He replied he had not, and that he would telephone her when his meeting adjourned. Andy paced the kitchen, unable to shake the worry that unpleasantness lurked ahead.

The kids arrived home from school within fifteen minutes of each other, and their questions about Kamila's whereabouts ebbed. "Uncle Andy, I got three gold stars on my story, the highest you can get." Olivia waved her short story in Andy's face. He read her tale about the little bunny that found a way to trick an aggravating fox by standing on a boulder and pretending to be an elephant. Andy thought it was clever and well written.

"You guys have lots of homework?" he asked.

"I don't," Olivia said, posting her story on the refrigerator at Andy's suggestion.

"That's because you're a dumbhead second grader. I'm in middle school. I get homework even for weekends."

"Make sure you do what you can before dinner so we can have a fun evening."

Mason was upstairs in his room, working hard on his schoolwork, while downstairs Olivia and Andy made hamburgers and home fries. Harden returned home from work early, close to five, and after eating and the kids' baths, the family gathered around the living room television with the lights dimmed and an oversized bowl of popcorn on the coffee table. Dressed snug in pajamas, the kids quivered and giggled in anticipation of the fun-filled evening, a special treat after their first week of school. Harden, sexy in his ratty sweatpants and T-shirt, readied the computer, which was cabled to the television. Andy sat with Olivia and Mason on the sofa, their warm cotton pajamas against his bare arms comforting and soft.

Olivia reached for the popcorn and spilled some onto the carpet.

"Watch that you don't make any messes," Harden told her in a lighthearted manner.

"Turn off the foyer light," Mason demanded. "It's making it too bright in here."

Olivia, leaving behind a small popcorn trail, jumped up and turned off the light. A blue-yellow flush permeated the room. "There's a full moon out tonight," Olivia declared, peering outside, where the grumbling of an engine came from the cornfield. "And Mr. Carelli's working."

"It's harvest season," Harden said, opening his arms to his daughter, who let the curtain dangle back into place and fell against him on the sofa. "He'll be out there night and day the next few weeks."

Harden pressed "play" on the remote, and everyone hushed. Andy had remembered to shut down his cell phone, which had been dinging with texts, mostly from Ken. He'd left them unread and ignored.

Their movie choice captured the somber aura that had nagged Andy throughout the week. A listless computer-animated ogre, frustrated with domestic life, fought a sinister world inhabited with folklore goblins who sought to cajole and lie for power, and a demanding damsel that reminded Andy of Lucinda Jamison.

Harden pointed out that one of the creatures had hair like Mason's and rubbed his head. Mason's dry protests brought about more tickles and giggles.

"Stop, Dad. I don't look like that."

"Hey, no throwing popcorn."

"Daddy, your breath smells like stinky coffee."

"Sorry, sweetheart."

Harden even gave Andy's butt a playful tap when Andy got up to use the bathroom. He returned and hunkered down, trapped in a tangle of legs and arms. Harden hoisted Olivia onto the spot closer to Mason, and he edged next to Andy, pressing against him.

Eventually, Harden draped his arm around Andy's shoulders, and Olivia shivered and giggled at the affection flanking her. Growing serious, she hushed everyone, as if they had been the ones to disrupt the quiet. Harden placed his index finger over his lips to mimic Olivia's call for silence, and winked at Andy.

Light pulsating from the television captured everyone in a misty stupor. Thousands of words were too inadequate to convey the bittersweet emotions flowing through Andy's soul. Midway through the film, a sleepy stillness settled over the living room. Before long, both Mason and Olivia lay on their sides, snoozing. While the end credits scanned the screen, Harden and Andy roused them awake and helped them to their beds.

Back downstairs, Harden and Andy tidied up before sleep. Harden stored the remaining popcorn, and Andy rinsed the empty glasses. In the midst of cleaning, Harden opened his arms, and Andy became absorbed by him. The beat of their hearts, mere inches from each other, came slow and rhythmic.

They broke off, and Andy made sure they'd cleared everything from the living room. He was carrying a half-empty glass of milk into the kitchen when someone banged on the front door. Andy guessed Dick

Carelli wanted to let them know he was working the field, although they'd already known by then he'd been spending many nights at a stretch plowing. But would Dick pound with such violence?

Harden hastened into the foyer. "Who the hell is that?"

Another round of loud banging.

"Is it Mr. Carelli?"

"I doubt it. I'll check."

Andy wanted to prevent Harden from moving closer. Something sinister came from those loud raps.

Harden hesitated before reaching the door. "It's Lilly," he whispered fiercely. "It must be her. She's come back, just like I worried."

Andy understood Lillian. The drugs had metamorphosed her into another creature. Crystal methamphetamine had injected her with rage and resentment toward the entire world, worse than what Andy had ever experienced. Yet the drugs had also rendered her into a lethargic mess who could barely move without someone carting her around.

"Maybe it's Kamila," he said.

"Can't be her." Harden shook his head. "Can't be."

Harden inched closer to the door. His shoulders rose near to his ears, and he held his arms away from his sides. He gestured for Andy to stay back. Slowly, he pulled aside the lace curtain hanging from the narrow door window that overlooked the porch and peeked outside.

CHAPTER
TWENTY-SIX

HARDEN peered out the window, but he saw only a tall, shadowy shape. The storm door was propped open by the stranger's back, and his fists were poised for additional banging.

Still rooted to the foyer and holding the glass of milk, Andy whispered, "Who is it?"

"Hard to tell with the porch light off."

"Turn it on."

"Best to keep it off," Harden said. "Stand back now." He leaned closer to the door. After a lengthy drawing in of breath, he said in his tough-guy voice, "Who's there?"

"I'm here to see Andrew Wingal. It's urgent. I'm a police officer."

Harden and Andy swapped looks. Andy's eyes grew wide, and his face went whiter than the glass of milk trembling in his hand. He set down the glass on the foyer console and brought his hands to his chin. Slow recognition crept over his shaky expression.

Harden sucked in more breath. "What do you want with him?" he shouted into the door.

"I want to see him. I see his van out here. I know he's in there. Let me talk to him."

His gravelly, dominating tone sent chills along Harden's arms and neck. He looked back to Andy. He still stood speechless, quaking.

Rubbing his eyes, Mason drifted downstairs. "What's all the racket down here?"

Andy gestured for Mason. Sleepy eyed, he obeyed. Andy kept his hands firm on his shoulders. Harden suspected he wanted to steady himself as much as hold Mason from getting in harm's way.

He scooted Mason toward the kitchen and moved to Harden's side. "It's okay, Harden. Let me speak with him."

"Who is he?"

"My… some guy I know from Chicago."

"What's he doing here? Are you in trouble?"

"Nothing like that. He's a friend who happens to be a cop. I'll talk to him real quick and send him on his way."

"He sounds hotheaded."

"He's all mouth. Go into the kitchen with Mason. Just let me speak with him a minute. It'll be okay. Trust me, please."

Mason stood, dwarfed by the kitchen's doorway. "Dad, what's going on?"

Andy nodded toward the kitchen. "Go on, Harden."

Confused and somewhat resentful, Harden ushered Mason farther into the kitchen. He instructed him to stand silent and Harden peered around the doorframe.

Andy was reaching for the chain. Nerves mixed with dread brought Harden's fists to his chest. The man on the other side knocked louder, rattling the lace curtains.

"Hold on, Ken," Andy said with a grunt. "Give me a minute, why don't you."

Slowly, Andy inserted the chain. He eased open the door and peered through the narrow gap. Harden could not see the man's face, for the door opened the other way, but Andy's expression revealed uncertainty and fear. The man hardly came for a kindly call.

"What are you doing here?" Andy whispered.

"Why haven't you answered my messages?"

"I turned off my phone. We were watching a movie."

"How quaint. Now will you open the door?"

"It's late, Ken."

All of a sudden, the door opened as far as the chain lock would allow. Andy pushed back. Harden moved to intervene.

"I'm coming out, Ken. Just wait. Geez! You'll break the door down."

Trusting Andy's instincts, Harden stayed back. But he remained close, ready. But ready for what? His mind began to roil with apprehension.

Andy reclosed the door, slid the chain out, and opened the door a sufficient width to squeeze through. For a moment, Harden wondered if he'd ever see Andy again.

Harden motioned for Mason, still standing like a scarecrow, to stay put in the kitchen. He moved to the door, which remained ajar. He nudged it open a few more inches to hear the voices outside.

"What on earth are you doing here, Ken?" Andy was saying.

"You've ignored all my calls, texts, and e-mails. What other choice did I have?"

There was a pause. Curious, Harden opened the door wider. Andy and his friend had moved to the driveway, where the full moon spotlighted a fiery red-faced man with muscles that stretched his short-sleeved collared shirt to the point Harden imagined it might rip into ribbons if he exhaled too much. The storm door muted their voices. Harden cracked it open to listen.

"Just because I haven't called you back," Andy said, looking ludicrous standing in his stocking feet, "you race out to Iowa like an escaped mental patient?"

The man Andy referred to as Ken stepped closer to him, fists tight by his sides. His red hair stood out in a blaze, as if he'd been running his fingers through it in a fit of agitation.

"Listen, Andy, I made a decision, and you're coming back to Chicago with me. Enough of this nonsense playing Farmer Joe."

In a gritty voice, Andy replied, "You're the one who told me to come here. You insisted I hightail it, remember?"

"That was a month ago, for chrissakes. Things have settled down in Chicago. Time you got home."

"And do what? The whole city, including you, wants to keep me from my South Side tours. You want to move in together, huh? You ready for that? We can legally marry in Iowa. Let's say you and me apply for a marriage license tonight. Right this minute."

"Married? What are you talking about? I just want you back in Chicago."

"What do you want with me there? So you can play with me, like some toy? You order me around like you own me, Ken. But you don't. You never have."

Ken gazed toward the orange moon, big and round, revealing his bulbous Adam's apple. With more conviction contorting his face, he turned back to Andy. "I'll be nice and give you two minutes to get your things. You can follow me in your van. We'll stop at a motel. You're coming with me tonight, no other option."

"I'm not going with you, Ken."

"That's how you feel, then?"

"I've made myself clear."

"Then screw your belongings."

Andy raised his forearms to block Ken's grabbing him. "Get off me, Ken. Stop acting like a bully. I've had enough. Now get out of here. Get in your car and go. Get off me."

Ken clamped Andy's arm and yanked. "I'm not leaving here alone."

Andy dug his heels into the gravel to keep Ken from pulling him to his car. "Let go of me, Ken. Let go of me."

Harden scurried for the kitchen. "Quick, Mason. Run to my bedroom closet and fetch my rifle and the bullets. Handle it the way I taught you."

"But...."

"Keep quiet, and don't wake your sister. Do as I say."

Puzzlement shimmering in his blue eyes, Mason hurried out of the kitchen and up the stairs. Squaring his shoulders, Harden marched back to the front door.

Andy was still struggling with the redheaded giant. "I'm not going with you, Ken. That's that. Now let go of me." Ken tugged harder, forcing Andy to wince. "Stop being so damn stubborn," Andy said.

"You better wise up, Andy."

"You're the nut, coming all the way out here. Now get off me."

Mason scurried downstairs and handed Harden the rifle and box of bullets. Harden whispered for Mason to return upstairs and stay in his room. With one eye on Andy and Ken, Harden loaded the Winchester with three bullets, set the box with the remaining two bullets aside, and creaked open the storm door with his foot.

Both men turned when Harden stepped onto the porch. The foyer light cast his shadow across the length of the stoop and near to where Andy and Ken struggled in the driveway. Rifle poised chest high, Harden stood, staring and waiting.

Ken's red eyebrows twisted with an angry fire. He studied Harden like a fox. All at once, he turned his attention back to Andy as if Harden had never ventured outside.

"It's time to come back to Chicago, Andy. Stop being difficult."

"Leave him alone." Harden gripped the rifle tighter. "He wants to stay."

Ken stopped and glared at him. "Who's this bozo?"

"That's Harden. He's my… my former brother-in-law. Harden, go back inside. I'll take care of this."

"Not until he leaves my property."

"I'll be happy to leave your property, as soon as Andy gets in the car."

"You put him in your car against his will and I'll blow your tires out."

"Nice." Ken sniggered. "A country bumpkin with his shotgun. Typical."

"It's a rifle," Harden stated. "I'd think that a cop would know the difference."

"You got the light to your back," Ken said, his face puckering. "Hard to see in shadows."

"No matter. Now leave Andy alone," Harden stressed. "Can't you see he doesn't want to go with you?"

Ken, his hand still clutched on Andy's arm, leered at him. "You're threatening a police officer. You know how much trouble you could get yourself into for that?"

"It's my property and you're not invited here. You're the one stirring up trouble."

Andy shook himself free. "I'm through with this, Ken. Stop acting like a pimp and go back to Chicago. I'm gone. See you." He turned for the house. Ken took one step and grabbed him by the shoulders, jerking his head backward.

Harden raised the rifle. "I'll call the police," he hollered.

"I am the police."

Heated blood pulsed through the veins coiling around Harden's neck and forearms. "I'm warning you. I'm not afraid to use this."

"I'm not afraid to use this either." Ken pointed with his chin to the holstered gun strapped on his waist. It was the first time Harden had noticed. He breathed, licked his lips.

Ken shook himself. "Enough of this bullshit. Come on, Andy."

Harden hoisted the rifle higher and stared down the barrel. Flexing his trigger finger, he took two steps closer. "Back away, get into your car, and drive off my property. This isn't Illinois. We're allowed to shoot intruders."

Ken relaxed, but Harden sensed he was merely collecting his strength. He was easily four inches taller and thirty pounds heavier than both he and Andy. Despite the rifle shaking in his hands, Harden suspected he could fire if need be. His grandfather had taken him and his two brothers shooting when they were boys. He was a bad shot against the silhouette sheets they'd used for targets. A large man might come easier, he considered, loosening his finger.

"Let's all stay calm," Andy said, holding his hand up. "No need for violence. Everyone stay calm. Harden, I told you, I'll take care of this. Now, please, go back inside and—"

"I want him off my land," Harden said, taking the first step down the stoop.

Ken squeezed his fingers into tighter and tighter fists, and his shoulders rose closer to his reddening ears. A small slit cut across his face. An open wound impersonating a smile. Nothing was heard but crickets and the sporadic song from the night birds.

"You shoot a cop and they'll put you away," Ken said, snickering. "Regardless of your hick laws. You'll be sorry, for sure. All I want to do is take back what belongs to me."

The words stung Harden worse than Andy's pained expression. He focused his watering eyes along the sight. "He belongs here. Now move out."

Ken's ugly smirk faded. "What's going on here? You two fooling around?"

Andy twisted to face Ken. "Listen to me. I'm going to march back inside that house, and you're going to get into your car and drive away and never come back here again. Okay? Good-bye."

Andy spun on his stocking feet and did as he'd declared. Ken stood planted in the driveway, watching Andy take Harden by his rifle arm and lead him inside the house. Andy slammed the door behind them. Mason and Olivia were huddled on the bottom step.

Andy wedged between them and pulled them to his sides. "Sorry about that, guys. It's all over."

"Does that bad man want to get us?" Olivia asked, sniveling.

Andy eyed Harden. "Don't worry. He won't hurt us. He's going away."

Harden leaned against the door, rifle clasped in hand. He stared at Andy and the kids. Pride and relief surged in his throat, and the tears that had boiled behind his eyes threatened to fall. He chuckled, picturing how Andy had finally stood up to that burly beast.

The front door jolted, almost knocking the gun loose from Harden's hand.

Harden cradled the rifle and pushed back, banging the door shut. Andy rushed to his side. Ken pounded the door, trying to force his way inside.

"Let me in! Dammit! Don't you walk away from me!"

Harden and Andy drove their shoulders into the door. Harden latched the locks, slid the chain in place, and turned to Mason. "Get you and your sister upstairs. Call 911 on your cell phone. Tell them we have an armed home invasion. If you can't get through on your cell, use the landline in my bedroom. Stay clear of the windows. Go now!"

Hesitating only seconds, Mason seized Olivia's hand and fled with her up the steps by twos.

Unexpected quiet allowed Harden a moment to clear his mind. He studied Andy's gaping dark-blue eyes. He wanted to console him, but fear glued his shoulder to the door.

Something crashed in the living room. Harden ran toward the sound. Shattered glass crunched under his slippers. Ken had broken one of the french door windows. "We've called the police," Harden hollered outside. "Now beat it! Stop harassing us! I'll shoot you. I swear I will."

Harden aimed the gun through the shattered window. His finger twitched. A shot blast echoed in his ears. Bewildered, he brought the gun closer to his face. Smoke curled from the end of the barrel. Andy dashed to his side.

"Did you hit him?"

Disbelieving, Harden stared down at the trembling and smoking rifle. "I... I'm unsure. I couldn't have. I didn't even see him."

Heavy steps stumbled down the porch. Andy glanced outside through the broken window. "I think you only shot out the porch light," he said. "It looks busted, unless Ken did that too."

But before Harden could speculate, more sounds of breaking glass came from the kitchen. They raced over. A softball-sized rock lay among the shattered glass scattered across the linoleum. The blinds were gnarled and rattling in the wind.

"He's gone crazy," Harden said in a furious whisper. *Maybe full moons do make people nuts.*

The latest attack was followed by a string of strident curses and demands from somewhere near the cornfield for Andy to come outside. Andy rushed for the front door. Harden held him by his arm.

"What are you doing?"

"I'm going out to him. Look what I've brought you here. Let me go to him so you can live in peace."

"Are you crazier than him?"

"I wish I had never come here," Andy said, shaking his head. "I've brought my Chicago troubles here."

"Stop dramatizing. I told you, you haven't brought us any troubles. You can't go with that lunatic. I meant it when I said you belong here."

"Kamila was right. I'm a horrible influence for the kids."

"Their own mother is a horrible influence to them, Andy. This isn't anything new for us, believe it or not. We all have our demons haunting us. Mine is an ex-wife. Right now, yours is an ex-boyfriend. You might as well blame me for Lillian, then." Harden detected the flush darkening Andy's face. He wanted to embrace him, to underline his sentiments, when more shouting from outside jerked his attention toward the broken window.

"Come out of there, Andy Wingal! Come out of there! I'm taking you back to Chicago with me, like it or not! I'll camp out here all night if I have to."

Andy pulled out his cell phone and switched it on. He inhaled, waiting for it to come alive. Harden watched, knowing what he planned to do. Andy tapped a few buttons and brought the phone to his ear. "The police are on their way, Ken. You better leave now. I don't care what you have to say. You've crossed the line big time. Stop harassing us!" He clicked off the phone and shoved it into his pocket, breathing as if he'd scrambled up a telephone pole.

Two gunshots punctuated Andy's last words. Harden reassured Andy with a light touch to his shoulder. "He's shooting into the sky, burning off steam," he said. "I can see the sparks flying upward."

"The kids are upstairs."

"We'll wait for the police with them."

They found Mason and Olivia in the corner of the master bedroom, away from the windows, clutching each other and shaking. The landline phone sat on the floor beside them. Harden asked if they had called the police, and Mason nodded, his eyes wider than pools. Olivia sniffled into his shoulder. Mason was growing up, Harden noted in a flash. Before long, he would abandon him, followed by Olivia.

He set the box of bullets and rifle aside. "Come with me," he said, motioning for the kids. "Let's get you someplace safer." He shepherded the kids into the master bathroom, where the sight of Andy's toiletry bag made Harden's face burn. Andy had been leaving it there since they'd begun sharing the bedroom. Would the children notice, or care if they did?

"Stay in here," he said. "You'll be okay. We'll be right outside the door. The police will arrive any moment."

Ken continued to holler from somewhere around the edge of the cornfield. Andy was staring out one of the windows. Next, he fired a worried look toward the door, which Harden had moments before locked. Rifle in hand, he stood guard with Andy, glimpsing out the window in time to see the fuming Ken move to the side of his car.

"Where did you get a rifle?" Andy asked, eyeing the gun in Harden's hand.

"We live out in the boonies. Out here, sometimes we need to take matters into our own hands. More for the foxes and coyotes than crazy people, though."

"But Mason called the cops."

Harden hesitated. "They'll take a good twenty minutes to get here. I know firsthand from when I used to call them…." He paused and pictured Lillian. "I just know from experience how long it'll take them. That's all."

Andy returned to peering out the window. "Maybe he's finally going to leave."

"Let's hope." Harden squeezed the gun butt. "I want to keep an eye on him in case."

Andy's text message tone sounded. Harden had become accustomed to the *ding ding*. By Andy's expression, Harden guessed who had texted.

"What does he say?" Harden asked.

Andy gulped and flushed. "He told me to come outside before he ransacks the house."

Harden tightened his grip on the rifle. "That's what I was afraid of."

"I'm sorry, Harden. I'm so sorry."

Harden leaned the rifle against the wall and at last took Andy into his arms. "Stop apologizing. It's not your fault. It's not."

Andy repeated his regrets, and Harden held him, whispering over and over that he wasn't to blame. Harden grasped his shoulders and focused on his eyes, which now shone like sapphires. "Don't let that guy get to you, Andy. That's what punks like that want."

Wiping his nose, Andy attempted to smile. He fixed his gaze out the window. His eyes widened, and he pointed. "What's that?"

Two specks of distant light emerged through the cornfield like a prowling tiger's eyes at night, growing in intensity and size. A growling noise accompanied the lights. The bathroom door swung open, and Olivia raced to Harden. Mason chased after her.

"I told you kids to wait in the bathroom."

"I don't want to," Olivia said, sniveling on Harden's shoulder.

"She wouldn't listen to me," Mason said.

"Stay clear of the window." Harden shielded them from the rifle. "Squat down behind me."

Andy kept his gaze pinned outside. "Is it the cops?"

The strange lights blazed a narrow path through the cornstalks, and the roaring increased. Harden and Andy shielded their eyes with their forearms from the lights suddenly lurching skyward. Next the lights swept down and moved to the right.

Harden began to chortle. "It's Dick Carelli," he said, gathering the children tighter against him. "You see? It's Dick."

Mason wiggled loose and pressed his palms against the windowpane. "He's going to run over that crazy guy."

Dick Carelli, at the wheel of his old tractor, headed straight for Ken. Ken's silhouette jerked sideways and stood petrified with obvious confusion and panic. As the massive machine appeared out of the corn, Ken ran off, in hot pursuit of his own elongated shadow.

Harden squat-shuffled to Mason's side and shared his widening grin. Shoulder to shoulder, they watched. Olivia rushed to the window and gaped alongside them. Ken stopped fleeing and aimed his gun at the machine's immense tires, but only empty, dull clicks cleared the barrel. Ken had run out of bullets from shooting up the sky.

The sixty-plus-year-old Dick Carelli might have been slow on his feet, but behind the wheel of his four-ton John Deere farm tractor, he was Hercules. Soon the sounds of the family's cheers joined the blaring sirens of the two police cruisers careening down the gravel driveway. Ken, trapped between corn and man, raised his hands and surrendered.

CHAPTER
TWENTY-SEVEN

KEN got his wish. He hadn't left Burr Oak Farm alone. Two Dover County deputies escorted him to sheriff's headquarters in Concord. A tow operator confiscated his car an hour later. To Harden's relief, his rifle shot had missed him. Andy almost wished it hadn't. But for Harden's sake, he supposed Ken had received fair comeuppance.

The kids were too wired to sleep in their own beds. Harden allowed them to crawl into his. Or was it also Andy's? Mason and Olivia showed no surprise that Andy stretched out among them. Of course, Uncle Andy would want to sleep with the family after their crazy night too. They acted as if they were on a camping trip. Excitement had replaced the fear and apprehension Ken had caused.

Neither bothered to ask who the "bad man" was. "Kids only ask questions if you lack answers," Harden had once told Andy. Mason and Olivia giggled and hunkered under the bedcovers. They quivered and squirmed, but soon the long night won and cajoled them to sleep.

Andy awoke with Olivia's elbow in his nose and Mason's face against the sole of his foot. Harden had gone. Andy left the kids sleeping and found him in the kitchen. He'd torn down the cardboard they'd duct taped to the broken windows the night before and, with a warm, gentle breeze blowing into the kitchen, was now removing glass shards from the frames piece by piece with leather gloves.

He looked up at Andy. "You sleep okay?"

"As good as expected."

Harden turned back to pulling out the glass chunks. "I wanted to get a head start for the window installer coming this morning."

Andy watched Harden a moment longer, appreciating his strong hands flexing and turning with the grace of an otter's neck. Similar to when he'd observed him grilling during the corn roast and Andy had been unable to turn away from him. His strength and steadfast dedication, anachronisms in action.

Andy poured a mug of coffee and inspected the kitchen and living room. They had swept and vacuumed before bed, but Andy was unsure they'd gotten all of the glass shards. He'd clean more once the window installer left.

Surveying the boarded up french doors and the twisted Venetian blinds, he fought back the guilt over Ken. Why bother to mention his remorse to Harden? He would dismiss him for being overdramatic. At breakfast, the kids raved about the previous night as if they'd experienced an adventure matching one of their silly cartoons. Harden patronized them, but Andy wished they would change the subject.

About the same time the window installer arrived at eleven, the sheriff telephoned. Andy showed the workman the french doors while he eavesdropped on Harden's conversation. He heard Harden hang up the kitchen landline and excused himself from the installer.

"The sheriff released Ken on bail?" Andy asked Harden in a low voice.

Harden nodded. "They returned his car. He should be halfway to Chicago."

"I'm kind of relieved," Andy said, casting his gaze downward. "I don't want anyone to make a fuss over this."

"He'll probably have a court date sometime for February. Sheriff says most likely the Chicago Police Department will suspend him a few weeks."

"Reasonable enough, I guess."

Harden ogled him. "Has he tried to call or text you since last night?"

"I turned off the phone after his threat." Andy reached into his front pocket and turned on the cell phone. It took a solid thirty seconds to croon awake. His voice and text messages were empty. Relieved, he stuffed the phone back inside his shorts and reported that Ken must have gotten the point.

Lance arrived shortly after the window installer had left. So much for Andy's hopes that the ordeal would be forgotten like a bad dream. Being a fireman, Lance had heard the scanner reports. Dick Carelli had probably recounted his heroics to a dozen people too. Each of them would tell a dozen people. Before long, everyone in northeastern Iowa would learn the news.

Three of Harden's friends showed up behind Lance. Harden reassured them, laughing, nothing too thrilling had happened. The kids' enthusiasm while recounting the incident entertained the visitors more than alarmed them. "Crazy full moons," Burt Anders from down the road said. Andy overheard Lance mention Lilly's name, and Andy exhaled in both shame and relief, thinking everyone might blame the entire episode on her rather than him. But didn't they associate him with her?

The long Labor Day weekend plunged ahead. By Sunday morning, Friday's events seemed to have faded along with the cornstalks. No one had visited since Saturday afternoon, and the phones remained mute. Harden took the kids to Mass, while Andy declined. He'd yet to attend church with Harden and the kids. He'd been tempted. Wanted to. Liked the idea of the kids sitting cozy between them, their chins raised respectfully toward the pulpit. But how could he? Especially after Friday night?

He settled at the kitchen table and gazed out the newly installed window, shiny and clean with the markings indicating the window's size and style left on. His van sat in the driveway, unmoved from when he'd last met Harden for lunch on Wednesday. The etching on the side, visible to anyone who visited: "Andy Wingal's South Side Tours." Along with a dozen bullet pockmarks.

Monday morning, they attended Mason's final baseball game, postponed from an earlier rainout. Andy sat in the stands with Harden and Olivia. He would have stood out like a movie starlet at a country bake sale had he attended a Catholic Mass. But he refused to miss Mason's third-place baseball contest.

Harden's mother sat directly in front of them with a coworker friend, a grandmother of one of Mason's teammates. Mrs. Krane had smiled at Andy when they'd met briefly in the parking lot. Had it come from blame or pity? She had asked about the kids' first week of school, as if he'd know more about their lives than she. And, at that point, wouldn't he? She never mentioned the ordeal from Friday night. He was sure she knew— everyone knew—but how much did she grasp? If she did blame him, she gave him no reason to suspect.

He nudged aside his ego and eyeballed the longhaired boy wearing a constant smirk and playing third base. Mason had pointed him out to Andy the last time he'd attended one of his games. Mike Tuelong might badger Mason into another fight, particularly since the entire community must have heard about Lillian's visit from a mere few weeks before too.

"With me here, that punk should behave himself," Harden whispered into Andy's ear after Andy had expressed his concerns. Harden nodded two o'clock, five seats down. "That's his mom, the orange shirt."

"Now, that lady looks like a monkey," Andy muttered.

Harden patted Andy's shoulder right when a whistle signified the start of the game. The innings unfolded, and Andy enjoyed himself, although his mind wavered from the game to the man who drove the scary black van with tinted windows parked in front of the Krane house.

Bottom of the fifth, Mason launched a ball toward left field, camouflaged by the milky sky. It reappeared during the downward arc and landed in a cornfield. A three-run homer.

They jumped to their feet and howled. Olivia, her hands full of cotton candy, stomped her feet. Mrs. Krane turned around, shared an exact gaze with Andy, and cracked a healthy grin.

Back home, Andy held Mason from jumping out of the Jeep. "Wait a minute, okay?" Harden and Olivia moved ahead, and Andy gestured for

Mason to climb out. He walked alongside him, deliberately slowing their pace so that Harden and Olivia would enter the house first. "Good game," he said.

"Fourth place isn't too bad out of eleven teams."

"You gave an awesome effort."

Mason, his cleats in a plastic bag slung over his shoulder and ball glove in hand, looked at Andy from under his baseball cap. "Is that all you wanted to say?"

Andy stopped him and placed a hand on his shoulder. "Remember when we went swimming and Randy Lederman started picking on you?"

Mason nodded toward his sandals. "Sure." He grinned at Andy from the recollection. "You really told him off. You said his mom was a monkey swinging from the trees."

Andy suppressed a desire to laugh. "Have you ever heard of a self-fulfilling prophesy?" Mason shook his head and Andy continued. "It's when you become what someone says. It's a form of self-defense, in a way. But eventually, you're giving in to your enemies. The best advice I can give you is what I did was wrong. Next time one of those bullies pesters you or your sister about your mom, or for any other reason, either politely tell the boys to back off or ignore them altogether. If you don't do that, then you risk becoming like them. Do you get what I mean?"

Mason bit his lower lip. "But they always start it."

"That's my point, Mason. They push and poke specifically to get a reaction from you. They want you to sink to their level."

Mason squinted away from the sun, appearing to contemplate. His bright blue eyes lit up, and he peered at Andy. "They are making me want to do something like punch them, even though I normally wouldn't?"

Andy nodded. "Now you got it. Let's say someone kept calling me a bad name. One day, in self-defense, I cuss them out and give them a good slug. Now, they can say that I'm a bad person. Just like they always said I was. I fell right into their sneaky little trap."

Mason dipped his head sideways. "Dad would always yell at me for getting into fights and say I was stronger than Mike Tuelong and the others. I thought he meant stronger physically. He meant stronger mentally, right?"

Andy rubbed the top of Mason's cap and moved him forward. "Your dad gives you good advice. You understand that, don't you? That he loves you and Olivia more than any two people on earth?"

Mason shrugged. "I guess. Sure. I know that."

"You understand why he had to keep you from seeing your mom, don't you?"

Mason crinkled his nose. "I get why. Just wish he wouldn't have to."

"For the rest of your life remember how hard it is for him, and that he does things like that to protect you. Promise now. The rest of your life, remember how he sacrifices and loves you."

"Sure, I'll remember."

"And tell him now and then how much you love him, okay?"

Mason and Andy reached the house, and Mason trekked upstairs. Harden was blocking the kitchen doorway, as if he were holding up the house on his shoulders. A smile stretched his cheeks.

"What were you two conspiring about?"

"Just guy talk."

"Guy talk?" Harden threw his head back and laughed. He left for the upstairs, leaving off with a sweeping caress on Andy's back.

Despite the good feelings the baseball game had forged between Andy and Mrs. Krane, Andy declined Charlie and Vivian Marshall's invitation to their Labor Day barbeque. He remained at home—with Olivia. Harden decided, since Andy wasn't going, it would be best for Olivia to stay behind too. Already spent from a half day under the hot sun and a belly sated with sugar, she was more than happy to hang with Uncle Andy.

Outside, after Harden and Mason had left, Andy nudged her down the slide a few times and next pushed her on the swing. He asked her, "You like living here at Burr Oak Farm?"

Olivia kicked her feet higher, since Andy's pushing had slackened off. "Of course," she said. "I live here."

"I'm glad you like it," he said.

"Don't you?"

"It's a wonderful place."

Grinding her sneakers into the dirt to a stop, Olivia jumped off the seat and said she wanted to see her favorite fish. Hand in hand, they walked to the creek. Olivia peered through the clear water, searching. The light tinkle of water mimicked the sound of pouring wine. For a time, he watched Olivia straddle the creek, her little chin pressed against her chest, and he savored the peaceful moment.

"Do you know who makes life at Burr Oak Farm wonderful?" Andy said, wanting to finish his thought from the swing set.

Olivia, still searching for her fish, glanced at Andy. "Who?"

"Take a guess."

Olivia peered toward the tree branches hanging above. Leaves had begun to turn crisp, and one fell before her eyes and floated down the creek, out of sight around a bend. Placing a finger to her puckered mouth, she said, "God?"

Andy snickered through his nose. "That's true too, I suppose. But I was thinking of someone more down to earth."

"Well… Great-grandma and Great-grandpop, for giving the farm to Daddy after they died, and Kamila because she does stuff like keeping the house clean…. Oh, and Daddy, of course."

Andy threw open his arms. Olivia instinctively fell into him. She still smelled of peanut butter from their small snack before venturing outside. Her long ponytails tickled his nose.

"Your daddy sacrifices a lot for you." Andy tweaked her nose. "But that's because you're such a sweet, special little girl."

Olivia blushed and made one of those "aw shucks" looks.

"He loves you. Even when he tells you things you might not like, it's to protect you."

Olivia tilted her head. "Daddy tells me lots of things I don't always like, like to wash my hands and take a bath, but I listen. Mason sometimes doesn't. He fills the bathtub with water but doesn't always get in. Do you think Daddy yells at us sometimes when he's feeling tired?"

Taken aback by her insight, Andy said, "We adults can take out our frustrations on kids, for sure. But that never means your daddy doesn't love you. Remember that, okay?"

"I know." Olivia giggled. She pointed toward the creek, and her face beamed. "There it is! See? That's him. The one with the big brown and yellow spots."

Andy admired the fish, although he knew that many of the creek's fish sported spots. He went along with her game, and then together they wandered back to the house.

Mason and Harden returned a few hours later and rustled their gentle evening with clatter and commotion. They described the barbecue's delicious spread, and Mason mentioned the "goofy big man" who'd tripped and almost fell into a pie. "But they saved it," he added, wide-eyed.

"What about the man?" Andy asked, chuckling.

Mason snickered. "We were more concerned about Lucinda Jamison's strawberry pie."

The name struck Andy like a dagger. He had failed to imagine Lucinda attending the barbeque. Of course she would. Charlie Marshall was her boss too. For a moment, he wished he'd gone. But for what purpose? Harden was busy at the refrigerator, putting away leftovers Mrs. Marshall had given him, when Mason had retold the story of Lucinda's pie. He'd glanced up for only an instant. Andy patted Mason's head and finished cleaning his and Olivia's dinner dishes.

With the kids tucked in later that night, Harden and Andy crawled into their own bed. Andy no longer kept a towel wedged under the door.

Nevertheless, he'd made sure to lock it. Leaning against a pillow, Harden described the quality father-son time he'd spent with Mason. Andy listened. He was glad life at Burr Oak Farm had rounded a positive corner.

When Harden finished, Andy pulled in his lips and peered at his restless fingers lying in the hollow of the covers between his legs. "Harden," he said, working the spit in his mouth, "it's time for me to go."

Harden patted the bedcovers on top of Andy's left thigh. "Go where?"

Andy wanted to speak his mind undaunted, to state the thoughts that had pestered him for days. "Chicago, where else?" he said. "My life is there. It's not practical for me to stay here, Harden. Not really."

Harden did not budge. His hand halted on Andy's thigh. Slowly, he removed it. "Christ," he whispered, "you say that now, after everything?"

"I can't play games with you."

"But you said you wanted to stay. I heard you speak to Ken."

"Going back to Chicago has nothing to do with Ken. He was a bad habit. I just can't stay here, that's all. We couldn't live together like we have been. Not in a small town."

"You'd be surprised how few people around here care about those things." Harden shot him a wide-eyed look. "Vivian even asked why you didn't come to the barbeque. She acted disappointed."

"If Dover County threw us the world's largest coming out party, I'd still have to make a living. I have payments to make on my van. I have an apartment with a lease. Mail is piling up, and I certainly can't trust Ken to handle that for me now. For all I know, he might be at my apartment right this minute trashing everything I own."

"Go back and tie up all those loose ends and come back. The kids don't want you to leave. I'm sure of that. They love you here."

Andy heard a rumbling rise from the field. Dick Carelli was back at work. The corn had grown brittle and wan, and the harvest was in full swing. In a few weeks, the farmers would thresh the kernels, according to Harden, and sell the feed to dairy farmers and beef raisers. Soon the fields would lay bare. Another season behind them. Winter would be on them fast. Snow and ice would cover the ground, tucking in hopes and dreams until next season.

Andy gazed toward the ceiling, one he'd become more accustomed to than the one in his Uptown studio. He recognized the mildew stains and the tiny blisters underneath the white paint. "You told me Kamila agreed to return to work Wednesday afternoon," he said. "I'll be leaving that morning."

"So that's what this is about? You don't want to face Kamila? I told you when I spoke with her she didn't mention anything about seeing us kiss. She agreed to come back. But I'll call her back and tell her not to. If you're that uncomfortable with her, I'll let her go—"

"This is not about Kamila, and it's not about Ken."

Harden's cheeks darkened. "Do you feel uncomfortable being Lillian's brother? Is that it? If I were some stranger that you'd met, someone in Chicago, wouldn't things be different?"

Lillian and Harden's portrait sat on the bureau in plain sight. Since sharing Harden's bed, it had been a point of confusion for Andy. His sister ogling them while he and Harden had made love—doing things she probably never had considered—often had driven him to ravish Harden more completely. Other times, she had made him want to stop and slam the photograph facedown.

Andy snickered. "Lilly's ghost isn't helping matters. But it's not about her either. It's about me. I'm from Chicago. That's where I live. That's where I have a business." He was careful to keep his voice low to prevent the kids from overhearing. "The past week I've moped about, antsy and listless, realizing I have to go home. As much as I love spending time with you and the kids, I have to go. Our worlds don't belong together. Friday night proved that."

"It's late," Harden said, forcing an odd smile that sliced through Andy's heart. "Why don't you sleep on it? Okay? Sleep on it."

"Harden, I've *been* sleeping on it. For over a month. I have to get back to my life, my livelihood."

Harden leaned back, and the billowy pillow swallowed his ears. "Some business you have waiting for you. Escorting people around, searching for death."

"Don't berate me, Harden, please. Before I came here I was making more money than I ever had."

Harden began thumbing Andy's cleft chin. "And you left because of thugs, right? You don't want to go back there. I know you don't."

Andy clamped Harden's hand to the mattress. "You're not even gay. Or are you?"

Harden shook his head. "It doesn't matter. You're like a... a third sex. Honestly, I'm unsure if I'd be attracted to you if you weren't gay."

Andy snickered. He'd heard the "third sex" analogy before and hadn't been offended then or now. He was no third sex, however. He had the same body parts as Harden. But Andy allowed Harden to rationalize in a way that provided him comfort. "What if Lillian rehabilitates and wants her home back?" he said. "What then?"

"We're divorced. And she hated living here."

"And the kids?"

"No one could be as good with them as you. They love you, Andy, and I... I...." He looked toward the curtains. "I want you to stay."

Andy shook his head back and forth over the pillow. "It's no good, Harden. It's no good. I made my decision. You have to understand. Please, you of all people. We both know how this started. We know."

Before Andy had a chance to remind him that he had merely wanted to provide Harden oral relief for one lousy night, to satisfy his own curiosity about what it might be like to kneel before his former brother-in-law and behold his sex, Harden placed his hand over his mouth.

"Let's not talk about it now. Okay?"

Harden began to fidget with the bedcovers. He peeled them down, exposing their nakedness. They always slept naked together, finding it easier than undressing and redressing each time they wanted to have sex.

Harden rolled on top of him and, with his arms wedged under Andy's legs, forced Andy's knees to his shoulders.

Andy resisted with a meager squirm. The action opened him more to Harden. Disregarding their bedside lube, Harden pushed the tip of his girth into him. Andy muffled a cry of initial pain. Closing his eyes in submission, he allowed Harden to take him, perhaps for the final time.

Harden wrapped his arms around him, squeezing tighter and tighter with each penetrating thrust. Andy, groaning, dug his dull, short nails into his back. He bit Harden's shoulder, and Harden pushed deeper. Pain more than pleasure drove Andy. He held Harden more firmly to him, locking his legs onto his arms like a vise. They did not kiss. Merely breathed heavy and bit at each other's hot flesh until Harden threw back his head and groaned to the ceiling.

He collapsed on top of Andy, panting. Andy remained still, their hearts thumping against each other's. Ultimately, Harden slid out of him, and he rolled to his back, still breathing heavily.

"Andy...."

Andy shrugged out of Harden's reach. He jumped to his feet, pulled on a pair of shorts, grabbed his toiletry bag from the bathroom, and descended to his former basement bedroom, where he lay alone, battling a fitful night of sleep.

CHAPTER
TWENTY-EIGHT

DURING breakfast the next morning, Andy explained his plans to the kids. "I'll stay on until tomorrow," he ended, pouring more orange juice for Olivia. He placed the pitcher aside and sat next to her. "Kamila will be back by then. Won't it be nice to see her again?"

Harden kept silent. Dressed in his shirt and tie, he sat with them at the table, like any morning, eating cornflakes and drinking orange juice and coffee. He had already started pouring cereal into bowls for the kids when Andy came up from the basement. Harden had looked at him, more surprised, like his first morning at Burr Oak Farm, but without the sparkling eyes.

"You were here a long time, but you can stay longer." Olivia dribbled milk on the table while she spooned cereal into her mouth. Harden moved to reprimand her but leaned back in his chair and refocused on eating.

"I appreciate the invite, sweetheart," Andy said, blotting Olivia's mess with a napkin.

"He said he was going," Mason snapped above his bowl of cereal. "Stop pestering people, Olivia. We all want him to stay, but you can't guilt trip people into doing things."

In his short stint with the Kranes, Andy noticed how Mason had matured into a little man. "Thank you, Mason," he said. "Well put."

"Will you visit?" Olivia asked.

Andy stared directly at Harden, who captured his eyes for the first time that morning. Harden's expression, open and yielding, possessed a beseeching desperation that forced Andy to look away. "I promise I won't stay away for as long as I did last time," he said, smiling at Olivia. "I'd love for you to visit too, as often as you like. You can see the tall buildings and pretty parks."

Harden stood with a scrape of his chair on the linoleum and carried his empty bowl and coffee mug to the sink.

"What about Daddy?" Olivia asked, following her father with her eyes. "Who will be here with him?"

Andy's gaze flowed along with Olivia's. He observed Harden, stiff-shouldered, while he rinsed and stacked the dishes. He closed the dishwasher with his knee and readied his briefcase at the table. As if seized by a profound consideration, he froze, his hands stiff inside the briefcase's gaping mouth. He jerked himself alert and said, "Come on, kids. Eat up so we can get out of here." And he snapped the briefcase shut.

The kids gobbled the last bites of their breakfast, and they leaped from the table. Feet scurried up and down the stairs, through the kitchen, landing in the foyer. Andy made sure Olivia carried her Bubble Guppies lunchbox, loaded with a thermos of milk, peanut butter and jelly sandwich, banana, small bag of pretzels, and butterscotch pudding. Mason, a big middle schooler, was too sophisticated to carry a lunch to school. He always bought a cafeteria lunch for two and a half dollars.

Harden escorted the kids down the driveway. A few minutes later, while Andy cleared the table, the first school bus, visible from the kitchen window, pulled alongside the driveway and disappeared. Right behind that one, the second came. Andy watched Harden walk back up the driveway and hop directly into his Jeep for work.

Andy finished the dishes and spent the remaining morning readying for his Chicago return, although he had a modest amount to pack. Somehow, he'd ended up with Harden's dark-blue, basic board shorts tossed in with his clothes. Kamila must have confused them for his when she'd last washed them. He held them under the overhead light and looked back on his first full day on the farm when he'd squeezed into them, and later when he'd spent the day with Olivia and Mason at the aquatic center.

Shaking his head from the needless remembrances, he threw aside the trunks and stomped upstairs. During his free time, he answered the newer e-mail inquiries for his tour business, and some older ones he'd neglected. By the time he signed off the computer, he had twelve confirmed passengers for that weekend. Pretty good for a six-week hiatus.

The remainder of the day, he prepared dinner, making extra spaghetti sauce and meatballs for leftovers. He knew the family tired of Kamila's protein-rich cooking.

His last night at Burr Oak Farm, Andy played Pictionary with the kids. Harden sat at the computer, sipping a beer, with a televised baseball game buzzing behind him.

"You never answered my question," Olivia said between turns.

"What's that?" Andy said, tearing off a used drawing sheet.

"Who's going to take care of Daddy?"

Andy glanced at Harden's back. "You, of course," he said, turning back to the board game. "Haven't you always? Just like Mason and Kamila and Grandma and Lance, and lots of his friends and neighbors."

"I guess so."

"Take a card from the deck, Olivia, it's your turn."

Olivia complied with her brother's grumbling and studied the next card. She slapped it to her chest, as was her way, slid it down her belly, over her leg, and onto the carpet. Tongue curled toward her right nostril, she signaled for Mason to flip over the sand timer, and she began to draw.

They played another hour, and Andy saw the kids to bed, spending extra time with Olivia. He read from her favorite picture book, and this time he took his time reading each page, and eventually Olivia fell asleep on him. Downstairs, he sat up with Harden, watching television. Few words had been shared between them since Harden had returned home from work. Nothing changed with the kids asleep. The lights were dimmed, and the television covered them in a rich glow. Andy observed

Harden, longing to speak but curbing himself each time he parted his lips with a crack of spit.

Their television show ended and Andy said good night. He descended into the basement to sleep for a second consecutive night alone. He found Harden seated before the computer the next morning. Blue light from the visual display veiled his face in a pasty hue. Andy asked if he wanted breakfast. Harden, his mouth tense, shook his head.

A half hour later, Harden peered around the kitchen doorway. "Kids, I'll walk you down the driveway before I go. Get ready in a few."

"I'll do it." Andy said from the table. "I want to. It'll be my last time."

The kids finished eating, and Andy helped them gather their school supplies. The usual early morning chaos swirled around him. He gulped back one last swig of coffee and walked with the kids to the road. Mason's familiar bus appeared around the curve first. Andy made sure to give him an extra tight hug before the bus pulled up.

"Remember what I told you about your dad, right?" he whispered into his ear. "Treat him well and know he loves you."

"I know all that." The bus pulled up, and the driver opened the inward-swinging door. Mason turned to Andy with his foot poised on the first step. "Thanks for everything, Uncle Andy."

Andy waved as Mason boarded the bus. Inhaling strength from the few remaining cornstalks that lay in shallow gullies, he grasped Olivia's hand tighter.

Once Mason's bus left the two of them standing alone, Olivia said to him, as if perceiving the notion for the first time, "You won't be here when we get home from school."

"That's right, sweetheart. I won't," Andy said bluntly.

Olivia released a deep sigh, one that sounded odd coming from a little girl's mouth. Her bus arrived, and she let go of his hand. Andy's palm suddenly went cold, and he found himself shaking. He hugged and kissed her, then shuffled her aboard, blowing more kisses. "Be good for your daddy and stay sweet," he said after her. He waved to her through the window and turned back for the house, refusing to watch the bus grow smaller.

The past few weeks he'd grown bored with each morning's tedious walk up and down the driveway. Now, realizing he was making his last trip, he wished he could extend the driveway to Lake Michigan. His parked van gave him pause. The entire summer blurred in Andy's mental rearview mirror. He breathed in the sweet country air, accented with the typical livestock dung, which he barely noticed anymore, and scaled the porch.

Harden was standing at the storm door, peering through the window.

They faced each other. Staring. Silent. Awakening birds trilling from the trees heightened the hollow space between them. Harden stepped aside and allowed Andy to enter. Andy had carried up his duffel bag and laptop when he'd come upstairs. They sat catty-corner in the foyer, leaning against each other, waiting.

"You're really leaving," Harden said, more resigned than questioning.

Andy pursed his lips. "You'll come visit, won't you?" he said, hoping to keep his voice steady. "I meant what I said yesterday. The kids will love Chicago. Summertime's the best time, but even Christmas with the lights is nice."

Harden's Adam's apple rose and fell. "This time of year, I'm often bogged down with additional work."

They stared at each other, so close Andy could smell the coffee on Harden's breath. Andy extended his hand for a shake. Then, realizing the ridiculousness of the gesture, he embraced him.

Harden stood stiff like a pole, his arms locked. Before long, Andy felt his arms wrap around him and tighten as the seconds passed.

They drew apart, hands grasping each other's arms. Andy found himself battling a sudden bout of bashfulness. Unable to meet Harden's bright blue eyes, he peered toward Harden's shoulder, where a speck of lint stuck to the fabric of his light-blue Oxford. Trembles shook them. Andy was unsure if they originated from him or Harden. Or perhaps both.

Andy patted Harden's burgundy necktie, swept the lint from his shoulder. Harden moved back, smiled tightly. Devoid of words, he turned and walked upstairs.

Maybe sixty seconds elapsed before Andy willed his legs to move. He loaded his luggage in the van and climbed behind the steering wheel. He made the typical U-turn, gave one final, fleeting toot of the horn to whoever cared to listen (perhaps Harden gazed at him from the master bedroom upstairs), and pulled out of the driveway.

CHAPTER
TWENTY-NINE

THREE bullets whizzed past Andy's van. He white-knuckled the steering wheel, keeping the two shooters in his rearview mirror. The target, a black Escalade, sleek like a panther, zigzagged down Sixty-Eighth Street toward Racine. Andy U-turned and hastened after it. The shooters separated and sprinted out of sight. Two blocks down the road, the Escalade veered onto the sidewalk and struck a three-story redbrick building at about forty miles per hour.

Andy idled to a stop. Smoke poured from under the Escalade's gnarled hood. Two of its passengers leaped from the backseat and fled. The driver and front seat passenger remained stationary, their heads slumped forward. Sirens screamed from close behind. Andy circumvented the road debris and headed far from the cops.

He dialed 911 on his cell phone, reported into his headset what he'd witnessed, and clicked off before the operator had a chance to ask for his name. Sighing with a chuckle, he glanced into the rearview mirror. His six passengers were shaking and chatting and woofing. He'd feared, after driving the Englewood streets for close to three hours without a single incident, that his first tour since returning to Chicago might end on a dud. As soon as he'd decided to head home, the shooting had erupted, mere feet from the van. The passengers (four friends from Schaumburg, a solo from Kentucky, and a man from Austria whose apathetic wife had decided to stay behind at the hotel) had hardly believed their eyes.

The police scanner Andy tuned to through his cell phone crackled with the bantering between a female dispatcher and a male police officer. The Chicago PD had arrived at the Escalade crash scene. Andy strained to decipher their garbled words. The Austrian, probably used to paying extra attention since English was his second language, interpreted.

"The driver and passenger are dead," he declared with a thick German accent.

Overwhelmed with a sudden tiring of his arm muscles from clenching the steering wheel, Andy decided his passengers had seen enough. He dropped off the Austrian and Kentuckian at back-to-back Loop hotels, and the four suburbanites at the Clock Tower parking lot in Lakeview.

Back home, lounging on his futon, he counted his first pay in more than a month. He'd pocketed one hundred forty-five dollars in fees, plus thirty-three dollars in tips. Not bad for a four-and-a-half-hour night. Perhaps by next week his income might double, burgeoning through word of mouth after tonight's excitement.

He thought about Dover County nearly every day since returning to Chicago, but he was beginning to compartmentalize his experiences and appreciate making up the lost money. Like one might a precious keepsake, he'd take Iowa out of his mental treasure chest, muse over the pleasant emotions, and then shut everything tight, focusing on real-world issues.

He'd witnessed that real world of fight or flight firsthand most of the summer, and he had again tonight. After his six-week sojourn, little had changed in Chicago. But the struggle for life was not restricted to Chicago's ghettos. Hardship found victims everywhere, whether Bosnia or Burr Oak Farm.

Lillian still hovered around his thoughts. He worried about her from a distance. Imagined with a cringe what she might be doing from moment to moment. Selling herself for crystal meth, living in squalor, perhaps sleeping in that beat-up Toyota she'd arrived in at the Kranes'. Or worse, wasting away in jail.

His sister had fallen. Andy intended to soar. Choices had to be made. Andy opted to move with the currents rather than fight them. The alternative? To be dragged underneath and drown.

He fanned the money under his nose, inhaling the scent of bills. Yes, he'd returned to Chicago, where he belonged. His pulse had quickened, near to racing, and the city's congestion began to bleed into his consciousness once more. It was almost—*almost*—as if Ken had never forced him to leave. Looking back, he realized Iowa was nothing but a blip in his life's radar screen.

The next day, red-eyed and uneasy, he met his friend Skeet for lunch at an Andersonville eatery.

"You look like you're possessed," Skeet said once he sat opposite him at the outdoor dining area. Mid-September temperatures had risen above sixty, and the sun beat hot on Andy's face.

He wiped sweat from his brow with the thick paper napkin. "Nice to see you too," he said. "Sorry, I didn't get much sleep last night. I'm trying to get back into my old sleep schedule."

"The South Side Tour Guide," Skeet muttered. "See any murders last night?"

A death databank scrolled through Andy's mind. "Nothing too much," he said, preferring to speak about other subjects under the full brightness of day.

The waiter crept up behind Andy and startled him. Skeet, the type who noticed every wince, every twitch, shook his head and asked the young waiter to take their orders in a few minutes.

"Wake up there, jittery boy," Skeet said, snapping his fingers before Andy's eyes. "Maybe you need a lunchtime cocktail."

"Or a lunchtime—" Andy closed his mouth. He was in no mood for crude banter with his best friend, who he'd first met at a gay bar when he'd moved to the city ten years ago. Andy had made it clear from the start he wanted friendship, nothing more. He suspected Skeet still desired something physical, and he avoided leading him on with dirty jokes. "How's Chicago treating you?" he said instead.

"One hell of a hot summer, but not always in a good way," Skeet said. "I still have a job. That's the best news. Tell me, why on earth were you gone for so long? I thought summer was the high season for your weird tour business."

"There were issues to deal with. And then Lilly showed up. One thing led to another." A bus screeching to a stop made Andy jerk. He calmed his breathing and tried to laugh off his skittishness.

"You act like you're afraid of everything," Skeet said.

"A person adapts to things fast, I guess. I'm not used to loud noises, especially in the middle of the day. Took me a while to acclimate to driving the South Side last night too, but then it came back to me, like riding a bicycle. I'll be cool in a few days. In Iowa, things are a bit slower and quieter."

"I can imagine." Skeet sipped his ice water. "And more boring."

Andy looked off down Clark Street. The collage of shops, vehicle traffic, and Saturday strollers filled his view. He shrugged. "It's not too bad."

"I couldn't picture myself living in a place like that," Skeet said. "There's no nightlife."

"After a while, I grew to like some of the differences," Andy said. "My niece and nephew were a lot of fun. They're the cutest kids. They're like tiny adults, and much better conversationalists," he said with a sardonic lilt while eyeballing Skeet. "Living way out on a farm, they have few neighbors or nearby friends. They play outdoors by—"

"What about the brother-in-law?"

Tall grass in oblong planter boxes separating the eating area from the sidewalk captured Andy's attention. He watched the green blades, soft like corn tassels, sway back and forth and coil against each other, imitating the smoke from an extinguished taper candle.

"Yoo hoo," Skeet said, snapping his fingers in front of Andy's eyes again. "What about the brother-in-law?"

The flaming flush came too fast for Andy to control. Skeet deciphered it right off. Andy's cheeks burned further. He tried to hide behind his menu, but Skeet slapped it down.

"You got the hots for your brother-in-law!"

"Shut up, will you? He's my ex-brother-in-law, and I don't have the hots for him."

"My God, you're simpering!"

"Skeet, people can hear."

"Strangers aren't interested in your sordid illicit affairs," Skeet said. "But, my God, I am. I can't believe you held back from telling me about this. What does he look like?"

"Is that all you think about?" But the question spurred Andy onto a grand and sweeping ride, allowing him to recall the best of Harden Krane. His different stances, postures, expressions, the clothing he wore. His magnificent, pouchy jowls.

And what had become Andy's favorite, Harden's girth, matching a corncob's thickness.

"Yoo hoo. You're still in Iowa, my dear," Skeet said, waving his hand before Andy's face.

"I guess my head's left behind."

"What other body parts did you leave? Tell me the truth. Did you two do anything?" Skeet studied him. Next he slapped the table, rattling their water glasses and flatware. "My God! You did! I know that look." It was Skeet's turn to flush. He turned redder than the fire truck that raced past. Andy cupped his ears, and Skeet allowed the blaring to fade before going on. "I can't believe it. It's true. Now I get why you were gone for so long. My God! Why didn't you tell me this before? Details! Details!"

"Calm down, Skeet. There's nothing to tell. He's a nice guy. I helped out with the kids. You know about my sister, about her issues. I owed him one."

"I bet. Did he enjoy it?"

The waiter returned and took their orders. Once he left, Skeet repeated his request for the nitty-gritty.

"We played house for a while," Andy said, sighing. "A fun diversion, that's all. He got too comfortable with me being around, and the time came to back off and come home."

"You were a farmer's wife. Like that old movie. What's it called?"

"You're thinking of *The Farmer's Daughter* starring Loretta Young. And it wasn't like that. Stop joking. Harden is a great guy."

"Well, tell me more about your husband."

"He's a hardworking, educated man," Andy said, disregarding Skeet's characteristic sarcasm. "He rents his farmland to this man named Dick Carelli. He's a real nice old guy once you get to know him. Most of the people out there are like that. It takes them awhile, but once they warm up to you, they're really good, dependable people." Andy sipped his water and leaned back in his chair. "Harden's got this great big burr oak in the backyard. The farm's named after it. The land used to belong to his grandparents, and they left it to him in their will. Sad thing is he can't farm right now, what with caring for two small kids. That's why he rents the land to Dick. But someday—" Andy shook his head and snickered. Skeet was gawking at him as if his face had sprouted purple polka dots. "Sorry," he said, "I'm going on and on like an idiot."

"Sounds like you're in big-time love with the whole state," Skeet said.

Andy grinned. *A little corner of paradise, nestled among the cornfields of northeastern Iowa.* Maybe life did come down to doing one little bit on one little patch with one person. But how much sitting on a porch swing listening to the corn grow could a man stand?

He shrugged. "I started to appreciate how people look at life out there, that's all. It's different. Like how they think and do for themselves. Here, we expect someone else to do the thinking and doing for us. If our toilets stop up, we call the maintenance man. We need our dogs walked, we hire a service. There're no challenges."

"Heavens, my dear. You moving back or what?"

Andy scoffed and gazed at the foot of the neighboring table, where a blade of grass labored through a sidewalk crack. "Move back to Iowa?" he said to the struggling grass. "Me? Not likely."

"And?"

"And what?"

"Okay, I'll let you off the hook for now. But I expect details about you and this brother-in-law of yours later. Tell me, what about you and Ken? Are you going to still see him after what he did?"

"Even if he hadn't made a fool out of me and himself, I think I'd still have dumped him before Halloween."

"I never did like him." Skeet scrunched his face. "He's one of those macho closet cases. You can never trust gay men like that. They're always on edge, ready to explode."

"With Ken, it was always an image issue," Andy said, pondering. "For other men… well, sometimes it's a privacy one."

Skeet made one of his exasperating bogus pensive looks that Andy knew too well. "Other men? Hmm…. You mean other men like wannabe farmers who live in certain Midwestern states?"

"Skeet…."

Their lunch arrived, and Andy picked at his Hawaiian burger while Skeet described his summer highs and lows. Not too long ago, Andy might have been amused by Skeet's elaborate narrations. Now, his tales tired him as much as Andy's details of Iowa seemed to have bored Skeet.

An hour and three beers between them later, they hugged good-bye on the corner of Clark and Berwyn and planned for another outing later next week. Andy returned to his apartment, napped for two hours, and prepped for his Saturday night tour. Another six passengers were lined up. All but one showed.

By midnight, he was escorting them through the bowels of the South Side. An hour into the tour, a gunshot came from Kedzie Avenue. Andy did not share the information with his passengers. They appeared ignorant.

The three Lake County suburbanites and two tourists from Wisconsin couldn't distinguish a gun blast from a belch, he suspected.

Rather, he drove down his favorite South Side block, the one with the tall evergreens and maple trees and Victorian homes outlined in gingerbread and latticework. He pointed out the planter boxes on front stoops brimming with bright flowers that seemed to glow at night, and the white picket fences that looked like something from a postcard.

"Where's the crime?" one man said, gaping out the tinted windows.

A mere block away, the passengers saw what they'd come for. A house party had turned violent. The narrow one-way street teemed with teens shouting and shoving. Intermittent wrestling matches erupted. Andy pulled into an alley and parked with the lights off, allowing his passengers full view of the spectacle. At last, someone brandished a knife. Within minutes, a gunshot split the night. The teens spread like butter on a red-hot frying pan.

The police were headed for the scene (Andy had heard through the scanner they'd been dispatched before the violence had even started), and he drove down the alley and turned left onto the adjacent street, out of sight.

With his passengers cheering and breathing heavily, he headed for the Dan Ryan Expressway, eager to return to his Uptown studio. He collected forty-seven dollars in tips. Surprised how little he cared, he filed away his earnings for later deposit and fell across his bed.

He was dozing when the door opened. A shaft of light from the hallway blinded him before the dark figure closed the door. Andy peered through the shadows. The figure stood by the kitchen counter, clutching the key to Andy's apartment.

Andy sat up, rubbed his thighs. "How did you know I was back?"

Ken remained by the counter. "I texted Skeet, and he told me. Besides, my friends on the force mentioned your business is up and running. They've seen your van cruising the South Side again."

"What do you want?"

"You're not going to even say hi?"

"Hi. Now what are you doing here?"

"I'd think you'd be more accommodating after what you put me through," Ken said.

What I put you through?

Andy locked his thoughts inside himself. What difference did it make if he hurled abuses at Ken? Numb with indifference, Andy muttered, "Sorry." Same response he might have given him any other night. He'd take the full blame, shoulder every wrong. Responsible for atrocities in Chicago and the entire world.

"You should be sorry," Ken said, stepping closer to him. "I had to pay a ten-thousand-dollar bail bond and have to stand trial in that hick town those bozo deputies dragged me to, not to mention the force suspended me for an entire month without pay and confiscated my Glock. What a damn mess. I can't believe I'd even consider taking you back."

Andy snickered. "I didn't ask you to."

The old lady upstairs sneezed. Andy could almost feel her spray soaking the back of his neck. He wanted to race to her apartment and slap her. All of a sudden, he longed to console her. Did she suffer from loneliness too?

After an irritating pause, Ken said, "You're saying you don't want to try again?"

"Try what again?"

"What's wrong with you? Listen up. I'm trying to save what we have."

Ken moved to hug Andy. But he shifted his shoulder away from Ken's touch, and Ken jerked his hand back.

"What's the matter?" he said. "Don't you want it anymore? Or are you getting it from someone else? You got your Farmer Joe living with you now?"

"I'm not getting it from anyone, as you so eloquently put it, and no one is living here but me. Now why don't you go, Ken. I'm not joking."

"I apologized for Iowa, if you'd bothered to read my text messages or e-mails. Besides, if you had listened to me and come home when I told you to, none of that would have happened."

"You ordered me to leave, you ordered me to come back. I'm not a slave. Yours or anyone else's."

"What are you saying?"

Andy sniggered and shook his head. "I don't want to see you anymore, Ken. Period. Take a hint."

The scarlet shade spreading over Ken's face matched his hair. "You better know what you're doing."

"You terrorized my family, Ken. My little niece and nephew were home when you started to act like an escaped mental patient. You scared the wits out of them. And you want me to pretend it never happened?" Why was he even bothering?

"I wanted you home, that's all. How else was I to get you back?"

"I'd already decided to come back to Chicago before your stunt." Andy waved a hand. "It doesn't matter one way or the other. Just go, please."

Ken crouched before him, taking an uncharacteristically gentle hold of Andy's forearms. He massaged Andy's elbows, his breath sour. Ken's thigh muscles stretched his tight jeans, expanding against his haunches. With Ken positioned perfectly between Andy's legs, Andy only needed to sink back and let him envelop him with his brawny arms. Eventually, they'd roll around, strip off each other's clothes, and Ken would push into him until Andy worried his neighbor would bang on the wall for them to quit. Good hot sweaty sex. Andy could use some too.

Andy rested a hand on Ken's shoulder, licked his lips, and gazed into his eyes. "Ken…."

"What is it, Andy?"

"Get… out… of… my… apartment."

In a flash, Ken stood. Andy fixed his eyes on Ken's knees, feeling his searing scowl on top of his head.

"I knew you were trouble when I first ran into you at that damn bar," Ken said. "I knew you were bad news."

Ken spun for the kitchen. Andy lifted his head, watching Ken reach into his pocket, slip a key off his key ring, and slap it down on the counter.

"You were a punk months ago," Ken fumed, facing him, "and you're a punk now." He turned, stopped with his hand on the doorknob, and said over his shoulder, "But you'll call me. I know you. You'll wise up and call me. You'll be begging me to take your key back." And he was gone.

The sense of loneliness that had stunned Andy moments ago intensified with Ken's swaggering out the door. He dropped to his side and battled for sleep the rest of the morning. He was none too surprised when Ken texted him around noon. "Did you wise up?" Andy sniggered, shook his head, and deleted the message, although Andy refrained from deleting Ken's name and number from his phone's address list. He noticed the key Ken had left on the kitchen counter, and an odd sense of regret sapped his breath.

Sunday night, Andy carried four more passengers. They witnessed no actual shootings or stabbings but saw the aftermath of an armed robbery. Five police cruisers blocked all but one lane of Marquette Road near the liquor store. The police officer conducting traffic snarled at Andy as he idled past.

A half hour later, they witnessed an old-fashioned brawl at a neighborhood park. The two Texans seemed thrilled with their experiences and didn't complain when Andy hopped on the expressway at one thirty and dropped them off at their Michigan Avenue hotel. The other two passengers, locals from Lakeview, said they'd seen worse after a night of Halsted Street barhopping. Andy collected a total of sixteen dollars in tips.

On Monday, three colleagues from Toronto, in town for a digital animation convention, called Andy for a last-minute tour. They were noticeably inebriated when they piled into his van at the Grant Park Best Western. Disappointed when they saw not a single felony after two hours of patrolling the streets, one of the men tried to hop in the front passenger seat and roll down the window. "Somebody shoot somebody!" he kept shouting at pedestrians. "Somebody shoot somebody!" Andy used humor and a few light shoves to force him back.

Though it was only twelve thirty, Andy drove toward Grant Park and pulled up to their hotel's front entrance without their expecting it. They complained Andy was "fucking the dog" and that he had ripped them off, while staggering out of the van. Andy headed north on Lake Shore Drive, indifferent to the obnoxious two-dollar-and-twenty-three-cent tip among them.

He drove straight for the Clock Tower parking lot, although he had no other passengers to drop off there. He wanted a place to park without worrying about street congestion. He slipped on his jacket, paid the meter, and headed for Broadway, a street that might have activity even on a late Monday night.

He wasn't disappointed. A healthy number of pedestrians pressed up and down the street, heading home from bars, friends' homes, or late-night eateries that opened on Mondays. The evening was mild, and people seemed to want to enjoy the weather before a cold, gray Chicago winter locked them indoors.

The typical North Siders passed by. One man had his shirt half-tucked in his stained pants, walked with a strange limp, and mumbled to an invisible companion. Another dressed in so many fashionable layers, Andy wanted to rip his own clothes off in protest. A reeking mist of L'Uomo Amore wafted in his wake, mixed with the smell of the limping man's urine-stained clothes.

Unexpectedly tired, he sat on a corner bench at Roscoe and Broadway, his forearms resting on his thighs, and watched the strollers. A lifetime seemed to have gone by from moment to moment, when last Friday he had been sitting, cozy, on the sofa between Harden, Olivia, and Mason, watching a movie, to the present, sitting alone on a Chicago public bench at one o'clock on a Monday morning.

I'm where I belong. Grabbing life by the balls and yanking hard.

He rose again and wandered farther down Broadway. A college-age girl cut him off from a side street and strolled in front of him. She was chatting on her cell phone and complaining to whoever listened on the other end that her father had yet to pay off her credit card bill.

A large group of fun-seekers brushed passed him, laughing about nothing he could decode. A couple sauntered down the street from the other direction. The woman clung to her male companion's forearm to keep from stumbling. More and more people scuffled by, streaming from the north and the south. Some were talking about their dreams of moving to Europe, others retelling what a famous movie star had said in a recent interview, a few more mentioning the best places for sushi. One solidified blur of Lakeview humanity.

"Self-awareness is my worst enemy."

The cell phone talker turned and leered at Andy when he muttered those words aloud. He wanted to laugh in her face.

"What's going on with me?" he said directly to her, frightening her down a street that clearly she had no intention of taking. "I blew what could've been a lucrative night," he said after she'd long disappeared out of sight. *A bunch of out-of-town drunks with money to burn.*

The urine-smelling man passed him again. He was wandering the streets, aimless. Wasn't Andy?

Andy took the same street the phone-talker had, and he came to where the tall condominiums lined up facing Lake Michigan.

One after the other, as far as he could see, the high-rises jabbed the nighttime sky, heaving with the city's illuminated breath. A tight, sturdy row, shoulder to shoulder. Some old, others recent construction. The buildings did not visibly bend. They were designed for give—one inch, maybe less, to sway with the constant winds off Lake Michigan.

He envisaged what it might be like to live in one of those sturdy towers with plush carpeting lining the lobby and a doorman who addressed everyone by name. Did the residents ever tire of looking out over the lake from the top floors? What might it be like to lounge alongside rooftop pools in summertime while listening to old ladies reminisce about their winter sojourns to Florida?

He laughed aloud, leaving off with a headshake and snicker. A man and a woman waving for a cab glanced at him. They probably cared little if he were a nutcase wandering the streets loose, like that man with the stains on his disheveled trousers, or thousands of others on a balmy September night in Chicago. He turned toward the pedestrian underpass for his van, realizing he minded even less.

When he cleared the tunnel for the Clock Tower parking lot, he noticed the mark of a deceptive society. He circled in closer, inspecting his van, his left ear near his shoulder.

Someone had slashed each of his four tires.

CHAPTER
THIRTY

THE first action Harden wanted to take when he heard news of his dad's death was to inform Andy. But there was little point. Andy had only left five days before. Instead, he sought condolence from the world he knew, the world he'd grown up in and had dreamed to become more a part of by living on his grandparents' farm.

His father had been raised on that farm. Now that he was gone, his little boy's presence seemed even more fixed. The rooms, the hallways carried the sounds of his tiny voice and footsteps, like Mason, demanding attention or something to eat. The towering burr oak, the tree in which he'd once told Harden he'd climbed far too high and had crashed to the ground, breaking his leg in two places, stood as a monument to his pastoral boyhood.

Harden imagined the burr oak incident was one reason why Dad had always disliked the farm and, once coming of age, had wasted no time leaving for town.

The kids were handling his death well. They had loved their morbidly overweight grandpop—a man far removed from the tree-climbing youth—and wished he could have moved easier in his retirement years. Yet they'd enjoyed his doting presence whenever they had visited the house in Duncan. Olivia had drawn his portrait, more muscular-looking than obese. Almost like an unintentional rendition of a sarcophagus.

Harden was happy to see his youngest brother, Jordan, who'd traveled from Kansas City with his wife and kids for the funeral. His last visit had been nearly a year ago last summer. He had more kids than Harden and Lance combined, with a fifth due in April. The youngest always embodied more domestic traits, Harden mused.

Lucinda comforted him at Mom and Dad's house after the funeral. She never once took her eyes off him her entire two-hour stay and provided him solicitous attention when he sat beside her. Before she excused herself to leave, he asked her out to dinner. Starry-eyed, she practically left on her toes.

And it was good they went on a date that next Saturday. If Lucinda Jamison harbored any illusions of Harden beyond what he represented, they ended that night.

Harden did not sulk. He was who he was: a laidback country boy who talked the same talk at work as he did at home, with a quieter voice, perhaps. Lucinda, sitting across from him at dinner and later next to him on her living room sofa with her jasmine scent choking him, never appeared more ill at ease.

She mentioned needing to rise early, and Harden, happy, understood the hint. He left for Burr Oak Farm, never more eager to send Alicia Anders from down the road on her way home and play Monopoly Junior with Olivia and Mason until their eyes glazed over with tiredness.

Funny, when talking with Andy, Harden never experienced inadequacy or awkwardness like he had with Lucinda during their date. Sure, Andy and rural life sometimes butted heads, but he acted more like a chameleon than perhaps Andy ever wanted to admit. His spontaneity, his keen understanding of his environment, was what Harden had always admired most in Andy. Perhaps that insight was what had made Andy bitter toward life.

He was at first surprised when Andy texted him with condolences a week after Dad's death. At breakfast, Harden mentioned the message, and Mason admitted he'd texted Andy with news of Grandpop.

From that moment, Andy began to send Harden short greetings about two or three times a week. *How's the kids?* and *How's work?* and *Did Olivia study her cursive?*

Waiting sometimes several hours before replying, Harden would write *Kids r great* or *All's good.*

Harden grew excited, then frustrated, whenever he'd see Andy's name appear. He'd inserted his name along with his phone number (the one with the 312 area code that a few months ago he hadn't recognized) into his phone's address list the day Andy had asked to visit the farm. He'd dared deleting it after Andy had left for Chicago but never got around to it. They texted, but never spoke on the phone. Too much of a commitment, Harden suspected. It was easier to maintain a safe distance without hearing each other's voices. Andy's texts came less frequently with the onset of October.

He pictured him now and then, driving his sleek black van through dirty, crime-ridden city streets. But the same worries had ground into his mind after he'd kicked Lillian out of the house. He'd run out of emotions for her. He supposed he might with Andy too.

Was it possible for him to have fallen in love with another man? The more Harden reflected, the more he realized Andy's presence at Burr Oak Farm had evoked positive changes for him. Was it wrong to have expressed that appreciation, that harmony, through physical communication? And Andy was gay. That made the big difference. Didn't it?

Harden had tried to stop analyzing what had happened between them. Don't think too hard on things, Andy had warned.

The kids mentioned his name as if he continued to live among them.

"Uncle Andy used to…." Olivia would say without fail nearly every day. Even when she'd watch *Thumb and Thumbelina* alone, she would laugh and talk to the cartoon characters on screen in that odd way of hers, bringing up Andy's name.

"Now, Uncle Andy would laugh at that, yes he would."

Months after their mother's leaving, the kids had spoken of her in a similar fashion. Her name falling from their lips had dwindled to a rarity. Harden reasoned the same would occur with Andy.

Kamila remained closemouthed. They barely spoke to one another. The employer-employee relationship sputtered forward. If Kamila had ever expected a relationship with him beyond business, she now accepted that it could never happen.

But she lingered, cleaning and cooking and, most importantly, watching her first loves, Mason and Olivia. Hearing them mention Andy's name caused her to falter, and her shoulders would rise and her brow furrow. And then a strange look of empathy would seem to gleam over her dark countenance.

The kids' school activities stirred the household into a blur of bodies and raucous voices. Mason began flag football with the Dover County Athletic Youth Club, since the middle schools no longer afforded interschool sports. He was gone longer hours and often required Harden to drop him off or pick him up when Harden couldn't remain and watch the scrimmages.

Olivia's second grade-class seemed to have one project after another. The latest—searching for different types of tree nuts. One weekend Harden took her to the creek with a plastic bag, collecting what they could find.

"We aren't taking the squirrels' food away from them, are we, Daddy?"

"No, sweetheart," Harden said. "They have plenty to fill themselves before winter."

"Don't they get tired of eating the same old stuff?"

"They aren't spoiled like humans can be," Harden said, catching himself smiling when he recalled Andy once uttering the same words years ago.

In addition, the kids demanded to partake in the pumpkin tosses and tractor pulls local farmers threw to earn extra cash. Parents of friends drove the kids to distant farms. Closer to home, Burt and Alicia Anders opened their pumpkin patch to the public for three dollars per pumpkin. After church Sunday, Harden hiked with Olivia down the road to search for the perfect potential jack-o'-lantern.

They returned an hour later smelling of vinegary apple cider, which the Anders provided free to paying guests, and peppery fertilizer. They spent the next two hours carving an unintentional likeness of Arty Ficklemeyer. Noticing the uncanny resemblance, Harden cut a small hole near the mouth and inserted a sheet of rolled white notepaper for an added touch. Olivia, and Kamila too, clapped and giggled.

The remainder of the evening, Harden, scratching from rummaging through the spiny pumpkin patch, worked on the computer. The kids watched Disney cartoons behind him, and Kamila was busy preparing dinner. He was grateful when Mason pulled his attention away from his latest ethanol research.

"Dad, can I have a dog for Christmas?"

"Dogs are too much trouble," Harden stated vacuously, irritated with the commercial selling Christmas toys one week before Halloween.

"I want a rabbit," Olivia declared, rolling back and forth on the floor.

"Dad, tell Olivia to stop messing up my notebooks. She keeps rolling on them."

"If you have homework, Mason, go to your room. That's why you have a desk."

Sighing, Mason collected his schoolwork and trudged upstairs. Olivia giggled and began mumbling to herself, a habit Harden had noticed frequently. He watched her. She tilted her head, made an "oh, stop that" gesture with her hand, and moved her lips, devoid of audible words.

Innocent enough, Harden figured. Who else was she to converse with on a farm, miles from her closest friends?

With the kids tucked in bed and the dinner dishes stacked, Harden carried a cold beer to the front porch, standing alongside the Arty-o'-lantern. Dick Carelli had finished the harvest a week before, and the field lay flat and barren. Green clover popped through the remaining scattered duff, and birds fed off the leftover kernels. The cornstalks were gone, but life forged ahead. Soon, spring would arrive anew, as it always had. Good things always returned. Or some good things.

The wan fields also meant a drive to garner substitute income sources for next year's yields. Harden hadn't gone back on his word to Charlie Marshall. He spent most of his working hours digging for justification to subsidize the alternative fuel.

He was in the middle of working on one such proposal the next morning when Arty popped his head in his office. The ever-present stench, both on Arty and the office, was thick in Harden's face.

"How you doing, Arty?"

"Good. Lunch later?"

"Sure, Arty. Come get me."

Harden worked through the morning and broke for coffee around ten o'clock. He had skipped coffee at the house since Olivia needed a drive to school extra early to prepare for a pageant. She was going to play a candy cane in the school's annual holiday spectacle to open the week before Thanksgiving. *Wouldn't Andy love to see that!*

"Hi, Harden." Lucinda turned from putting away a snack in the refrigerator. "Good weekend?"

"Hi, Lucinda. Busy one, that's for sure. Took the kids to a pumpkin patch."

She stood tall. "Where did you go?"

Harden hastened to make a single-serve coffee. "Down the road."

"Crowded?"

"Not too."

"Well, great seeing you again, Harden."

"You too, Lucinda."

Lucinda continued to smile and be polite at the office. Nothing excruciatingly uncomfortable stuck between them, merely because Harden refused to let it. The very first day back to work after their disastrous date, he'd looked her straight in the eyes, smiled, and had said with a hearty voice, "Hey, Lucinda, how's it going?" Of course, he didn't dare ask her how her weekend had gone. They both had an answer for that.

What else do you say to a coworker when a date flops? A small discomfort compared to Harden's other concerns.

Relieved she'd gone, Harden waited for the coffee to brew, headed for his office, shut the door, and focused on work. Ethanol reports. Heaps. Investors from Brazil and Japan wanted information. Fast. A succinct e-mail from Charlie Sunday night italicized the urgency.

He pushed himself so hard on the project, he never lifted his eyes from his desk until Arty stopped by, reminding him of lunch.

Fifteen minutes later, relaxing on the smooth faux leather booth seats at Ferdia's Diner, Harden breathed for the first time in.... Weeks? His neck and eyes ached from staring at reports, and he looked forward to comfy food and idle chitchat with a sociable colleague.

"Your head is on our front porch," Harden said to Arty. "Olivia and I carved a pumpkin last night, and it came out looking like your twin."

"I should sue for use of my image."

Harden laughed. "He's handsomer than you. Don't blame me if it becomes a Halloween sensation."

They studied their menus a moment in silence. Then Arty asked, forcing Harden to jerk his head up, "Whatever happened to that brother-in-law of yours?"

"Why on earth would you ask that?"

Arty continued to scan his menu. "Thought he might move here, he was with you long enough."

"He's a former brother-in-law," Harden corrected, more for his sake than Arty's, "and he lives in Chicago. You know that."

Harden's breath fogged over a section of the plastic-coated menu. Arty's question brought back the old longings he'd wanted to suppress, and there was little he could do but sigh and slide farther into the slick seat.

Arty kept his nose between the folds of the laminated menu. "I'd go nuts if my brother-in-law lived with us for that long," he said. "Probably would have moved out myself. Maybe move in with my sister-in-law."

Harden chuckled, appreciating Arty's sarcastic wit. "Andy is family, Arty. The kids loved seeing him."

"So you'd let him stay longer? Move in permanently, with you and the kids, if he asked to?"

Harden had pictured Andy living at Burr Oak Farm many times. His gut roiled as he thought about it now, a roller-coaster ride of angst. Struggling to look indifferent, he said, "Sure. Like I just said, he's family. Wouldn't you cave to your higher ethics and let your brother-in-law move in with you, even a former one?"

Arty sipped ice water, wiped his mouth with the back of his hand. "If Loretta were no longer in the picture?" He shook his head. "Gary and I get along well enough, but…. Nope, I can't imagine."

"Why not, Arty?" Harden glanced at him above his menu. "Is your brother-in-law that bad?"

"He's a big overgrown lazy slob," Arty blurted. "Nothing like…."

Harden relished the unusual pallor that stained Arty's features. "Nothing like what, Arty?"

Squaring his shoulders, Arty lifted his menu higher to conceal his face. "Nothing like Andy."

Harden's head flew back against the seat, and he let loose a howl. A few patrons glanced at him. Felt good to laugh earnestly again. But what was so hysterical that even Arty ogled him and then turned away, redder than a maple leaf in autumn?

Coughing a few lingering chuckles, Harden said, "Arty, if you ever travel to Chicago, I'm sure he'd be more than happy to play tour guide for you."

"Never considered that," Arty said, peering outside the window, where a truck careening down Main Street shook the diner. "He does that strange crime tour business, doesn't he? The one where he takes people into the ghetto?"

Harden flexed his menu and continued reading, although he paid scant attention to the itemized offerings. "With the economy the way it is," he said, clearing his throat, "people have to make do with creative ways of earning a living. He's not so different from any of us at Marshall. Look what we're trying to sell."

Arty turned away from the window, his eyes flashing above his menu. "Corn has its share of controversy," he said, shrugging and smirking. "Not too long ago the big hoopla was genetically modifying corn to become insect resistant. Now, it's standard practice. The whole world eats the beef and drinks the milk from livestock that feed off that corn. See? The world hasn't stopped rotating."

Harden glanced up toward the fluorescent lights. *No*, he wanted to say, *just seems like it has*.

The waitress took their orders and they ate, bantering back and forth about work and family, yet after they had discussed Andy's unconventional career, Harden's mood seemed to have settled into a dark channel.

His somber spirits shadowed him into November. The gray days, the fallow, tawny fields, colorless and cold, always left a hole in his spirits. This time, they pressed heavier on his shoulders. Thanksgiving dinner at his mother's failed to improve his disposition.

It was the family's first Thanksgiving without Dad. Mom wore a plastic smile most of the day, ensuring everyone had enough to drink and snack on before the feast. She had accepted Dad's passing quietly, settling into a private bereavement, as was her way.

Harden suspected she relished the extra attention from friends and family. And indeed he and his brothers had spent added time with her since Dad's death. Once or twice a week, Kamila would stay later so that he might swing by the Duncan house after work. Lance, the eldest, shouldered the brunt of the responsibility. *Thank God!* And Mom had her Health Foundation job, which kept her busy alongside attentive coworkers.

Jordan did not show for Thanksgiving, since he had already made the trip from Kansas City in September. He promised to come up for Christmas instead. The rest of them played Hearts while Damon and the kids let loose downstairs, waiting for the turkey to cook. The snug house, warm with delicious aromas, held them in a weary reception of death and time's passing.

The family adopted Dad's demeanor. Not a fan of mawkish sentiments, Dad had dealt with issues—not feelings. His name, spoken in passing, was usually followed by a gentle sigh, and the subtle silence would shift to louder voices—usually Lance's—calling for another beer or more smoked chickpeas.

After the abundant meal, Harden walked off his stretched belly by wandering to the garage. He peered around the chilly, empty room, which Dad had used more as a den. It still reeked of his Don Diegos. Harden could almost see the yellowish smoke brushing the ceiling.

Back inside the house, Lance scooted over to make room for him at the Hearts table. Mom dealt the cards, squared her hand, and fanned them before her eyes.

"You still seeing that Lucinda girl?" she asked Harden.

Harden peered over his hand and inhaled. "I was never seeing her, Mom. We went on one date nearly two months ago."

"I worried she was a bit young for you," she said, swapping one card's position for another. "But she seemed nice enough. It was thoughtful of her to have brought a pie over for your dad's funeral."

"I wish I had her figure," Holly said toward her cards.

"I never liked skinny girls," Lance said.

Holly huffed. "You saying I'm fat?"

"Yes," Lance said, his eyes tacked on his cards. "That's exactly what I'm saying. You're a big, fat tub of lard. Now pass your cards."

Everyone chuckled, and they had played two more hands when, to Harden's surprise, someone else other than the kids again mentioned Andy. This time, Mom.

"You heard from him lately?"

"Not in a while. He texted condolences for Dad."

"Men are like that, aren't they?" Mom said, examining the cards Lance had passed her with a scowl. "Women send flowers or bake pies, men text. How did a man send his good wishes before the invention of the cell phone?"

"Most men are married," Holly said. "Their wives do things like send flowers and greeting cards on their behalf."

Mom held her hand closer to her chest and glanced upward. "I wonder if the sentiment is the same. I mean, between a bouquet or a greeting card and a text message?" She made a grunting noise, shrugged, and refocused on her hand.

Harden played one more hand, then stood and stretched, hoping to dodge the inevitable. His mom flashed him a pained expression. He'd taken from her one of her glories—the right of a mother to poke into her children's private lives.

But Harden did not wish to discuss his empty love life or who might one day send greeting cards and well wishes on his behalf. If she only conceived who he'd been thinking of since August, she'd most likely fall off the chair and chip a tooth.

Harden's self-revelation still failed to shock him. He smiled inwardly, drawing strength from the image of the two of them making love. He turned away from the card table, carrying with him the flush on his cheeks.

December fifth was Harden's thirty-eighth birthday. His face hurt from grinning after reading Andy's text message, the first he'd sent since responding to the picture of the kids in their Halloween costumes Harden had sent him on his cell phone.

He'd written a simple greeting: *Happy bday, Harden.*

Andy had taken the time to spell out and initially capitalize his name. A small gesture, but one Harden noted and appreciated. Andy possessed an old-fashioned spirit, but he eschewed sentimentalities like exclamation marks.

"We're a society full of empty affection," Andy had once told him a few years after they'd first met. Harden had grown to value Andy's unusual philosophy.

Christmas season made him consider driving to Chicago to visit Andy and show Mason and Olivia the bright lights. But the more he pondered the idea, the less he imagined following through. Besides, what if it snowed? Passage through northwestern Illinois and its anomaly of uplifts could be treacherous for the kids. Andy had also stopped texting again. Harden supposed he'd encouraged Andy to stop. Other than the picture of the kids, Harden had never once sent him a spontaneous text. He only responded to Andy's.

"Daddy?" Olivia said, sprawled before the decorated spruce tree a week before Christmas. She was doodling in her pad, and the soles of her stocking feet paralleled the ceiling.

Harden was watching the Sunday afternoon football game and nursing a beer on the sofa. "What is it, sweetheart?"

"Is there really no such thing as Santa Claus?"

Harden squirmed. How he hated that question. Four years prior, he had faced the same dilemma with Mason. He'd struggled for diplomacy, not wishing to crush childhood fantasies. They would have so few once they attained adulthood.

After taking a sip of beer for courage, he said, "What do you think?"

"I think there is, but Christina and Natasha said he's made up."

"Some Santas are made up, but somewhere out there, there might be a real one." A little bit of truth, a little bit of lies. Kind of how Harden approached hawking ethanol. And maybe everything else in life.

"I thought so," Olivia said, her pencil point flowing over her doodle pad. She remained quiet several seconds, and Harden hoped her Santa quandary had ended. Then she said, "That Santa you took me to at the shopping mall, that was a made up one, wasn't he?"

"That one was fake, yes."

"But I told him what I wanted for Christmas. How will the real Santa know?"

"All the fake shopping mall Santas work for the real one. They report to him what the children have told them."

Olivia's hand stopped moving, and she rotated her eyes upward. Harden was pushing it. Even for a seven-year-old, too many lies induced skepticism. He snickered under his breath. "Somewhere out there, a real Santa listens to your dreams. There's a Santa for us all, okay, sweetheart?"

Later at dinner, Olivia recounted what she'd learned about Santa to Mason. Maturing each day, Mason gave Harden one of those "whatever" looks but pursed his lips.

"Sounds pretty good to me, Olivia," Mason said, using a "big brother" patronizing voice, perhaps for the first time.

The kids were growing faster and faster, and they were piecing together more of the world spiraling around them, including the dubious existence of Santa Claus. And what if Lillian gave them troubles now and then? Mason no longer viewed his father as the ogre trying to keep their mother away from them.

"You don't have to protect me anymore, Dad" was his new phrase whenever Harden lectured him. "I understand. I know you love me. I love you too."

At that exact moment, ruminating on the kids' maturing and the characteristic fears of an unpredictable tomorrow, Harden heard the crunch of gravel from the driveway.

He peered out the window at a dusty black van pulling to a stop alongside his Jeep. The front yellow brake lights disengaged, and Harden could tell whoever had arrived had come on purpose. His heart quickened. He found himself standing, cocking his head.

Please, not Lilly. Please, not now. Not another Christmas disaster like last year.

The door opened, and a foot wearing a sneaker appeared. Olivia jumped from her chair, nearly upsetting her milk, and rushed for the front door.

Mason raced after her, leaving his half-eaten hotdog looking dejected.

As if in a trance, Harden followed, unable to move faster than a shuffle. Somehow, he made it to the storm door. Olivia was jumping up and down, eager for Andy to lift her. Harden watched, willing his feet to move. Eventually, his legs carried him across the threshold and onto the porch and miraculously down the five steps.

Olivia slid from Andy's arms. He patted her butt, whispered something into her ear. Giddy and smiling, she ran past Harden inside the house. Andy's gaze stopped Harden. When Olivia reappeared outside wearing her boots and purple winter coat, Harden and Andy had still yet to move closer or speak.

"Are you here for Christmas, Uncle Andy?" Mason asked.

Andy, staring at Harden, said, "If you want me."

"We want you," Olivia said, dancing a little girl's two-step.

Their voices roused Harden. He inhaled and trusted that his voice would not waver. "Surprised to see you," he said finally.

"Hope you don't mind me popping up unannounced this close to Christmas."

"You're taking a holiday break?"

Andy stared, his eyes like blue carnations set against the pallid landscape. He inhaled the country air that Harden felt enter his own lungs, and turned to face the kids, eager and thrilled. "Who wants to help me carry some of these presents Santa left for me?"

Andy slid open the van door, and Olivia's jaw dropped. She looked to Harden, who stood a few paces away, observing and absorbing. Digesting the sight of Andy Wingal again, interacting with the kids, as if he'd never left. Harden smiled and nodded, giving his consent to his youngest. Andy hoisted Olivia into the van, placed a hand across Mason's back. Natural gestures, as pure as the bending of the elm and oak branches in the breeze.

Olivia and Mason hopped out of the van. Armfuls of gifts blinded Olivia as she passed Harden. "Careful with the steps, sweetheart."

Mason, doubling her gift count, walked at her heels. "I got her back," he said.

Alone with Andy, Harden moved closer. He caught a whiff of Andy's woodsy scent, the soap they'd often used when they'd showered together. His face heated against the nippy December air.

"You sure you're okay with me being here?" Andy said, almost too bashfully for Harden to take. "You don't have other holiday plans?"

Harden tightened his lips. "We were going to spend the night at Mom's Christmas Eve, but we can go in the morning. Lance and Jordan will be there. No one will mind." He retrieved Andy's duffel bag from the van. "Did you find us okay?" he said, walking with him toward the house.

"Remembered every square inch, of course," Andy said, his voice in tune with Harden's light sarcasm. "Didn't even need the Magellan."

"Hit any snow?"

"There were some flurries west of Freeport. Other than that, a smooth ride."

"We've been dry as a bone here." They climbed the stoop. "What made you decide to drive out?"

"Long story. Will bore the pants off you."

Harden stopped before opening the door. "Are you here only for Christmas?"

Andy looked penetratingly into his eyes. He was trying to convey a message to him, unspoken words intended for the two of them. Harden allowed one side of his mouth to rise. He turned for the door and gestured Andy inside.

For what seemed an eternity, they stood at the bottom of the steps. Sweat built on Harden's palm from clutching the handle of the duffel bag. He was unsure in which direction to move. The basement or his upstairs bedroom?

Mason and Olivia were placing Andy's gifts under the Christmas tree, their knees tucked under their bellies and their bottoms sticking out. Mason jumped to his feet and scurried over to them in the foyer. He grabbed Andy's duffel bag from Harden and began to haul it upstairs.

"What are you doing, Mason?" Harden's eyebrows almost brushed his hairline.

"I want to get Uncle Andy settled so he can fix my new app," Mason said. "Hurry up."

Harden and Andy swapped looks. Andy shrugged and, patting his laptop strapped across his shoulder, climbed the stairs. Shaking his head, Harden followed them to the master bedroom.

CHAPTER
THIRTY-ONE

"TO YOUR left is one of the few basilica cathedrals located in a small town anywhere in the world," Andy said, pointing to the Catholic church with the two towering steeples that could be seen rising above the cornfields miles outside of town. "Usually you find churches like that in large cities, like Chicago or Paris, France. It was built in 1889 to meet the needs of the Germans and Scandinavians immigrating into the area." He parked across the street and allowed his latest group of tourists, mostly retirees, to ease out of the van and snap photographs of the impressive Gothic structure and the panorama of "Main Street."

Leaning against the van, he propped his Oakleys atop his head, folded his arms across his chest, and waited for his passengers. The twitch of a smile tickled his sun-warmed cheeks. Not as exciting as his old South Side tours, but a wholesome and gentle affair. His emerald-green van with the words "Andy Wingal's Iowa Tours," stenciled in gold to emulate sunshine, on both sides and the back still made him chuckle. He had had the detailer repaint the entire van and replace the silhouette of the gun-toting criminal with the profile of lavender cornstalks. The bullet indents had been turned into stamen for yellow flowers.

Business was slow the first two budding weeks, but he expected an uptick after Memorial Day. The local press had given him a write-up and more interested tourists were calling or e-mailing. He hoped to encourage Skeet's old acquaintance, a reporter with the suburban Chicago *Daily*

Herald, to write a story about his new tour venture. Chicagoans, eager to escape urban sprawl, might find a farm-belt weekend with a gregarious tour guide to their liking.

He peered along the cathedral's massive twin steeples. Same church Harden and Lilly had wed in. Other than a subtle pinch in his gut, the recollection failed to bother him. He looked away and inhaled the crisp April air. The corn outside of town had already reached knee high and was turning a richer shade of green each day. How nice to see the landscape fill again, after a snowless winter which had left blank, wan fields.

One by one, the tourists meandered back to the van. Andy aided them inside and prepared them for the next stop, another small town with a soaring cathedral a mere five miles away. The cathedrals of western Dubuque County towered even above the silos and grain elevators. He explained how the Catholic immigrants had wanted to build churches that duplicated what they'd left in the Old Country. After that, he herded them again into the van and set off for his tour's grand finale. Like he had Chicago's South Side streets, Andy had learned the rural back roads in no time. He switched on his GPS only when passengers requested a special detour.

He turned down the famous touristy site's long driveway and waved to a man riding a lawnmower. The man waved back. He'd recognized Andy by then. Andy had brought them a dozen tourists, the most popular destination on his tour, and the proprietors were more than thrilled. Andy grew to find the tour boring, but he did enjoy absorbing the rolling landscape while waiting for his passengers to experience the place.

Sitting in his van alone, his cell phone dinged. Mason had texted he was about to start his baseball team's first practice. How fitting, Andy reflected, looking over the celebrated baseball diamond surrounded by cornstalks made famous by the Hollywood film. Nice that Mason trusted him enough to share his excitement. He had sent no mass text either. Mason had addressed him "Unc Andy."

"How long you going to stay with us?" Andy recalled Harden asking him after the kids had torn open their gifts Christmas morning and they'd stood shin-high in shredded wrapping paper and gaping boxes.

Andy had shrugged. "I don't know. Probably not too long."

Andy had attended Christmas Mass with the Kranes. He hadn't wanted to feel like one of those leftover Christmas gifts that sit under the tree until after New Year's. His first time in the pews with Olivia and Mason between him and Harden had evoked a sense of purpose for Andy. Harden's mother and two brothers had sat in front and behind them.

Later, at the Duncan house, Andy had continued to participate in the family fun, refusing to allow his misgivings to ruin the festivities. Jordan's children had warmed to him, and the two middle sons had called him "Uncle Andy" more than once. Holly and Jordan's wife, Courtney, had even begun to prefer his company. Three "in-laws" seeking each other's solace in a cauldron of relative strangers.

With the passing of Christmas, Andy had become the surrogate "other" parent. The go-to guy. Not as he once stood for the Chicago PD, but as a friend, confidante, and mentor to his niece and nephew, who had suffered heartache and upheaval. A dependable fixture in a home that demanded calm.

"But what can I do here?" Andy had asked Harden two days before New Year's Eve while they'd sat at on the living room sofa, planning how to celebrate. "How can I make a living?"

"Waterloo and Dubuque aren't far. Lots of people around here commute there. And Dyersville and Duncan are growing like crazy. Maybe you could get a communications job with the tourist bureau. You have experience in public relations."

"It's been such a long time," Andy had said into his coffee. "Who will hire me after more than a year underemployed, and in this rancid economy?"

"You could check with the local chamber of commerce," Harden had said. "You might find something there."

Andy had figured that unlikely. In mid-January, he'd told Harden he must return to Chicago.

"And do what?" Harden had said, his shiny blue eyes wide and glazed. He'd been preparing his briefcase at the kitchen table after Andy had escorted the kids to their school busses, but had frozen, peering at Andy.

Andy had smiled. "I have a court date. I'm a witness to a triple homicide, remember?"

Harden had smirked, one Andy had taken for as relief, and two days later when Andy had pulled his van out of the driveway for Chicago, Harden had stood on the porch, signaling a thumbs-up, but with a shaky smile.

A neonate in a courtroom, Andy had acclimated to the dry heat and the lowbrow questioning. The defendants had sat to his left while he'd answered questions. Two toughs who'd looked more ridiculous in their trial suits than Andy had felt in his. They'd exchanged brief, penetrating glances. Andy had garnered strength from the trial judge, who'd showed a respectful, professional charisma that the prosecutor had lacked.

Despite Andy being on Miss Steinen's side, she had interrogated him from an angle that suggested Andy had been the bad guy. Her questioning had pierced him worse than the defendants'. Ignoring her insolence, he'd provided the truth with a terse and steady voice.

Yes, he'd remembered the make and color of the car. Yes, he had recognized the baseball cap one of the defendants had worn. Yes, he'd been certain the shots had come from the Buick. No, he had not seen the faces of the shooters.

It hadn't mattered. Prosecutors had claimed only two men had been in the car, and both guns had fit the forensic evidence collected from the scene. Three more days of testimony, and the trial had ended. Andy had lacked the interest to wait around for the verdict. But that evening, he'd forced himself to watch the local news and learned that jurors had found both men guilty of second-degree murder. All that trouble for two seven-year sentences. Typical Chicago.

Harden had grinned when Andy, pulling into the driveway with a U-Haul trailer behind him, had returned. Andy had decided to cancel his Chicago lease and pack his belongings. Most of it was junk. "We could store some of it in the garage or barn, or perhaps have a yard sale once it warms up," he'd suggested to Harden. "It doesn't mean I'm staying," he'd said. "I just need a place to toss my hat for now."

While in Chicago, squeezing his things into his five-by-eight U-Haul trailer with Skeet's haphazard help, Andy had decided to continue his tour enterprise—but in a new locale. Andy, the South Side Tour Guide, peddler of bloodletting and societal decay, would become the Iowa Tour Guide, purveyor of cornstalks and pastoral beauty. Harden had applauded the idea.

"It's just temporary," Andy had emphasized. "Until a better opportunity comes along. Who knows? I might have to move back to Chicago."

He couldn't charge people touring Iowa thirty-five bucks a head like he had in Chicago. But fifteen dollars per person with the lower cost of living—and a man to depend on for extra support—never seemed more lucrative to Andy.

After a half-hour wait at the baseball site, Andy dropped off his passengers at the meet-up point, Duncan's public library parking lot. Next, he headed for....

Did he dare call Burr Oak Farm home? The kids never seemed to expect him to leave. He still questioned whether his remaining was a good idea, for any of them. At least a brighter perspective had peeled away the dark veil of malaise that had blurred his vision for so many years. The world seemed a happier place, one with satisfying principles.

Pocketing eighty dollars total in tips and fees, he found everyone home from school and work. Mason had just arrived from his baseball practice and was heading for the kitchen, and Olivia and Harden were throwing together dinner. He looked for Kamila but realized her car was missing from the driveway. Harden must have sent her home early since it was Friday.

Who were these people, Andy wondered, watching them from the kitchen doorway. Harden was cautioning Olivia not to spill the opened can of mushrooms, and Mason was pouring a tall glass of plum juice. Two of them shared a small portion of his blood, the other... Harden? In a sense, he and Harden shared much more.

Perhaps that never became clearer than when Mason had carried his luggage upstairs the first day of his return, assuming Harden and Andy would share a bedroom. And then again, after Mason and Olivia had opened the family's brand-new flat-screen television Christmas morning, and Mason had mentioned the old TV might do well in "their bedroom," referring to Harden and Andy's master suite.

Then came Ken's court appearance in early February, and Olivia had commented, after they had learned of Ken's pleading "nolo contendere" to lesser charges, that her father was much better for Andy than that "bad man." Five thousand dollars poorer, Ken had returned to Chicago, and Andy couldn't have had agreed with Olivia more.

They'd celebrated Mason's twelfth birthday the weekend after Ken's court appearance. The entire family and most of Mason's school friends had gathered. Mrs. Krane had exhibited a youthful energy, doling out cupcakes and gifts. She'd been going to casino junkets in Dubuque and south of Waterloo with her girlfriends on weekends, and it had enlivened her. Everyone had become accustomed to "Uncle Andy." Any hesitant wonderings had been concealed behind wide eyes and stiff, veiny necks. But Mason's nascent adolescence had stirred additional worries for Andy.

"What will their friends say if they ever think we're together like a married couple?" Andy had asked Harden the night after the party while they'd sat up in bed. "They sometimes poke fun at him because of Lilly. Imagine what they might say about us."

"I suspect there might already be some gossip."

"And that doesn't bother you?" Andy had shaken his head, waiting for Harden to show a semblance of unease.

But Harden had shrugged. "The reality is, Andy, we very well could be a married couple. Two men can legally get a marriage license in Iowa, you know."

Andy had felt his face heat, similar to when Harden had kissed him at the kitchen sink in Streamwood. Wanting to shake off the sudden timidity, he'd said, "That's not the point. You know what I mean."

Harden had responded with a soft brushing of two fingers over Andy's lips. "Didn't you tell me once not to overthink matters too much?"

Noticing Andy staring at them from the kitchen doorway, Harden smiled. He asked how his latest tour had gone, and Andy answered affirmatively. Harden mentioned his flushing cheeks. The afternoon was warm, Andy said. He added they might have a balmy spring night. The kids were eager for a fun-filled weekend. Maybe they'd ride their bicycles tomorrow, Harden suggested, and Mason and Olivia cheered their support.

Accustomed to the trek, Andy went upstairs to shower. He allowed the water to wash away the smells of farmland and earth. He enjoyed smelling like spicy farm soil and livestock dung after work more than city dirt. Yet concerns about sharing a bedroom with Harden continued to dog him.

"What about Lillian?" Andy had said to Harden in March while they'd sat on the porch swing, snug in sweaters and sipping coffee, after the kids had gone to bed. The hushed house had had a hot, desperate feel, restless for the eruption of spring, and both men had longed for fresh air.

"We'll worry about that pothole once we come to it," Andy remembered Harden having said.

"What if she comes back a changed woman?" Andy had pressed. "What then?"

"Then I'll be glad for her, happy that maybe she can begin a promising relationship with Olivia and Mason."

Andy had felt Harden's eyes burn into the side of his face. "I mostly worry for the kids."

"I do too," Harden had said. Then he had chuckled. "Olivia made one of her comments again today before you got home. She said that, with a new daddy, she worried Kamila might no longer be needed. Isn't that priceless?"

"That's another thing," Andy had said, trying to suppress the giddy lift to his soul that Olivia's words had given him. "What about Kamila? She's inserted herself pretty tight into this family."

"And she'll always be a part of it for as long as she wants. This summer, once you begin working more hours on your tour business or if you get another job, we'll still need her around. I think we can afford her. She likes you now. I can tell. She admires the love you show the kids."

"She knows about us."

Harden had shrugged. "And?"

"Doesn't any of this bother you at all?"

"Does it bother you?"

Andy failed to remember his exact response, if he had made any.

Wrapped in a towel, he stepped out of the bathroom. Harden was standing in the middle of the bedroom, waiting for him. He had shut the door, and now he gestured for Andy to sit beside him on the bed. Facing Andy with a subtle gleam in his blue eyes, he told Andy how he'd talked to the kids earlier that day.

"Talked about what?" Andy asked, his heart quickening for an unknown reason.

"I wanted to alleviate some of your concerns," Harden said. "I also wanted to ease up on the secrets. Families need honesty to survive. So I seated the kids in the living room before Mason left for his baseball practice, squatted down to eye level, and asked them how they felt about our relationship."

"What did they say?" Andy managed to eke past his tightening throat. He glanced over Harden's shoulder, noticed for the first time that the photograph of Harden and Lillian had been removed.

Harden told him Olivia had wanted to know if he was mad at women because of Mommy. "I told her no, that sometimes relationships between two consenting adults are about love and commitment and loyalty and friendship. It can fit all pegs. It's not about anger."

"Why's it a secret?" Olivia had asked. Harden said to Andy that her perceptiveness had always taken him aback.

"It's not really a secret, sweetheart," he'd tried to explain. "More private. There's a difference. A secret is something you never want to tell anyone. Something private is—"

"Nobody else's business," Mason had jumped in, itching to take off for his game.

Andy ruminated on his new stage in life through dinner, surveying the kids, perceptive of their awareness of his role in the family more than at any other time. All of a sudden, he realized that Mason had texted him that day *after* his father had confessed about their relationship.

"Next Friday is my school's spring recital," Olivia said as she shoved Tater Tots into her mouth one after another. "You two have to come. All the parents will be there. It's at night, so you don't have to worry about work. Everyone has to come, Kamila too."

Harden smiled at Andy. "We'll be there, sweetheart. We can't wait to see how pretty you'll look dressed like a daisy."

The following Monday, with coffee in hand, Andy walked the kids to the bottom of the driveway to await their school busses. He returned once the last one left and remained standing on the porch, enjoying the first genuinely warm morning offered by the emerging spring. Harden stepped outside and kissed him on the cheek, leaving behind the scent of his spicy aftershave. Andy watched him climb into his Jeep. He honked, and the wide tires kicked up gravel as he pulled out.

From his altar, Andy sipped more coffee and stared into the vast farmland. Dick Carelli had returned to Burr Oak Farm, working day and night since the advent of daylight saving time. Dick's corn had grown another few inches, from the look of the tassels tickling the blue sky. The cornhusks, the size of babies' forearms with fuzzy little heads, were beginning to bud nicely from the stalks.

Andy imagined his mother would be less accepting of his moving in with Harden and the kids full time. Then again, she seemed oblivious to most of the world these days. Rejected by a husband twenty-five years ago, who she still remained legally married to, she lived alone in her Streamwood rancher and spent her free time with a tight circle of coworker friends. She never seemed to glean anything from her life's experiences, as if she were an observer, never a participant. Numb to the world.

Andy studied his shiny green van. He was glad another work week loomed ahead. Six passengers had signed up for his new tour. Three on Wednesday, a solo on Friday, and two more on Saturday. He wondered how much more tedious it might be, escorting middle-aged folks and retirees around to the same sites over and over. But wasn't all work monotonous?

Squawking crows settled atop the barn roof. Andy gazed at them and pictured Lillian finding escape in that barn, the epitome of the life she had loathed and sought to soften through drugs. How long had it taken before Lillian could no longer endure her life? Andy shook his head. She probably would have found fault with Hawaii too, like he'd once told Harden. When had he said that? During one of their late-night chat sessions?

Sweeping his gaze over the expansive cornfield, Andy seemed to have discovered something less weighty than Lilly. Ken might have done Andy a favor forcing him to Iowa. Or maybe the city's thugs (for Andy was certain the city had sent his assailants, including those who had slashed his tires, to stop his business) deserved his gratitude. They had booted him from their city and inadvertently helped him discover a new land with a new meaning.

He denied he was trying to justify his relationship with Harden. What remained in his life to rationalize? The more he pondered, the more he realized Harden was perhaps the most decent endeavor he'd experienced.

Through Harden's probing tongue and the genuineness of his embraces, Harden was forcing Andy to a higher level of living—not a lower one. Knotted in the arms of Harden Krane, former husband to his only sister, Andy found himself drifting from the shelter of his self-loathing world to Harden's reassuring, vital one.

Harden, bundled in thoughtful movement, symbolized motion. Life had kicked him hard—more than once—and he'd collected himself and soldiered forward. Many others, when faced with obstacles and challenges, chose to revert to backward ways like Andy and Lilly had. Not Harden Krane.

Like the farmer that Harden yearned to become, he plowed ahead, sowing new life from dirt. Harden was a man of unadulterated action, even in his most silent, static state. Dreams propelled him. Almost animallike in his subconscious quest to live, day to day.

The first time Andy had knelt before him, Harden had lain back and submitted to the pleasure. He hadn't fought but a moment, a singular spasm evolved into acceptance and wanting. A man who, without weighty philosophies and ideologies to leave him bitter and corrupted because the world he'd created in his mind had failed to live up to his lofty expectations, lived to live.

There had always been decay, death, and misery in the world. Harden, like perhaps his ancestors who'd settled the prairies, understood how to navigate through it. He exemplified the best of mankind.

The sun rising higher shortened the house's shadows. Andy walked inside, with the gentle slap of the storm door behind him. Even before reaching the kitchen to clean the family's staggering breakfast mess, he presumed life alone in his studio apartment would be far worse. But fantasy wasn't the same as reality. He'd often imagined that he and Lilly would be little children forever, and spend their lives licking sweet, sticky Pop-Ice and climbing mulberry trees.

He clung to such wavering thoughts the entire week. Deliberating. Questioning. His tour business brought in another one hundred forty dollars. One passenger gave him a twenty-five-dollar tip after he'd persuaded Andy to take a special detour to the Trappist monastery south of Dubuque. Maybe Andy might add the site to his permanent tour. Perhaps even coordinate tours with local wine growers. Or include the nearby farm-toy factory. Endless possibilities stretched before him.

After Andy had dropped off the last group at the Duncan Public Library on Saturday, he arrived home, the smell of smoking lighter fluid thick. He crossed under the shadow of the silo on the side of the house and found Harden in the backyard, standing before a smoldering grill.

Harden looked up and smiled. "Such a nice day, the kids and I decided we'd grill for dinner tonight. Okay?"

"Sounds good," Andy said, chuckling inwardly at Harden, the grill sergeant.

An hour later, they were eating barbeque chicken breasts and grilled sweet corn. Next, the kids raced for the swing set. Olivia slid down the slide a few times and joined Mason on the swings, shouting she could reach higher.

"Watch us swing, Daddy and Uncle Andy," Olivia said into the wind that whipped her long ponytails.

"We're watching," Andy said.

Harden stood straight, chest thrust out. "You're swinging better than anyone on earth," he called.

They watched as the kids swung higher and higher, the tips of their sneakers aiming for the denim-blue sky.

"What do you think?" Harden asked Andy.

Andy shrugged. "I think it's time to clean up."

Andy moved toward the table, but Harden grabbed him around the waist and landed him on his back, where he began to tickle him. The kids leaped from the swing and jumped in. Andy kicked and squirmed, then fought back by tickling the closest body. He yelped when his lower back rolled over the green acorns that had fallen from the burr oak. Andy poked Mason and Olivia's ribs until they giggled and squirmed. The ground and the sky nestled them, holding them into a coalescing ball of energy.

The two-year-old mutt Andy had talked Harden into getting Mason for his birthday, rescued from a shelter in Concord, trotted to them, tracing the boughs on the burr oak with his tail. Mason had named him Stretch, because of his unusually long midsection. The shelter attendant had guessed he might be part German shepherd, part basset hound. He poked his cold, wet snout into Andy's face and barked.

Andy peered through the tangle of limbs. He struggled to release himself, but Harden buried him further. He straddled Andy and stroked Mason's and Olivia's hair. Giving in, Andy threw his head back and laughed, and relented to Stretch's cold tongue. Covered in grass, the kids rolled off, hopping and guffawing while Stretch leaped alongside them.

Filled with unlimited energy, Olivia began spinning and twirling. Like a prairie twister, she moved about the yard, laughing. Mason and Andy began to twirl with her, their arms held out, heads tossed back. Andy whirled and laughed until the sky above spun into a dizzying blue vortex and the three of them, including Stretch, collapsed into another heap.

"Listen, everyone. I have a great idea," Andy said, wanting more than anything for a chance to breathe. He sat upright, panting, and petted Stretch's muzzle. "Why don't we camp out tonight, right here out back? It's forecasted to be in the fifties, perfect temps for the sleeping bags."

"That's an awesome idea," Harden said. But instead of providing Andy a breather, everyone jumped on him anew, cheering him for his perfect proposal. Stretch bounded into the fray and woofed in his ear.

By nightfall, the kids had spread out their sleeping bags under the burr oak, snug around the small wood-burning fire in Harden's makeshift fire pit: the grill with the legs removed. Crickets chirped in the field and by the nearby creek, which Andy heard gurgling when the chirping or their laughter waned.

"What insect curses in a low voice?" Mason, nestled inside his sleeping bag, said.

Andy brought his knees under his chin and chuckled. "That's a tough one. I give up."

"Stumped, Mason," Harden said, raising his palms to the night sky.

"A locust. Get it? A low cuss."

"Horrible, Mason," Harden said, rolling his eyes and snickering.

Andy hushed them. "I've got a good insect riddle. What bug is similar to the top of a house?"

"A roof bug," Olivia said, giggling alongside Mason.

Andy waited, and when they all stared at him, wide-eyed and mouths agape, he answered. "A tick. Don't you get it? Attic."

"You and your silly house riddles," Harden said, giving Andy's belly a light pat. "That one's worse than Mason's."

"You seem to be an expert on what makes a good riddle," Andy said. "You tell one."

Harden, gazing into the fire pit, rubbed his hands together. "Okay, here you go. Why shouldn't you tell secrets on a farm?"

"You told us this one before, Dad," Mason said.

"Let your Uncle Andy answer."

Andy grinned and shrugged. "I give up. Why shouldn't you tell secrets on a farm?"

"Because the corn has ears."

Andy flung up his arms and joined the others in hoots of sardonic laughter. "That was bad," he said. "Very, very bad."

All of a sudden, their laughter settled, followed by an incisive silence that descended upon them like a warm blanket. Even the crickets seemed to have quieted. Andy noticed the whites of everyone's eyes glowing in the firelight. The flames hissed, as if they were telling secrets, intended for human ears shielded under the canopy of night. The earth rushed ahead, spinning, yet they remained as still as the corn and the elms and oaks in the breezeless night.

Mason and Olivia slid lower into their sleeping bags, and their father's rich voice, as he began retelling a story he'd once heard as a boy about an old woman who ignited a rumor of her village's impending doom that so terrified the inhabitants they burned down the village, lulled them to sleep.

While the kids and Stretch snoozed, Harden and Andy sat up, shoulder to shoulder, heads inclining on pillows against the wide trunk of the burr oak.

"The other day, I overheard Dick mentioning to you he's thinking about retiring," Andy said toward the fire. He stretched, and his head slipped to rest against Harden's crooked arm. "Might be the perfect opportunity, don't you think? I could be responsible for keeping the books, since I know business, and you, of course, would be the agricultural expert. It'll take some effort, but I'm certain we can do it."

Harden twitched, and his warm breath fell over Andy's neck. Andy sensed he'd shifted his eyes downward to look at him. He fondled Andy's hair and leaned in to kiss his dimpled chin.

"*Volim te*," he breathed in Andy's ear.

"*Volim te*, Harden," Andy whispered in response.

And they settled back against the burr oak, staring off into the starry sapphire sky, the fire warm on their faces, the kids breathing gently in their sleeping bags within arm's reach, and together they planned for the future.

SHELTER SOMERSET's home base is Chicago, Illinois. He enjoys writing about gay and bisexual men who live off the beaten path, whether they be the Amish, nineteenth-century pioneers, or modern-day idealists seeking to live apart from the madding crowd. Shelter's fascination with the rustic, bucolic lifestyle began as a child with family camping trips into the Blue Ridge Mountains. His "brand" is anything from historicals, mysteries, and contemporaries. When not back home in Chicago writing, Shelter continues to explore America's expansive backcountry and rural communities, where he has had the pleasure of meeting many fascinating people from all walks of life.

Also from SHELTER SOMERSET

ALASKA HUNT

STATE TROOPER

Shelter Somerset

http://www.dreamspinnerpress.com

Also from SHELTER SOMERSET

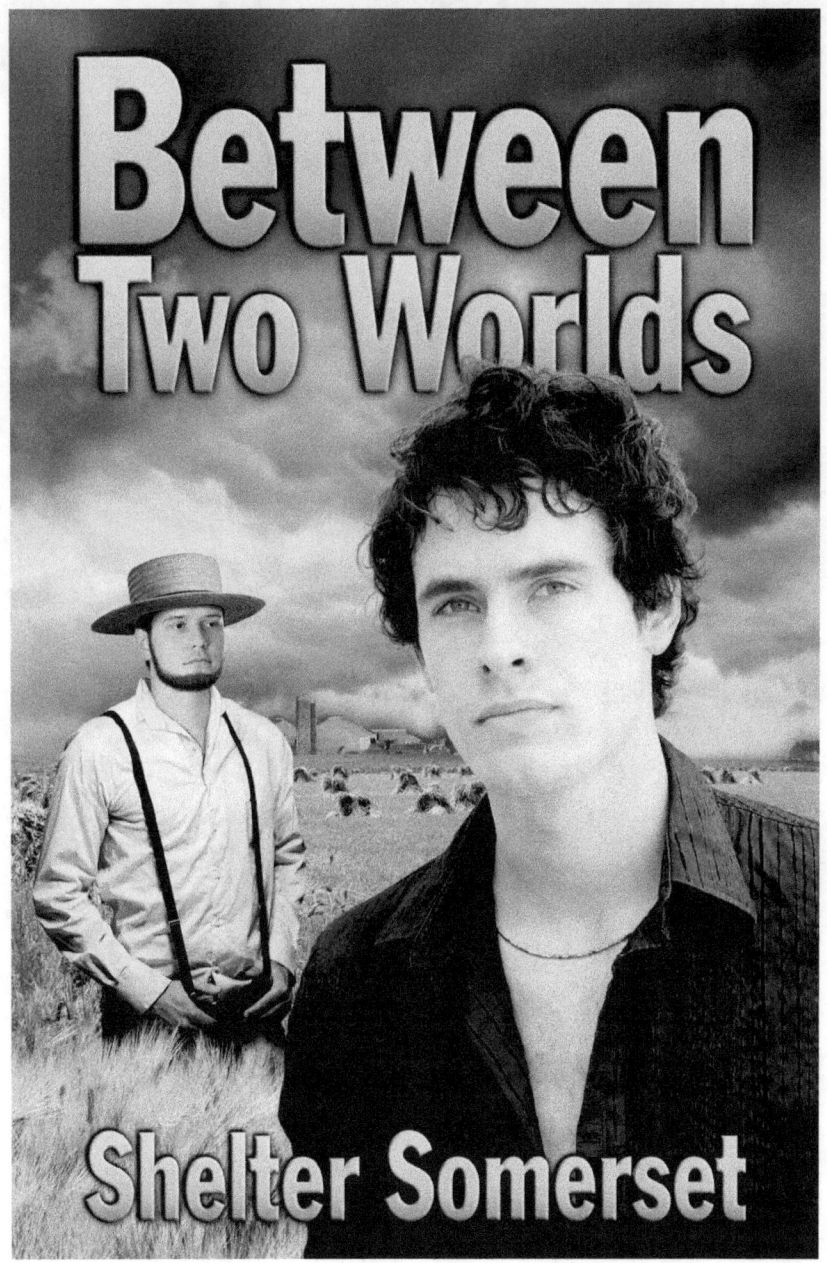

Between Two Worlds

Shelter Somerset

http://www.dreamspinnerpress.com

Also from SHELTER SOMERSET

http://www.dreamspinnerpress.com

Also from SHELTER SOMERSET

www.ingramcontent.com/pod-product-compliance
Lightning Source LLC
Chambersburg PA
CBHW070055030726
47506CB00002B/472